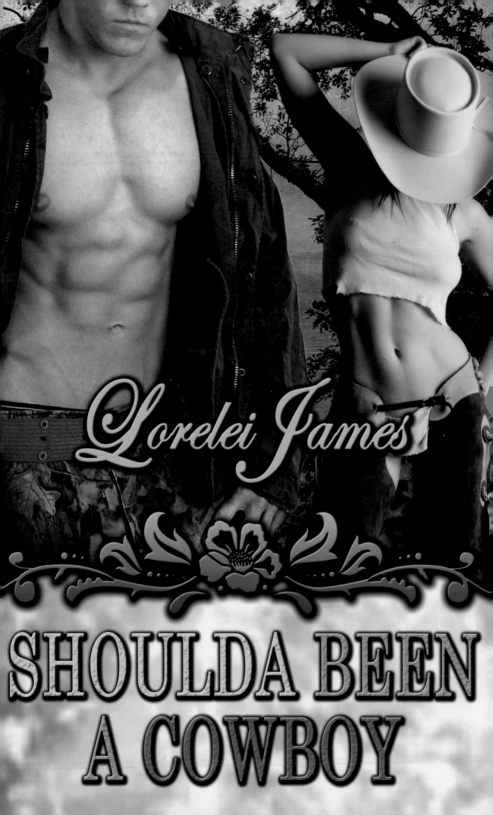

Lorelei James

SHOULDA BEEN A COWBOY

Praise for Lorelei James's
Shoulda Been A Cowboy

"You're going to need two things before you sit down to read Shoulda Been a Cowboy: a fan for the heat and a box of tissues for the tears. I can't remember the last book that had me swinging from one emotion to the next more times than I could count. Lorelei James creates her stories and characters with such raw realism. If you're thinking that Rough Riders has to be losing some of its shine with seven books in the series, you'd be wrong...Shoulda Been a Cowboy is the best book yet...one of the best books I've read all year..."
~ *Fallen Angel Reviews*

"Sigh...I have been waiting for Cam's story for a few books now, and the wait was definitely worth it. I thoroughly enjoyed how Ms. James tied this 'non cowboy' into the rest of the family and dealt with all the issues that would come from being injured while serving our country. Domini was just the type of strong woman he needed to move to the next stage of his life. I think Shoulda Been A Cowboy is the best of the seven Rough Riders books to date..."
~ *Joyfully Reviewed*

"...pacing was perfect and the plot was diverse...The author delves into some controversial issues as well as tragic ones and blends them into the romance superbly. The ending was everything I had hoped for..."
~ *The Romance Studio*

Amber—

Shoulda Been A Cowboy

Lorelei James

A Samhain Publishing, Ltd. publication.

Samhain Publishing, Ltd.
577 Mulberry Street, Suite 1520
Macon, GA 31201
www.samhainpublishing.com

First Samhain Publishing, Ltd. electronic publication: August 2009
First Samhain Publishing, Ltd. print publication: June 2010

Dedication

To all the men and women in uniform, we owe you for your dedication and sacrifice. And to all the families of military personnel, who hold it all together at home...this book is for you too...

Prologue

Crash.

Bang.

Thump thump thump.

Silence.

Another loud thud followed the distinctive sound of breaking glass.

Not good.

When the whole building seemed to shake with the next *crash-bang-thump* combo, Domini Katzinski panicked.

Call the police, dummy.

Good plan.

She scrambled for her cell phone on the nightstand. She dialed and hunkered underneath the covers, counting the rings.

Pick up. Please pick up.

"Domini?" Cam McKay said with a surprised tone. "What's goin' on?"

The deep timbre of his voice allowed her to focus on something besides her fear. "I think someone is breaking into the restaurant. There's loud noises and breaking glass—"

"Are you locked in your apartment?"

"Yes. Should I—"

"No. Don't move. Stay right there, do you hear me?"

Domini started to answer but he beat her to the punch.

"I mean it," Cam said sharply. "Stay put and stay quiet until you hear from me. Keep your phone close to you and on vibrate. Promise me."

"I promise."

"Good. I'm on my way." *Click.*

For the next thirty minutes, Domini cowered in her bed, hating that the incident had transported her back to the sleepless nights of her childhood. Hearing the violence in the streets below. Sirens in the distance.

As terror beat in her chest like a living thing, trying to claw its way out, she realized she hadn't exorcised that scared little girl at all. No place on earth was far enough away from those horrid memories because she carried them inside her.

Domini's phone buzzed in her hand and she nearly screamed. The caller ID read: Cam. Thank God. "Hello?"

"I'm outside your apartment. Let me in."

She tossed back the quilt and raced to the living room. After releasing the deadbolts, she opened the door. The gigantic silhouette slunk into the room and she instinctively backed up, because the guy took up a serious amount of space.

Cam McKay was imposing, even in near darkness. The dominant male animal. The ultimate guardian. A pillar of strength. A bona fide warrior.

His deep frown and shrewd gaze read all business. "You okay?"

I am now. "I guess."

He kept looking at her as if he expected her to get hysterical. "Domini—"

"I'm fine. Really. Just shaky. I'll umm...make tea."

Tea? How lame. But she was so flustered from being scared, and from Cam being right *there*, she wasn't thinking straight.

"Maybe you need a shot of whiskey," he muttered as he followed her into the kitchen.

Maybe I need a shot of you to settle me down.

Domini filled the kettle and fired up the stove. Her hand shook like crazy when she put a jasmine teabag in each mug before she faced him, knowing she looked calmer than she felt. "I didn't hear sirens. Does that mean there wasn't a break in?"

Cam watched her carefully and shook his head.

Her relief warred with frustration. "I didn't imagine those noises. I'm not the type of woman who just—" she gestured distractedly, searching for the right phrase, "—who just calls the law on a whim."

But Domini hadn't called 911...she'd called Deputy McKay.

At home. Did Cam think she'd tricked him to get him to show up alone at her apartment at midnight? On a night she knew he hadn't been on duty? Her chin fell to her chest.

"Hey." Cam shuffled closer. His warm fingers tipped her face up. "Don't you think I know you'd never cry wolf? Don't you think I know what type of woman you are, Domini?"

No. I don't think you have a clue.

"You didn't imagine anything. You heard somebody throwing stuff in the Dumpster. Inside the container were a bunch of broken glass and rotten wood from old window frames. Either the Dumpster rolled away as they were loading the bigger stuff into it, or they used it as bumper car, because it's crossways in the alley."

"Really?"

"Yep. There are a couple of big chunks out of the sandstone where the Dumpster smacked into it."

She blinked at him. "But that was it?"

"For the most part."

"You probably think I'm just another paranoid woman who overreacted."

"Not even close. I heard the fear in your voice when you called me. That's what got me over here so damn fast."

And despite her resolve not to act wimpy, Domini launched herself at him. She circled her arms around his neck, pressing her face into his sturdy chest as she shuddered with relief.

It took a minute for Cam to respond. Then one hand stroked her hair with gentleness that belied his size, and his other hand gripped her hip.

At five foot ten, Domini had always been considered tall. But sheltered within Cam's height and breadth, she felt positively petite. Surrounded by his warmth and his scent she felt completely...safe.

Neither one said a word. But their body language spoke volumes. Cam's heart thumped wildly beneath her ear. Her breathing was as choppy as his.

Domini angled her head back gradually, not wanting to scare him away from touching her. When he sensed her looking at him, those sinfully long eyelashes lifted and he studied her from beneath the half-lidded gaze.

Here's your chance. Take it.

11

She stood on the tips of her bare toes until their mouths were a breath apart. "Thank you for coming, Cam." Without breaking eye contact, Domini brushed her lips over his. Slowly the first time. Even more leisurely on the second pass. The third time she'd intended to leave her mouth pressed to his, just to see if he'd kiss her back.

But Cam stole that third kiss from her. His velvety tongue snaked out and traced the seam of her lips. She gasped and that wicked tongue dove straight into her open mouth.

For so long she'd wondered what Cam tasted like. Now she knew—delicious. All hot musky male. The kiss wasn't aggressive, but a curious dance of tangling tongues and sliding lips. When Cam playfully suckled her tongue, her curiosity vanished and spiraled into hunger.

Cam's fingers tightened in her hair. He tilted her head,, devouring her mouth with wet sucking kisses. The hand on her hip slid around to caress her lower back. The heat of his rough palm on her bare skin was as potent as an electric charge as his hand glided beneath her pajama bottoms. His middle finger used the crack of her butt as a sensual guide until just the tip of his finger rested on her tailbone. Then he urged her pelvis closer to his by pressing on that bone.

The odd pressure on that erogenous spot, coupled with Cam's greedy kisses set her blood on fire. The man could inflame her entire body with just one finger.

He briefly lifted his lips. "More," he growled against her mouth. "Give me all of you." Cam kissed her harder. Deeper. Plastering her body to his. Grinding their hips together in a show of raw sexual power. He cranked her need higher, tighter, hotter with each consuming kiss.

Yes yes yes. This is what she'd been dying for.

Domini dug her fingernails into his scalp, returning his passion. Then she let her eager hands drift down the angular lines of his skull to cup his face between her palms. She traced the outer shell of his ears. When her thumb brushed the raised ridge of the scar on his left cheek, he quickly turned his head away.

The teakettle whistled and Cam abruptly released her.

She understood without looking at him the foray into testing the water as lovers was over.

"Domini. I'm..."

Don't apologize. Don't you dare apologize.

"Look. I didn't mean for that to happen."

"But it did."

Silence.

"Sorry. It shouldn't have," Cam said tightly.

Great. He'd reset his persona back to Cam, the helpful deputy, a far cry from Cam, the demanding man who'd just turned her inside out with a simple kiss. Now he'd run. Was he running from her? Or from himself? And would she just let him go?

After removing the kettle from the burner, Domini mustered the courage to meet his eyes. "I assume you're not staying for tea?"

Cam shook his head.

"Well, thank you for showing up at this crazy hour. I appreciate it."

"No need to thank me, princess. That's my job."

"Forgive me for saying so, but your job sucks."

"You have no idea how true that statement is right now."

Cam's gaze scanned her from bedhead to bare toes. He rubbed his mouth with his knuckle, almost as if he was wiping her kiss from his lips and his memory.

Enough.

Domini kept her emotions in check as she walked to the living room. She stood pointedly beside the open door.

Cam said, "Look. Don't—"

"I know what you're about to say, Deputy McKay. I won't forget to lock the door behind you."

"That's not what…" He sighed. "Fine. Good night."

Immediately after Cam cleared the doorjamb, she slammed the door, flipped the locks and stomped back to her bedroom.

Idiotic man. He wanted her. She wanted him. So what was his problem?

What's your *problem? Why can't you just tell him you want him?*

I did! I kissed him first.

And it hadn't changed anything—unless she counted how fast he ran out on her. Evidently actions didn't speak louder than words.

Maybe she should just be patient. Maybe now that she'd

made the first move, Cam would jump on board and take their flirtation to the next level. Or jump on her.

Domini just hoped it wouldn't take another two years.

Chapter One

Eight months later...

At times like these, Deputy Cameron McKay suspected his life would've been easier if he'd stayed a simple cowboy.

Whoosh.

He managed to stop the woman's wild right hook from connecting with the man's jaw. Grabbing her fist, he jerked her arms behind her back. "Assault in front of an officer will get you tossed in jail tonight, Opal, guaranteed, so knock it off."

"I've known you since you were in diapers, boy, don't you dare smart mouth me," Opal retorted.

Yep, riding the range alone, dealing with animals that didn't talk back...some days Cam regretted not taking the offer to join the family cattle business. His gun dug into his hip as he shifted off his bum leg to reach his cuffs.

"Opal. Leave the poor deputy alone," the man behind him snapped.

"Why ain't you arresting him?" Opal demanded. "He started it!"

"I did not, you crazy old bat."

"See? He's calling me names again."

Cam glanced at the gray-haired man holding an ice pack to the goose egg on his forehead. "Now, Ralph, you know I won't tolerate that kinda talk."

"Hah! Told you he'd be on my side," Opal said gleefully.

Ralph muttered.

"There are no 'sides' here, Opal. I haven't made an arrest. *Yet.* Not until someone tells me what happened."

"She—"

"He—" the couple said simultaneously, and started arguing simultaneously.

Cam tried to listen to the heated exchange, but the accusations flung back and forth had nothing to do with the issue at hand: Opal Stancil smacking Ralph, her husband of five decades, with her umbrella. Why Opal had an umbrella handy when Crook County had suffered from severe drought for the last ten years remained a mystery.

Domestic disturbance calls weren't a mystery or all that unusual. Most incidents were cleared up fairly quickly once the participants were forced to talk to each other in front of an unbiased third party.

It also helped that Cam wore a gun.

But Opal and Ralph were too busy shouting to listen to each other, let alone him.

Cam let loose an ear-piercing whistle. "I'm out of patience. Ralph, since you're injured, you can ride up front with me. Opal, I'm gonna have to cuff you and you'll ride in the back."

More silence. Then a meek, "You mean, you're gonna arrest us? Both of us?"

"Yep." Cam waited. Rumor in the Crook County Sheriff's office was Opal and Ralph repeated this same row on their anniversary, every summer, going back fifty-four years. But as there were no arrest records, none of his fellow officers would confirm or deny. They'd just laughed when the call came in on his rotation.

"I can't stomach the idea of her goin' to the hoosegow." Ralph lowered the ice pack and dropped his double chin to his chest. "Aw, Opal, you know I didn't mean it when I said I wished I woulda married Marion Lutter. She ain't never held a candle to you in the looks department."

"And she can't cook worth a damn either," Opal said.

"Makes you wonder how she's so gol-durned, fat, huh?" Ralph peeped at her, wearing a hangdog look.

Opal cackled. "You're so bad, C-bear."

"I'm sorry, snooker-pie. I shoulda stayed outta the whiskey on our special night," Ralph said.

C-bear? Snooker-pie? Sweet baby Jesus. He'd rather jam sticks in his ears than listen to geriatric foreplay.

"Good thing my aim ain't what it used to be."

"Amen to that." Ralph squinted at Cam. "I reckon you can let her go now, Deputy, since I ain't pressing charges."

"You sure?"

"Yep." Ralph patted the floral couch cushion. "Why don't you come on over here, my bee-yoo-ti-ful blushin' bride, so we can kiss and make up proper?"

Opal blew Ralph a kiss. "Give me a minute to see him out." She practically shoved Cam off the porch. "Sorry to trouble you, Deputy. Say hello to your folks from us."

Then she slammed the door in his face.

Stunned, Cam stood on the steps. But when giggles, grunts and the sounds of slapping flesh drifted through the living room window, he practically ran to his patrol car.

Dust kicked up behind him as he drove away. Fast. His radio crackled before he'd gone too far. "McKay."

"Deputy, this is dispatch. Do you need backup for...snooker-pie and C-bear?" Deep belly laughs and kissing noises echoed in the background.

Assholes.

Mindful of being on the radio where anyone with a scanner could hear his response, Cam said, "That's a ten-four," rather than his usual, "Fuck off."

"One other thing. This just came in."

"What?"

"There's a situation over at the Twin Pines."

"What kind of situation?"

"Looks like a bar fight."

It figured. Nothing cowboys liked better than a good fight. "I'm on it." Cam spun a U-turn. Maybe he'd stick around for a stiff drink after he broke up the brawl. God knew he needed one now.

∗

"Let's toast." Keely McKay held her bottle of Bud Light to the center of the table. "To Hudson McKay, the newest addition to the family. The darling boy of Colt and Indy. He's beautiful and healthy, but damn, do I wish one of ya'll would birth me a niece."

Laughter rang out as bottles and glasses chinked together.

"The last thing we need is another wild McKay girl," Skylar said dryly.

"But nine boys in a row? Ten, if I count Chassie's precious Westin? Come on. There's something in the water in Sundance for sure." Keely skewered her sisters in law, Channing, Macie and AJ, with a look. "Maybe ya'll oughta grab your collective spouses—my beloved brothers—and head over to Moorcroft for a night or two when you plan on getting knocked up again."

"Bite your tongue, Keely McKay," AJ replied haughtily.

"Uh-huh. We're done for a while," Macie said. "A *long* while."

Channing piped in, "Us too."

"Right. If you three aren't pregnant again by the end of the year I'll kiss a pig."

"Is that a challenge?"

"Yep. Remember not all pigs are of the bovine variety." Keely grinned and downed her beer.

Domini sipped her rum and Coke, secretly pleased to be included in the first annual "Cowgirl's Night Out", the brainchild of wild child Keely.

Keely had arranged the shindig at a semi-private table in the back room, inviting her brother's wives, Channing, Macie, AJ and India, as well as her cousin Kade's wife, Skylar. Domini didn't know Quinn McKay's wife, Libby, or Luke's wife, Jessie. Poor Jessie appeared as wide-eyed as Domini felt.

In addition to Keely's cousins, Chassie West Glanzer and Ramona West, the group included Ginger Paulson, a local attorney who was pals with Libby and Dr. Joely Monroe. Domini was grateful the chatty doc sat on the other side of the table. The woman had rubbed her the wrong way from the first time they'd met.

Wrong. You're just jealous because you think she's been rubbing on Cam McKay, not in an official medical capacity, even when he claims they're just friends.

Yeah, Cam was friends with everyone it seemed.

Cam. He'd rocked her world with that stunningly passionate kiss months ago. Since then? Nothing. Deputy McKay still showed up at Dewey's every day, friendly as ever. Her own hide-in-the-kitchen reaction bothered her more than his nonchalance. Why couldn't she just buck up and proposition him?

Because you made the first move last time and he scampered away like a scalded cat. Obviously he's not interested in you. Get over it and move on.

Stupid voice of reason. She scowled at her drink, wishing it were pure rum.

India warned, "Slap on a happy face, Domini, or Keely will whip out the party games."

"Oh no."

"Oh *yes*. Keely and Carolyn have this bizarre fixation on forcing everyone to play games at family gatherings. God save us from suffering though another round of 'pin the dick on the cowboy'."

"They really play that?"

"If Keely's in charge we do."

Domini beamed a totally fake smile at India. "Better?"

"Uh-huh. Just keep it up."

"Who are you guys conspiring against?" Macie demanded.

"No one. Just having a rip roarin' good 'ol time," India answered.

Domini's toothy grin widened and she gave Macie two thumbs up.

"I don't care what you two are up to. This is fun." Macie downed her drink. "It's been ages since I've been out with adults."

"In a place without placemats to color on and balloons bobbing everywhere," Channing added.

"Oh pooh, you guys wouldn't have it any other way," Keely inserted. "Am I right?" She elbowed AJ, who'd just knocked back another shot.

"Totally. I love my guys, but I forced myself not to skip out the door because I was *so* looking forward to this girl's night. Damn this is good. What is it?"

"A cherry bomb. Blake got me hooked on them over at the Rusty Spur."

"Does Blake like living in Nebraska?" Doc Monroe asked Keely.

"Yep. He's bought into his buddy's bar. He's head over heels in love with Willow. She's a real firecracker. When he returned to load up his stuff, I've never seen him more...content. He deserves it."

"Amen," Ramona West said, lifting her glass.

Keely ordered another round in Blake's honor and insisted everyone but India drink up.

Everyone bowed to Keely's will. Keely McKay was a force to be reckoned with, a whirlwind of fun, a woman who seized life by the balls and did whatever struck her fancy. Not for the first time Domini wished she could be more like Keely. Freer. Looser. Bolder. Willing to go after what she wanted.

Willing to go after Cam.

Right. Like that'd ever happen. Domini had overcome many things in her life; unfortunately, shyness wasn't one of them.

Someone cranked the music. They all got up and danced, the booze and the laughter flowed freely as they cut loose. But even a semi-private room didn't stop every cowboy in the place from sauntering over to flirt with Keely, who flirted right back. Easily. With complete confidence. Domini could hate her if she wasn't so much fun.

When Keely tucked away yet another hot cowboy's phone number into her jeans pocket, Chassie said, "You're so bad."

The bad girl batted her eyelashes. "Why, whatever do you mean?"

"How many men do you have on a string right now?"

"That's rich, coming from a woman who lives with two guys," Keely shot back.

"Ooh. Ouch," Ramona said with a wince.

Chassie bumped Keely with her shoulder. "I'm living with *three* guys if you count my sweet baby Westin. He's at such a cute stage right now. Trev and Ed are always—"

"Can it, Chass. No baby talk tonight. Remember?"

"Fine. But most of us here do have babies."

"What about you, Jessie?" Skylar asked. "You and Luke talked about kids?"

Jessie shrugged. "Off and on. We're 'off' right now. We've got some really cute baby llamas. You should bring the girls over to see them."

"Llamas?" Domini repeated.

"Jessie was the saving grace for the llamas Chase won in some rodeo last fall. He dumped them off with his folks and expected Charlie and Vi to take care of them." Libby pointed with her beer bottle. "Good thing your father-in-law didn't get his way. Quinn said he was pissed you kept them."

"Casper is always pissed off at me about something I've done. Or not done." She frowned, dipping her head toward her drink so her hair obscured her face.

As the time and drinks passed, Domini couldn't remember when she'd had such a blast. Even India, who rarely set foot in a bar/supper club, was still hanging out two hours later.

Domini heard her name and broke her conversation with Jessie to focus on Skylar and India.

"Even if you are my sister, and I love your offbeat sense of humor, you can be mean."

"When am I ever mean?" India demanded.

"What you did to Kade was mean," Skylar chided. "Kade actually told people that Domini was a refugee because she was kicked out of Bosnia for political persecution."

"But Kade embellished it, claiming she barely spoke English, so any shit he got for sharing misinformation was well deserved," India retorted. "And people around here don't know the difference between Bosnia, the Ukraine and Timbuktu. A foreigner is a foreigner."

How true that was. Because Domini had shared a house with her friend Nadia, who'd emigrated from Bosnia, everyone assumed they were from the same country. Everyone except for Cam. Cam had pegged Domini's accent and country of origin right away. Not that it meant anything.

"Kade wasn't the only one India pranked. She told Lettie from the Golden Boot that Domini was a dethroned Russian princess and to never say the word *vodka* in front of her or she'd burst into tears and go on a bloody rampage."

Domini smiled. That'd been a good one. In fact, that's why Cam had taken to calling her princess—a nickname that'd stuck even after he'd ferreted out the truth.

"That wasn't as bad as what she told Dewey." Macie leaned forward. "India swore Domini was a former Soviet spy posing as a chef. And she was in Wyoming hiding from her checkered, murderous past with the Russian mob."

India snorted. "Come on, can you blame me? People were gossiping about her. I just made the gossip more...colorful. I added a virtual tattoo to her, if you will."

Skylar groaned. "Does everybody have to be tattooed in your world?"

21

"Yep. It makes the world so much more colorful."

"Has anybody ever guessed the truth?" Jessie asked. "Or does everyone believe you're a deposed Russian princess who used to be a knife-wielding Soviet spy and who was kicked out of Bosnia?"

Domini squirmed at their curious looks and being the rare center of attention. "If they ask I tell them I immigrated to the U.S. from the Ukraine with a church group when I was eighteen, which is the boring truth. So that's why I didn't mind when India created a more dynamic...virtual tattoo for me."

"At least I didn't make up a tale about your past as a hot Ukrainian mail-order bride," India said.

Dr. Monroe's pager went off and she bailed. Then Jessie turned milk pale when a group of women blustered into the restaurant and insisted on departing immediately. Skylar begged off since she had the longest drive. Libby was the next to take her leave.

Keely sighed. "Looks like things are winding down. Maybe I should take—" she dug in her pocket for the folded piece of paper, "—Davis up on his offer of a midnight rendezvous. It really sucks goin' home alone."

"Tell me about it," Ramona said. "Although, I imagine I go home alone way more nights than you do, little cousin."

"You'd be surprised if you knew how untrue that statement was in the last two years," Keely said softly. "Especially since I don't have a place of my own to go home to when I'm in Sundance. I'm pretty sure Dad would disembowel any man he found me havin' wild monkey sex with in my bedroom."

"I beat you both," Domini said. "I haven't gone home with any man since I moved to Sundance and I've never had wild monkey sex."

Silence.

Shoot. Maybe she should've kept her mouth shut.

Keely's brooding expression vanished. "So nothin's goin' on between you and Cam? Not even a fuck buddy type thing?"

"Keely!" Macie said.

"Ignore her." AJ added, "*We* all do."

"No, Domini, I'm serious. Whenever I'm in the diner with Cam, he can't keep his eyes off you. And you do some serious staring and stammering of your own. So what gives?" She paused thoughtfully. "Does his handicap bother you?"

"Keely!" that protest came from Channing.

But Keely ignored her sister-in-law, focusing intently on Domini. "Don't you think he's a little bit attractive?"

Domini nodded.

"So what's the problem?"

"Why don't you ask him?" Domini said evenly.

The air went still.

"Get out. Big, bad, bold, take charge Cam...?"

"Runs as hot and cold as the broken pie case when it comes to our comrade Domini," Macie said wryly.

Keely rolled her eyes. "I hoped I'd have a least one brother who wasn't a complete bonehead when it came to women."

Channing, Macie, AJ and India pelted Keely with snack mix and booed her.

"What happened with Cam that he's shied away from you? 'Cause, honey, you're gorgeous. And sweet. Plus, you have that sexy, mysterious accent. Hell, you can even cook. You're like, perfect for him."

"Keely, leave Domini alone," India warned.

But Keely was undeterred. "If you're not interested in the down and dirty details, Indy, maybe you oughta conjure an I-just-got-laid virtual tattoo for her," Keely retorted. "However, *I* wanna know why she and Cam aren't knocking combat boots."

There was no way Domini was avoiding this conversation. Maybe that wasn't such a bad thing. Despite her embarrassment, she told them how Cam had backtracked after he'd kissed her, apologized and never approached her again.

Another bout of silence lasted a minute and then they all chattered at once.

"Cam's got it bad for sure," Chassie said.

"Uh-huh. No wonder he's always working out. Working off all that sexual frustration," AJ said.

Ginger Paulson cocked her head. "Is that why Cam passed off the cooking lessons he won from you to Buck and Hayden? Because he—"

"—cringes at the thought of being alone with me?"

"Or a better explanation is he's scared he won't be able to keep his hands *off* you if you're alone together," Ginger countered.

Keely squinted at India. "Has Cam said anything to Colt about this thing with Domini?"

"Are you kidding? Guy talk is sacred. Colt wouldn't tell me anything, especially when it comes to divulging details about his precious little wounded hero brother, Cameron."

AJ nodded. "Cam isn't talking to Cord about anything either."

"Or to Colby," Channing added.

Wow. Maybe Cam's rejection had nothing to do with her. Sounds like he steered clear of his family too, which made no sense because his family was great.

"Put Carter on the 'no talking' list. However, I'm impressed you've managed to stay professional around him at the diner, Domini," Macie said.

"Real professional. I want to jump that man every single time he walks through the door," Domini muttered.

Ramona grinned. "So do it. Grab him by the hand, drag him upstairs and force him to finish what he started."

"You know, that's not a bad idea," Keely mused. "You're a modern woman. Take control."

Domini understood what these helpful, experienced ladies were saying...in theory. But the truth was, she needed Cam to take charge. That's what had attracted her to him from the start. His bold, bossy nature.

Advice was bantered about. Keely angled forward and spoke very softly just to Domini. "I'll bet a million bucks you both want the same thing. Cam is staying away from you in some misguided attempt to protect you—probably from himself. Tell him what you need, Domini, and he'll move heaven and earth to give it to you."

"And if he doesn't believe me?" *Or want me?*

"That's where actions speak louder than words. Never ever underestimate the power of getting naked. Get him alone, strip to nothin' but skin, and I guarantee he won't look away, let alone walk away." Keely scowled at someone over Domini's shoulder. "Is Cam on duty tonight?"

"Uh-huh. Why?"

"No reason." Keely pointed to Domini's empty glass. "You ready for another drink? Something with more kick to it?"

Bizarre conversational change, but then again, it was

typical Keely behavior, so Domini went with it. "Umm. Sure."

"Cool. What the hell happened to our waitress?"

"I wondered the same thing, K," Ramona said.

"No worries. I'll be right back." Keely popped up and exited into the main part of the bar.

While she was gone, the ladies dispensed more detailed advice on how to handle Cam. Some of the raunchier suggestions made Domini blush, but were very intriguing. Mostly because these seemingly mild-mannered mothers were obviously very sexually satisfied with their McKay men. Hard not to be even more jealous of them.

Keely returned with a pack of unfriendly women on her bootheels. She slid the tray on the table and faced the gatecrashers.

Ramona hopped up in a show of support. "What the fuck are they doing here?"

"Grazing," Keely said.

"So this is where the skank meeting is," a chubby blonde sneered.

"We saved a seat for you, Amanda, but damn, I don't think your fat ass will fit in the chair," Keely shot back.

India coughed to cover a laugh.

"You could always get on your knees," Ramona suggested, "since we all know that's a natural position for you."

"Fuck you, Ramona. Your mouth has always been bigger than your brain," another woman snapped.

"You think I'm all talk, Margo? Try me."

Holy cow. Domini had never seen a real live bar fight, let alone seen women in a bar fight.

The sneering blonde—Amanda—crossed her arms over her chest. "I'd still break you like a twig. I'll spare you the pain and humiliation in front of your friends."

"Generous of you. But you're a fucking idiot if you think I'm scared of you now. I no longer play nice because God and Mommy say I have to."

Domini swallowed a laugh. Man. She'd lived that statement.

Amanda shuffled closer. "Bring it. I owe you serious payback anyway."

"Payback for what?" Ramona asked innocently.

"Don't pretend you've forgotten, after you rubbed it in my face for months afterward."

Ramona shrugged. "It's pretty sad that you haven't gotten over it by now. Old news, Amanda."

"Gotten over what?" Ginger asked.

"Me and Ramona banged their boyfriends a couple years back," Keely said. "Some people hold a grudge."

"Ryan and me were practically engaged!" Margo shrieked.

"Not according to him. Besides, it's not my problem your lover boy couldn't keep his little winky in his pants," Ramona cooed.

Amanda's upper lip curled with disgust. "Sluts."

Keely and Ramona exchanged a look and laughed. "Was that supposed to be an insult?"

"Only a McKay would take that as a compliment," Margo said. "Everyone in the entire state knows a McKay or West will fuck anything that walks."

"Except for you, apparently," Keely retorted. "How many of my brothers and cousins have you propositioned? And how many turned you down flat? All of them."

"Not all." Margo smiled nastily. "Apparently *you* haven't been talking to Luke lately. Where is sweet little Jessie? Did she run on home? Does she even know where her husband is?"

The group of women behind the two in the front guffawed.

Keely's stance changed, as did her demeanor—to absolute fury. "Get the fuck out of my sight, Margo, or I will beat you bloody."

"Oh, I don't know. The odds look pretty good." Margo's gaze swept the women seated around the table. "None of your other 'friends' have jumped in to save your smart mouth from getting your dumb butt kicked."

"That's because Keely knows we have her back," AJ said, and stood up on the other side of Keely.

Amanda's eyes widened with recognition. "Amy Jo Foster. Still a McKay hanger-on I see. How pathetic."

Chassie pushed to her feet. "No one here gives a shit about your opinions, so crawl back to the swamp you slithered out of."

"So the little squaw is allowed to speak?" Margo tsk-tsked. "But I see they're still makin' you sit at the back of the table."

Domini caught Chassie as she lunged at Margo.

More laughter.

"Why don't you load up your freakshow friends—" Margo jerked her head toward India, "—and get the hell out of here."

Keely didn't budge. "Make me."

"Remember you said that when you're cryin' for your mama, McKay."

No one moved.

This was going to get ugly.

"Afraid to take the first swing?" Margo taunted.

Casually, Ginger said, "Keely? Can I offer a suggestion?"

"Sure."

"Kick her ass. I'll bail you out."

All hell broke loose.

Keely lunged for Margo; Ramona charged Amanda. Chairs were kicked aside. Tables fell over. Drink glasses and beer bottles crashed to the floor. Shrieks, grunts, sounds of flesh hitting flesh, cries and curses bounced off the concrete walls.

AJ, Chassie, and India yelled encouragement to Keely, while Domini, Channing, and Macie closed off the circle, keeping Margo's friends from joining the fray.

Someone pushed Domini from behind. She turned and got a fist to the jaw. Rather than turning the other cheek, she slammed her hands on the woman's shoulders and sent her flying with a terse, "Don't touch me."

Macie said, "Whoa. You okay?"

"Yeah." Domini touched the spot and winced. "Maybe."

The fight didn't last long. The noise brought staff running from the restaurant to break it up.

But not before Keely McKay beat the living crap out of Margo. Margo's hair stuck up every which way. Her shirt was ripped. Her mouth was bleeding. She'd curled into a ball on the floor. And she was crying, not Keely.

Ramona had pinned Amanda's arms behind her back. Some man separated them and immediately herded Ramona through the wall of people between the two warring groups.

When Keely wobbled backward, her head smacked into Domini's jaw and Domini sucked in a surprised breath. Holy crap that hurt.

"Sorry."

"Maybe you should sit." Domini snagged a napkin and handed it to Keely. "Your nose is bleeding."

"Thanks." Keely half swayed, half fell to the floor. She patted the open space. "First bar fight?"

"Uh-huh." Domini hunkered down next to her.

"They get easier." When Keely tried to smile, she hissed in a breath and blood trickled out of her mouth. "Damn. I'm getting to old for this shit."

The room buzzed with confusion and excitement.

Ramona ambled over, a shit-eating grin on her face, still looking as if she'd just stepped out of a western fashion magazine. Not a wrinkle on her clothes, not an auburn curl out of place. Her brown eyes sparkled with victory. "You okay, cuz?"

"Never been better. You?"

"Awesome. I've been wanting to do that forever."

"Me too. Felt good. Damn good. And we're the ones who owed *them* payback."

At Domini's quizzical look, Keely explained, "This rivalry has been going on forever. We didn't go to the same school but we attended the same church. Summer church camp was torture. Our moms forced us to go every year until we got kicked out."

"You guys were kicked out of church camp?"

"Yep." Keely and Ramona high-fived each other.

"Fighting with them was totally worth whatever time we spend in jail."

Keely scowled at Ramona. "Jail? What the hell are you talking about?"

"You'll be goddamn lucky if hauling you to jail is *all* I do to you, little sis."

Domini looked up.

An infuriated Cam loomed over them.

Chapter Two

"I can explain," Keely said.

Cam held up his hand. "Save it."

"But—"

"Not another word, Keely West McKay, or so help me God, I will cuff you *and* gag you."

Ramona snickered.

He whirled on her. "Got something to say, Miz West?"

"Nope, cuz. Umm. I mean, no, sir, Deputy, sir." Ramona snapped to attention and mimed zipping her lip.

Chassie giggled.

Cam's gaze encompassed the motley crew of women, who were trying very hard to look...sober. "Sweet Jesus. Are you all drunk?"

"Hey. It was a party. We're in a bar. You do the math," Keely responded with a loud hiccup.

Which sent them all into gales of laughter.

"I'm not drunk," India said.

AJ waggled her fingers. "I am."

"Me too." Macie laughed. "Those cherry bombs were the bomb, Keely."

"No kidding." Channing swayed as she craned her neck to look toward the bar. "Think we can have one more for the road? To toast Keely's victory?"

"No one is sucking down any more booze," Cam barked. He glared at Domini. "What about you?"

"What about me?"

His gaze landed on a bump on Domini's jaw. Briefly his focus jumped to her succulent mouth—*bad idea*—and lust squeezed his balls. "Were you in on this bar fight too?"

Those full pink lips flattened. Those aquamarine eyes became chips of ice. "Never confuse being soft-spoken with being weak-willed. I stand up for my friends. I don't run away."

A female chorus of *ooooh* rang out.

"Fine. All of you stay here while I straighten this out." He tossed a quick look over his shoulder and dropped his voice. "And off the record? Thanks a helluva lot. You think I wanna call my brothers and tell them their wives got drunk and were in a bar fight tonight? While I was on duty?"

Silence.

Then they descended on Cam like a pack of hyenas.

AJ drilled him in the chest with her finger. "FYI Deputy McKay, I'm a big girl. And if I wanna get shitfaced, I'll get shitfaced, so back off."

"Don't you dare call Carter in Canyon River, or so help me, I will ban you for *life* from Dewey's," Macie warned.

"Yeah," Channing chimed in. "If you tattle to Colby before I have a chance to explain, I will call your mother and suggest *weekly* instead of monthly McKay family dinners."

Chassie swayed in front of him. "What they said. Times two, 'cause I got two ornery guys to deal with."

Domini just blinked those exquisite icy blue eyes at him.

Damn women sticking together. It'd been easier when Keely was the only woman in the family. Then the McKay boys could band against her.

Right. Keely always had the upper hand, she knew it, and she played it well. Now they were outnumbered.

Cam stalked off, but not before he heard another round of high fives and drunken whoops of victory.

No one pressed charges, no surprise. It didn't take long to assess the damages. He handed his sister a piece of paper.

"What's this?"

"They're keeping your deposit for the party and you've been banned from Twin Pines indefinitely."

Keely shrugged and folded the paper. "The food sucks here anyway. And if Margo and Amanda are regular customers? Then their clientele sucks too."

Cam took India aside. "Bein's you're sober, can you get the rest of your sisters in drunken arms home? Since I've been barred from calling their husbands to pick them up?"

"Sure. I'll take Chass too, since we're neighbors." India's gaze flicked between Cam and Domini. "You'll make sure if Domini's walking home she gets there all right?"

He snorted. "Domini ain't walking home. She's riding with me when I drop Keely and Ginger off."

"Why?"

"So I have witnesses I didn't kill my baby sis and dump her body out in the boondocks for her latest stunt."

India whistled, directing the women riding in her SUV to the side door. She scorched Cam with a look. "Don't be stupid, Cameron McKay. You've been fucking with her head long enough. Either go for it, or let her go. But it's selfish to try and have it both ways." She didn't wait for a response, but spun on her heel and left.

No explanation necessary. Only one woman had him tied up in knots. His gaze automatically sought her out.

Domini was already staring at him.

He crooked his finger at her.

She sauntered over without delay. "Yes?"

Cam had a hard time breathing when she looked at him like that. Like she'd do anything he asked her. Anything he demanded of her. His gaze roamed over her pretty face, she could be a princess with her regal looks: jutting cheekbones, a high forehead, a thin nose and a delicate jaw. Pale skin, pale eyes, pale hair. Domini should look washed out. She should blend into the background. But she didn't—she was a beacon of light and beauty in the darkness.

"Cam? Can I go now?"

He refocused on her arctic blue eyes. "No. You're riding with me."

"I can walk home. Unless there's a law against that?"

God. Her voice alone could bring him to the edge of ecstasy. The measured enunciation, accented with the sexy, husky hint of her native tongue. Did she cry out in English when she came? Or in Ukrainian?

"Stop staring at me, Deputy."

"Not a chance. Come on."

Keely and Ginger waited by the door.

"Where's Ramona?"

"She caught a ride from a friend."

Outside, Cam opened the rear door of the patrol car. "You two are in the back."

Ginger climbed in without objection. Not his mouthy baby sister. Her protest, "Hey! That's not f—" was lost in the cab as Cam slammed the door.

Smiling, he shoved his key in the door lock on the passenger's side. His belly jumped when Domini placed her hand on his forearm.

"I can open my own door."

"Not without a key you can't. It's self-locking for security reasons."

"Oh."

Cam glanced at the stubborn slant of her mouth. His gut twisted seeing the bump on her jaw. Without thinking, he cupped her neck, stroking his thumb across the swollen spot. "Next time, stay out of the line of fire, princess."

"Is that a direct order, Deputy?"

"Yes." He lightly swept over the protrusion again, just because he could. "I'm bossy. It's a habit, I'm afraid."

"That's what I like about you. How easily you take charge."

He didn't look away even when his head screamed retreat and his dick pulsed against his zipper.

Domini didn't look away either. "Does it mean anything? You touching me like this?"

"Like what?"

"Like you don't want to stop."

God help me, I don't want to stop.

"Do you want it to mean something, Domini?"

"Yes." Her lashes fluttered. "Maybe it's liquid courage allowing me to say this, but do you know how many times I've imagined the different ways you'd touch me? Softly. Firmly. Sweetly. Roughly."

Cam's heart beat a million times faster. He wanted to pull her closer and devour her mouth. He wanted to trace her every curve, with meticulous attention to every dip and hollow. He wanted to see her elegant fingers mapping his body with equal curiosity.

Four loud smacks on the rear window brought him back to reality. He reluctantly let his hand fall from her face and opened Domini's door.

Ginger and Keely gabbed nonstop during the ride. Domini didn't say a word, choosing to gaze out the window into the darkness, her hands primly folded in her lap, the picture of sweetness. Of innocence. Of perfection. Of total fucking hotness.

That's what I like about you. How easily you take charge.

He half feared, half hoped she'd been telling the truth.

"Turn here," Ginger said.

Ginger's one-level ranch house had a detached garage off to one side and a wheelchair ramp running the perimeter. The sight of that wheelchair ramp caused Cam's stump to twitch and the word *never* to echo in his head.

Keely said, "Hey. Isn't that Buck's rig?"

"What? Yes. But he's supposed to be camping with Hayden." Ginger yanked on the door handle. "Goddammit let me out!"

"Hang on." Cam shifted his weight, getting out of the vehicle with his bum leg was harder than climbing in. By the time he'd opened the door, Buck met them in front of the patrol car.

Ginger nearly plowed Buck over. "Where is he? What happened?"

Buck set his hands on Ginger's shoulders. "Whoa there, Red, settle down. Everything is fine. Hayden's stomach was actin' up again, so we canned the campin' trip. No biggie. I gave him some 7-Up and soda crackers. He's sleeping in his room."

"Then why are you still here?"

"Hayden was worried about you. He said you never go out. He made a big ruckus about the *never* part of it."

She muttered, "That little tattletale."

"Anyway, I promised him I'd wait until you were home safely." Buck glanced at the patrol car. "Maybe you oughta tell me why my cousin is bringing you home in a cop car."

"Well, I had a little liquid fun with your cousin's wives and then there was this bar fight..."

Buck squinted. "Is that Keely waving at me through the cage?"

Cam nodded.

"Then that explains everything. Thanks for bringing Red back. I'll take it from here." Buck steered Ginger toward the porch. She tried to jerk away from his hold, but he just yanked her flush with his body and spoke in her ear.

The second Cam was back in his patrol car, Keely bombarded him with excuses, explanations, and justifications, until he said, "Enough."

She sighed despairingly. "Look. I know you're mad as hell at me right now, Cam."

"Yep."

"I know I have no right to ask this."

"Nope."

"Just hear me out? Please?"

"Fine. You've no right to ask me...what?"

"For a favor."

He laughed.

"I'm serious." Keely spoke through the steel cage. "Even though I'm an adult, if I show up drunk, bloody and bruised at Mom and Dad's, they'll both have a fit. It'll be a big ugly scene and I cannot deal with it tonight."

"So what do you expect me to do? Run interference for you, Miz Adult?"

"No! Let me stay at your place. Please? Just for one night? I'm so tired I'll probably crash and I promise I won't be any trouble—"

"Trouble follows you everywhere, so no dice."

"I get that your house is your haven, but Cam, you have an extra bedroom that no one uses. You won't even know I'm there, I swear."

"Keely—"

"Domini, help me out here," Keely pleaded.

Domini faced him. "I think you should listen to her since she is letting you off the hook."

"How is allowing *her* to crash at my place letting *me* off the hook?"

"If you just dump her off at your parent's place, they'll be angry you didn't come in and explain why Keely is a drunken mess. If you escort her into the house, your parents will still be angry and expect you to explain why she's a drunken mess. So calling them to say she's staying with you is the best solution all around."

Damn women sticking together.

"See? It makes perfect sense," Keely said. "Except I'm not that much of a drunken mess."

"Right."

"Cam? Please? I'll never ask you for anything ever again."

"Uh-huh."

"Please?"

He gave in. He always did when it came to Keely. "Fine. You can stay one night. But if one thing is out of place in my house, or if I see any other person besides you in my home? I will tell everyone in the family and the whole damn county what I saw at Colt and Indy's wedding reception."

Keely gasped. "You wouldn't!"

"Oh, I most definitely would. With absolute glee." Cam flashed her a cocky grin. "So do we have a deal, little sis?"

"Yes, but I am entitled to point out you're a lot meaner than my other brothers."

"No, I'm just not buffaloed as easily as they are."

Keely harrumphed and remained unusually quiet for the rest of the drive.

When Cam pulled up the driveway leading to his house, he experienced a sense of joy, a swell of pride, a feeling of peace. This place was the first thing he'd owned outright, finally obtaining the space, freedom and solitude he'd given up during his years in the army. He'd spent his adult years living in barracks or in tents with just a cot and a footlocker to call his own. Meals, showers, hell even sleep was a group affair.

Not here. Cam rarely had visitors and he preferred it that way. Sometimes on his days off he stretched out on his couch and stared at the walls in complete silence just because he could. He'd created an island of peace for himself even surrounded by the turbulent sea of his family.

He parked on the concrete slab and the yard light clicked on. His dog, Gracie, raced back and forth along the fence, yipping with excitement. Cam turned to Domini. "Sit tight. I'll be right back and then I'll run you home, okay?"

"I didn't know you had a dog."

"There's a lot you don't know about me, princess."

"The same could be said about me, Deputy," she murmured.

Was that a...challenge? From sweet Domini?

"Are you gonna let me out, or what?" Keely complained. "I hafta piss like a racehorse."

"Classy, Keely." Grumbling under his breath, Cam exited the car quickly, wincing at the sharp pain in his hip. Upon opening the rear door, he heard, "—what I said about getting naked."

Don't ask what Keely is babbling about. You're better off if you don't know.

At the front door he rattled off, "Stay out of my room. Stay out of my bathroom. Stay out of the liquor cabinet. Don't fuck with my TV. Leave Gracie outside. I'll deal with her when I get home in a little bit."

"There's no need for you hurry back, bro. I can take care of Gracie." Keely stepped into the foyer. "In fact, I hope I don't see you until well after the sun rises."

"Brat."

She grinned and slammed the door in his face.

Cam counted to ten and backtracked to the car. He took his time getting in, not because he was stalling, but because his stump was starting to chafe inside the socket.

As soon as they were on the paved road, Domini said, "Is your leg hurting?"

How had she picked up on that so fast? "You wouldn't think so, bein's half of the damn thing is gone."

Silence.

"Sorry. It's been a long day."

"Are you off duty now?"

"Yeah. I've been off since I finished up at Twin Pines."

"I'm sorry you have to drive me home."

I'm not.

The conversation died. Cam flipped on the defroster. Why was his windshield fogging up at the end of freakin' August?

Because Domini Katzinski is smokin' hot. She makes your heart pound. She makes you sweat. She makes you breathe hard. She makes you imagine what it'd be like pounding into her, both of you covered in sweat as you breathe in the scent of her.

Dammit. Think of something else. Do something else.

He fiddled with the police radio. Then he drummed his fingers on the dash.

Domini placed her cool palm over his knuckles.

Cam looked at her. "What?"

"Do I make you nervous, deputy?"

Yes. "No. Why?"

"Because you constantly fuss whenever you're around me."

"It's just a habit."

"An annoying habit." She threaded her soft fingers through his until her palm rested on the back of his hand. "Can you keep still now?"

He shrugged. But he didn't remove his hand. Actually, he was shocked she'd touched him so freely. Domini was usually so...reserved.

Normally silence didn't bother him, in fact, Cam preferred it. But tonight, he wanted to talk, if only to hear her voice. "Did you have fun before the cops showed up?"

"Yes. We danced and drank and gossiped. I've never actually seen a bar fight."

Cam snorted. "You must not hang out with Keely much. That girl is always finding trouble."

"She seemed pretty pleased she'd popped my cherry tonight."

He nearly wrecked the car. "What?"

Domini blushed. "It was my first Wyoming bar brawl. Keely came up with the cherry-popping phrase, not me."

"It figures. I'm curious. What else did you ladies gossip about?"

"Family. Babies. Men. Sex." Domini's gaze pierced him. "You."

"Me? What about me?"

"Your sister asked if something was going on between us."

His stomach dropped at the thought of his family gossiping about him. "What did you say?" Cam eased the patrol car alongside her building.

"No. But I did say I wished something was going on between us."

Cam didn't know how to respond. Evidently saying nothing was the wrong response, because Domini attempted to bail out of the car.

"Forget it."

"Ah-ah-ah." Cam caught her wrist, holding her in place. "Wait just a damn minute. You don't get to say something like that and then just leave."

Domini just stared at him intently.

"Why would you want to start something with a gimped-up, scarred man like me?"

"That's not what I see when I look at you."

Fuck. This is what unnerved him about Domini. She saw too much. "Maybe you need glasses."

"Maybe you're the one who's blind."

He winced internally, but managed, "What's that supposed to mean?"

"I see the fire in your eyes when you look at me, Cam. I feel it when you allow yourself to touch me. Yet, you won't take what you so badly want." Domini cocked her head. "Why? Are you a martyr? Or a masochist?"

"Neither. I'm just a man." *Not even a whole man.*

"If I begged you to prove your manhood to me you'd run again, wouldn't you?"

Heat rose up his neck. "I didn't run."

"No. You apologized first and *then* you ran. Which was way worse."

Shit. He had no idea how much she'd misunderstood his reaction to her months ago. "Domini, let me explain—"

"No. Stop right there." She drew away from him until her back rested against the door. "No more excuses. You either want me, or you don't. You will either come upstairs right now and we can explore this—" she gestured to the space between them, "—or you can drive away and we will never speak of it again."

Cam's anger surfaced. "And if I drive off, you'll what? Find another man?"

Her shoulder hitched in a half-shrug. "Perhaps."

"Who?"

"Harold Henderson is always flirting with me."

"If I ever see that fucking pervert looking at any part of you, I'll gouge his goddamn eyes out," Cam snarled.

"Then you'd better add Deke Nealon to that list because he asked me to a movie last week."

"I've arrested Deke before and got no problem doin' it again if he messes with you." His head spun. No one touched Domini but him. No one.

Really? You haven't been touching her either. She's supposed to wait around for you to get your head out of your ass?

India's comment, *Either go for it, or let her go. But it's selfish to try and have it both ways,* haunted him because he knew she was exactly right. The time had come for him to fish or cut bait, as Colt always said. "Who else?" he demanded.

"Last night Marshall Benson offered to take me to Ziggy's."

"Marshall Benson? He cheats at pool!"

"So do I. You going to arrest me too?"

"Hell yes, if it'll keep you from going out with a loser like him." *Stay calm.* "What are you trying to do, Domini? Piss me off by naming all the guys who want to do you?"

She jabbed her finger at him. "You asked, Deputy. And I'm tired of waiting for you to come to terms with what *you* want to do to me. I especially want you to get over your mistaken belief that I am somehow...too fragile to handle you. I told you I like that you take charge, Cam."

"You really wanna see that side of me, princess? The rough man who expects his demands to be met without question or hesitation?"

She nodded.

Lightning fast, Cam curled his hand around her neck and hauled her close enough to kiss. "I don't play at this. It's not a phase, not bedroom games. This is who I am."

"Then that is who I want," she said softly.

His resistance shattered. "I'm giving you one last chance to change your mind."

"My mind has been made up for a lot longer than yours has."

He put his mouth on her ear and growled, "Get upstairs. Get naked. Wait for me."

Domini slipped from the car with such grace and determination Cam wondered what he'd gotten himself into.

After he plodded up the staircase, he stopped to catch his breath. Why could he run ten miles with no problem but a climb up a set of stairs made him ache like he'd scaled Mt. Everest?

Because you're a cripple. You'll never be the man you were.

Cam gritted his teeth against the voice of that bitter man inside his head, the voice who usually won the argument.

Not this time.

Domini hadn't known him before his war injury. She knew him now. She wanted him now. That thought gave him the courage to open the door.

The creak sounded unnaturally loud in the stillness of her apartment. Cam was shocked he'd heard anything above the swift beating of his heart. "Domini?"

"I'm here."

His head whipped around to see her perched on the couch.

Naked.

Holy fucking shit. She was beautiful. And even better, she was obedient. He grinned and crooked his finger at her.

Domini pushed to her feet and sauntered over.

"You're naked."

"You told me to be."

He traced the line of her jaw down her throat. "What are you thinking right now?"

"I can't believe you're really here." The desire darkening her pale blue irises staggered him. "What are you thinking?"

"This." Cam gripped her shoulders and crushed his mouth to hers.

The sweet taste of mint teased his tongue as he dove straight in for a hungry, openmouthed kiss that was eight goddamn months overdue.

Domini wound her arms around his waist, kissing him back with greediness only matched by his. Her tongue dueled and retreated as she kissed him from every possible angle. Her fingertips dug into the muscles of his back.

As much as Cam ached to explore every inch of her sinuous body, first with his hands and then with his tongue, he had to demonstrate from the start his take-charge side was his real sexual side.

Cam's lips meandered to her chin. He let his mouth skim the curve of her jaw, taking a minute to kiss the welt she'd received at the bar.

Domini's soft moan stirred the air by his ear.

"Couch. Now."

She laced their fingers together, not caring his left pinky was gone as she tugged him to the living room.

Cam trailed his fingertips across her collarbone, then he took a step back until his right calf hit the bottom of the couch. He'd already removed his gun and stashed it in the car. Next he unclipped the cuff pouch and tossed the handcuffs on the cushion behind him. Almost in slow motion, he pulled the end of the belt out of the first loop and released the buckle.

Her gaze never wavered from his crotch.

He unsnapped the button on the waistband of his uniform pants and eased the zipper down. Jesus. He needed relief; his dick had been straining against his pants for an hour. The two halves of fabric separated, exposing his white boxer briefs. He watched her expression change as she caught her first glimpse of his cock.

Cam kept his pants and briefs high on his upper thighs as he lowered to the couch, but he yanked them down his ass in the back. "Turn around and put your wrists together." Two quick snaps and the handcuffs were locked behind her back. "Face me."

She looked amazing completely naked, half bound and fully willing.

And she'll look damn good with your cock in her throat.

"Just so you know. I received a clean bill of health last month when I was at the VA in Cheyenne. What about you?"

"I haven't...been with anyone since I moved here from Denver a few years back."

He lifted a brow. "A bunch of real sorry guys around these parts who let a beautiful woman spend her nights alone."

"Do you include yourself on that list, Deputy?"

"Yes."

Domini smiled serenely.

"I want your mouth on me. I don't care if you weren't the swallowing type before, because now, you are. On your knees."

She dropped between his thighs and Cam noticed she was careful not to bump his prosthesis. Or was she avoiding touching it entirely?

Shoving aside his doubts, Cam swept the hair from her

flushed face, crushing the silky, fragrant strands in his hand. He wanted an unobstructed view of her mouth working him because he'd fantasized about this for too damn long and he was damn impatient to have it all right fucking now. "Lick the head."

Her tongue darted out and rimmed the tip, lapping at the bead of moisture gathered in the center. She suckled the ruddy head, flicking her rough tongue over the sweet spot.

Cam hissed. "I like it wet. I wanna feel you sucking me all the way into your hot mouth. Slowly. Make it last."

She sucked. She licked. She used her teeth. Her tongue. Oh man, that wicked, naughty tongue might break him. She kept her lips tight around his shaft from tip to base. Saliva ran down her chin and neck as she bobbed her head. Over and over. Domini worked Cam over until he could barely see straight and his dick was ready to explode.

"You really do get off with me telling you what to do, don't you?"

The affirmative noise vibrating in the back of her throat settled in his balls, drawing them up tight.

He traced the outline of her upper lip as his cock plunged in and out of that wet, suctioning heat. He lost track of the number of strokes but the buzz began in his balls and zipped up his abdomen. He shoved until her mouth was around the root.

Domini gagged.

"Breathe through it, baby. Come on. That's it."

When she'd relaxed her throat muscles, he pulled out halfway and rammed in again. Faster, but with shallow thrusts.

"Tighten your lips more. Fuck, that's good. Goddammit, here it comes." Lost in sensation, he plunged deep and hissed, "Swallow. Now. All of it. Let your throat muscles work me." Cam kept his grip on her head as his seed pulsed out and she swallowed every spurt.

As he floated back to sanity, the arousing scent of her body drifted up. His hands fell away. His cock slipped from her mouth and he sagged into the couch cushions. Sweating. Breathing hard. Totally spent.

But nowhere near done.

Chapter Three

Domini watched pleasure soften the harsh angles of Cam's face. She'd fantasized about this moment, but fantasies paled in comparison to the reality of being bound and on her knees before this strong, sexy, demanding man.

Surrender created the rush she'd been searching for.

"C'mere." Cam's big hands curled around her upper arms and he helped her to her feet. "Lemme touch you."

Please. Yes. Now. Everywhere.

He settled her high on his lap, a knee on either side of his hips.

His cock, still semi-erect, rested against his abdomen. The heat from his groin tempted her to grind hard into that thick shaft.

"Domini. Look at me."

Her gaze tracked the line of brass buttons from the bottom of his khaki uniform shirt to his face. His eyes were usually bright blue, but right now, those eyes were dark with lust.

Domini's heart rate accelerated.

Cam's hands glided down her arms, behind her back to her wrists. "The cuffs aren't chafing you?"

Cuffs? What cuffs? Oh. Right. She was handcuffed. How had she forgotten that?

Because you were immersed in a blissful, sexual haze.

"My hands are fine."

"Good to hear. Although, we seemed to've lost our momentum," Cam murmured. His fingers trailed beneath her bound arms. He spread his hands across her naked back and gently urged her forward.

"Wait. I'm falling."

"I won't let you. Trust me."

He leaned closer, but his lips didn't seek hers. His mouth zeroed in on her right nipple.

She gasped when his wet tongue flicked the tip. Again and again. She arched and began to rock into him, trying to connect her sex to his.

Cam lifted his mouth long enough to command, "Stay still."

How was she was supposed to stay still with the soft suction and heat of his hungry mouth? And the rasp of his five o'clock shadow on her flesh?

"You are as perfect everywhere as I imagined." Cam lightly scraped his teeth over the beaded tip.

"You imagined me...naked?"

He tipped his head back. "All the damn time."

"Really?"

His eyebrows drew together. Comprehension dawned. "You didn't honestly believe I wasn't attracted to you."

She nodded.

"Why in the hell would you think that?"

Because I redefine insecure. "Because you left after the one time you kissed me and never attempted to touch me again."

"That wasn't because I wasn't attracted to you. That was out of self-preservation."

"Why? Because you thought I might hurt you?"

"Not even close. But I ain't exactly in the mood to talk about it."

"What are you in the mood for?"

Then Cam was kissing her fiercely. One hand held her in place by the back of the neck. His other hand skimmed her torso and his fingers slipped straight between her legs.

Domini canted her hips, allowing him total access to whatever part he desired, giving him everything without having to ask.

Cam stroked her pussy with soft exploratory touches. He kissed a path to her ear. "You're wet. Did you get off havin' my cock in your mouth?"

"Yes."

He reconnected their lips as his middle finger swirled in the cream coating the mouth of her sex. He dragged that wet finger up and drew circles around her clit.

Domini's thighs clenched and she suppressed a moan.

As Cam's mouth languidly moved over hers, he pushed one finger inside her slick channel, then two. He pumped the digits deep, stretching her delicate tissues, while the base of his thumb continually rubbed against her clit.

She'd never felt such urgency, yet didn't want the probing touches to end. The heat and fullness of his stroking fingers inflamed her as much as his lazy, seductive kisses.

Cam's lips broke free and he nuzzled her throat. "Come apart for me, Domini." More kisses sizzled across her skin as his fingers worked magic inside her. "Tell me what'll get you there."

"I-I don't know. Just...don't stop. Please."

"I won't make you beg for it—" he licked the cords straining in her neck, "—this time. Next time I'd like to string you along and see how long it takes before you unravel."

His words rushed her to the next level of need. "Cam—"

"I'll take care of you. Arch back."

His rhythmic fingers, his sucking kisses, his confidence in seeing to her pleasure, unlocked a place inside her she'd never trusted another man to access. She closed her eyes and let go.

When the first searing ripple started, she tightened her thighs, her interior muscles, her butt cheeks and cried out as the strength of the orgasm sideswiped her.

"Look at me."

Obeying Cam's gruff command, she stared into his fiery eyes while her pussy pulsed around his skillful fingers and saw her satisfaction and lust reflected on his face.

"That's it, princess. Give it all to me."

After the last throb faded, Domini wanted to bury her face in the side of his neck. Lick the salt from his skin, familiarizing her senses with his taste, drown in his scent. Memorize every intimate detail about him.

But Cam had other plans. He fumbled for the handcuff key. A soft *snick* sounded and her arms were freed. The cuffs plopped on the couch cushion and he urged, "Put your hands on my shoulders."

Domini wished Cam had ditched his shirt, allowing her a chance to explore the sculpted muscles of his chest. But when he widened her knees and pressed his cock into her cleft, she forgot about everything except the sensation of the hard length of his shaft grinding against her clit. She countered his rocking motion, sliding down as he thrust up, increasing the friction.

Cam plunged two fingers into her pussy from behind, stroking with unerring accuracy the hot spot inside her vaginal walls that sent heated shivers of need spreading outward.

Panting, mindless, she lost herself to the moment. The smooth, fast glide of his velvety cock against her swollen sex. His greedy mouth sucking on her throat.

They rocked in tandem. In opposition. He nipped, licked and rubbed on her neck like a gigantic cat. A hungry cat if the scrape of his teeth from her earlobe to her nipples was any indication.

But Domini liked that he hungered for her. She liked his unintelligible mutters that sent tingles racing across her bare skin. She liked everything about being with this man.

Her belly tightened in warning. Gripping his closely shorn scalp, Domini tipped Cam's head back and smashed her mouth to his, kissing him crazily as her second orgasm hit.

He swallowed her cries and his rhythm never faltered as he rode out the storm with her.

Just as she was about to rip her mouth free, a shiver worked through Cam like he'd been zapped with an electric current. Hot liquid spurted on her belly as he came with a drawn-out groan. His hips bumped up three more times, slowed, and stopped.

He nestled his forehead in the curve of her neck and breathed hard. She breathed hard.

Her whole body shook with the glow of two fantastic orgasms. Would Cam run if she told him he was exactly the type of lover she'd been searching for?

Probably. Especially since he'd played it cool for months after that steamy kiss.

Yet, another part of her wondered if he'd run if she *didn't* say anything. If she didn't reassure him that she didn't want this to be a onetime thing.

Take a chance. Tell him the truth.

Domini hitched her shoulders back. Her smile died and her hopes fell when she noticed Cam's face read pure panic.

In fact, he stayed frozen, not even looking at her face.

She ignored the urge to flee. Instead she slowly swung her left knee over his lap and rolled to her feet. Keeping her back to him, she tried to figure out what she'd done wrong.

Why do you always assume you're to blame?

When Domini faced Cam, she noticed he'd already yanked his pants up and was hastily stuffing the handcuffs in the leather pouch.

Maybe Cam was just distracted and he'd murmur something sweet and normal when he wasn't so flustered.

But it seemed to be a long wait.

Almost nervously, Cam rubbed the top of his head and glanced at his watch. "Wow. I didn't realize it was so late."

Lame excuse, Cam.

Domini retreated to her bedroom for a robe, allowing Cam time to get his head in order. He stood by the door when she returned. If he'd worn a hat, he'd be wringing it in his hands.

"I better get home and see if Keely has destroyed my house."

"I understand." *Liar.* "Drive safe."

"Thanks. Remember to lock up after me."

"The second you leave, the door will be shut, locked, and I won't reopen it for you, Deputy. Not even if you beg."

Cam frowned at her rare sarcasm but didn't comment. "Good. I'll see you." And he was gone.

After Domini slammed the door and flipped the locks, she listened as he lumbered down the stairs. She pressed her head to the cool wood frame until she heard him land safely at the bottom. Stairs gave him fits with his prosthesis, not that he'd ever admit it.

Maybe he's the type of man who won't ever admit anything, especially his feelings.

The outer door shut. She listened. Sure enough. Cam tested the outside doorknob to make sure the door locked behind him.

Why was he so concerned about her safety if he didn't care?

Because Cam McKay is a cop. He cares about everyone's safety.

The truth of that statement didn't sit well with her.

Domini trudged into the bathroom and didn't like the confusion and bleakness staring back at her from the mirror.

Her hair was a tangled mess. Her lips were swollen from giving Cam a blowjob and his harsh, deliciously wicked kisses. Marks from his razor stubble scored her chest. He'd even sucked a big purple hickey above her collarbone. Under other circumstances, with Cam standing behind her, kissing his passionate marks, she might've laughed. Or begged for more. But now? She just looked used.

Used. Right. Cam didn't even want to have sex with her. He got off and he got gone.

Why?

You're defective. He knows it. He doesn't want to get tangled up with you because it can't go anywhere. So if he comes back for more, retain the upper hand. Keep it casual.

Come back. Right. Cam had left so fast he'd probably scorched her carpet.

Better burn marks there than on your heart.

True. She clicked off the light and crawled in bed.

Domini hadn't scheduled herself to work in the diner the next day. But after spending part of the morning at the park with her friend Nadia's son, Anton, while Nadia ran some mysterious errands, she knew she'd go stir-crazy sitting in her apartment, obsessing over Cam's retreat.

Cooking appeased her. She waited until the lunch rush ended and snuck into Dewey's kitchen.

"Just can't stay away, can you?"

She smiled sheepishly at Beatrice, her second-in-command.

Beatrice set her elbows on the steel prep counter. "Please tell me you're whipping up goodies full of chocolate and sugar."

"Yes, ma'am."

"Goody! Lucky me."

"No, I'm lucky to have you and that sweet tooth as my secret taste tester."

"Almost as good as having a secret admirer." Beatrice winked, casting a look over her shoulder. "Lemme know when you need me to lick the spoon."

Creaming butter and powdered sugar together released a familiar sugary scent, way better than any expensive aromatherapy. Domini sifted the dry ingredients into the industrial mixer. She poured in white chocolate chips, and butterscotch chips and hand stirred the thick mixture, keeping the consistency between cake batter and cookie dough.

She dumped the mix into a rectangular cake pan and set it on the middle rack of the smallest oven. She grabbed a saucepan, determined to nail down a souped-up version of mole sauce she'd been messing with for months.

After the timer dinged, she deposited the brownies on a wire rack to cool. She'd finished the sauce but wasn't sure if she'd gotten the proportions equal. She yelled, "Bea, could you please come here?"

Beatrice peered around the corner. "You bellowed?"

"Yes." Domini waved a spoon coated with dark sauce. "Taste."

"At your service." Beatrice popped the spoon in her mouth. She swallowed and licked her lips. Then her face became fire-engine red. She sputtered, "Too much chili powder!" and raced for the sink to gulp from the stream of water.

Domini sighed. "Sorry. I always screw this up."

"I know the feeling," came from behind her.

She whirled around.

Cam.

And didn't he just look good enough to eat? Talk about hotness and sweetness perfectly proportioned. He wore faded jeans and a black tank top that showed off his beefy biceps, triceps and bulging pectorals. His hands were jammed in his back pockets and he watched her with a guarded expression.

"What do you want?"

"Domini!" Bea gasped. "What on earth is wrong with you?"

Yeah, snapping was so unlike her, but she couldn't quell the surly feeling.

Beatrice wiped her mouth on her apron. "She's always testy when things don't turn out the way she'd hoped."

"Kinda sounds like the way my night went last night," he said softly, never taking his eyes from Domini's.

Her heart beat as fast as a mixer on high speed.

"Beatrice, could you give us a couple of minutes?" Cam asked.

"Sure. I'll just be out front icing down my tongue." She flounced off.

When Cam remained quiet, Domini said, "Why are you here?"

"I've been waiting in the dining room for you for over an hour," Cam said. "You ignoring me?"

"Hard to do when I didn't know you were here."

Cam edged closer. "I wouldn't blame you if you were avoiding me after the shitty way I acted last night." His gaze dipped to the collar of her shirt. "I'm here to apologize."

"For what?"

"For what?" Cam's brow furrowed. "I think it's obvious."

"It's not obvious to me, so why don't you explain it?"

An incredulous look appeared only to be replaced with an irritated one. "What? You expect me to grovel?"

"No. I expect nothing from you, which is why it's so ironic that I'm disappointed."

"Now wait just a damn minute—"

"Just go." Stupid chili pepper powder must've blown in her face; her eyes smarted with tears. She sidestepped him, muttering, wishing she was the type of woman who could rant and rave and throw things to relay her frustrations.

Cam wheeled her around, boxing her between his body and the steel door of the walk-in cooler. "Will you at least let me apologize before you storm off and start swearing at me in Ukrainian?"

"That was Russian."

"So I'm an idiot all the way around, okay? Look, I'm sorry..." His gaze lingered on her neck. "I'm so goddamn sorry I was such an animal and marked you last night. First thing. You deserve better than a man who mauls you."

Her stomach swooped at the self-recrimination in his words. "Cam—"

"This is why I stayed away from you, Domini. You're so soft and sweet. And I'm too—"

"—much man for me to handle?" she supplied.

Cam's eyes narrowed. "I'm serious."

"So am I. At any point last night did I say, 'Cam, you're

hurting me.'"

"No. But—"

"Do you think I am incapable of being honest with you? Do you think I am so desperate for your touch that I would allow you to...hurt me?"

"Dammit. You're twisting my words."

"No, I am being honest. And you still don't get it, do you?"

"Get what?"

She searched his eyes. "The only thing that upset me about last night was that you left again."

He stared at her with complete confusion. But he didn't back away. "Really?"

"You know I'm not very bold, which means I've been waiting to see if you would make a move on me. And when you finally did, and I saw the passionate, demanding side you keep hidden because you think I can't handle it—"

"You can't handle it."

Domini snapped, "You haven't given me a chance to prove otherwise, have you?"

"Whoa. I didn't mean—"

"Yes, you did. You assumed. Did you consider I have needs and desires that *you* might not be able to meet?"

Cam's face slackened with shock. Then his male pride leapt to the surface all hot and dangerous and in her face. "Oh, princess, don't go there. I can satisfy all your needs and desires and then some."

"Prove it."

A pause followed as Cam looked at her. Almost as if he was seeing her for the first time. Then Cam framed her face in his large, rough hands. "You deserve a man—"

"—who makes me come so hard I see stars?"

"Domini."

"Cameron."

He muttered, "I'm so goddamn tired of fighting this."

"So don't fight it."

The soft brush of his lips over hers was in direct contrast to the heat in his eyes. "All right. You win."

"I think we'll both be winners, Cam."

"You're coming home with me right now."

Cam grabbed her hand and strode out the front door,

towing Domini behind him. He opened the passenger side of his truck and loomed over her. "You're sure you want to get involved with me?"

"It doesn't sound like I'm the one having doubts."

"I'm not." He bent to kiss the hollow of her throat. "I still say you're too good for a broken war bum like me."

"Trust me, Deputy, I know a thing or two about being broken." Domini didn't wait for his response before she climbed in.

Chapter Four

Domini mashed herself next to Cam in the cab. The air from the open window blew wisps of her silky hair across his cheek, teasing him with a reminder of her fragrant softness. It was damn close to heaven being alone with her, with dust kicking up behind them and miles of grazing lands on the horizon in front of them, beneath the cloudless Wyoming sky.

She hadn't said much on the drive out to his place. Most women would be compelled to fill the quiet with mindless chatter. Not Domini. Her silence wasn't unsettling. In fact, Cam found it comforting.

Cam parked on the concrete slab in front of the garage and shut the truck off.

Domini faced him and smiled softly.

Every time she gazed at him as if she could read his soul, his breath stalled in his lungs.

"Thank you for the moment to clear my head."

"No problem."

"Are we going to talk first? Or..."

"Or what? You think I'm gonna truss you up and fuck right out here in the truck? Give me some damn credit, Domini. I do have some damn restraint."

"Too much restraint sometimes."

In another bout of silence between them, his dog yipped along the fence.

"Gracie," he yelled out the window. "Hush. We'll be there in a sec so you can sniff her and make sure she's not a threat."

Domini's whole body went rigid beside him.

"Are you afraid of dogs?"

"Yes. You probably think it's silly—"

"Hey." Cam bent his head to peer into her alarmed eyes. "Nothin' silly about it. I'll keep her in the yard if it'll ease your mind."

"If you do that, the dog will have another reason to hate me."

"Luckily Gracie doesn't hate anybody." He smiled. "Just let me know when you're ready to meet her, okay?"

"You aren't going to assure me she is the best dog ever and I will immediately love her?"

"No. Although she *is* the best dog ever, I'm serious about not pressuring you about her. I know what it's like to have that 'just get over it' mentality thrust at you."

"Thank you."

Cam's gaze descended to her lips. He couldn't resist stealing a kiss. Her mouth was so warm and supple moving beneath his that he stole another one. And another.

She sank into him, welcoming his attentions with a dreamy sigh.

After several long, deep, wet kisses, he playfully nipped her bottom lip. "Let's take this inside."

She paused at the base of the stairs. The bottom was divided into two sections. Half was a set of steps, half was a wheelchair ramp. "I've never seen you use a wheelchair."

"That's because I don't use one." *Ever.*

"Then why have a ramp?"

"It's a daily reminder I could end up in a chair if I don't work hard every damn day at staying out of one."

"Did you build it?"

Cam shook his head. "Blake did at Colt's request. Right after I got back to the States and was discharged."

"Did Colt think you wouldn't walk again?"

"No. But he knew I needed a place that was accessible just in case."

She curled her palm over the handrail. "It must be nice to have that kind of unconditional support from your family."

"I guess. But living around all of them can drive me nuts." Domini didn't avert her eyes as Cam ascended the stairs, and oddly, her scrutiny didn't bother him. He opened the door. "After you."

Domini ducked under his arm and stopped on the edge of the carpet, taking it all in.

Cam tried to see his refuge through her eyes. His cousins Chet and Remy West had gutted the inside of the house after he'd purchased it from Colt and Buck. Any resemblance to the infamous Boars Nest party house had been completely eradicated.

The structure of the living room hadn't changed much, besides replacing the sagging bay window with a newer, larger window. Modern track lighting ran along the center of the ceiling. The rectangular room was anchored at one end by a gigantic flat screen TV and a stack of audio/visual components, and on the other end by a fireplace. A wood coffee table was centered between reclining chairs and a plush, oversized couch the color of tobacco.

"This is awesome. Did you pick out the colors and the furniture and everything?"

"Keely helped. Said she didn't want me living in a man cave with white walls, a TV and cheap bean bag chairs."

Domini laughed.

"Come see the kitchen."

The wall between the formal dining room and the kitchen had been demolished, creating one large open space. New appliances, pine cabinetry, bigger windows and tile flooring showcased modern amenities, yet the eat-in breakfast bar uniting the two areas retained a rustic, country feel. A sliding glass door led to an enormous covered deck that wrapped around the entire backside of the house.

"Please tell me you use this fabulous kitchen for more than zapping microwave meals and cooking frozen pizza."

"Um. Not really."

She scowled at him.

"What?"

"I wish you would've taken the cooking lessons you won. It would be a dream to teach you to cook in this kitchen."

Cam slid his hands around her hips to cup her ass and urged her lower body against his. "You really think we would've gotten any cooking done? Or maybe I just would've spread you out across my table and feasted on you. 'Cause princess, you look mighty tasty."

A shuddering breath left her lungs.

He kissed the corners of her mouth. "I want you like crazy. I wanna tie you to my bed for days. But before any of that happens, we need to get some things straight."

She nodded. "Can we sit outside and talk? It's such a beautiful day."

"Sure. Would you like a beer?"

"A beer would be fine."

"Head out onto the back deck and I'll bring it to you."

Cam heard the sliding glass door open, forgetting Gracie was penned in the backyard until Domini shrieked. He turned just in time to see Domini leap on the antique oak table.

Gracie barked and raced around excitedly, thinking it was a game.

"Gracie! Sit."

A disbelieving whimper sounded and then the Border collie obeyed.

"Good girl." Cam crossed to the dog, ignoring Domini crouched like a cat about to pounce. He ruffled Gracie's silky ears. "Listen up, pup. Domini hasn't been around dogs as cool as you, so give her some time to adjust. Be on your best behavior and before you know it, you'll have Domini sneakin' you treats and rubbing your fat belly. Understand?"

Gracie barked twice.

"Good girl. Stay." Cam grabbed a new rawhide chew out of the pantry. The second Gracie saw it her tail thumped. Her tongue flopped past her gums in a doggie version of a smile. He couldn't help but grin. The damn dog cracked him up. "If I let you out in the pasture, you can't be sneakin' up on Colby's cattle."

A tiny, sad noise hummed from Gracie.

Domini said, "She'd do that?"

"Yep. Her breed is great for herding. Since I don't have cattle she tries to herd everyone else's cattle. Back here. The first couple times my brothers were amused. After that, not so much."

Gracie whined pitifully again.

"I mean it, Gracie. No chasing cows."

Two more barks.

Cam shot a look over his shoulder at Domini. "Be right

back without the mutt. Grab the beer and I'll meetcha outside." He whistled loudly and Gracie raced out of the house hell bent for leather.

When he returned, Domini had curled up in a lounge chair in the far corner of the deck. Sunglasses covered her eyes and she'd wrapped both hands around a bottle of Bud Light.

He snagged a beer and eased himself into the chair beside her. "Sorry about that."

"Not your fault I freaked out about a dog. I should be apologizing because I jumped on the table like a spooked cat." She muttered in Ukrainian and gulped her beer.

"We all have fears, princess."

"Even you?"

"Especially me." Cam pried her fingers away from the beer bottle so he could hold her hand. "But maybe you oughta come clean about what happened that makes you so afraid of dogs."

Domini gazed off into the distance, as if gauging her words. "When I was six, we were relocating from Kiev to Kharkiv because everything was in chaos due to the Chernobyl incident. We were waiting outside the train station, when two Soviet policemen showed up with a German shepherd police dog. A big, mean, snarly attack dog. Although I'd done nothing wrong, I...ran."

Cam's throat closed up.

"The dog chased me until it caught me. By the time the police and my parents separated me from the dog's jaws, I was already bleeding badly. I remember little of the hospital except the excruciating pain when they stitched me up. The next day the same Soviet police came by and wrote my father a ticket."

"For what?"

"Some trumped-up missing paperwork charge. Mostly they needed an excuse to explain why a dog that was supposed to be protecting people, attacked a child unprovoked."

"Jesus. The police twisted it around so it was your fault?"

"Stuff like that happened all the time when we were under Soviet rule. Law enforcement there is nothing like it is here. So, we had to stay in Kiev another three weeks, during which I got an infection." She shuddered. "I ended up back in the hospital and almost died. I've had...issues with dogs ever since, which is why my first instinct is to run."

Rage filled him. Yet he managed a calm, "Where did the dog bite you?"

"You asked, I answered, so can we drop it now? It doesn't matter."

Cam stood. He braced his hands on the armrest of her chair and demanded, "Where did the dog bite you?"

Her pale eyebrows lifted above the rims of her sunglasses. "The first mark is on the back of my left shoulder and the second one is on my hip."

"Lemme see."

"Cam. It's not important."

"Then it shouldn't be such a big goddamned deal to let me see it." Why was he pushing her on this?

Because you want her to be physically scarred, same as you. You want to see it so you don't feel like such a freak.

In angry, jerky movements, Domini slid the shirt down her left shoulder. She dropped her chin to her chest, leaving the nape of her neck exposed.

Oh fuck. His stomach clenched. The jagged edges of the white scar tissue showed where the dog had ripped a huge chunk of her skin off. Whatever sawbones had treated her in the Ukraine managed to piece it together, but not very well. How had he missed feeling those ridged scars last night?

Because you were selfish and then you were gone.

Seeing that broken section of her skin broke something inside him. He placed his mouth against her warm, sweet-smelling flesh and tenderly pressed kisses across every inch of the scar. And when he finished the first pass, he did it again.

Domini's breath caught.

Cam dragged his mouth over the sexy arch of her neck, pushing aside the baby-fine strands of hair. He brushed his damp lips to her ear and murmured, "See, that wasn't so hard," before easing back and retaking his seat.

She hadn't removed her sunglasses, but he knew she was watching him very closely.

"So what's churning inside that pretty head of yours, princess?"

"I was just thinking I still run from situations that scare me. Dogs. People."

"Do I scare you because I'm a cop?"

She shook her head.

"Good."

"But that's not entirely true. I've never been in this situation before."

"What situation is that?"

"Asking you for something."

"You afraid I'll deny you?"

Domini shrugged. "Given our past...situation, maybe I am a little afraid you'll think I'm weird for what I want."

Cam reached out to reassure her, but thought better of it. Now was the time for talking, not touching. "Try me."

"It's about sex. At least, I'm assuming we're going to have sex."

Sweet Jesus. Hopefully she wasn't one of those stump fetish freaks who could only get off with amputees. He'd never been with a woman like that, but lots of guys he'd met at the VA talked about being approached by women—and men—with that bizarre fetish. "So if I say, yes, I'm ready to nail you right now...you'd say?"

"Yes." She removed her sunglasses and locked her gaze to his. "I'd say what I really want is for you to take control of me during sex. Just like you did last night when you handcuffed me, pushed me to my knees and made me suck you off."

His heart began to race. "You liked that?"

"Yes. A lot."

"Why?"

"I've never been able to really let go in any kind of sexual situation."

"Why not?"

"I used to think it was because I was with a church organization for a lot of years and they taught us sex—wanting it, doing it—was totally wrong. But my real problem is I worry too much I won't measure up because I'm so inexperienced. And if you haven't realized it yet, I'm also shy."

Cam smiled. "Really? I hadn't noticed."

Domini rolled her eyes. "So I've always fantasized about finding a man who will take away my choice, who won't let me be shy about any aspect of sex. A man who will command me to please him and myself, but who won't physically hurt me."

"You looking at playing master and slave? The boot licking,

collar-wearing type of role-playing and pretend punishments?"

"No. I just...don't want to have to think about sex. I want to surrender my body to a man who pushes me to my sexual limits so I can experience the ultimate pleasure and give it back to him in return any way he wants it."

"Have you ever been in this type of sexual relationship?"

"No. I haven't had many lovers."

"How many?"

"Three."

It figured. Domini was as innocent as he'd feared. "So if you've had little sexual experience or exposure to a dominant male, how do you know so much about this?"

Color tinged her cheeks. "I don't...well...besides reading romance novels with a bit of a domination theme. I realized that type of sexual relationship was what I was looking for."

"Submissive?"

She nodded.

"Say the word. If you want to be submissive to me, you'll say it."

"Submissive."

"So if you're submissive, that makes me...?"

"Dominant."

"Exactly. Do you know what it means to be under the rule of a dominant male, Domini?"

"No. But I know you'll teach me. I *want* you to teach me."

That little remark made his dick hard. "You wanna know why I stayed away from you? Because I couldn't imagine you—sweet, kind, timid Domini—letting me have my way with you however I wanted. Letting me fuck your mouth, your cunt, your ass. I couldn't fathom you'd be willing to let me call the shots and play rough."

"How rough?"

"I'd never use my rougher edges as an excuse to hurt you. Spanking your ass with my hand is one thing, making you bleed by punching you in the face falls into a whole nother realm.

"For example." He leaned forward, using his voice as a lure. "If I wanna handcuff you to my bed all night or all day, I will. If I wanna fuck you against the truck, I will. If I want you to go down on me in my patrol car when no one else is around, you will. If you agree to this, my rules are simple. Any time, any place, any position I say, you say, 'yes'."

"Yes."

He bit back a growl of approval. "You oughta know I'm beyond demanding when it comes to getting what I need from my lover."

"Have you been in a relationship like this before?"

Cam debated on how much to tell her. But if he expected honesty from her, he'd better reciprocate. "Yes, I've been in several. Not since—" *I lost my leg and my nerve,* "—my injury."

Domini regarded him pensively. "So we would fulfill each other's sexual needs and that's all? No relationship beyond that?"

Hell no. Little did Domini know now that he'd uncovered this surprising side of her, after he got her in his bed, he'd never let her out. She'd belong to him. But his reassurance he wouldn't attempt to turn this into a traditional dating relationship seemed important to her. It went against everything Cam was to lie. But because he wanted her with an acute ache, an unfathomable need, a sense of rightness he'd never felt in his life, he lied with a straight face.

"It's a small town, Domini. If my truck is parked outside your apartment all night people will know something is goin' on with us. Denial would just increase the speculation. So I ain't gonna hide the fact we're seeing each other. What we do when we're alone together ain't anybody's business. I don't tell locker room stories."

"That's why I trust you."

"Okay, but I'm curious. Why don't you want a relationship?"

"Because any kind of long-term relationship always falls apart. Always. I watched my parent's marriage implode before they died. I saw my friends in the Ukraine marry themselves off to the highest bidder and they were no better off than a prostitute or a maid. I witnessed verbal abuse repeatedly in so-called Christian marriages and relationships, actions that were sanctioned by the church. And don't get me started on the physical abuse issues Nadia suffered before she escaped that awful relationship. So I'll pass on the trappings of marriage, because from what I've seen, it is a trap."

Cam let her vehemence sink in. It chilled him to the bone.

"I'll never get married, Cam. That's not the life for me. Do you understand?"

No. "Completely. And we are on the exact same page, there, princess. I've worked hard to turn my house into my sanctuary, and it might make me a bastard, but I'm not eager to share."

Relief softened the hard set to her mouth. "I'm glad. And I'm good with pretending we're dating, when we're really having lots of hot sex."

"Which brings us back to my next question. What about birth control?"

A stark look briefly flashed in her eyes. "We are covered as far as no accidental pregnancy and I haven't had a lover in three years, so no STDs."

It'd been nearly that long on the "no sex" wagon for Cam too, but confessing the truth smacked of desperation. "So, we agree no condoms?"

"Yes."

"Good." Cam finished his beer. He set it on the table and stood. "I'm done talkin'. How about if I finish the rest of the tour?"

Domini clasped Cam's outstretched hand and followed him back into the house.

Chapter Five

A house tour.

Maybe Cam would show her his bedroom. And then demonstrate how wickedly ruthless he can be in bed.

Focus, Domini.

That was nearly impossible when the ragged edge of Cam's thumb continually stroked the inside of her wrist—an erotic touch she felt between her legs. As they meandered the brightly lit hallway, Domini looked up to see skylights spaced a foot apart. "Those are unusual. I like them."

"I had Chet and Remy add them. I can't stand living in darkness." He gestured to the bathroom. "Pretty much everything from here back is a total remodel."

"Why not just build a whole new house?"

"I like the location. The house has a solid foundation. It just needed a little cosmetic work and someone to care about it." He pushed open a door that'd been left ajar. "Spare bedroom." The plaid denim bedspread hung off one end and pillows spilled onto the carpeted floor. "I see Keely managed to bail without cleaning up after herself again."

"Do you really hate having people in your house?"

"Not hate. It's just...I went from living at home to living in barracks and tents. I've never lived by myself. I tend to get protective of my space. My family doesn't get that. So I had to state the rules about them staying away without a specific invitation from the moment I moved back here." Cam opened another door and hit the lights. "Here's my bedroom. We combined the two smaller bedrooms into a larger one."

The bed dwarfed the room. Rising from each corner of the bed frame were thick wooden posts. A plain cotton quilt in a vivid bronze covered the massive space from headboard to footrest.

A pair of crutches were propped between the headboard and the nightstand. Contrary to what he'd said, Domini suspected the real reason Cam preferred to be alone in his house was so he could wander around minus his prosthesis without embarrassment.

Domini refocused on the furniture. A tall rough-hewn pine dresser, with wrought-iron accents, matched the nightstands book-ending the bed. An oversized, overstuffed corduroy recliner faced the window rather than into the room.

"What do you think?"

"I think I could crawl right into that puffy bed and take a nap."

"Princess, when I get you in my bed the last thing we're gonna be doin' is sleeping."

His husky tone dripped of raw sex and sent a shiver of fresh desire rippling through her.

The door she assumed led to a closet was actually a pocket door that revealed a sun-drenched bathroom. An enormous slate-tiled shower, encased in glass blocks, took up one side of the room. A deep Jacuzzi tub the other. A toilet was secreted behind half walls in the corner. Along the back wall was a double sink in a soft gray, sunk into a glossy, black, high countertop and surrounded by mirrors. She checked out the bathtub, looking longingly at the jets and nozzles. Outside around the rim, a conglomeration of silver-colored tubes were imbedded in the tiled floor, curving around the front end and backside of the tub.

Domini started to ask Cam why he needed so many handrails, when she realized climbing in and out of a slippery tub with one leg would be difficult. She'd forgotten about his handicap. A positive sign in her mind, but she knew Cam wouldn't appreciate her mentioning it so she didn't.

She faced the mirror and Cam wedged his body right behind hers, nestling his groin into her butt. He gripped her hips. "Bend forward until your palms are flat to the wall."

Keeping their gazes connected in the mirror, Domini did as he told her.

Cam's eyes glittered. "Compliant. I like that." He rocked his pelvis, grinding his cock against the cleft of her ass. "I'm gonna fuck you like this, Domini."

"Now?" *Please. Now.*

He shook his head. "Soon." Cam tugged her upright, keeping her back pressed against his chest as he trailed openmouthed kisses up her throat. "I knew this countertop height would be perfect."

She was dying to ask if he'd had other women in the bathroom to test the height and strength of the marble. Her gaze flickered over him and she had her answer. A man as sexy, virile and commanding as Cam McKay wouldn't lack for sex partners. Ever.

"Come on. Let's get back to the kitchen. I could use another beer. Maybe we could play cards."

"Cards?" she repeated.

"Yep. The best way to get to know a person is to play cards with them. You learn their tells—" he licked the cord straining in her neck and she moaned, "—like that one. Or figure out when they're bluffing." He slid his hand into her hair and pulled.

Domini stiffened with surprise.

"You don't like that, do you?"

She tried to jerk out of his hold, which only made her scalp sting worse. Then she attempted to relax.

"Answer me."

"I-I don't have much experience with aggressive—"

Cam increased his grip and pulled again. Harder.

"Ouch. Let go."

Immediately his hand dropped. He scattered sweet kisses across her scalp. "You don't bluff worth a shit, Domini," he muttered.

"Is that good or bad?"

"Good."

"Why?"

"I'll be able to tell if I've pushed you too far." He spun her and sealed his mouth to hers in a hot, wet kiss.

Domini arched her breasts into his chest, rubbing the center of her pelvis over his erection, tempting him to forget all about card games so they could indulge in other games.

His deep groan vibrated in her mouth. He slid his lips across her cheek to whisper, "Soon," and abruptly dragged them from the bathroom.

An hour later, Domini was ready to climb out of her skin. Talk about extended foreplay. While they played cards, Cam touched her. Constantly. Running his callused palm down her arm. Trailing his fingertips up the ticklish inside of her thigh. Twirling a section of her hair around his fingers. Letting his thumb linger on the pulse points of her throat. Tracing her soft, damp lips after he'd scrambled her mind with a powerfully seductive kiss.

She was holding her cards without really seeing them. His husky command, "Domini, look at me," completely destroyed what little concentration she'd managed. She raised her gaze to his.

Cam stood, grabbed her hand, and brought her to her feet. Then he swept the cards from the table and lifted her onto it, crushing her lips beneath his.

Domini gave herself over to him, aware he'd already built her to a level of sexual awareness she'd never experienced.

He broke the kiss. "Lie back."

When her legs dangled off the table, and she stared at the antelope-horn chandelier above her, Cam spoke again.

"Prop yourself on your elbows."

She looked at Cam across the length of her body.

He curled his hands around her knees and set her feet on the table. In a purposefully drawn-out and sexy move, he teased her sundress up over her thighs and hips until it bunched at her waist.

Thank God she'd worn decent underwear.

Cam idly traced the triangle of fabric stretched over her groin. "I wouldn't have pegged you as the black lace type. But it looks damn good against your snowy white skin." He urged to her raise her hips, slipped the scrap of lace from her body and tossed it aside. Cam lowered his head and kissed her belly button. He paused at the surgical scar below it.

Please don't ask. Please don't ask now.

"What's this from?" His thumb followed the white slash.

"Appendix," she said automatically.

"Huh. That's a weird place for it." He tickled it with his tongue. "They must do surgery different in the Ukraine, huh?" While he teased her skin with little licks and nipping kisses, he noticed the other dog bite scar on her hip. Next thing she knew, he lovingly placed sweet, healing kisses over every inch. Her heart soared as she melted.

"Cam."

"I know, baby, I'm getting there." The kisses ventured southward, over the blonde hair covering her mound. He stopped to suck the hidden nub at the top of her sex, just once, very gently. Then he used his tongue to separate her pussy lips until the tip of his tongue hit the mouth of her sex. He groaned. "You taste as sweet and hot between your legs as I imagined."

Her entire body trembled.

"I'll let you come fast this first time." He burrowed his tongue deep into her channel. Once. Twice. Three times. "After that, the wait'll be longer but the payoff will be sweeter." His hands slipped under her butt cheeks and he brought her weeping sex to his mouth. "Watch." Cam lapped. He licked. He sucked. He fucked her with his tongue, lavishing attention on every quivering millimeter of her swollen flesh...except her clitoris.

So much for letting her come soon. Her disgruntled sigh caught his notice.

"Something you need, princess?"

"To come! You said fast. This isn't fast, this is torture!"

He chuckled. "Oh, I'm gonna have *such* a great time teaching you patience."

"Can I learn it later?"

"Yep. Now hold tight." He formed a small circle with his lips and pressed his mouth directly over her clit. He flicked his tongue across it. Let his teeth graze it. Cam closed his eyes as if he were in heaven and started to suck.

Domini's pelvis shot up at the escalating rhythmic pulls of his mouth. The slow hum of sensation beneath the surface of her skin picked up heat and speed. Her hands, her thighs, her teeth clenched hard and then all at once, she detonated.

Cam steadily sucked through every twist of her hips, every hoarse cry tumbling from her lips. Sweat coated her body, blood pounded in her ears. When the last pulse weakened, Cam nuzzled the inside of her leg. Domini flopped back on the table and tried to catch her breath.

But her respite didn't last more than fifteen seconds. The heat from Cam's body radiated above hers. "Domini."

She pried her eyelids open at the sexy sound of her name rumbling from his throat. The passion in the depths of his eyes sent a shiver through her.

He drawled, "My turn." He slid her down and flipped her on her belly. "Grab the edge of the table. Like that. Don't move your hands, your body, anything." Cam widened her stance. Even as tall as she was, her tiptoes barely touched the floor. She felt a little wanton. A little helpless. More than a little turned on.

Cam rolled the dress up to her hipbones. "I've been thinking about goin' down on you since the first time I saw you in Dewey's with a smudge of flour on your cheek." He traced her moist cleft and he plunged one finger inside. "I wondered how you'd taste. Now every time I look at you I'll remember the tang of you on my tongue. The smell of your sweet juices on my face."

Her pulse spiked hearing the metallic jangle as he unbuckled his belt.

"When you started to come against my mouth? Showing me you're not shy about grinding that juicy pussy into my face, showing me how much you loved what I was doin' to you...I damn near came right along with you."

Domini almost came again from his dirty-talking play-by-play.

A long zip was followed by the shuffling whisper of his clothing hitting the floor. Then all that hot, male hardness was crowded against her backside.

When Cam leaned closer to bury his face in her hair, she wished they were naked so she could feel his chest against her back. He didn't move his body even as she felt tension vibrating within him. "Cam? You okay?"

A kiss bussed the top of her ear. "I'm exactly where I've wanted to be for too damn long." He positioned the tip of his cock at her entrance and worked his thick shaft inside to the hilt. Cam pulled all the way out. He eased back in as slowly as he did the first time. Twice more. Without warning his hips flexed hard, rocking her to the core as he rocked the table.

Cam's hands were curled around her hips to protect her hipbones from banging into the table edge. He never altered in his pace. And Cam had been right in one respect: this time was all about him. No sweet kisses. No murmured words of encouragement. No loving caresses. Just pure fucking.

Domini's vision wavered. She wanted to wrap her fingers around some part of Cam's hard body, not the hard table. Even the stroke of his hand on hers would deepen their connection.

There is no deeper connection. It's just sex.

Her body didn't care about any kind of connection beyond purely physical. A small orgasm pulsed and the contraction sent Cam over the edge, he grunted and bumped his pelvis as his cock emptied, coating her insides with a blast of liquid heat.

Neither attempted to move. Their labored breathing was the only sound in the room.

Finally, Cam said, "Hang on. I'll get a towel." A gush of wetness ran down her leg. She heard him yank his pants up and fumble with the belt. Water ran in the kitchen sink.

She pushed up, unnerved by his rapid retreat. Would he reset the distance between them again? An anxious feeling bloomed, but when she spun around, Cam was right there. Kissing her in that sinful way of his. Gently mopping the stickiness between her thighs.

"You said it'd been a while. Are you sore?"

"A little."

"Sore enough to keep me from having you again?"

Immediately her nipples hardened with interest. "Right now?"

"If I could get it up right now, it'd be right now. And then I'd wanna do it again right after that. But I need a little recovery time first." He smoothed her dress down. "I'm getting old."

"How old are you?"

"Between thirty and death," he deadpanned.

"Funny." She spied her panties on the floor. As she reached for them, Cam's rough-skinned hand circled her wrist.

"Huh-uh. No panties while you're here today."

"I hope we're not going horseback riding."

He chuckled. "Nope."

"If I'm minus an article of clothing, you should be too."

A cool appraisal settled on Cam's face. "Oh yeah? Like what?"

"Ditch your shirt."

Cam didn't budge.

Chances were good Domini didn't have the nerve to push him on this issue.

"I'm not backing down. Show me your chest."

Secretly pleased to see feistiness lurking beneath her placid demeanor, Cam yanked the tank top over his head.

She whistled.

He blushed, grateful she didn't focus on the ugly shrapnel marks and gouges marring the skin on his belly. And on his chest. Marks that were all over the goddamn place.

Those marks aren't nearly as ugly as your stump.

She flattened her palms on his chest and kissed his scowling mouth.

Naturally his stomach chose that moment to rumble with hunger. "Sorry."

"I'm hungry too. What do you have to eat?"

"Not much."

"I'm sure I could figure something out. Mind if I poke around in your kitchen?"

"Have at it."

Cam stood behind Domini as she surveyed the meager contents of his refrigerator. Milk. Beer. Condiments. Cheese. Lunch meat. Grapes. A half a loaf of wheat bread.

"Pretty sad, huh?"

"What do you cook?"

"I don't cook."

"Why not?"

"Never needed to learn."

She tossed sandwich fixings on the counter and washed her hands. "Some of us had no choice."

"Is that why you know so much about cooking?"

"Yes. Can you get me a knife?"

Cam rummaged in a drawer and set a dull butcher knife and a bread knife on the counter. "Where did you learn?"

"Hands on mostly. The church group that brought me to the U.S. had missionary outreach posts all over the states. We traveled a lot. We'd have to fix three meals a day for the church leaders and members who were out spreading the word."

"How long did you do that?"

"Day in, day out for years. Until I realized I could apply for citizenship and escaped." She gestured to the cupboards. "Will you grab plates?"

"Sure." Cam didn't ask questions but he knew there was way more to the story than the bits she'd shared.

They sat side by side and ate. His ham and cheese sandwiches never tasted this good, even if he used the same damn ingredients. Might be sappy, but little domestic things like this made him feel cared for, probably because these cozy moments were so rare in his life. He glanced over at her and his glass of milk stopped halfway to his mouth.

Domini's fingers fondled the two fat purple grapes left on her plate. Gauging the tightness and fullness of the globes containing all that sweet juice, she plucked one from the vine and popped it in her mouth.

Lust slammed into him. Instantly Cam envisioned her long fingers rolling his balls like that. Teasing them with feathery touches. He imagined the moist heat of her breath, down low between his inner thighs, right before she sucked the sac into her mouth.

He must've groaned because Domini whipped around.

Her eyes widened as if she'd peeked inside his brain. But he didn't see shock in the pale blue depths, just interest. When her mouth softened, Cam couldn't keep his hands off her another second.

His glass hit the counter. He stood and lifted her to her feet, then his mouth claimed hers in blistering kiss. God he loved how wickedly eager her tongue was sliding beside his. How recklessly and hotly she writhed against him.

So crazed was his need for her, his hands trembled as he yanked her sundress down. It fluttered to the floor, allowing her pert breasts and hard-tipped nipples to fill his greedy hands.

Domini sucked in a surprised breath.

Cam flicked little whips of his tongue around the point of her left nipple. Each lick, each suckling touch of his mouth to any part of her breasts drove Domini wild. She gyrated her hips. She gouged her fingernails into his shoulders. He changed it up, keeping her guessing on whether he'd use his teeth, mouth or tongue. Her sexy purrs caused everything male inside him to roar with primal need to satisfy her.

He pushed her back to the fridge, still sucking on her sweet little tits. "Now. Right fucking now."

She just moaned.

Cam moved his hand between her legs and he found her hot and slick and ready. No reason to wait. She was wet, he was hard. Cam held her wrists behind her back. He let his tongue tease the shell of her ear until she shivered. Oh yeah, he was learning all her secret hot spots.

He turned her, and pressed her against the refrigerator door.

Domini gasped when her bare breasts met the door's cold metal front.

"Feels good and naughty on your hot skin, doesn't it?" Cam placed her palms flat on the top of the door. "Keep your hands there and spread your legs."

Domini's feet slid out.

Cam layered his face to the side of hers while he quickly worked his belt and pants. They hit the tile with a resounding thud. His right hand snuck around her hip and flattened over her abdomen, urging her pelvis to angle back. His left hand guided his cock to that tight channel weeping for him.

He drove into her hard and deep.

"Oh. God. Yes."

Using his right hand to stroke her clit, he followed the line of her arm up with his other hand and threaded his fingers through her left hand braced on the top of the refrigerator. Then Cam began a series of shallow thrusts. Slow thrusts.

Her head fell onto his shoulder. "Your bare chest feels so good against my back."

"Your cunt feels hot and wet and tight around my dick." He pumped his hips and circled his finger over her clit, wondering how quickly it'd take to get her off.

"Cam. Please."

"Please what?"

"Harder."

"Lucky for you, that's what I had in mind."

Domini groaned.

As much as he'd love to build her to the point of detonation, chances were high once he began pounding into her, he wouldn't last either.

"Let's kick this up a notch."

Between the constant attention to her clitoris and the deeper thrusts, Domini's body trembled, she cried out as she shot like a rocket.

Cam blinked the sweat from his eyes and managed to hold off until the tail end of her orgasm. The internal vibrations jerked him right over the edge into sweet oblivion. They were still locked together, with Cam scattering kisses across the sexy slope of her bare shoulder, when he heard his work cell phone ringing. In his pants. On the floor.

Shit. Perfect fucking timing as usual.

He eased out of her and jerked his pants up, fastening them in record time. He dug for his cell phone but it'd already quit ringing. Before he hit call back, he scooped up Domini's clothes and grabbed a couple of napkins from the counter. "Here."

"Thanks."

Cam called the station and paced to the sliding glass door. "What's up? No. That sucks. I understand. I'll be there in half an hour." He sighed and walked back to the kitchen.

Domini's hair obscured her face while she righted her dress. She didn't acknowledge him at all.

Screw that. They'd had too many misunderstandings already; he'd be damned if this would be another one.

Cam crowded her against the refrigerator until she looked at him. "I'm sorry, that was a pretty abrupt dismount, huh?"

She allowed a smile. "But the ride was good while it lasted, cowboy."

"I'm not a cowboy, I'm a cop. In fact, that's what the call was about. Another deputy is sick, they're shorthanded so I've been drafted to duty." He smoothed her hair back from her face. "Which is too bad because I was kinda hoping we could hang out the rest of the night."

"You liked beating me at cards that much?"

I liked being *with you that much. Too much.* He let his lips toy with hers. "I knew the sex would be smokin' hot between us."

Domini peered up at him. "You sure it wasn't...ho-hum for you?"

"Ho-hum? Jesus. My cock gets as hard as a fucking bullet if you so much as look at me, Domini. I've fucked you twice in an hour. If I wasn't goin' to work, I'd probably fuck you at least twice more. So ho-hum is the last goddamn *way* it is between us."

A flirty, smug smile tilted her lips. "Good to know. You can make it up to me later. Now put your shirt on, Deputy."

Cam grabbed his uniform. He'd change at the station. Once again Domini sat right next to him in the truck, constantly touching him, but not saying much.

✳

It never failed. This shit always happened on his shift. Even when it was a fill-in shift.

Since they were short-staffed, both he and Sheriff Shortbull responded to the 10-54.

The red and blue lights threw shadows on the pavement. His patrol car sat sideways in the road, Sheriff Shortbull's patrol car sat sideways three hundred yards down from his. Between the two vehicles? A herd of cattle. Cattle, which weren't moving at all, hence the dispatch call.

Cam wiped his brow and punched the talk button on the radio. "Dispatch, how we coming on that cattle prod?"

"With all due respect, Deputy McKay, no one is bringing you a cattle prod."

"How about a bull whip?"

"That's a negative, sir."

"So I'm just supposed to sit here and shoo them outta the road with my bare hands?"

"Deputy, sit tight. The owner is en route."

"You've been saying that for thirty minutes."

"If you have an issue with the time frame, Deputy McKay, I suggest you bring it up with your cousin, Luke McKay, once he arrives."

"Ten-four."

Cam tossed the handset on the seat. Headlights bobbing up the road caught his eye. Too close together to be a truck. He waited and a big Yamaha four-wheeler parked. The driver ripped off the helmet and long brown hair spilled out.

"Jessie? What're you doin' here? I thought Luke was coming?" Cam said.

"So did I, but apparently he's screwing around again, who knows when he'll make an appearance. You guys have better things to do than to look after our cattle. Especially since Luke was supposed to fix this section of fence last week so this wouldn't happen."

"I know you guys are busy, we just don't want anyone getting hurt." Two years previous, loose cattle wandering into the road had caused the deaths of a young married couple and their baby. Escaped cattle were a fact of life in Wyoming, but a fact that shouldn't be ignored.

Jessie reached into the back of the ATV and extracted an enormous pair of bolt cutters. "I'll cut that bad section of fence away so I can herd the cattle back through it."

She didn't wait to hear his opinion on her solution; she just took off on foot. Five minutes later she returned and tossed the cutters in the back end.

"If you guys turn on your sirens, the noise will make them uneasy and I can probably get them rounded up easier."

"Sure thing." Cam whistled at the sheriff and relayed the message. Once the sirens were on full blast, the cattle began to get restless. They started to move when Jessie honked and circled them with the ATV. She chased one cow through the broken fence line as a signal for the rest of the cattle to follow.

Within twenty minutes, steaming piles of cow shit were all that was left. Sheriff Shortbull drove off. Just as Cam rounded the front end of the patrol car, another set of headlights approached. The truck parked and the owner jumped from the cab, leaving the vehicle running.

Cam wasn't particularly surprised to see his cousin, Luke McKay. Although Cam had always gotten along fine with Luke, the man's late appearance rankled.

"Hey, Cam. Did you round up my cattle?"

"No, we waited on you, but Jessie handled it."

"Jessie?" Luke's laugh sounded bitter. "Gotta hand it to her, sometimes that girl shows all sorts of gumption."

Cam waited for Luke to clarify the condescending comment, and when he didn't, Cam said, "Gumption or not, Jessie had it under control in no time flat." *No thanks to you.* "You should be proud of her for handling it when you weren't around.

"I can hardly freakin' wait for the silent treatment the next week because she had to *handle* it." Luke rubbed the section of skin between his eyebrows. "Be the smart one in the family, Cam, since you're the last of your brothers who ain't wrapped

75

that ball and chain around your ankle. Don't get married. Ever."

That shocked the crap out of Cam. He had no clue what he was supposed to say. Luke and Jessie had only been married a couple of years and they were already having problems?

You'd know what was going on if you kept up with family business.

Luke squinted at the gaping hole in the fence line. "I suppose she'll give me hell about that too."

Cam thought Luke deserved all kinds of hell, but he didn't see sweet, soft-spoken Jessie standing up to him. "How long has the fence been down?"

"Why?" Luke's gaze snapped back to his. "Did Jessie say something to you about it?"

"I've got eyes, cuz. I'll remind you the rest of your damn fences can be falling down all over the place, but it's your responsibility as a landowner on this section of highway to keep these fences maintained. It's dangerous to let 'em go."

"Yeah? Maybe you oughta mention that responsibility to your brother, Cord, as there are plenty of rickety-ass sections of fence line runnin' along his portion of the highway."

"I will mention it to him, trust me. Meantime, if this fence isn't fixed within forty-eight hours, I will ticket you, Luke, count on it."

Luke didn't snap off another comment. He merely nodded, climbed in his truck, and roared off.

Chapter Six

Ah, the glamorous, exciting life of a single woman.

Domini had scrubbed her apartment from top to bottom and finished laundry. Then she'd indulged in a long, hot bath in perfumed water. For dinner she'd grilled a juicy steak, loaded a baked sweet potato with butter and brown sugar, poured a glass of Shiraz and finished off the meal with a slice of chocolate peanut-butter pie.

Normally she'd consider that a perfect day. The sense of accomplishment balanced with a touch of personal indulgence. But after spending yesterday afternoon hanging out with Cam McKay, she couldn't shake the feeling her life lacked something.

Was it just sex? Or was it something scarier? Like the beginning of a relationship?

Nah. Definitely sex. Cam was a confirmed bachelor. He wasn't looking for a white picket fence, a wife and two point five kids any more than she was.

Not that she could pop out even the point five portion of a kid. Was that why she'd gone off on a tangent about the evils of marriage? Probably. She excelled at deflection. She swirled the claret-colored liquid, studying the light refraction in the crystal facets of the wineglass.

Soft rapping jarred her out of her melancholy. She straightened the lapels of her silk robe as she strode to the door.

"Domini? It's Cam."

She unlocked the deadbolt. Man, he looked positively lip smacking in his uniform.

Cam smiled. "Hey. I was hopin' you were still up."

"I was just about to head off to bed."

"Princess, don't say stuff like that to me. It gives a man all sorts of ideas." His eyes traced the V neckline of her robe. "Whatcha wearing under that silky robe?"

Her pulse spiked. "Nothing."

That was all the invitation Cam needed. Before she blinked, his hands cupped her face and his mouth was hungry on hers.

Domini's body seemed to go completely boneless.

The kiss evolved from ravenous to seductive. His hands drifted. One lightly circled her throat as he idly swept his thumb back and forth over the pulse point. The other slipped straight down the center of her body. His middle finger coaxed her clit.

She must've moaned because Cam ended the kiss, but he didn't move his hands. He kept fondling her, gauging how each stroke between her legs caused her pulse to jump beneath his thumb.

Domini wanted to demand he quit playing and whisk her off to bed. But this was a test of her obedience. She forced herself to stay still.

His breath tickled her ear. "I've a mind to reward such good behavior."

"How?" escaped before she could bite it back.

"You'll see." Cam nuzzled her jawline. "I need you to do something for me. Dig out a scarf or two. Something that's soft and won't chafe."

"Chafe what?"

"This beautiful skin of yours." He paused, allowing that to sink in. "After you find what I need, wait on the bed." Cam pecked her on the mouth and stepped back.

She chanced a look at his face.

The lust burning in his eyes stole her breath.

"Go on," he rasped, "before you make me lose my ever lovin' mind and I fuck you standing up right here."

The robe flapped around Domini's hips and she forced herself to take measured steps to her bedroom. She frenetically searched her dresser drawers for the articles of clothing he'd demanded.

Demanded. Oh wow. Was she really ready for this?

If the swollen folds of her pussy and the slickness coating the inside of her legs were any indication, the answer was a categorical *yes.*

She unearthed a striped silk scarf and one crafted from combed cotton with fringe dangling from the edges. She'd just seated herself on the edge of the bed when Cam sauntered in.

He still wore his uniform. No matter how sexy and commanding Cam looked in his deputy duds, she wished he'd taken them off.

"Now that's a look I love to see on your face. No fear. Just anticipation."

"Should I be afraid?"

"I'd say I'd cut off a limb before I'd ever hurt you, but that seems a little farfetched coming from me, huh?" Cam tugged the satin tie free from her robe. "I'm gonna need this one too. Stand up and turn around."

The first thing he did was tie the satin scarf around her eyes. She tried not to panic at the sudden darkness and the sense that nothing was familiar—even in her own bedroom.

"Tell me if you can see at all. Light, anything?"

"No."

He kissed the dog bite scar on her bare shoulder as he used the tie from her robe to bind her wrists behind her back. "Hang tight."

Domini heard the soft rustle of clothes. Would she finally get an up close and personal view of Cam's body?

Shoot. She was blindfolded.

"Climb on the bed and lay on your back, facing the ceiling."

She struggled with the position.

"Tip your head off the end of the bed. Good. Stay just like that."

Domini flinched when his hands palmed her breasts and his cool lips landed between her belly button and the start of her bikini line. Then she smelled the heady, intoxicating male aroma that was uniquely Cam.

"Part those pretty pink lips for me."

The instant her lips parted, the bulbous tip of his cock forced her mouth open wider. That thick, male hardness brushed the soft palate on the roof of her mouth, slid over her tongue, and stopped when it hit the back of her throat.

The gag reflex wasn't as pronounced in this position and she managed to swallow.

"That's it. Breathe through your nose. Jesus, it's hot as hell seeing you take me this way. It keeps your neck arched at the perfect angle when your hands are underneath you."

At her humming noise of agreement, he hissed in a breath.

"You can take me. All of me. Which means I'm gonna pick up speed." As Cam pulled out with every fast stroke, his hand dipped between her thighs. "Extend your legs so I can touch you."

Coherent thoughts deserted her as Cam's cock shuttled in and out of her mouth, and her face was pressing into his groin. She couldn't see. She couldn't move. She had to remember to breathe. She couldn't do anything but feel.

And oh what a feeling, she'd never been so thoroughly...taken. So thoroughly controlled.

Cam traced the outline of her pussy lips and plunged one finger into her core. She bowed up only to get his hand planted in the center of her chest, pushing her back down.

"Huh-uh. I'll get you there. This is part of surrender. Trust me."

As soon as his words took meaning, he added another finger and matched the rhythm in her pussy to how he fucked her mouth. "So wet for me. You're liking this, aren't you?"

Yes. Enjoying her own helplessness was as shocking as her quick acceptance of how much her submission pleased Cam.

He withdrew his fingers from her cunt and began to pinch her nipples. Harder than she was used to, but she existed on a whole new plane of sensation, part pleasure, part pain.

"As much as I wanna feel those gorgeous throat muscles teasing my dick as you swallow every drop of my seed, I want to see my come marking you."

At his visual, Domini sucked harder. With his cock halfway out, she used her teeth on the sensitive rim lining the head. She relaxed her jaw when his pelvis thrust and he buried his cock balls deep in her throat.

"Fuck. I'm not gonna last."

His cock disappeared from her mouth and she heard the fast *slap slap slap* of Cam's fist beating on his shaft as he jacked off. "Oh yeah."

A guttural groan rumbled, followed by warm liquid splattering on her stomach and nipples. One droplet landed on her chin. Given the angle of her head, the sticky bead rolled to the curve of her lower lip. Domini's tongue darted out and she moaned at the salty proof of Cam's passion.

He swore and his thumb smeared more come over her lips. "Lick it off." His harsh breathing echoed above her. She sensed him gloating at the image of his come cooling on her skin.

Before Domini could speak, Cam pushed her upright. He licked the shell of her ear and his hands tracked her bound arms from her shoulders to her wrists. "Sweet Domini, who has a hankering to be dominated, I am so gonna fuck you until you scream. But first—" he tugged her arms down and sank his teeth into the nape of her neck, "—I'm gonna play hard and dirty with you."

A whimper escaped.

"On your knees." Cam rolled her to her side, then he hiked her hips up. Way up. He managed to wedge a pillow under her knees, arranging her at the angle he preferred.

Domini gasped for breath beneath the mass of hair covering her face. Her cheek was pressed into the comforter. Her ass, her pussy—every intimate inch of her was completely exposed. She should be blushing, but the buzz of anticipation overruled any other feeling besides need.

His gentle hands brushed the tangles free from her damp face, allowing her to suck in a lungful of air. With sweetness and tenderness, he kissed her temple, letting his warm lips follow the curve of her jaw before he retreated.

The wait for his next move was excruciating. Her body throbbed with pent-up sexual need. Cam wouldn't hurt her, but she figured he'd drive her to the point where she needed to come so badly it might actually hurt.

Without warning, the fringed end of the scarf swept across the bottoms of her feet, then her calves and the backs of her thighs. Cam arced the scarf so it tickled the outside of her hips, the inside of her arms and her shoulder blades. The change in his demeanor from demanding to teasing didn't calm her; it electrified her. With each lingering pass of the fringe, new goose bumps arose. Did Cam plan on changing things up with a dreamy, lazy bout of lovemaking?

His big hands landed on her ass with a loud smack.

Domini jumped.

Then Cam's fingers were holding her pussy open so he

could lick her sex. The wet sounds of his sucking kisses caused her belly to quiver and sent another rush of cream flowing into his mouth.

"I could lick these sweet juices from you all damn night. I lose my mind when I hear your sexy squeaks and moans when I'm tasting you."

His mouth was everywhere. His teeth, oh man, the gentle scrape of his teeth across her clit brought every bit of her body's focus to that throbbing bundle of nerves.

He stopped his intense attention and licked straight up the crack of her ass, rubbing his face over her butt cheeks, first one side, then the other. The razor stubble felt coarse on her skin, which was in direct contrast to the soft kisses and hot breath he bestowed to every inch. Of her butt.

"Damn I love your ass. I wanna bite it." He sank his teeth into her left butt cheek. "I wanna feel every curve of it on my face." Cam rubbed his cheek and chin from the top of her right hip and down to the back of her right thigh. "I wanna kiss it." He placed loud smacking kisses on each butt cheek. "I wanna lick it." Once again his tongue traced the crack. When his tongue met the hidden pucker, he swirled the very tip around it.

Domini gasped. Loudly. She'd never... Lord she couldn't think straight. It felt so strange. So naughty.

So damn good.

"But mostly I wanna mark this ass as mine, Domini. I wanna suck it, fuck it, spank it." He used the flat of his tongue to slowly lick down.

"Yes," burst out on a breathy sigh, before Domini realized it wasn't really a question.

"There's my obedient girl." Cam buried his face in her pussy, zeroing in on her clit. The delicate butterfly licks morphed into continual sucking.

Her limbs shook. She was so primed that the orgasm didn't build slowly; it blindsided her. Starting at full throttle and escalating to warp speed.

And Cam didn't let up. She didn't know how he took a breath because the angle of his head seemed all wrong, but man-oh-man was it ever right.

After the last orgasmic twinge, Cam knocked the pillow from beneath her knees, and scooted her lower half off the edge of the mattress. With the pillow bracing her belly, he canted her hips and impaled her.

"You feel good. So wet and tight, like you were made to take me like this." Cam's hips hammered into her.

Covered in sweat, shaking from head to toe, surrounded by the *slap* of flesh meeting flesh and the intimacy of total darkness, Domini was dangling by a thread again.

Cam sensed it. He jerked on her restrained wrists, lifting her upper body off the bed as he kept fucking her. "Come for me again. Come hard. Lemme hear you."

Her clitoris rubbed on the pillow and matched the cadence of his energetic thrusts. She was blind and bound to everything but the pleasure bombarding her from all sides. It was too much.

Domini flat out screamed as the orgasm rocketed through her, setting every nerve ending in her body to the same frequency as the vibrations shocking her from head to toe. Never in her life had she experienced something so earth-shattering. A feeling so addictive she'd do anything to have it again and again.

Cam's primal roar followed and the heat of his ejaculate prompted another tiny orgasm to flare, which he prolonged with short snaps of his hips.

She went limp as the synapses in her brain shorted out. Cam released his hold on her. After she fell face first on the mattress, Cam withdrew and a rush of wetness trickled down the inside of her thigh.

Undone. She was completely spent. He'd most likely ruined her for all other men the sex was so volatile. In the hazy aftermath of such explosive passion, she heard the sound of clothing being righted.

No. That couldn't be right. Cam wasn't just...leaving after he'd screwed her nearly unconscious, was he?

He tugged the robe tie, freeing her arms. He massaged her shoulders and slid the silk scarf off her eyes.

Blinking several times, Domini let Cam roll her onto her back. Very gingerly, he untangled the strands of her hair covering her face. Then his thumb followed the arch of her eyebrow as he cradled her head in his hand. "Jesus, Domini. You're beautiful. You stun me."

Not what she was expecting. Nor did she anticipate his achingly gentle kiss that lingered on her mouth and seemed to seep into her soul.

Domini lifted her hand, needing to touch him, but the second her fingers connected with the scar, he retreated.

"I have to go," he said, as if he were trying to convince himself. "Sleep well and I'll see you tomorrow."

Before she pushed herself upright, she heard the door close and he was gone.

What the hell had just happened?

She'd done everything he'd demanded or asked of her— true, she'd done it because she'd wanted to, not just because he'd commandeered her sexual responses as his right.

Why had Cam dressed fast and raced out like he suddenly remembered he had another engagement?

Dressed. Wait a minute. That was the third time they'd had sex. The fourth time they'd had sexual contact if she counted the time they'd messed around on the couch. By all rights she should've already explored his remarkable body. Sucked his nipples and raked her fingernails down his muscular back. Licked the bulging muscles in his arms. Traced his rippled six-pack abs with her tongue. Kissed her way from his belly button to his hipbones. Scraped her nails down his thighs. Nibbled on his knees. Tested his feet to see if they were ticklish.

Knees and feet? Cam only has one knee and one foot.

Domini clapped her hand over her mouth as the truth jarred her. His reaction tonight wasn't an oversight in a moment of passion; it'd been calculated, like all their sexual encounters had been.

Cam, that sneaky jerk, didn't want her to see his prosthesis. Tonight he'd blindfolded her so when he did strip down, she couldn't see anything.

Domini tried to wrap her head around the fact he always bent her over the closest horizontal surface. He'd not allowed additional touching, no eye contact. And by bending her over, three freakin' times now, she wouldn't feel the difference of his artificial leg as he pounded into her from behind. She'd just remember how hot and kinky it was that he fucked her so thoroughly.

Don't move. Keep your hands just like that.

If he commanded her during the actual act of sex as well as foreplay, then she'd be less inclined to disobey and reach back to grab his thigh. Or the stump where his thigh used to be.

Damn him. Cam could continue keeping her off balance by seeing to her sexual needs, especially when she'd already given him control. Was Cam hoping all Domini would remember in the aftermath when she was alone was the blazing hot sex?

Yes.

Well, she had news for him. Not happening. Next time he'd come to her honestly, with the same trust she'd shown him, the same willingness to put himself out there, or he wouldn't come to her at all.

And neither of them would come.

Domini grabbed her robe off the floor and hoped a shower would cool her burst of anger.

But somehow she doubted it.

Chapter Seven

"Domini, can I have a glass of milk?"

She set the blue marker in the crack of the coloring book. "Pretty soon you'll start mooing."

Anton shrugged. "I like it."

She ruffled his blond hair. "To be honest, your milk addiction gives me an excuse to keep cookies around." She filled Anton's favorite Denver Broncos mug. As she plunked it on the table, she peered over his shoulder at what he'd been working on with such diligence.

Her jaw dropped. She'd always considered Anton's artistic skills advanced for a seven-year-old boy, but this was beyond anything she'd seen so far. It was a pencil drawing of the road leading out of town. In the left hand corner was a small rendering of the building she lived in, which had a glow about it.

The depth perception was incredible, the telephone poles, the fence line, the pavement decreased in size and breadth, fading away until it was barely a speck. The landscape was stark and minimal, but it was the overall tone of the picture that left Domini feeling bleak.

Did Anton feel that way? Or was this just a picture?

Domini realized he'd gone utterly still. Was he waiting for her to criticize his work? "Anton, this is amazing. Did you just do that today?"

He reached for his milk and his legs began to swing under the table again. "Uh-huh."

"Can I have it when you're done with it?"

A beat of hesitation, then, "You really want it?"

"Sure. Why wouldn't I?"

"'Cause it's not happy. My mom only wants the happy pictures I draw."

"I like all kinds of pictures." Domini couldn't resist smoothing his cowlick. "What were you thinking about when you drew this?"

Another drink of milk. "Sometimes I watch out the back window when mom is driving home. I keep watching until your building is tiny. Just like this." He pointed at the drawing. "I'm thinking about you because I miss you." He paused and said softly, "I wish you still lived with us."

"I miss you too. But I understand why your mom wanted to have a place for just the two of you."

Anton's head whipped up. His pale blue eyes shone with accusation. "But it isn't just the two of us. *He* comes over all the time now."

Domini froze. Only one nameless *he* in Anton's life. "Your father has been there?"

"Betcha she didn't tell you that, huh?"

"No, she didn't." Nadia and Rex. There was a good reason Nadia kept her contact with her ex to the absolute minimum— the man was an abusive asshole. "Is she trying to make you spend time with him?"

His shoulder lifted. "No. He doesn't talk to me at all, but I don't care. Really. I don't."

Although she was upset with Nadia, she pasted on a smile for Anton. "Well, I'm glad she's letting you spend time with me, even if my artistic skills are limited to coloring inside the lines."

Anton hopped up and used a magnet to attach the picture to the fridge.

Domini set her hands on his shoulders. "Looks good, doesn't it?"

"Yeah." Anton cranked his head around and smirked. "So were you lyin' about the cookies?"

"Talk about impatient." She snagged a cookie from the breadbox and slid it into the microwave, so the dough would be warm and the chips inside gooey, just the way Anton liked it.

After the snack, they watched TV. Domini covered Anton up with an afghan when he conked out.

About ten o'clock, Nadia knocked on the door. "Is he

asleep?"

"Yes. You want a cup of tea before you go home?"

"Sure." Nadia dropped into a dining room chair with a heavy sigh.

Domini turned up the kettle and gathered her thoughts as she lined up mugs, sugar cubes and milk. She poured and sat across from her friend.

She and Nadia had met in Sundance right after Domini relocated. At the time, Nadia had been in an abusive relationship with her ex-husband, desperate to get out. After Nadia wised up, left the man and filed for divorce, she and Anton had moved in with Domini.

Things had worked out well as roommates, but something changed and Nadia started hinting about finding a new place to live for just her and her son.

Around that same time, India Ellison married Colt McKay, and the apartment above the restaurant sat vacant. Domini let Nadia take over the lease on the house they rented and moved out. It eased her loneliness that she saw Anton frequently, but the close relationship she shared with Nadia had cooled considerably. Now Domini knew why.

Nadia sighed after the first sip of tea. "I miss having tea with you."

"Me too." Domini fingered the handle of her mug, dreading this conversation. "I'm worried about Anton."

"Why?"

"He doesn't seem the same the last couple times I've seen him. Tonight he told me..."

"What?" Nadia asked sharply.

Domini's eyes connected with Nadia's. "That Rex has been coming around a lot lately. Is that true?"

"So?"

"So?" Normally the "stay out of it" train of thought won out and Domini would shut her mouth and seethe in silence. Not this time. "Do you really need me to remind you that Rex used to beat you? And verbally abuse you? And a big part of the reason you left him was because you were worried about Anton's safety?"

When Nadia's gaze fell, Domini's hopes fell right along with it.

"He's changed."

No he hasn't! Domini bit the words back even when it seemed she'd choke on them.

"He loves me. He wants me back. He wants us to be a family again."

"What about what Anton wants? Does that matter to you at all?"

Nadia became defiant. "Anton is seven years old. Rex is Anton's father. He has a right to know his son. And Anton needs to get to know his father."

"Even if that means going back into an unsafe situation?"

"It's not unsafe. He's changed," Nadia repeated stubbornly.

"This man threatened to kill you."

"That was in the past."

Domini dug her fingernails into her palms to keep from grabbing Nadia and shaking her.

"He's asked me to give him another chance," Nadia said softly. "I'm just supposed to say no?"

"Damn right you should say no. I'd say no."

Nadia drained her tea. "I'm not you. I'm tired of being alone, Domini. Maybe if you don't know what you're missing, it's not so bad, living alone all the time. But I do know what I'm missing. I want someone to hold me. I want an adult to talk to at the end of the day. I want to share my life with someone. We have a history. That means something."

"You have a violent history," Domini retorted. "And if I remember correctly, he used to hold you down and smack you. That is not *holding* you, Nadia. Is that really what you want? For yourself? For Anton?"

"I knew you wouldn't understand." Nadia stood stiffly. "I'm tired. Thanks for watching my son tonight."

Domini wanted to keep the dialogue open, but she knew Nadia well enough to recognize the conversation was over. She swallowed her anger. "You're welcome. I love having him. You know that."

Nadia's defiant posture softened. "I do. Sometimes I think you've been his mother more than I have been."

That didn't sound like something Nadia would say; that sounded like something Rex would say to undermine Nadia's confidence. But pointing it out would be...pointless.

At the doorway, Anton hugged Domini fiercely before allowing his mother to lead him out into the night.

As Domini tidied up the kitchen, her gaze landed on the picture on the refrigerator. Was Anton facing backward in the car, watching her building disappear? Fearing she'd disappear?

A sob escaped. She slid to the floor, curled into a ball and cried, not for herself, but for the little boy who'd bear the brunt of his mother's bad decision.

Her cell phone buzzed in her back pocket, jarring her out of her crying jag. She dug the phone out and stared at the caller ID. Cam. She debated on answering, but if she let the call roll to voicemail, he'd stop by to check on her. She couldn't face him right now. "Hello?"

"Hey. Sorry to be calling so late."

"I was just about to go to bed."

Silence. "What's wrong?"

"Nothing. I'm just tired."

"Bullshit. You sound like you've been crying."

The man had radar-like instincts when it came to reading her emotions. Part of being a cop? Or part of being so tuned in to her needs?

Right. Wishful thinking.

"Cam, it's been a long day, but I appreciate the good night call. I'll talk to you tomorrow."

"Don't you hang up on me."

Domini sighed. "Look, Cam—"

"I'll be there in five goddamn minutes. Stay put. I mean it." Then he hung up on her.

Pushy jerk.

By the time Cam arrived, Domini had worked herself up into a rare frenzy. She flung open the apartment door before he knocked. Once he was inside, she sidestepped him before he had a chance to grab her, kiss her, and cool down her temper.

"What happened?"

"What makes you think something happened?" she volleyed back.

Cam lifted an eyebrow. "Well, for starters, you're pacing and snapping like a dog on a leash."

"Tell me you did *not* just compare me to a dog."

He winced. "Shit. Sorry. But you know what I mean."

"No, I don't. I don't know why you're here."

His mouth opened. Then shut.

Domini scanned his clothes. Sweat pants. Tight T-shirt, the armpits and neck hole ringed with sweat. "Where were you?"

"Working out with Colt."

"This late?"

"Colt waits until Hudson and Indy are asleep before he comes to town. So are you gonna tell me what's wrong? Or are you gonna keep changing the subject?"

"I didn't ask you to come over."

"I know, princess, that's why I'm here. I knew you wouldn't ask me."

The soft concern in Cam's eyes did her in. Tears fell again. Before her sobs became incoherent, Cam enclosed her in his arms. He stroked her hair as he rained kisses on the crown of her head. "Talk to me, baby."

Don't be such a pushover. You'll never tell him what's bugging you if he's touching you.

She wiped her eyes and attempted to retreat but Cam wouldn't release her.

"No harm in letting me hold you until you calm down, is there?"

Yes. I'll start to depend on you for comfort and support and that's never turned out well for me.

Domini squirmed away. "I'm fine."

"Then talk to me. You watched Anton tonight, right?"

She nodded. "He was really quiet. He's been that way the last couple times I've seen him. So he let it slip his father has started coming around again."

"Shit."

Domini didn't have to explain to Cam what a bastard Rex DeMarco was. The man had harassed her a couple of times when she'd lived with Nadia and Anton. But Rex was smart and careful enough not to step over the legal line.

"I asked Nadia and she admitted she's considering reconciling with him."

"Why?"

"Nadia claims he's changed. He quit drinking. Now he wants them to be one big happy family. She just doesn't see it. Men like him don't change." Her eyes searched Cam's. "Do you think he can change?"

Cam sighed. "That's a tricky question. Even my own family didn't believe my brother Colt had changed. Only recently have they accepted Colt is not the same guy he was. So on one hand, yes, I honestly believe some people can change. But this guy? My gut reaction is no. Rex has way too many issues, coupled with a history of violence and..."

"And what?"

"When Nadia had you as a roommate, Rex didn't have much chance to be alone with her. My worry was for you in case he decided to push this issue. So I was goddamn glad to hear you'd gotten out of that dangerous situation."

The warmth of Cam's concern didn't loosen the fear knotting her belly. "Nadia said she's lonely. She claims I don't understand loneliness because I've never been in a long-term relationship."

"Lots of people are lonely even in a relationship."

"I know! So it's ridiculous and sad and...*stupid* she's willing to go back to a man who beat her just because she doesn't want to watch TV alone."

"See? That's why this asshole doesn't want you around her, influencing her to think for herself."

"I hate this. I hate that she's putting Anton's needs last."

"And you would put Anton's needs first." Cam's fingers caressed the side of her face so tenderly she felt tears welling again. "He's been blessed to have you in his life, Domini."

She'd been blessed. She loved that sweet little boy. He was the closest she'd get to having a child of her own. "Thanks."

"You're welcome. Now can I kiss you hello?"

Domini parted her lips and Cam's velvety hot tongue slipped inside her mouth. She wanted to make love with him like this—face to face, skin to skin, mouth on mouth.

After scrambling her brain for several tongue tangling minutes, he broke the kiss. "Bedroom. Now."

"Maybe I want to drag it out." Her hands floated down his chest. "Strip you slowly. Lick and taste and tease you all over. Maybe you should make me do it."

His body went stone still. Then his voice was low, warm and persistent in her ear. "I said bed. Now. We do this my way. Remember?"

Domini recognized this wasn't about sexual control with Cam. Heck, it wasn't even about her. She stepped back and challenged, "And how is your way, Cam? With me bent over the table, or against the refrigerator, or on my knees, or draped face first across the bed? Or are we actually going to have sex some other way for a change?"

His eyes tapered to fine points. "For a *change*? What the fuck is that supposed to mean?"

It was difficult to stay the course, faced with his angry surprise, but she dug in her heels, bracing for a fight. "Every time, every single time we've had sex, it's been from behind. I've never kissed you, or whispered in your ear, or even touched you when you got me off."

"Is that a complaint?"

Don't back down. She notched her chin higher. "Yes. I guess it is."

Color dotted his cheekbones and his eyes glittered with something that looked like resentment, but she suspected was embarrassment.

"You told me you wanted to surrender to me, Domini. *Me.* Which means I get to call the shots."

"Evidently that also means you get to hide."

"Hide?" he repeated.

"I've never seen you naked. Never. You can blame it on being tied up or blindfolded or whatever you did to restrain me, but the truth is: you're hiding yourself from me.

"I've opened myself up to you, Cam. More than I ever have with any man. And while I'm grateful you proved my trust in you was justified, I know you don't feel the same about me."

The muscle in his jaw jumped as he stared at her with those hard, dark, cop eyes that scared the crap out of her.

"You don't trust me, do you?"

No answer.

Domini purposely let her gaze drop to his left thigh. She let it linger before she looked at him again. "You think I'll laugh when I see your prosthesis? Or are you afraid I'd be grossed out by your missing leg and run? Help me understand, Cam, because as much as I like you and trust you, I can't do this anymore. It's all or nothing."

Two-hundred-odd pounds of aggressive, challenged male

was right in her face. "Why are you pushing me?"

"Because you need it."

Silence.

"So what's it going to be?"

The air stayed still and quiet.

It broke Domini's heart to see him retreat. To watch that strong, chiseled face lower to his chest, almost in defeat.

After a couple minutes passed, Cam said, "You're right."

Her heart beat again; she breathed again.

"I've hidden my injury, my stump, my disability, whatever the hell you wanna call it, from everyone, not just you."

"Why?"

"It embarrasses me that I'm...broken. Most the time when I'm wearing the prosthesis and it's covered with regular clothes I can pretend I'm normal. But when that shit is off and I'm completely naked? I see I'm not a whole man. I can't lie to myself. And I sure as hell can't lie to you."

His anguished tone nearly broke her resolve. *Be strong for him now because he needs it.*

"The only person in my family who's seen it is Keely. And that's only because she moved to Cheyenne and became my personal physical therapist. She kept everyone in our family away. She helped me deal with all the doctors and the prosthetic specialists, the millions of prostheses fittings, the excruciating rehab and learning to walk again. She...pushed me.

"Keely wouldn't let me give up even when I wanted to give up on myself." He briefly squeezed his eyes shut. "Jesus, did I want to just fucking hide myself and my ugly stump from the world."

Even though Domini ached to go to him, she stayed put.

"After a few months of Keely working her 'rah rah you can do anything' magic on me, I tried to reclaim the sexually charged guy I'd been." He laughed bitterly. "What a joke. I had sex one time after I had the hang of walking on my prosthesis. One. Fucking. Time."

"What happened?"

"I got her clothes off. I went down on her. She came. I thought all was going great...then she reached for the button on my jeans and I totally fucking panicked. I mean, the type of panic that's pure debilitating fear. I knew I should've told her about my stump. I knew I should've practiced getting naked because when faced with it with a stranger the first time...I couldn't fucking do it."

Domini was well versed in those types of panic attacks, but she still didn't go to him. He needed to get this all out.

"I'm thinking to myself, what a fucking loser I am. Somehow, I managed to pull it together and insisted we do it from behind. I only dropped my pants far enough she felt my cock and a little of my upper thighs. I fucked her fast and left. She probably never knew. But I did. The worst part was I realized I'd never be the same man. I'd be half a man. I never wanted to try again...until I met you."

A million thoughts raced around in her head and she couldn't seem to voice a single one.

Finally, Cam said, "Say something. Your silence is killing me."

"Well, as encouraging as it is that you want to return to being that sexually charged man with me, you've still been selfish."

Cam's head snapped up. "Excuse me?"

No doubt he'd expected her to coo sympathy. To be sweet, soft-spoken and pat him on the head while clucking *there there, it'll be all right little soldier, all is forgiven.*

Wrong.

"Not sharing your body or yourself with me is selfish. Oh, I understand you wanting to maintain the illusion of male perfection, but know something? I don't want an illusion, Cam. I want a real man. I want you. I don't care what kind of lover you used to be. I care what kind of lover you are *now*. And I can't be the kind of lover you need if the only part of you I'm allowed access to is your cock."

He stared at her with absolute shock.

"Surprised?"

"Uh. Yeah. Usually you're so s—"

"If you say shy I'll brain you," she warned.

"No." He smiled slyly. "I was gonna say subtle."

"I am subtle and diplomatic most of the time, but there comes a point where in your face is the only option."

"So Miss In-Your-Face, have I fucked this up completely by

being a selfish and clueless dickhead?"

"Not by a long shot. Not since you're willing to admit some things need to be different between us."

Cam released a long, slow breath. "Thank you. I...I'm sorry." He laughed self-consciously. "What do we do now?"

Humbling, that this formidable man looked to her for direction. The sudden boost of confidence allowed her to erase the distance between them. She twined her arms around his neck and held him until he stopped shaking. "First we get completely naked. Then we see how smokin' hot it is to have sex in missionary position. Then we test out my cowgirl skills as I ride you. All within the parameters of your control, naturally."

"Naturally."

"Sound like a plan?"

"Sounds like the best plan I've ever heard." Cam lowered his head and kissed her stupid.

Chapter Eight

Sweet baby Jesus. If Cam was crazy about Domini before, it was nothing—*nothing*—compared to the way he felt about her now.

He flat out fucking loved her.

Loved. Her.

The woman had guts. No one in his life said shit like that to him. Not even his in-your-face sister, not even at his lowest point. And the hell of it was she'd been exactly right. He *had* been a selfish bastard in bed. Even Domini's surrender had been about him.

No more. He would lay himself bare for her. Completely. He ripped his mouth away and mumbled, "Stay with me tonight. At my house. All night."

"Maybe. It depends on a couple of things."

He ignored the spike of fear and said, "Anything. Name it."

"Well, can I touch you as much as I want? Because I have a lot of catching up to do."

"As much as you can handle."

Cam tried to remain calm at the thought of her waking up and staring at his stump while he was still asleep.

This is about trust. You have to start someplace or you'll lose her and never have to worry about her staring at any *part of you.*

He headed downstairs and waited for her while she grabbed her stuff.

She bounded around the front end of his truck. Moonlight glinted off her hair, making her look like a goddess. An angel.

Mine, roared in his head, *she's all mine.*

Not that Miss I'm-Never-Getting-Married would appreciate

his claim on her.

Domini climbed in, scooting right next to him like she always did. He grinned. She was cuddly as a kitten. Oh yeah, this woman was most definitely his, whether she knew it yet or not, whether she liked it or not.

On the drive Cam draped his arm across the back of the seat and his fingers toyed with her hair.

She said, "You nervous?"

"Yep. Do you think that makes me a pussy?"

"No. I think it makes you real."

"Meaning what?"

"Meaning...I sort of lied when I said I wasn't afraid of you."

Cam frowned.

"Sometimes you scare me, the larger than life persona. Cam McKay, the injured war hero. The model cop. The dutiful son and brother."

"You're makin' me sound like John Wayne or something."

"Does that bother you?"

"I don't know. I am who I am."

"That's who I want."

He nudged her shoulder. "You sure you don't have some sweet-talkin' cowboy heritage hiding in that Ukrainian background?"

She laughed.

When they pulled up to his house, he said, "I'll let you inside but I've gotta take care of Gracie first."

A moment of silence followed and then she blurted, "Can I come with?"

Cam squinted at her. "Seriously?"

"Ah. Sure. You're facing your fears tonight, maybe I should face mine too."

"Sometimes you scare *me*, Domini Katzinski."

"Why?"

Because I'm so in love with you that I'm afraid I'll do anything to keep you forever.

"Cam? Are you going to answer me?"

He grinned. "Nope."

Gracie was penned in the backyard. Although Domini winced when she heard the happy yips, she trucked along.

"Hey Gracie. Sit. Good girl." He glanced over his shoulder at Domini. "Give me your hand."

"She isn't going to chew it off, is she?"

"No. However, she probably will slobber all over it."

Domini held very still as Cam guided her hand through the chain link fence. Gracie sniffed. And sniffed. Then she whimpered and licked Domini's palm. "That tickles."

She petted Gracie as if she'd done it a million times before, but he knew what a huge leap of faith it was for her. Cam said, "Go inside. I'll finish up and be right there."

He cleaned up before he headed to his bedroom. Damn. His heart was pounding something fierce. He froze in the doorjamb at the sight of Domini stripped to nothing and perched on the edge of his bed.

"Hi."

"Hi," he said back, feeling totally lame. "Man. I am more nervous right now than I've ever been."

"I understand. But I'm not backing down. So strip. Oh, and come closer so I can see every muscle ripple. Because you can't know how often I've wanted to lick you from head to toe." She smiled cheekily. "With your permission, of course."

"Of course. I doubt I'll deny you anything." Keeping his gaze on hers, he yanked his T-shirt over his head and tossed it behind him.

Domini reached for his bare chest. She made a little purring sound as her hands skated over his pecs and his ribcage, then lower to trace the defined lines of his abs. "Do you do anything when you're off duty besides work out?"

"I harass my favorite cook."

"Lucky me." She met his gaze. "Lose the sweats."

Blood rushed into his head as loud as a raging river. His heart galloped a million miles an hour. His body quaked. Hell, even his voice was thready. "I—I...Domini...Dammit. I don't know if I can—" Shit. He was such a fucking pansy-assed loser.

"It's okay. Hold on to the post and let me do this for you."

Cam nodded and shut his eyes.

Cool fingers traced the elastic band sitting low on his hipbones and his belly quaked from her gentle touch. One fast, hard tug and the sweats were down around his ankles.

"Lift your right foot. Good. Now your left. Good."

How many times had he suffered the dream where he'd gone to school naked? A dozen times perhaps. This was worse. *Way* worse. Standing naked before a beautiful woman and exposing his flaws?

A tender kiss landed on his belly button. Followed by a series of harder, insistent nipping kisses as she moved south. But she didn't go straight down his groin. She didn't kiss or lick or nuzzle his cock. She detoured to his left thigh.

His whole body flamed with embarrassment. He wanted to apologize for being crippled. To tell her to stop.

But she didn't. Domini kept going until she reached the band of the sock above his stump.

Cam gathered the courage to open his eyes. He looked down at her. And saw nothing but concentration. He smoothed her hair away from her cheek. "What?"

"You don't wear that to bed, do you?"

"No."

"Will you let me watch you take it off?" When he frowned she added, "I don't have some kind of weird stump fetish, okay? It's part of you. I don't want you to feel uncomfortable with me or in your own bed. Especially if I'm going to be in your bed often."

He growled, "I may never let you out of my bed."

Domini smiled.

Cam didn't look at her while he went through the play by play of removing the prosthesis. The thick prosthetic socks. The silicone sleeve. Releasing the suction that attached his residual limb to the socket.

But at the moment of truth, when his limb would be out there uncovered, scarred, naked and ugly, he hesitated.

Domini didn't. She hopped off the bed and stood in front of him. "What do you do with it at night? Turn it into a crazy leg lamp like in that movie *A Christmas Story*?"

He laughed with relief. "No. I just toss it on the chair and make sure my crutches are close by." He jerked his stump out and waited.

"Can I touch it?"

"Umm. Sure." He'd had the prosthetic specialist touch it. Nurses touched it. Doctors touched it. Even Keely had touched it. But never a lover. He found himself holding his breath as her fingers connected with his skin.

"How much can you feel?"

"Everything from about two inches up."

Domini seemed absorbed in the process. Just when he was starting to get freaked out, she pressed her mouth to his and kissed him with the same softness and consideration as she caressed him. When the kiss heated up, she pulled back. "Will you tell me all about this robotic leg after?"

"Ah. Sure."

"Good." She scrambled back into the middle of the bed. "We're both naked. I want to feel you on top of me, Cam. In me."

Goddamn. He was so touched by everything she said, everything she did, everything she was, he felt tears stinging his eyes.

Don't be a fucking cry-baby. Man up. Mount up.

He sat, swung his right leg up and was flat on his back, thinking about his next move, when Domini straddled him.

His cock jerked toward her like a heat-seeking missile.

"Tell me what to do."

"For now, just let me touch you."

His hands mapped the curves of her body, starting with her breasts. He played with her nipples, watching the tips pucker beneath his stroking thumb. "Bring them to my mouth."

Domini placed her hands above his head on the mattress. She teased his lips with the peaks, one side, then the other until he sucked her deep and hard. She arched her neck, sending her silken hair cascading down her back as her eyes closed in bliss. It was the sexiest thing he'd ever seen.

He clamped his hands on her hips and brought the hot, wet, center of her sex down on his cock. He urged her to slide along the length of his shaft as he lavished attention on her breasts.

Her breathing changed and her body went taut. Cam knew she was about to come. He lifted her up.

She emitted a protesting squeak. "What are you doing?"

"Making this last more than fourteen seconds for both of us, Miz Impatient. Slide your legs down. Hold tight." He carefully rolled them using his right leg, so she was on the bottom.

Domini blinked up at him. Then her hands were

everywhere. On his shoulders. Traveling down his back. Gripping his ass. "You have such an amazing body." She lightly whapped him on the butt. "Do you know what torture that was for me? Knowing you were built like this? You're the sexiest, hottest man I've ever known and I wasn't able to get my hands on you?"

"You can touch me all you want now." He nuzzled her neck. "Spread your legs wider." Cam kissed her as he pushed in to the hilt. He groaned. She groaned.

At first it felt weird in this position, one foot bare, one foot not there, as he steadily rocked into her. Cam used his upper body strength to propel him into her tight sheath with each thrust. "You feel good, Domini."

"I like looking in your eyes and feeling every part of your body rubbing on mine."

He crushed his mouth to hers and used his tongue the same way he was using his cock. Slowly and steadily. Waiting for that moment when Domini's body signaled him to pound into her.

She ripped her lips free and whispered something low and husky in Ukrainian in his ear.

Cam lost it. He slammed into her.

Domini arched, meeting his every hard stroke, keeping her legs wrapped around his hips. "Yes!" She gasped and started to come; her pussy muscles squeezed his cock, sucking it in deeper.

He rode out the waves with her. When the tension left her body, she gave him a dazed smile. "Wow."

Cam pushed up off her, separating their chests. "You wanted to touch me, princess. Play with my nipples."

Domini didn't use her fingers; she used her mouth. She sucked, licked and bit his nipples until his balls drew up tight and he bowed back as he came in long, slow bursts of liquid heat.

His arms shook and he collapsed, sinking into the soft cushion of her body. He breathed in the perfume of her skin mixed with the musky scent of sex filling the air.

He didn't know how much time passed as they remained intimately connected, caressing and kissing, but it was long enough for his cock to stir with intent. Cam pinned her hands above her head and growled, "Again."

This go around wasn't sweet and lazy. It was an intense pounding, thrusting, clash of bodies. Of wills. Cam made Domini come twice before he followed suit in a blinding rush of pleasure that left him exhausted and lightheaded.

Then Domini's mouth searched for his, kissing him so sweetly, but with such underlying hunger that Cam knew he'd take her at least one more time before dawn broke.

"I'd say you fucked me so thoroughly that I can't feel my legs," Domini muttered, "but that seems sort of unfair to you."

He chuckled. "Here I thought you were shy."

"Oh, I'm plenty shy. Look how long it took me to work up the courage to approach you. Almost two years."

"But offering yourself up to me any way I wanted was a great icebreaker, princess."

He flopped onto his back and sighed. He hadn't felt this good, this sated, this relaxed...since before his injury. Maybe not ever.

Domini rolled to her side and propped her head on her elbow. "Will you tell me about your injury and recovery?"

Cam rarely talked about his war experiences. Mostly because people who hadn't lived it wouldn't understand it. But with Domini growing up in a turbulent eastern-bloc country, she wasn't innocent to the harsh reality of the world outside the U.S. borders.

"It was a late patrol in Baghdad. I was teaching one of the new kids protocol for an unsecured urban area when a bomb went off in front of us. We stopped and got out, only to have another detonation behind us. The dirt and debris cut us off from the rest of the caravan. Before we'd gotten too far off the road, I heard that distinctive whistling noise that meant someone had launched a rocket. I grabbed the kid, Jenks, and we hit the ground. But not fast enough. The jeep exploded behind us.

"It's kind of blurry after that. The explosion knocked us both out. When I came to, I had a big chunk of metal embedded in my left calf. It was bleeding, but I knew if I tried to pull it out, I'd bleed out, so I left it in. I couldn't hear, I could barely see, but I knew there was still fighting going on all around us. I also knew we were sitting ducks after the ambush. We limped our way off the road into an abandoned building, figuring we'd sit tight until the fighting died down and we could reestablish radio contact.

"No one realized we were missing until they did a head count at the base later that night. By then the gates were locked up and they couldn't come back looking for us. Then a three day sandstorm hit that kept us cut off from any rescue attempt. Which was good and bad—the Iraqis weren't able to find us any more than the patrols were.

"Jenks and I stayed put. It wasn't like I could walk anywhere with a big hunk of metal sticking out of my leg, even though it was mostly numb. Once we realized the storm had ended I told Jenks to leave me because he only had surface injuries, but he wouldn't. Then a goddamn rainstorm hit, which is how he managed to get water for us when we didn't have food. The week of unscheduled leave was a gritty haze of pain."

"How'd they find you?"

"My buddy, Brock, wouldn't give up on finding me—either dead or alive. Once the storms passed, he was out looking discreetly, randomly checking through the buildings in the area, so as not tip off anyone there were a couple of American army soldiers MIA. He stumbled across us after we'd been gone for six days. Shrapnel wounds coupled with being a pint or so low on blood, a low body temp and I was in a coma when the medics got a hold of me. When I woke up four days later, I found out they'd removed my lower left leg below the knee, as well as my pulverized left pinky." He shuddered. "I still have goddamn nightmares about that."

"I'll bet." Her gaze moved to his stump. "But you don't have a knee."

"They got me stabilized, called my family, and put me on a plane to the amputee specialist docs at Walter Reed as soon as possible. I was only there a couple of days before another infection set in. The docs decided it'd be better in the long run to remove my knee joint entirely."

"Did you have a say in it?"

"I was so doped up and in so much pain that I didn't give a shit." And he was seriously pissed off about the wrong turn his life had taken. At first he'd refused to talk to anyone. Then he went a step further and denied all access to him. No visitors. Period. Cam knew it'd hurt his family, but at the time he didn't give a rat's ass. He wanted to be left the hell alone.

But his sister wouldn't accept his decree. She'd charmed

her way into Ward 57 at Walter Reed Hospital and chewed him out, refusing to leave until he made some decisions about his life.

Talk about being yanked up by his bootstraps. At the time, he'd almost hated her.

Now Cam admitted he wouldn't be where he was if not for Keely. If she'd shown up bawling her eyes out and wringing her hands, he'd've kicked her to the curb without apology. Her grim determination made him face the harsh realities. His life as a soldier was over. Period. He was handicapped. Period. So in Keely's mind, that meant the sooner he learned to live with his disability, the sooner he'd be able to live a better life.

Keely rented an apartment for them in Cheyenne after he'd been discharged from Walter Reed and his medical records transferred to the VA hospital. She ran interference with their family. She dealt with his doctor appointments, his army discharge paperwork, his VA benefits. And she personally oversaw his physical therapy, including convincing a prosthetic specialist from Denver to offer Cam a second opinion. She pushed him until they both broke down. She was there when he took his first steps on his new prosthesis. She argued with the doctors about the fit issues when he probably would've walked away and suffered in silence. She gave up six months of her life for him and never once complained. Never once did she throw her sacrifice in his face. It humbled him.

"Cam? You okay?"

"Yeah." He ran his hand down her body, pleased when her skin broke out in goose bumps. "It's late. We should probably try to get some sleep."

"True. I'll get the lights."

The bed dipped and Domini snuggled into his right side, forcing him to wrap his arms around her. Not that he minded. He couldn't remember the last time he'd held a woman in his arms all night.

Domini was quiet, but it was a purposeful quiet.

"What are you thinking?"

"It's almost more intimate to share a bed with someone than it is to have sex, isn't it? Because when you're asleep you're vulnerable. It's back to that trust thing."

Cam kissed her forehead. "Sleep. You're safe with me."

"Maybe I wasn't talking about me, Cam."

How the hell was he supposed to sleep now?

The scream woke him. Disoriented, Cam realized it'd come from him.

Shit.

Not now. Please. Not now.

Too late. His body was covered in sweat, yet he trembled so violently with cold that the mattress shook.

"Cam? What's wrong?"

Rather than look even more weak, he turned on his side, away from her and shivered like a wet dog. Squeezing his eyes tight didn't stop the images from flashing in his mind. Fuck. He hated this nightmare shit. He kept waiting for it to go away and it never did.

"Ssh. It's okay. I'm here." She stroked his back in silence. Supporting him. Calming him. Soothing him.

Pink and orange rays lightened the bedroom windows as the sun rose. Finally he quit shaking, but he hid his tearstained face from her.

"If you don't want to tell me I'll understand. But if you do want to talk about it, remember I'm not going anywhere, Cam. Nothing you can say will make me leave you like this. I'll be right here if you need me. For as long as you need me."

It wasn't like her to push and it wasn't like him to blurt out every horrid fucking detail, yet he found himself doing just that. "I was back there, helpless, knowing what was coming but unable to stop it from happening."

"Stop what?"

Say the words. Say them out loud.

"The amputation. I woke up in the hospital and the docs said my leg was gone. But I felt it. I knew it was there but no one would listen to me. They called it phantom limb pain but they were all a bunch of fucking liars. I fought so hard to get out of that goddamned hospital bed. I couldn't breathe and when I finally sucked air in, all I could smell was dirty flesh and blood and antiseptic. Then the nurse put me in restraints. That much is true. That really happened when I woke up. But then the dream...changes.

"I'm lost, walking on a road in Iraq, the same road where

the RPG hit us. I'm wearing my new leg and a...Jeep pulls up behind me. Full of American soldiers. I'm relieved to see them until I notice they're all holding chainsaws.

"They knock me to the dirt. One guy puts his boot on my chest to hold me down. The others..." Cam swallowed. "They start to cut off my other leg. Then they cut off both my arms. I can feel every fucking inch of that chainsaw blade digging into my skin and slicing through the bone. I'm screaming. Not only can I see my blood leaving puddles where my limbs used to be, I smell it. I smell the sand and the heat and my own blood and the exhaust from the Jeep as they drive off and leave me there to die. That's when I always wake up."

Domini tugged on his shoulder until he rolled to his back. The horror and sympathy—not pity—in her eyes punched him in the gut. She wiped the beads of sweat from his brow, the tears from his eyes and traced the curve of his jaw. "What can I do?"

He whispered, "Make it go away. Please, just help me forget."

She fell back to the mattress and attempted to yank him on top of her, apparently forgetting half his ability to balance was propped against the chair.

"Be with me now. Like this. There's nobody in the world but us, Cam. You're safe with me."

The movement of her body was so sweetly urgent, so loving and caring that Cam aligned his cock and plunged into her without preamble. "Hold on to the headboard. Don't let go."

When Domini arched back for it, Cam anchored his foot against the footboard and fucked her so hard the headboard slammed into the wall. Over and over. And since he was sprouting morning wood, he felt as if he could fuck her for hours. Fuck her until she passed out. Fuck her until he forgot every shitty thing in the world but her.

The first orgasm rippled through her quickly. He sank his teeth into the delicate sweep of her neck and bit down on the magic spot that sent her spiraling into a second orgasm.

"Cam."

"I know, baby. Again. Come for me again."

"This was supposed to be for you."

"It is for me. Being with you like this is the best thing that's happened to me in a long time."

"Such a sweet-talking soldier."

"Only for you." His hair was damp, as were the sheets as their bodies slapped together. The sexiest, neediest sounds tumbled from her perfect lips.

When she started to bear down on him during her third orgasm, Cam rammed into her and let her swollen, pulsing pussy muscles milk him of every last drop of seed. Milk every single care in the world clean away.

Eventually their breathing returned to normal. Domini's hands traced the contour of his spine. "Better?"

He smiled against her neck and scattered kisses across her shoulders, down to her breasts and back up to her mouth. "Much. Thank you." He breathed in the scent of her, let himself absorb her softness and strength.

"My pleasure."

He pushed up on his palms. "I've got to get ready for work."

A sneaky smile crossed her face.

"What?"

"Need some help getting a leg up on your day?"

"Har har." He smooched her nose, secretly thrilled that she was already comfortable enough to tease him...and he was comfortable enough to take it. "Just for that comment, I expect breakfast." He kissed her nose again. "A big breakfast. Pancakes. Eggs." One last kiss. "And you will hand feed me while you're nekkid."

"Is that an order?"

"Yep."

"Then I'd better get cracking, huh?"

Chapter Nine

Cam dropped Domini off in the alley behind her apartment with a promise he'd see her later.

She rested her forehead against the tile wall in the shower and the let water beat down on her. For such an outwardly resilient man, Cam had a wide streak of vulnerability. As much as she hated to see him hurting, it gave her a sense of...purpose that he'd leaned on her, confided in her, needed her. That he could rely on her to be the strong one for him for a change.

During the course of the day would Cam decide he needed a break to regroup after opening himself up to her? Especially after she'd seen him reliving his worst nightmare?

She'd ached for him, knowing exactly how it felt to wake up in the hospital with a piece of yourself missing.

Why didn't you tell him?

Because the early morning breakdown wasn't about her or what she'd experienced, it was about what Cam needed.

Clean, dressed, loaded with caffeine, Domini grabbed her laptop and tackled the grocery order for the following week. She emailed the invoices to Macie in Canyon River, along with a note about payroll changes.

After juggling next week's employee schedules, Domini powered down her computer. She locked up her apartment and paused at the bottom of the staircase when she heard a baby wailing. She grinned and detoured to the back door leading to India's Ink and Sky Blue. "Indy?"

No answer.

Chances were good given the baby boy's set of lungs that India hadn't heard her. Domini followed the crying to the retail store at the front of the building.

But India wasn't holding the squalling baby. Colt was.

"Colt?"

He circled around slowly as he continued to pat Hudson's back. "Tell me he wasn't loud enough that you heard him clear upstairs."

"No. I was in the stairway. I thought India was closing the shop today."

"She is. We're just waitin' for Mama to get back."

The drop-dead gorgeous cowboy looked like hell. Colt wore stained cut-off sweats, flip-flops and a wrinkled sleeveless T-shirt. The ball cap pulled low on his forehead didn't hide the dark circles under his eyes. The second he quit moving, the baby fussed.

"Is everything okay?"

His bleary gaze connected with hers and it hit her that Colt and Cam had the same midnight blue eyes.

Colt smiled at her crookedly. "Everything is fine, except Hudson doesn't sleep much. Which means Indy and I don't sleep much." He dropped a kiss on the baby's dark head. "Not that I'm complaining."

She wouldn't either. "Where is India?"

"At Doc Monroe's getting her post-baby check up—three weeks late."

Domini bit back a smile. "My offer to babysit any time still stands."

"You're gonna be shocked when we take you up on that one of these days." Colt gave her an odd look. "So, what's goin' on with you and Cam?"

Domini blushed. Dammit. She was pretty sure red cheeks and stammering was a dead giveaway something was going on.

"That sneaky little shit," Colt said. "He hasn't told me nothin' about this."

How was she supposed to answer? What if Cam didn't want his family to know? "Maybe there's nothing to tell."

"Right. Seein' as his pickup has been parked outside your apartment late at night for the last week...well, sweetheart, that's not something that's gonna escape notice in this gossipy town or in the gossipy McKay family," Colt drawled.

"In that case, I guess it doesn't matter that my shades are drawn?"

Colt grinned. "Oh, I wouldn't go that far. There's lots of shocking things goin' on behind closed doors that are better left to the imagination."

No kidding. "Tell Indy I said hello," she said and ducked out the back door.

Domini snuck in the delivery entrance to Dewey's. She watched David's knife flash as the scents of onions and green peppers filled the prep area.

David didn't look up when he said, "Hey, Domini."

"Hey, Dave. How's it going?"

He shrugged. "I'm good."

"Did lunch go okay?"

"Slow. So I have a feeling you'll be busy tonight."

"Why's that?"

"Because you're cooking."

She groaned. "I forgot. Is there any chance—"

"Nope. I'm prepping until five and then I'm outta here."

"Please?"

"No way. I have a date with a hot number from Spearfish. She's staying over at my place and everything."

"Lucky you."

"Yep." David scooped the mix into a white plastic bucket.

Domini wandered out front. The place was empty, typical for the time of day. Myra, the night waitress, sat in a booth rolling silverware. "Need some help?"

"I won't say no if you're offerin'."

She slid across from Myra and grabbed a stack of napkins. "How was the lunch crowd today?"

"Eating someplace else according to Bea." Myra peered at her over the rim of her leopard-print eyeglasses. "Bobby is slacking big time when you're not around."

That was disconcerting. "I haven't heard customer complaints."

"That's because they don't bother to complain. They just don't bother to come back in."

"David says we'll be busy tonight because I'm cooking."

Myra rolled the silverware into the napkin and dropped it into the bucket with a muffled clank. "Why don't you hire another cook if you don't want to do it anymore?"

"That's the thing. I'd rather just cook. It's the management stuff that I don't want to do." Domini almost clapped her hand over her mouth. Why had she admitted that? To an employee?

"Why don't you tell Macie? I'm sure she'd understand."

"No, she wouldn't. After what happened with Cat, she needs someone she can trust to manage this place. I had to promise David the moon to stay on as a prep cook because no one else has applied. I know it's the exact same story on the management side." Domini sighed. Unemployment rates may be skyrocketing everywhere else in the country, but not in Wyoming. For the most part, skilled workers in the restaurant industry could pick and choose where they hung their apron.

The doorbell chimed.

"Right on time." Myra's eyes sparkled. "Chin up, boss. Maybe a knight in shining armor will ride to your rescue and sweep you away from this mundane existence."

Domini didn't have to turn around to know who'd walked in.

Cam.

Silly, but her heart did a little flip.

"Hey, Deputy," Myra called out. "Want coffee?"

"Please."

She waited until Myra delivered Cam's coffee before she sauntered over. Her body flushed hot as the griddle when his hungry eyes ate her up. "Deputy. May I join you?"

"I'd be disappointed if you didn't."

"Would you prefer I sat beside you or across from you?"

"Depends."

"On?"

He blew across his coffee. "On which side offers the easiest access for me to cop a feel."

"A cop copping a feel?"

"Yep."

She sat across from him. "How has your day been?"

"It started off with a bang." His sexy bad-boy grin made her stomach cartwheel.

"I'll say."

"How's your day been?"

"Good. I saw Colt and Hudson a little while ago. Colt grilled me on what was going on with us." She swiped his mug and took a drink. "The rumor mill has been churning."

"Yes, it has. My mother called today."

"What did you tell her?"

"Nothin'. I didn't answer her call. I just..."

Don't want to tell her it's just sex between us?

Cam sighed. "I want to keep you to myself for a little bit longer before they start meddling. Does that sound stupid?"

"No." Before she choked up at another glimpse of the sweet side of this gruff man, she changed the subject. "So, did you arrest anyone today, Deputy?"

"I ticketed two kids for drag racin' out by the old cemetery. Then I finished paperwork. I got tired of listening to Shortbull and Reeves arguing about baseball so I took a break and came here. What time do you get done?"

"Ten thirty. I'm cooking tonight, which I'll admit I am not looking forward to."

"Funny, I always look forward to your cooking."

"Ah. So is that why you've been coming in at least once a day for the last two years? Because of my culinary skills?"

"I'm a bachelor. Half the time I eat Cap'n Crunch for supper."

Domini leaned across the table. "That is not an answer, Cam."

"I know. But I don't guess you'd like to hear how seeing your pretty face never fails to make my day, no matter what else happens to me during the course of that day."

"You're wrong. Sometimes I want to hear mushy stuff."

Cam touched her face. "Anything you want, Domini. Name it."

The doorbell pinged. Cam dropped his hand and threaded their fingers together. Before Domini tore her gaze away from Cam's compelling blue eyes, a blond ball of energy stopped short of tackling her in the booth.

"Guess what? Mom said next week I can spend the night and you can take me to school—" Anton caught sight of Cam. His teeth clamped together so fast Domini feared he might have chipped a molar.

"Hey, Anton. Do you know Deputy McKay?"

Anton shook his head.

Cam stuck out his right hand. "Pleased to meet you Anton."

He shook Cam's hand, albeit reluctantly.

The bell pinged again and Nadia hustled in. The second Nadia saw Cam, she froze too. She gathered herself and stood behind Anton.

"Nadia, you remember Deputy McKay?"

Cam returned Nadia's quick nod of acknowledgment.

"What brings you guys by?" Domini asked to fill the silence.

"We were out and about and thought we'd see if you had time to eat with us."

"Shoot. I'm working in the kitchen tonight—"

"No big deal, it was a spur of the moment idea anyway. Another time." Nadia squeezed Anton's shoulders. "Let's go home." She aimed a cool gaze at Cam. "Deputy."

Then Nadia and Anton were gone. Weird.

Half a dozen people came in. She sighed. "Time to get to work." Domini tried to tug her hand free. Her breath caught when Cam brought their joined hands to his mouth, licking and nibbling her knuckles like he was kissing her sex.

He flashed her a cocky grin. "See you at ten thirty."

Cam's cell phone rang right after he'd climbed into his patrol car. "McKay."

"Is this Cam McKay? The war hero?"

He grinned. "Brock Tennyson, you bastard. Were your ears burning? Because I was just talking about you last night."

"Yeah? I hope you were talking me up to that hot sister of yours, because, man-oh-man that cowgirl she has got it going on, whoo-ee."

"Don't make me hurt you after you saved my life. I will rip your arms outta the sockets and beat you with them if you lay so much as a single finger on Keely."

Brock laughed. "You're so easy to rile, McKay. So what's up with you? Been busier than a one-legged man in an ass-kicking contest?"

"You're a fuckin' riot."

"Admit it. You miss my humor. How goes the deputy job?"

"Great, most days. Better than chasing cattle, that's for damn sure. What about you? It's a little early to be calling about setting up our bi-annual hunting trip."

"Actually, I apologize for giving you such late notice. I'm on my way to Seattle and I've got an extra day to burn, so I thought I'd stop off in Sundance, see if you're gonna be around."

"When?"

"Day after tomorrow."

"I'll be here. I'm scheduled off that day so if you wanna hit Colt's fishin' hole—"

"To be honest, I'd rather chill. Drink a couple of beers. Shoot the shit. Relax."

The word *relax* wasn't in Brock's vocabulary. Cam's alarm bells started ringing. "Is everything okay, B?"

"Yeah. No. Hell, some stuff I need to figure out, which is why I'm driving across country instead of flying."

"You're welcome to crash at my place for as long as you need."

"Thanks. I appreciate it. Look forward to catching up."

"Me too. Drive safe."

"Will do." Brock hung up.

Cam stared at the screen on his phone listing missed calls.

Besides Brock, his mother had called. Twice. That was it. Sad really, that his brothers and cousins weren't ringing him up just to chat. Even Keely had given up calling him for the most part.

Can you blame them? You don't exactly encourage that type of behavior with anyone in your family.

Big fucking deal. Didn't matter anyway.

He shut the phone off and returned to work.

Chapter Ten

Cleaning the grill was her least favorite part of shutting the restaurant down. Thank God she was done. Domini scoured the grease from her hands and fantasized about a hot sudsy shower. Right. Like that'd happen. She'd sent Cam upstairs to wait for her an hour ago. He'd had that look in his eye then and she expected cooling his boots had only increased his ardor.

A tremor of desire rolled down her spine.

As Domini scaled the stairs to her apartment, she wondered if she should've doused herself with perfume. Did she reek like a fryer?

The door opened. Cam wore the look of an impatient man. He circled her wrist and tugged her inside, immediately scorching her lips with a blistering kiss. He released the band holding her hair, and used his fingers to loosen the strands.

Okay. Maybe fryer grease was an aphrodisiac.

Cam herded her until her back met the wall. Being on the receiving end of such passion was still so new and exciting, she welcomed the rush of moisture in her panties whenever this man touched her. Domini generated a hungry noise as she worked his buttons, *want want want* echoed in her head.

Cam ripped his mouth free. "Shirts off." Within seconds they were pressed naked chest to naked chest. His lips flirted with hers, sending an electric buzz from her mouth to her core. "I want to hoist you against this wall and fuck you right here, right now."

"Sounds good to me." Domini toed off her shoes. She unsnapped the clasp and her pants fell to the floor.

He groaned. "I don't think I can. It'll put too much pressure on my leg."

She shimmied out of her underwear and watched Cam watching her. "Where?"

"Couch. Now." He set her on the edge. It wasn't wide, but the height was ideal. Keeping their eyes locked, Cam unbuckled his belt, shucked his pants and his briefs.

His callused finger drew a line from the dent in her chin to the opening of her sex. He swirled two fingers into the stickiness and swallowed her gasp of surprise when those fingers slid in and began fucking her. He feathered his thumb across her clit. Slowly at first, and then quicker, shorter, more precise movements.

Every drop of blood in her body seemed to gather in the bundle of nerves. Just when she bumped her hips up, clenching her pussy muscles in anticipation of a killer orgasm, he stopped.

Domini whimpered.

"You'll come on my timeframe not yours. Watch."

She glanced down as he thumbed his erection and pushed the head of his cock into her.

"So hot. So wet." He fed her an inch at a time, both of them looking until they were completely, intimately joined.

When Domini raised her chin, wanting to see Cam's eyes, Cam's fingers squeezed her upper thighs.

"Huh-uh. Watch." He withdrew until just the tip rested in her opening. "Do you know what a fucking turn on it is to see your sweet cream coating my cock?"

Seeing the swirls of white smeared against the dark skin of his shaft was highly erotic. She couldn't remember caring what the mechanics of sex looked like; she'd only cared what it felt like. Yes, it felt amazing, but leave it to him to bring her every sensual nuance she'd missed.

"What if I told you to get on your knees right now? What if I wanted to see you licking the taste of yourself off my dick?" He alternately sucked and blew in her ear, sending tremors straight to her sex. "Would you do it?"

"I'd do anything you wanted."

"Right answer, princess." Cam kicked up the pace. He nuzzled the sensitive skin beneath her jaw, allowing his teeth to graze her neck. His hand slid up to the juncture of her thighs, while the other hand pushed against the small of her back, subtly changing the angle of her pelvis.

Domini dug her fingernails into his biceps when he started stroking her clit. "Oh God. I like that."

He pumped into her. Not faster but with precision and finesse. "Say my name when you come."

His harsh breathing in her ear, the sucking sounds of his sex driving into hers, the scent of his skin, the feel of his hard chest muscles and fingers and cock...she couldn't even think straight.

"I wanna hear you say it, Domini." Cam teasingly licked the column of her throat as his fingers strummed her clit. "Say it."

"Please."

"I can feel those cunt muscles gripping my cock, trying to bring me all the way inside you. Until all you feel is me. In you. On you." His hoarse whisper, "Say my name," was a sexy command she ached to obey. "Or better yet—" he lightly pinched her clit, "—scream it."

That tiny pinch of pain sent her rushing into pleasure so dark and sharp she did scream.

Cam hammered into her, whispering sweet, dirty nothings into her ear as her body pulsed around his. He slanted his mouth open wider and kissed her in a hot, wet, clashing of tongues. Her insides were flooded with the heat of his ejaculate.

Domini brought her arms around his neck and held on.

After he broke the kiss, he murmured, "You never fail to amaze me, Domini." He pulled out and stepped back.

Suddenly off balance, she windmilled her arms to no avail. She yelped, fell backward, narrowly missing kicking Cam in the head as she bounced on the couch cushion and crashed to the floor.

"Shit! Are you okay?"

Domini started to giggle.

Cam seemed wary of her laughter as he skirted the couch, fumbling with his belt buckle after he refastened his pants. He loomed over her. "Did you hurt yourself?"

"Just my pride."

He jammed his hands on his hips. "I'm sorry. I should've tried to catch you. It's just...I have this thing about falling. I did it a lot when I first... Sometimes I still fall and I fucking hate it. Makes me feel helpless."

"I should've been paying attention." She rolled to her feet, noticing he'd dressed his lower half. "So are you leaving now?"

No answer.

What was he thinking about with that far-off look? "Cam?"

Still no response.

Which ticked her off. "Is this where you tell me you hate to screw and run, but you've got to be up early tomorrow?"

Then Cam was right there. "Excuse me? Did I say we were done?"

She shook her head.

"Who has the say so in that?"

"You."

"And if I didn't say it, then we're not done, are we?"

"No." When her eyes darted away, he held her chin, forcing her to lock onto his dark and dangerous gaze.

"Maybe you need a reminder of who's in charge." He leaned forward, taking his time, until finally his lips grazed her hairline. "Go wait for me in your room."

"Cam—"

"Now."

Domini knew better than to argue. But the truth was, she didn't want to argue. She wondered if he'd dally. Probably not. Cam liked to play, but he didn't play games. Right after she'd arranged herself on the bed, she glanced up and saw him propped against the doorframe.

"Pull the covers back and get your vibrator."

His bossy tone shouldn't have hardened her nipples, made her wet, caused her skin to tighten with anticipation, but those short, terse, commanding words did it for her.

Boy did they *ever* do it for her.

Cam sauntered into the room. He set a bottle of vegetable oil on the nightstand. His gaze never wavered from hers as he dropped his pants and his shorts to his ankles. He sat in the chair and yanked them off.

Now they were both naked. Yet, they weren't on a level playing field because Cam had the upper hand. She allowed her gaze to drop to his cock.

His fully erect cock.

He wrapped his fingers around it and stroked. "Sit on the edge of the bed and spread your knees so I can see every bit of that sweet pussy."

Domini's heart raced at the wild look in Cam's eyes. This was the predator. The alpha. She, shy Domini Katzinski, brought out that beastly side in Cameron McKay.

"Have you ever masturbated for a man?" he murmured.

"No."

He emitted a pleased-sounding growl. "You will for me. Use the vibrator and show me how you get yourself off."

Even after all they'd done with each other, she blushed at the idea of performing such an intimate act in front of him. She turned the vibrator on and let the buzzing tip follow the rise of her pubic bone down to the opening of her sex. She rimmed the outer edges of her pussy, leisurely. Thoroughly.

"Do you always draw it out like that?" he asked.

"No."

"Show me how you do it when you're alone."

"You sure you want to see how fast I can get off with a vibrator?"

"Yep." Cam cocked his head. "You say that like my ego will take a hit when I see what battery power can do."

"It might."

"Darlin', when they manufacture one that can do all the things my hot, wet tongue and my soft lips and sucking mouth can do, well, then I might be worried." He grinned with pure male confidence. "Then again, maybe not."

Cocky man.

If Cam wanted fast, she'd give him fast. Switching it to high, Domini set it directly on the swollen nub of flesh. She rubbed up and down, back and forth mostly for show. The sensation of her tissues pulling tight built and her clit was pulsating beneath the vibrating tip. Her head fell back and she moaned. The short, intense orgasm was nothing like having Cam's cock pounding into her or his tongue bringing her to climax, but it was good nonetheless.

She peeked from beneath her lashes and saw Cam still stroking himself, still watching her.

"How soon before you can go again?"

"Usually one is enough."

"One is never enough."

"Umm. Well, it might take a while."

Cam shrugged. "I doubt it, but I'm in no hurry. Show me.

Now."

Another command. Another overpowering need to please him. Another wave of desire swamped her. Domini gave him a raunchy show as she played with herself and her vibrator. He'd been right; it didn't take long to get off a second time. After she clicked the toy off, Cam was there. Right there. All dangerous, hungry, challenged male.

"My turn." He pushed her flat on the mattress, slapped his hands on the inside of her thighs and set his mouth on her.

Oh he had something to prove. Cam used his tongue in so many naughty, delectable ways, keeping her dangling on the precipice of bliss. If he suspected she was close to careening into pleasure, he'd stop, yank her back to sanity, and start over.

While his busy mouth tended to her clit, his fingers pumped in and out of her wet pussy. She swore he was fucking and sucking her at the same time. And his wicked thumb brushed across her bottom hole, bringing her awareness to those sensitive nerve endings. She noticed his probing of that untried area became more insistent with each pass.

Her stomach muscles were quivering. Her legs were doing this weird, twitchy thing. And she absolutely couldn't take any more. "Cam. Please."

He lifted his face from between her thighs and his mouth was shiny with her juices. "Please what?"

"Please make me come."

Cam blew a cool stream of air across her hot, wet folds. Teasing. Tormenting. Proving his mastery over her.

Then he bent his head.

He'd kept her on the edge for so long, when he sealed his mouth to her clit and sucked, Domini started to come immediately. She gasped when a finger breached the first ring of anal muscles and slid deep.

That added stimulation catapulted her to another level of pleasure. She placed one hand on Cam's head, wrapping the other hand around his thick wrist, not sure if she was trying to pull that probing finger out, or making sure he kept it in.

As soon as the last twinge faded, she propped herself on her elbows and looked at him.

He wore a funny little smirk. "I've got nothin' to worry about from a piece of plastic, do I?"

"Umm. No."

"Good. Now that you're all relaxed, we're gonna try something new."

"New?" she squeaked.

Cam dipped his head to her right nipple. "Uh-huh."

"Does it involve the bottle of oil?"

"Yep." He lapped around the areola, loving her greedy hum of approval. His lips skimmed the shallow dent above her sternum and he licked the left nipple. Her breasts were small, but proportioned perfectly, and Cam never considered himself a tit man anyway. Give him a firm, shapely ass over enormous jugs any day. Speaking of ass...he wasn't surprised to see Domini looking down at him curiously as he enjoyed her body.

He kept eye contact with her. "You know what I want?"

Domini nodded.

"Say it. Straight up."

"My ass. You want to fuck my ass."

He smiled. "See? We're getting good at this communication stuff, ain't we?"

She threw her head back and laughed like he'd said the funniest thing in the history of the world.

Her pure, unrestrained joy was one of the most beautiful sounds Cam had ever heard.

He was past the point of no return with this woman and she hadn't a clue how he felt about her. Not a freakin' clue.

When Domini gifted him with a sweet smile, he kissed her. The glide of her lush mouth on his always brought his arousal to fever pitch, but it seemed sharper tonight. Deeper. Almost desperate.

Cam brushed his nose by her ear. He loved the feel of her silky, baby-fine hair on his skin. When wisps stuck to the whiskers on his face and tickled his neck. Or crushed in his hands and twined through his fingers. Trailing down his body. And the scent. Lord. The cool scent of her hair drove him insane. Or maybe it was the perfume of her skin that seeped into his brain, making him absolutely crazed for everything about her.

"Domini," he murmured against her throat. "I need this from you."

"I know. I want to give you what you need. I want to *be* what you need, Cam."

He forced himself from the temptation of her pliant body only long enough to grab the bottle of oil. His hand shook as he poured the golden liquid into his cupped palm and coated his cock and his fingers.

Her heels rested against the wooden footboard and he tapped her butt as a signal to lift her hips and he placed a pillow beneath her. The long expanse of her belly tempted him to lick and kiss until he reached those sweet, tasty little breasts. As he sucked on a peaked nipple, he lightly circled her anus. He worked his middle finger in a little at a time until it was imbedded to the webbing of his hand.

"Don't tense up, relax those muscles. There, just like that." Cam knew it'd take more than just one finger to prepare her, so he slipped another finger inside.

He caught Domini's gasp of surprise in a hungry kiss.

She squirmed as he scissored his fingers. Curling, twisting and stroking inside that tight channel, pushing her toward the sharp bite of pain that would turn into pleasure.

Cam slipped his fingers from her loosened hole and nipped at her bottom lip. He stood, hoping like hell he didn't look as unsteady on his feet as he felt. Goddamn he wanted this from her. Needed it. He circled her ankles in his hands and positioned her feet on either side of his shoulders. He stepped between her thighs, poising his cockhead at that enticing pucker.

Domini frowned.

He swept his hand across her belly. "What?"

"I thought we'd do this...from behind."

"No. As you've pointed out, we've done it from behind enough times. I want to see your face as I'm taking you this way. I want to touch your clit when I'm buried balls deep in your ass." Cam pressed the tip to the rosette and slid his hand beneath her butt cheeks, opening her ass fully. He pushed until the head of his cock disappeared inside the first ring of muscle.

Domini hissed.

"Breathe out, princess, come on, lemme make you feel good."

"It burns."

Going slow wouldn't make a difference now, so he shoved until his cock was lodged completely inside her.

She gasped.

Ah fuck. She was so tight. And hot. And tight. And goddamn he had the urge to rut on her. Slam into that vise-like heat. Feel that snug channel gripping his cock as he eased out slowly, so she felt every inch scraping against those tight tissues. Then he'd ram back in over and over. Hard and fast and deep. Relishing the loud slapping of his balls as he fucked her until she screamed.

Gritting his teeth, he held off on that raunchy scenario, allowing her untried channel to adjust around his impatient dick. Once he'd controlled his urge to pound into her without mercy, he glanced at her.

Her chest rose and fell rapidly. Her eyes were closed and her teeth were biting into her bottom lip so hard he expected to see blood.

"Domini. Look at me."

She opened her eyes.

"Touch me. I want your hands on me."

"If you lean closer will that put too much pressure on your leg?"

Leg? What leg? Cam froze. For the first time, he'd forgotten about his stump. He'd forgotten he wore a prosthesis. He'd forgotten to be self-conscious. He was so lost in her and all she brought to him he'd simply...forgotten.

She did this for him. To him. Domini made the world melt away. His vision wavered at the sudden rush of emotion.

"Cam? You okay?"

His gaze zoomed to hers. Hell. He sure as fuck hoped she hadn't seen him tear up. During sex. Yeah. That'd be sexy as shit. Bawling on her. While he fucked her in the ass.

That actually brought a smile to his face. Cam angled his head and kissed the inside of her left ankle, and then he kissed the right. He slid her feet down his biceps until they were braced in the crooks of his arms. He eased out, feeling the sphincter muscle surround just the fat head of his cock. He leaned forward and thrust into her ass to the hilt.

Domini gasped, pressing her palms against his pectorals, as if trying to push him back. "Dammit, Cam, I wasn't ready for that!"

He slipped his hand between their bodies and murmured, "Sorry, baby. Lemme make it up to you." He stroked her clit in the lazy way he'd discovered she liked best. "Better?"

"Yes."

Cam let the natural rhythm of their bodies take over. He flicked her clit with each thrust into her ass; she raked her nails down his chest, grinding her pussy into his groin on every upstroke.

That tight tingling in his balls indicated he couldn't last much longer. When the buzzing sensation brushed his fingers, his eyes flipped open.

Domini positioned the vibrator directly over her clit. "Let me see you lose that last bit of control."

And he did. He hammered into her without caution, without finesse, his head thrown back, sweat trickled down his throat and not into his eyes. *Almost there. Almost...*

Contractions from her orgasm tightened her cunt muscles with enough force he felt them in her bowels.

"Holy fuck." Cam shoved into her ass and went still. He groaned, hell, he howled when those rigid anal muscles clamped his cock and milked every drop of seed.

A bunch of nonsensical words filled the air and then she flopped back on the mattress.

Cam slipped out of her ass and pressed his lips to her throat. "You okay?"

"Mmm. Tired. Worn out." She cracked an eye open. "Sore."

"I'll refrain from swatting your ass tomorrow night."

"Swatting? I don't think so."

"Not into spanking?"

"No."

"Have you ever tried it?"

"No. Have you?"

"Yep. There's something sexy about seeing a handprint—*my* handprint—on your ass. Then the skin feels hot to the touch. Just think how good my tongue would feel cooling you down."

"But—"

"What would you do if I demanded you let me spank you?"

Her eyes held a rare challenge. "I'd let you...but I'd demand equal time."

"I'll keep that in mind. In fact, the thought of you smacking my ass turns me on. Everything about you turns me on, princess." He nuzzled her hairline and just breathed her in. "Stay put. I'll get stuff to clean up."

Domini stretched with that sated, smug expression of a well-fucked woman.

Heh heh. His well-fucked woman. If he had that cock-of-the-walk swagger, he'd earned it. About damn time too.

Cam washed up in the bathroom before he dressed. He brought a warm washcloth and teased Domini with flirty kisses as he swabbed between her legs. He tucked her between the sheets, wondering if she'd have regrets about his rough behavior when she noticed the finger-shaped bruises on her thighs tomorrow.

"You okay?"

"Mmm-hmm."

He kissed her forehead. "I must've done something right, because you were babbling in Ukrainian when you came that last time."

She blinked at him sleepily. "I wish you could stay with me tonight."

"Another time. Can I make it up to you tomorrow night? By taking you to supper? Someplace besides Dewey's?"

"Or I could cook for us here."

"Princess, we'd just end up in bed. And I don't see how you cooking for me is a night off for you."

"Are you asking me on a date, Deputy McKay?"

"Yeah, I guess I am."

That skeptical look returned to her icy blue eyes. "Why? You promised me this wouldn't—"

"Just say no if you don't wanna have supper with me tomorrow night, Domini."

"I don't want to say no."

"Good. Then I'll pick you up at six." He kissed her softly and left.

Chapter Eleven

"You're going out with him?"

Like Nadia had a right to judge her on men. Domini sighed quietly. "Cameron McKay is a good man, Nadia."

"He's also *police*," Nadia retorted, reverting to Russian in case Anton was listening. "Don't you remember what they're capable of?"

Domini absentmindedly rubbed her shoulder where the German shepherd had taken his pound of flesh. "It's not the same. He's nothing like the men who were terrorizing and brutalizing innocents."

Nadia muttered in Bosnian. Domini understood enough to realize she'd been called a fool. She let it slide and changed the subject. "So Anton likes school?"

"Being with kids his own age is better for him than being with the so-called 'babies' at Sky Blue daycare this summer." Nadia smiled at Anton over her shoulder. "He wishes he could ride the bus home."

"Is he making friends?"

She shrugged. "He doesn't say. He is disappointed he isn't hanging out with you tonight."

"I'm sorry I can't watch him and you had to cancel." Why had Rex insisted Nadia cancel their date? Wouldn't he encourage Nadia to bring his son along? Even one time? Especially if he was serious about making them a family again?

The thought of Rex living in the same house with Nadia and Anton turned Domini's stomach. She knew what Rex used to do to Nadia. She saw what he'd done to Anton and how that beating had finally forced Nadia into leaving the man for good.

Or so she'd thought.

"I'm sorry too. Anton likes coming here. You spoil him."

Spending time with Anton didn't equal spoiled in her book.

Anton raced into the kitchen. "Any cookies left?"

"No. You ate them all."

"It's time to go home anyway. Get your stuff," Nadia said.

"But we just got here!"

"Domini has a life, Anton, don't whine."

His chin fell to his chest.

"Hey." Domini tugged him until he was sitting on her lap. "You are part of my life too. You'll see me again soon."

"Promise?"

She smooched his head and laughed when he made a face. "I promise. Now vamoose, both of you. I need to get beautified for my date."

An hour later Domini fussed in front of the mirror. Why bother pinning her hair up? Cam would just undo it at the first chance.

She tidied the kitchen, setting the plates in the dish rack to dry as she waited for Cam to arrive.

Three distinctive raps echoed...forty-five minutes later.

Domini opened the door.

Oh yum. Look at the sexy man on her doorstep. Double yum. The spicy scent of aftershave drifted from the open collar of his white button-down shirt. He wore dark blue jeans, combat boots and a wolfish grin.

"Excuse me?"

Domini's eyes met his. "Um. What?"

"You said double yum and I'm wondering if that's some kind of Ukrainian slang for 'dumb ass you're late'."

"No. That's American slang for you look and smell yummy."

Cam actually blushed. The man could fuck her like an animal and demand all sorts of kinky things from her, but a compliment caused him to blush? She bit back a grin. "Come in. We must've been on the same wavelength because we even dressed alike tonight."

"I've often thought about how you'd look wearing my shirt...and nothin' else."

"Maybe later." She kissed his smoothly shaven cheek. "You want a beer?"

He groaned. "Shit. I was probably supposed to bring you wine or flowers or something."

"You're fine." In the kitchen she passed a bottle to him. "Need a glass?"

"Nope." He rested his backside against the counter and sipped.

She sipped.

Drip drip drip echoed in the silence.

"What's wrong with that faucet?"

"I don't know."

"How long's it been leaking?"

"Since I moved in."

Cam walked over and inspected it. "Just needs to be tightened. Checked for corrosion. Your landlord oughta be able to fix it pretty fast."

"Which would mean something if I'd ever seen the landlord. I send rent checks to a post-office box in Denver."

"Huh." Cam set down his beer. "I don't suppose you have a toolbox around here?"

"I think Colt or Blake left one in the utility room."

He left the kitchen and returned a couple minutes later with a rusty-looking toolbox.

"What are you doing?"

"Fixing it."

"Cam. You don't have to do this."

"I want to. It'll just take a minute and then we'll go, okay?"

"Okay."

He rummaged in the toolbox and fit the mouth of several wrenches to the base, discarding each one with a loud clank until he found the one that worked.

Cam muttered under his breath as he cranked the metal. Once the handle was off, he took a small steel bristled brush and scrubbed the inside. Domini couldn't see exactly what Cam was doing, but it gave her an odd feeling of domesticity to see him with his sleeves rolled up. She'd never had a guy around to do manly things for her.

She sipped her beer as he reassembled the parts and wrenched it all back together.

He grinned as he tested the handle. "See? No leaks."

"You didn't have to do that, but thank you." She frowned at

his chest. "Now you've got grease on that shirt."

Cam attempted to rub the spot away.

"No! Don't do that. Take if off and I'll get the stain out."

"Domini, you don't have to—"

"I want to." She began unbuttoning his shirt. "After spending my life working in a restaurant, I know a thing or two about removing grease stains."

"Or you just wanna get my shirt off," he drawled.

"That's a side benefit. Or it would be if you didn't always wear a T-shirt underneath everything. Maybe you could skip it next time." She waited while he peeled the shirt off and handed it to her. "Be right back."

Domini treated the stain and tossed it in the washer. Cam casually leaned against the counter, arms crossed over his chest defensively, not looking particularly happy.

"What?"

"I ain't exactly dressed for a night out. Not that I was Mr. GQ before but..." He sighed. "I always seem to fuck up."

"You haven't screwed up anything." She stopped in front of him and debated. If she ran her hands up his arms would he see it as a sexual advance? Or the reassuring gesture she intended?

Only one way to find out.

Domini set her palms on his biceps and perused the thick muscles to the wide curve of his shoulder. When he didn't flinch, she kept going until she reached his neck. With her hands at the base of his jaw, she feathered her thumbs over his jawline. Every inch of him was utterly masculine. Body. Face. Stance.

Cam didn't budge. He appeared to have quit breathing. But he watched her, very closely, with those dark, hooded eyes.

Her left thumb arced over his plump lower lip, and the dip in his full upper lip. Then both together until Cam's damp lips parted and she could feel the heat drifting from his mouth.

She shifted her hand to trace the hollowed shadow of his cheek beneath his cheekbone. She caressed his temple with her fingertips. His eyebrow. His hairline. That tender section of skin in front of his ear.

Before Domini touched the other side of his face, she locked her gaze to his. "Trust me. Let me."

His long, dark lashes fluttered as he closed his eyes in silent consent.

"No. Open your eyes. I want you to look at me, Cam. I want you to see it as I see it. I want you to watch me touching you."

Maybe she was a little surprised he'd obeyed.

Using a light touch, Domini followed the scar on the left side of his face. She smoothed the jagged edges from the corner of his mouth up to the ridged section where the scar hooked sharply. Then she slowly tracked the bump where it cut back and the gouge was deeper, the scar was thicker. She mapped every inch of his warrior's mark until it ended at the apex of his eye socket.

Before Cam could speak, or before she lost her nerve, Domini repeated the process with her mouth, scattering kisses from top to bottom and finally pressing her lips to his.

As she kissed him, she reveled in the sweetness of his surrender. Domini dropped her cheek to his chest, listening to the strong, steady beat of Cam's heart.

After a bit, he said, "I really don't want to go anywhere. But I imagine you're hungry since I was damn near an hour late."

"I have a casserole in the freezer I could pop in the oven."

Cam tipped her chin up to look in her eyes. "You sure?"

"Yes. If you don't mind tuna casserole."

"I love homemade tuna casserole."

If the domestic scene made Cam uncomfortable, he hid it well. They ate. They cuddled up on the couch and watched TV. She didn't attempt to wrestle the remote from his grasp. She didn't attempt to turn his closeness into something sexual.

The DVD clock flashed eleven o'clock. Cam kissed the top of her head and pushed to his feet. "I've gotta go. My buddy Brock is gonna swing through on his way to Seattle tomorrow."

"Thanks for a great date."

He snorted. "Some date. You washed my shirt, cooked me dinner, cleaned up and you didn't even get lucky."

She felt very lucky to have him in her life, even temporarily, but she'd never say it out loud.

Chapter Twelve

Gracie's barks forced Cam out of his easy chair. He opened the sliding glass, allowing her to check out the visitor from behind the safety of the fence in the backyard. Some guard dog. Gracie would lick him to death.

Cam watched as Brock's bright red Audi TT putted up the gravel driveway. Idiot babied that damn car. Although he probably rodded the piss out of it as he zipped across the country. Out here in the Wild West, where the paved roads were long and empty, law enforcement officers had better things to do than issue speeding tickets.

Didn't mean Cam wouldn't have enjoyed the hell out of writing him a ticket just because he could.

Brock's six-foot two-inch frame unfolded from the sports car. He wore his usual aviator shades, jungle print camo pants, and combat boots. The difference between this uniform and his official army uniform was the dark green tank top with "That's MISTER Asshole to you" emblazoned on the front.

"McKay, you ever gonna pave that goat path you call a driveway?"

Cam grinned. "Nope. It wouldn't be an issue if you drove a truck and not a wussy foreign car."

"Fuck off." Brock scaled the stairs in two giant steps. He dropped his duffel bag, threw his arms open. "What? Ain't you gonna show me the love, bro?"

"You're a scrawny thing, I didn't wanna crush you." Brock didn't allow one of those awkward male hugs, where they barely touched, beat each other on the back—hard—and then stepped away quickly. No. The bastard actually hugged him.

"I'm deeply touched by that sentiment, Hop-along." Brock

pushed the shades on top of his closely shaved head. His gaze swept Cam from crew cut to boots. "Seriously, man, how you doing?"

"Good."

"No issues with the new leg?"

Brock was one of the few people who'd seen Cam right after the amputation surgery in Iraq. He was also one of the few people Cam let visit him in Cheyenne during his rehab. Brock and Keely were the only ones besides hospital personnel who'd seen him without his prosthesis.

And now Domini was on that very short list.

Her tenderness and penchant for pleasing him was disconcerting because it had nothing to do with sex. Things had changed. Scary thing was, he wasn't sure if either of them were ready for those changes so soon.

"Cam? Buddy?"

Cam refocused. Although Domini was in the forefront of his mind, he'd make a concentrated effort to keep her out of any discussions with Brock today.

"Yeah, sorry, I spaced out. The leg is good."

"You still running?"

"Ten miles, every day."

"But you haven't tried one of those carbon fiber legs with the funky S-shaped foot yet? Man, I saw a guy who'd had both legs blown off in Afghanistan, and he could haul serious ass when he had those babies strapped on. He was a regular bionic man."

Cam snorted. "He'd have to be the six million dollar man to pay for it, because those super high tech prostheses are serious bank."

Brock looked at him quizzically. "You telling me the VA isn't ponying up cash for the latest advances in prosthetics for our injured war veterans?"

"That's exactly what I'm telling you. And since I'm a low-paid public servant, I ain't rolling in dough neither, so I'll be wearin' the leg I've got for a long damn time." Cam changed the subject. "Anything you're burning to do today?"

"Since a tumble in the hay with your sexy cowgirl sister ain't in the cards, I'm up for other suggestions."

"You hungry?"

"Nah."

"Been a while since I've taken the four-wheelers out."

"Sounds good." Brock hefted the strap of the duffel bag over his shoulder. "Lemme dump my gear."

They grabbed jackets before loading up. Gracie hopped on her usual place on Cam's ATV and Brock shook his head.

"You spoil her."

Cam ruffled the fur between Gracie's ears. "She deserves it. She's a good girl, aren't ya, Gracie?"

Gracie barked twice.

"I worry about you sometimes, McKay, out here alone in Wyoming, a dog as your only companion. You need a woman. And a whole houseful of kids."

Cam revved the engine, cutting off Brock's diatribe about how Cam needed to start "living" again. Wouldn't his buddy be shocked to hear how Cam had been spending his nights? Relearning how to be the sexual man he'd been in the past?

Except it's not all about sex with Domini.

Was that why he was hesitant to tell Brock about her?

Putting such girly thoughts out of his mind, he gunned it through the pasture, following the rutted tracks. Since there were plenty of paths to choose from, Cam picked one that zigzagged from the hills and the plains to the valley marking the end of McKay land.

They rode in silence, as was their custom. Brock's life as a soldier didn't allow much time for quiet contemplation. Everything Brock did had specific purpose—usually as a result of a direct order. When Brock was on patrol in the sandboxes of the world, he sure as hell wasn't enjoying the scenery. So Cam knew aimless wandering appealed to him.

A bank of clouds covered the sun and Cam shook off an odd feeling of...foreboding.

Brock shouted, "Up there?" breaking Cam's reverie. Cam nodded and dropped behind Brock's ATV.

They detoured to the top of the ridge and parked. Brock practically ran up the last hill. Cam lumbered to the ledge and let his gaze encompass the area.

A valley spread out below. The tall grass was mostly burned away from the summer sun; what remained was bleached out and trampled down. Outcroppings of boulders in shades of pewter and russet popped up across the rock-strewn field. No water ran in the empty riverbed, it was merely a deep gouge in the landscape. Scrub oaks and cedar brush sporadically lined the hillside. Clumps of sagebrush and yucca were scattered here and there. The wind blew, as it always seemed to do in Wyoming. Bugs and birds and critters were conspicuously absent.

"I forget how damn beautiful it is here."

"Hell, I live here and I never get used to it."

Brock swigged from his water bottle, staring across the vista. "Tell me, Cam. Are you happy? Living around home?"

Weird question, but if Brock asked it, he needed an answer. "Most days I guess I'm pretty content. My job isn't bad. I respect the hell out of the guys I work with. And they don't give me much shit for fulfilling the county's ADA quota." Cam paused. "Why?"

"I've gotta decide whether to re-up in the next couple months."

"Is that why you're headed to Seattle? To see if you could live around your family on a permanent basis?"

"Yeah. Lemme ask you something else. If you hadn't gotten injured, would you be here right now?"

Cam didn't hesitate. "Nope. I'd still be a soldier."

Brock nodded.

No further explanation was necessary.

A cold, damp wind whipped up from the canyon and they headed back. They'd crossed the halfway point when the skies opened and drenched them. Gracie couldn't stay on the back of the vehicle with muddy paws, so Cam had no choice but to let her run home. He kept turning around to check on her, ignoring Brock's taunts, "She's a dog! She's supposed to run!"

Cam's concern for Gracie meant he wasn't watching out for his own safety. Brock's warning shout about the sinkhole was too late. The front right tire of Cam's ATV hit the hole, bouncing the vehicle up and ejecting Cam out of his seat. He crash-landed on his ass right in a puddle of mud.

"Fuck!" That smarted. The kill switch from the ATV hung from his wrist and the vehicle was silent, flipped on its side. He shoved Gracie from licking his face with a stern, "No."

Brock parked close and slogged over. "Buddy, you okay?"

"Yeah."

"Need help up?"

"Nah. I got it." Cam pushed to his right side and rolled up. But he'd misjudged the angle of the hill. Once he was upright, all his weight was on his left side. He heard that familiar sickening pop and the suction broke, separating the socket from his stump. He fell into the mud again.

"Jesus fucking Christ!" He wasn't hurt so much as he was embarrassed and pissed as hell. *This* was what he fucking hated. He hated being helpless. He hated that someone had seen him helpless. He grabbed onto his useless leg and pulled. Nothing happened. "Fuck!" He yanked harder but his prosthetic foot was lodged in the mud. Great. Not only was he sitting on his ass, not even the sheer brute strength of his upper body would move the goddamn useless thing.

"Cam—"

"I said I've got it," Cam said through clenched teeth.

"Don't be so goddamned stubborn. Let me help you." Brock crouched. "It's me, remember? We've been down this 'I don't need your fucking help' road before and the result is always the same: you do."

"You are one fucking pushy-ass bastard, Tennyson."

"You can try and kick my ass for it later." Without asking, Brock gently worked the prosthetic out of the mud. Even though it'd mostly detached from Cam's stump, he still felt a sting of pain.

He hissed.

"Up you go." Brock clasped Cam's hands and hauled him upright. He wrapped an arm around Cam's back, steadying him as Cam bunny hopped to the vehicle. Brock's focus stayed on Cam's lower half, not the blush discoloring his face, and for that Cam was immensely grateful.

"Now, Hop-along, we're both gonna have to ride side saddle on the four-wheeler."

Cam lurched toward the ATV. He was sweating, muddy and livid he was gasping for air after walking ten fucking steps. Once his lungs weren't failing him, he forced words out through his compressed teeth, "Thanks. It'd be easiest if I sat on the left side so I can brace myself with my right leg."

"That'll work." Brock waited until Cam situated himself before he climbed on the four-wheeler. "Ready?"

"Let's go."

Brock drove like a little old lady. They bumped through the field so slowly that Gracie—who'd raced ahead—was napping on the back deck by the time they'd returned to the house. Cam fought another burst of temper while Brock trudged inside for his crutches.

At least Cam could hobble into his house under his own steam. He'd barely cleared the welcome mat when Brock spoke behind him.

"If you don't need my help, I'll run back and get that other four-wheeler."

"Run? It's like five miles in," Cam said.

"I haven't done PT today so it'll be good for me." Brock's pearly whites flashed. "Plus, it ain't often I get a chance to run in the rain *and* sling mud from the tires."

"Have a ball." Truthfully, Cam needed time to put himself back together. Literally.

A few hours later, after Cam and Brock cleaned up, they were glued to an MMA event on the big screen. Things were back to normal, placing bets and shouting insults about the opposing competitor. Cam's work phone buzzed in his pocket. "Shit." He hit mute on the TV. "McKay. Uh-huh. No. It's okay, I know exactly where it is. I'll be there in a bit." He shut the phone.

"What?"

"Deb can't find a file and since Sheriff Shortbull is in the office, she doesn't feel comfortable picking the lock on my desk to get it. So I have to go in. Won't take long."

Brock's gaze fell to Cam's left side. "You sure you're up for it? You did crash today. Maybe you should tell them—"

"I'm fine."

"Then you'd better get some beer while you're out. I'll just hold down the couch—ooh, Jesus that had to hurt."

Cam rolled his eyes. Brock was obsessed with MMA; he probably wouldn't notice Cam was gone.

Brock shouted, "Hey, pick up some food too. I'm starving and neither of us can cook worth a shit."

Domini had driven out to return Cam's shirt, which she'd washed, pressed and hung up. But Cam's truck wasn't around and a cute red sports car sat next to the garage.

And yes, maybe she wanted to meet the guy who hadn't given up on Cam in Iraq. But Cam hadn't invited her over. Maybe Cam didn't want his friend to know about her.

Just drop off the shirt and leave.

Cursing her flip-flopping behavior, she grabbed the plastic bag and headed for the front door.

Several minutes passed before a nearly bald man, wearing camo and a Vin Diesel scowl, loomed in the doorway. "Yes?"

"Is Cam here?"

"Nope."

"Oh. Well, I stopped by to drop off his shirt."

"Who are you?"

"Domini, umm Domini Katzinski. I'll just leave it—"

"How do you know Cam, Domini, umm, Domini Katzinski?"

What was with the sarcasm and the third degree? Was this guy a cop? Too bad she didn't have the guts to snap off, "I'm fucking Cam. What's it to you, asshole?" Instead, she said, "We're...friends."

"And your *friend* Cam just happened to leave a dress shirt at your house?"

Shoot.

"Does this happen often?"

"No. It was the first time."

His sharp gaze softened and those melted chocolate eyes widened. Then his mouth broke into an enormous grin that would've made her weak-kneed—if she hadn't already succumbed to the power of Cam McKay's smile. "Why don't you come in?"

"That's not nec—"

"I insist." The guy strong-armed her into the house. He flashed that devastating smile again. "I'm Brock Tennyson. Cam and I go back to basic training."

"Cam mentioned you'd planned to visit." This Brock guy was absolutely mouthwatering. Brown eyes and skin the color of rich coffee. He was built like a dream, deeply cut muscular arms, a contoured chest, trim hips and waist, yet he wasn't as impossibly muscle bound as Cam.

"Funny, Cam didn't mention you, sweet Domini."

"I'm not surprised." *Since it's just sex between us.*

"Cam'll be back any minute. Would you like a beer while you wait?"

Say no. "Maybe just one."

"That's a girl."

Domini followed Brock and froze in the entryway into the kitchen. "Is Gracie here?"

"She's sleeping on the deck out back. She did a lot of running today. Why? Did you want me to bring her in?"

"No! I mean, that's good she's outside. I don't really...get along with dogs."

"But Gracie isn't just any dog."

Where had she heard that before?

Brock popped the cap on a bottle of Corona and handed it over. "Didn't Cam tell you how he ended up with Gracie?"

She shook her head.

"When Cam was rehabilitating in Cheyenne, this do-gooder group began showing up with 'therapy animals'. At that time Cam was in his bitter stage and he didn't want anything to do with anyone, let alone an animal. He refused the therapy, but one day Gracie escaped from her handler and cowered under his bed.

"He didn't rat her out. He realized she didn't want to be a therapy animal any more than he wanted one. Long story short, they bonded and the people were more than happy to pass Gracie off to Cam, because she'd broken the rules and attached herself to one person."

"Cam."

"Uh-huh."

"I know how she feels," Domini muttered.

Brock's eyebrows drew together but he didn't comment.

Domini stayed mum and swigged her beer.

"You an MMA fan?"

"What's that?"

He sighed. "I'll have to whip that white boy for your lack of education. Come into the living room and prepare to be enlightened on the ways of the ring warrior."

She perched on the edge of the couch and watched two

guys beating the crap out of one another with punches, kicks and wrestling moves. Brock cheered them. Booed them. It wasn't her thing, but she saw how it'd appeal to men with an abundance of testosterone. Like Brock. Like Cam.

"So how long have *you* known Cam?" he asked.

"He's been coming into the restaurant I manage for a while. Only recently have we...started seeing each other outside of working hours."

"You're very diplomatic, Domini. Where are you from? Switzerland?"

"No, the Ukraine." Her head snapped up. Blood tinged her cheeks. "I get it. Neutral. Switzerland. Funny."

Brock shrugged. "I'm guessing it wasn't a picnic living in the Ukraine after the Chernobyl disaster and the fall of the Soviet Union."

"It was bad, which was why I left."

"Not as a mail-order Ukrainian bride, I hope."

"No. That was never an option for me."

"Why not?"

I'm damaged goods. "The Evangelical Church of Hope got their hooks in me before the marriage brokers did and they offered me a better way out of the country. I eventually found a way to escape them too." She chugged her beer and boldly changed the subject. "You've known Cam for a long time."

"Yep."

"Can I ask you something about him?"

"Sure. Doesn't mean I'll answer."

That flip reply might've stung if she hadn't suspected Brock's passive aggressive responses were his way of protecting his friend. "Was Cam always...such a..." Domini struggled with the right word.

Brock's eyes narrowed. "Such a what?"

"The type of guy who's loyal. Polite. Thoughtful. Generous. He'd walk a little old lady across the street. He'd jump in front of a bus to save a baby in a runaway stroller. He'd give up his seat to a pregnant woman. He'd..."

"Throw himself on a grenade to save your life?" Brock supplied.

"Exactly. Has he always been that way? Or did he become that way after his injury?"

"What do you think?" he asked without guile.

"I think he's always been the selfless guy who does the right thing. No matter what. No matter the personal cost."

"You'd be exactly right. And you're the first person who's picked up on that...except for me, of course."

"Of course."

"I owe him my life. He'll tell you the reverse is true, but it's not. He saved my dumb ass more times than I care to count. I will do *anything* for that man. Cam is one of a kind and he deserves the best—" his cool appraisal moved over her and he frowned, "—in everything."

Stung by his less than flattering perception that she wasn't good enough for Cam, she stood. "I should go. Please give Cam the shirt."

"Chill out. Finish your beer. I didn't mean to run you off."

She allowed him time to consider his statement, then challenged, "Didn't you? Didn't you really?"

Brock attempted to stare her down, but gave up and laughed. "Man, you ain't a pushover at all, are you?"

"Some people confuse a quiet nature with timidity. There is a difference, Mr. Tennyson."

"I see that now." Brock snatched her hand and kissed her knuckles with exaggeration. "Call me Brock. I owe you an apology, delectable Domini."

"Apology accepted."

His right eyebrow winged up. "I'm forgiven that fast?"

"No point in holding a grudge. You were only looking out for Cam's best interest and I can't fault you for that."

"Hmm. Gorgeous, quiet and forgiving. Will you marry me?"

She laughed. "Let's stick to being friends."

"Oh woman, I am so gonna try to change your mind. Let's have a toast to celebrate our new friendship." He leapt to his feet. "Have any idea where Cam keeps the tequila?"

"No. But I hope his liquor cabinet is better stocked than his refrigerator."

"You and me are gonna get along just fine."

Cam was surprised to see Domini's car parked in the drive. He was even more surprised to enter the kitchen and see Brock and Domini laughing over a row of empty shot glasses.

A possessive roar filled his head.

"Cam! My man. I was just telling Domini about the time—"

"I kicked your butt for drinkin' all my tequila?"

"No, about the time we got into that bar fight in—"

"I'm sure Domini ain't interested in hearing our old war stories, Brock."

"Yes I am."

Damn she looked good. Color on her cheeks. A sparkle in her eyes. Amusement tilting the corners of her mouth.

He forced a smile. "Looks like I have some catching up to do. Pass me that bottle, will ya?"

"Sure thing." Brock poured three fingers of tequila and slid it across the bar.

"Why don't you tell me one of your wild stories?" Domini asked him.

"I'll pass because I don't lie nearly as smoothly as Brock does."

"That's true," Brock said. "We called him George behind his back because of that 'I cannot tell a lie' bullshit."

Cam confided, "And we called him Pinocchio."

"Really? I'm stunned. All your stories have been an outrageous...lie?" she said with mock shock.

"Not all. Once I wrassled a bear with my bare hands. I have pictures." Brock peeped at her with those big, dark puppy dog eyes that always got him laid. "Wanna see them?"

"I assume you're bare naked on the bear skin rug after you killed the beast with your bare hands?" Domini mused.

"Yep, but unlike the pictures of those white boys who ain't smart enough to hunt bears the right color, like polar bears, my brown ass blends perfectly with the grizzly I slayed." Brock leaned closer. "Is this getting me anywhere with you, hot stuff?"

Domini and Brock continued to flirt like Cam wasn't in the room. This playful side of Domini fascinated him. He'd seen her various sides, sweet and fiery and obedient and occasionally pushy, but never shamelessly charming. Or was it just shameless?

Regardless, it was hot as sin watching her enchant Brock— a man who was not easily enchanted.

An hour later, Cam was on his third shot and Domini and

Brock had quit drinking entirely.

But they hadn't stopped the sexy banter, arguing the pros and cons of mail-order brides. "Not speaking the same language would be a huge bonus," Brock pointed out. "Then she couldn't nag me."

"You, Brock Tennyson, are trying to get under my skin."

"No, sweetheart, I'm trying to get into your pants." He waggled his eyebrows suggestively. "Is it working?"

She laughed—a little nervously—but she didn't say no.

"I'm gonna take your silence as a yes. Hot damn!" Brock grabbed her hand, acting like he was dragging her away.

"Stop. I know you were kidding." Domini sent Cam a questioning look. "Right?"

Tension hung in the air.

"You're a big girl, Domini. Do what you want."

"But..." She looked torn. "Don't...aren't you supposed to..."

Scream no, you're mine! Yes. Cam tossed off a cool, "Give you permission?"

She nodded warily.

Brock sucked in a breath. "Shit, Cam. She said you two had one date and I thought... Why didn't you tell me it was that way between you two?"

Domini spun on Brock. "What way?"

"Cam's way."

"How do you know—"

"Because I've known him a long time, Domini, and I know what he prefers."

Cam flashed Domini a wolfish smile. "Surprised?"

She shook her head before addressing Brock. "And you aren't like Cam?"

"No." Brock slurped from a water bottle. "I like to watch. Damn, do I like to watch. Sometimes I join in. When control freak here lets me."

Cam caught the flare of interest in Domini's eyes.

Whoa. That reaction was unexpected. But then again, Cam hadn't delved much into finding out Domini's sexual fantasies because he'd been fulfilling his role as her dominant lover and that'd been enough for him.

But was it enough for her?

Right then Cam knew he'd have to decide how far he was

willing to let them take this flirtation. He and Brock had shared women in the past. It'd been no big deal.

But now it was different. Could he orchestrate a sexual situation between his best friend and the woman he'd fallen in love with? Or would he want to rip the hands off the man who'd saved his life just because he'd put them on her?

Did Domini think she could handle a threesome?

Too fucking bad. No way in hell was Brock touching her, no matter what she thought she wanted. No. Way.

What kind of lover would you be if you didn't see to her sexual needs? Even if they are in direct conflict with yours?

Fuck that. She's mine.

Is she? Does she know that?

No.

Dammit. If he snarled and showed jealousy, not only would Domini realize he'd developed serious feelings for her, but so would Brock.

What better way to prove his control over her than to command her to satisfy another man? And bonus: it'd prove to Brock that Cam McKay might've lost his leg, but he hadn't lost his edge. He still owned the ability to bend a woman to his sexual whims.

Decision made, Cam casually asked, "Domini. Have you ever been with two men at once?"

"Umm. No."

"Does the thought of two men fucking you at the same time turn you on?" When her response was a long time coming, he said, "Answer me."

Domini didn't look away. "Yes."

"If I were to demand you blow me while Brock watches, you'd do it."

Not a question, yet she nodded anyway.

"Then come here."

She sauntered over, her head held high, her white-blonde hair flowing around her angelic face, her arctic eyes bright, her mouth curved in a small smile.

Cam curled his hand around her neck and centered her body between his legs. He brought his mouth down on hers hard, taking the brutal kiss he craved. When he'd thoroughly flustered her with his possessive kiss, he slid his lips to her ear.

"If you don't want to do this, princess, say so now."

Her voice was so subdued he strained to hear it. "I gave myself to you without restriction. Whatever you want, you can have."

"Good answer, baby. And you can show me. Now."

He walked to the fireplace in the living room, expecting Domini to follow. From the corner of his eye, he saw Brock flop on the couch. The move looked lazy. Bored. Cam knew it was anything but.

As Domini approached him, he unbuttoned his shirt. She didn't lower her eyes or keep her hands clasped behind her back. The subservient posture and attitude crap didn't appeal to either of them, thank God. But she did not balk at letting him have complete control.

She said, "You didn't wear a T-shirt."

Cam smiled. "See? I listen to you."

"I'm glad." Her fingers trailed over the sprinkling of chest hair. Her palms smoothed his pecs, his ribs, and his belly. She angled her head to lap at the hollow of his throat.

A tremor threatened to break free from that sexy innocent lick.

Domini's delicate butterfly touches were a stunning contrast to the hard nips and deep sucking kisses she used on his nipples.

"Enough. Unbutton my pants." The khakis were loose enough once she'd released the snap, they pooled around his ankles. "On your knees." She looked up at him and Cam couldn't resist brushing the hair from her face. "Your hands can be on my hips or my ass. Choose."

She peeled the boxers down and didn't spend significant time gawking at his prosthesis, but neither did she ignore it. She mouthed the length of his shaft, teasing it with hot breath and firm nibbles. Then she sucked it into the wetness and heat that never failed to make his breath catch.

Cam braced his right hand on the oak mantel and gathered her hair in his left hand, keeping a clear shot for Brock. He knew how hot the visual looked—Domini's bobbing head as his cock pumped in and out of her hungry mouth.

But the visual wasn't nearly as hot as the reality of her sucking him off.

"Baby, your mouth is pure heaven. You know how I like it."

Domini kept him wet, she kept him deep, and she kept sucking until Cam felt his balls lift.

He shoved his cock until her lips were stretched around the base. He tightened his hold on her hair, but not hard enough to sting her scalp. "Suck it all down, every fuckin' drop. Swallow. More, baby, don't choke. Breathe. That's it."

Hot pulse after hot pulse shot out the end of his dick, and she sucked in tandem to every pulsation, leaving him depleted. Sated. Dizzy. He would've staggered and probably crashed to the ground if not for the hold Domini maintained on his hips.

The supreme glow of satisfaction she wore whenever she'd pleased him was heady stuff and it humbled him. He murmured, "Thank you."

Wordlessly, Domini nuzzled his left thigh, then his right.

"Are you ready?"

She peered up at him. "Ready for what?"

"For me and Brock to fuck you."

Chapter Thirteen

Being with two men? At the same time?

A million thoughts spun crazily in Domini's head.

First: *yes! I want this.* Followed quickly by: *no! I can't do this.*

What about after the fun and sexual games ended? Would she be hot and happy in the moment but feel used when it was over? Could she look Brock in the eye without embarrassment? What about Cam? How would he react after his friend fucked her?

Even as Domini considered the repercussions, she knew she'd do it. Not for Cam, not for Brock, for her own curiosity.

Cam helped her to her feet. "Tell me what you're thinking."

"I'm nervous."

"Because you've never—"

"—done anything remotely close to this."

His deep chuckle vibrated throughout her body. "Brock and I have. Trust us."

She said, "Okay," in a breathless rush.

Cam placed his mouth on her ear. "Remember something. *I* decide what I'll let him to do you. Not you. Definitely not him." After a lingering kiss, Cam said, "Take your shirt and bra off."

Domini stripped and hated the burning in her cheeks.

"Brock, grab a towel and the vegetable oil from the kitchen. Get the captain's chair out of the dining room and bring it in here."

Brock grinned and returned promptly, setting the chair by the end of the couch and the other items on the side table.

Cam lowered into the seat and motioned to Domini. He

zigzagged his rough-skinned finger from her left hipbone to her right and her belly trembled beneath his sure touch. He clamped his hands on her waist and turned her sideways.

Brock sauntered forward. Naked. When had he gotten naked? His left hand pumped his cock, his gaze fixed firmly on her face. "I'd like to taste your pretty mouth, lick those full pink lips before I see them wrapped around my dick, but since that's not the way Cam plays...can I touch them?"

Domini opened her mouth to respond, only to have Cam answer for her. "Just her lips, nothin' else."

Cam's possessive answer sent a shiver through her.

Brock's right hand came up. He outlined her lips with a languid sweep of his thumb. He brushed it just far enough inside her mouth that the wet rim of her lip dampened the pad. He hissed when she darted her tongue and licked it.

"Ever had a black man, baby?"

"No."

"You know what they say..."

Brock laughed and ignored Cam's warning growl as his hand followed the line of her throat to her shoulder. He gently pushed until she fell to her knees.

Then that black cock was in her face. It wasn't as long as Cam's, which meant she'd have an easier time deep throating him. But the cockhead was plumper. The shaft was thicker. Brock's skin tone was beautiful, a rich dark brown. His shortly trimmed pubic hair was pure black. She had just latched onto his hips when Cam's voice broke through the sounds of Brock's heavy breathing.

"You hands are on me, not him." Cam circled her wrists and placed her hands behind her; one on Cam's right thigh, one high on the left. "I'll touch you while you're sucking him."

The position would've been awkward if not for the arch in her spine which caused her nipples to brush the bristly hair on Brock's legs and tingle deliciously in response. She smiled. Cam knew how much she loved nipple play. Even now he was seeing to her sexual needs.

"Open," Brock directed.

She closed her eyes, dropped her jaw in anticipation of all that smooth, hot, hard flesh pushing past her lips and teeth, over her tongue until it filled her mouth completely. Brock swirled the cockhead over her lips and plunged in to the root.

Domini started to gag.

Cam's voice drifted to her. "Relax. Breathe."

Brock wasn't expecting a slow tease. He pumped in and out in a smooth rhythm that Domini knew would get him off quickly.

Cam twined his hands in her hair, holding it out of her face. "You have no idea how fucking hot it is to see his dick in your mouth."

A slight hum from her had Brock groaning, "Jesus. Do that again."

She did.

Domini looked up at Brock. A little thrill shot through her, seeing him lost in pleasure. She understood Cam was giving this intimate moment to Brock as much as she was.

Was it easier for Cam to show his gratitude for his friendship when he was proving to Brock that Cam McKay was still one hundred percent dominant male?

"More, come on, take it all," Brock urged, forcing her to refocus.

As she created tight suction on every withdrawal, she slackened her throat muscles when Brock plunged back in to the root. His hardness filled her mouth over and over, sending her into hazy subspace where she existed on a whole different plane.

"You're beautiful," Cam whispered. "So damn beautiful I can't think for wanting you. Two men so fucking hot for you that we're both gonna fuck you at once. Me in that tight pussy. Brock in your tight ass. You're getting wet thinking about it, aren't you?"

She moaned. The sensations were devastating. The constant wet suction of Brock's slippery cock fucking her mouth. The rasp of her nipples against Brock's legs. Cam's hand fisted in her hair. The ache in her arms. The feel of Cam's rough skin as she dug her nails into his upper thighs. Three distinctively different breathing patterns distorted the air. Three different scents filled her lungs.

But it was the simple eroticism of Cam's words and his fingertips dancing up and down her arms that made her hot.

She saw Brock's hand reach between his legs and adjust his balls.

"I need it faster." Brock picked up the pace, and his fingers curled around her neck, his thumbs pressed on the spot her jawbone hinged, keeping her jaw open. "I'm so close..."

"Come on her chest."

Brock groaned and eased out of Domini's mouth. His left hand wrapped around his cock and he jacked off in short, fast strokes. The sound of his flesh slapping and his grunt of completion gave way to spurts of warm come landing on her chest as Brock watched through hooded eyes. His hand slowed, but didn't stop, as if he didn't want the moment to end. "Damn, woman. You're something."

Cam rubbed the quivering muscles in her arms. "Stand up."

Brock snagged the towel, intending to wipe his come from Domini's chest, but Cam snatched it. "Let me." After he'd wiped her down, those intense blue eyes locked on hers. "You ready?"

Her body trembled. Could she do this? She looked at Cam. Fire danced in his eyes. He wanted this. She nodded.

"Get rid of your pants."

Domini shimmied them off.

Cam hooked a finger under the elastic band of her panties and tugged her closer. "You're wet." He pressed his mouth to the section of skin below her belly button and sucked hard, holding her lower back so she couldn't squirm away.

Not that Domini tried to escape any time he put his hands or mouth on her. He'd sucked hard enough to leave a reddish-purple love bruise behind.

"My mark looks pretty on your creamy skin. I'd like to leave love bites all over you."

"I wouldn't stop you," Domini said, reaching out to caress the side of his face.

"I know." He kissed her belly one last time. "Climb up on my lap."

Cam widened his legs to fit outside of the chair legs. He brought her high up on his thighs; his erection nestled into the crack of her butt.

Domini tried desperately not to put weight on Cam's left side. She gasped when Cam hooked her legs over the arms of the chair, baring her most intimate parts completely.

"Look at that." Brock stood a few feet away, hot eyes drawn

to and devouring her sex.

"Pretty pink isn't it? Soft. Wet. Sweet."

"You offering me a taste?"

Again, Cam answered for her. "Yep."

"Hot damn." Brock dropped to his knees.

She couldn't seem to find her voice through the staccato beats of her heart.

Cam's large, work-roughed hands followed the curve of her legs from her ankles up to the crease of her thighs. He traced one finger up her slit and gently separated her pussy lips, exposing her clit.

Oh no. Surely they didn't plan on...double-teaming her.

Brock bent his head and lapped at the moisture pouring from the mouth of her sex, curling his long, pink tongue inside. Not only did Brock expertly use his tongue, the contrast of his dark face and light-colored mouth, centered between her milky white thighs, was an undeniably hot image.

Domini moaned when Brock wiggled his tongue inside her.

Then Brock licked the folds surrounding her core, suckling her pussy lips, stopping below the swollen nub throbbing for attention.

"How close are you to coming?" Cam murmured in her ear.

"A hair trigger away," she admitted.

A look passed between Cam and Brock, but Brock didn't look at her. He fastened his mouth to her clit.

No tongue swirling teases. No drawn out licks. Brock just kept sucking on that pearl until the orgasm steamrolled over her. Domini gasped through each strong pulse, listening to the sexy timbre of Cam's voice in her ear, which only heightened the heat in her groin. By the time the final throb ended, her body trembled. She wanted to crawl into Cam's big bed and sleep.

Naturally Cam and Brock had other plans.

Brock said, "Up you go," and lifted her off the chair and to her feet. After that orgasm she didn't have enough breath in her lungs to protest and hardly the wherewithal to even stand.

"We're both gonna fuck you now."

The fog cleared from her head at that command. "Here? But..." Why not in his bed?

"This is more stable for my leg."

"Oh." But she knew there was more to his reasoning.

He whispered fiercely, "My bed is our space, Domini. I won't share you in it. Ever. Not even for an hour." He used his teeth on her earlobe. "I'm pushing you to the edge you wanted. To the place where your body knows what it wants even if you're unsure." Cam drew his finger from her chin down to her belly button. "Trust me."

"I do."

As soon as Cam lay back on the sofa, she crawled up and managed to situate her legs on either side of his hips.

"You'll have to lean against me completely and angle your ass so Brock can reach you."

To please herself and to quell her nerves, she rubbed her breasts over his chest, loving his quick intake of breath when her nipples brushed his. "I like being pressed against you like this," she whispered. "Face to face."

"Me too, princess." Cam's lips drifted across hers in an almost kiss. "Ready?"

A tiny wave of apprehension flowed through her but she nodded.

"Brock? You suited up?"

"Yep. Suited up, slicked up and ready to go."

Cam sifted his fingers through her hair. "You're gonna have to do most the work since I'm flat on my back."

"Being naked with you is hardly work."

"God, woman, sometimes you undo me," he rasped.

Such raw emotion in his eyes. "Cam."

"I know. Let's do this. Lower onto me."

His cock filled her and she closed her eyes with a sigh. This was familiar.

Cam tapped her chin with his finger. "Eyes on me. Always on me." His avid mouth controlled hers and coupled with his greedy hands roaming over her bare body, Domini almost didn't notice a slippery finger circling her anus until it wiggled inside. Her gasp was lost in Cam's mouth when a second finger joined the first. Stretching her. Fucking her steadily.

Brock didn't say a word as he prepared her. It was surreal, feeling him so intimately, but not seeing him.

Both fingers disappeared. She stiffened.

"Gotta relax," Cam murmured against her mouth.

When Cam threaded his hands though her hair, kissing her like she was the center of his universe, she forgot how big the head of Brock's penis was until it pressed past the ring of muscle.

Burning pain followed. Domini fought the urge to break free from Cam and buck Brock off.

Cam sensed her panic. "You can take him. Just like you took me." He nuzzled her neck. Her temple. Her ear. "Loosen up, let go, let us make you feel good. Let me give you something you've never had." He licked and teased the pulse point at the base of her throat. "I love how you taste here."

"How do I taste?"

"Like fire. Like ice. Like mine."

Their gazes collided.

When Cam's tongue swept into her mouth, she fell headfirst into his powerful kiss.

Somewhere in the back of Domini's mind she realized Brock had been very quiet. Too quiet.

Cam kept a haze of passion floating between them she could almost touch. Then Brock snapped his hips and drove into her ass completely.

Oh God. Fire. Burning pain. Hot, deep thick burning in her rectum.

She ripped her mouth free and cried out.

"You okay?" Cam asked.

"Uh-huh. But I need a second." Domini attempted to relax and enjoy being stuffed with two cocks.

"We're not goin' anywhere." Cam nibbled her jaw, paying attention to the vulnerable skin beneath her chin that caused her to forget her own name.

Brock's fingers lightly traced each bump and hollow of her spinal cord. Waiting patiently for her to be ready, even when she felt tension vibrating from him. The male need for him to take what she'd offered.

You wanted this experience; it's not fair you're being skittish now. They're waiting on your signal.

Domini began to move on Cam in a rocking motion. The grind of her clitoris on Cam's pubic hair tightened her abdominal muscles and made everything more pleasurable, less painful, as she kicked up the pace.

Brock didn't start ramming into her until she focused on squeezing her anal muscles around his cock. "You're very good at nonverbal signals, Domini," he said and began to ride her relentlessly.

Because Domini was fucking Cam and Brock was fucking her, she and Brock choreographed the movement. Brock shoved balls deep when Cam's cock wasn't buried fully inside her pussy. He pulled out completely, letting his cockhead rest against her spasming anus when Cam's cock glided into her. When Brock first reentered her ass, he caused an acute spark of pain every time, but Domini went from holding her breath against it to anticipating it. Craving it.

"Gotta have more," Brock panted. "Domini, can you come like this?"

"I'd like to."

They all laughed.

When Brock's strokes lengthened, Domini let her head fall back in a soft moan.

"Look at me," Cam demanded.

Domini knew if she saw the possession in Cam's eyes it'd be over. She ignored his command, allowing Brock to take control.

Spreading her ass cheeks in each hand, Brock hammered into her without stopping. His cock jerked hard against her anal passage. He shouted, "Oh fuck," as he came. And came and rode her hard.

When Brock finally stilled, he sighed and pressed a kiss in the middle of Domini's back.

"Goddammit Domini. Look at me."

Sweating, panting, on the verge of meltdown, she opened her eyes.

Cam's eyes were wild as he pumped his hips. The tip of his cock seemed to zero in on her G-spot. "Come for me. Now." His rough voice unleashed the last string of restraint. She gasped as the climax ripped through her like a tidal wave. Her sex squeezed Cam's cock, her anal muscles clamped around Brock's dick. Her body pulsed from head to toe. She vaguely heard Cam's hoarse shout before she faded away into a blissful, relaxed, post orgasmic state.

Hands stroked and petted her as she floated back to earth.

"Wow. That was…"

No one else piped in. But some other wordless communication passed between the two men she was still sandwiched between.

Brock managed to sneak a quick kiss on her shoulder before withdrawing. "I'm exhausted. Domini, you sure wear a man out, girl. I'm gonna hit the shower and then the hay. I have a long drive ahead of me tomorrow. Thank you for tonight."

"I didn't mean to keep you from resting," Domini apologized.

"You didn't." Brock bussed her cheek. "I'd forego sleep for the rest of my life if it meant we could do this again. Damn, Domini. You are sexy and fun."

"More fun than wrassling a bear?" she teased.

His warm laughter tickled her ear. "Definitely."

After Brock was gone, Domini tried to get up, but Cam pressed her down until she was prone across his body. "What's the rush?"

"I hate to say it but I have to go too."

"Why? I thought you could spend the night."

"I have to work early shift tomorrow."

He sighed. "Doesn't that just figure? Because I'm on the noon to ten shift tomorrow." His fingers idly traced her spine. "What's your schedule the next day?"

"Early shift again, but I promised Nadia I'd watch Anton after work."

"Am I ever gonna have sex with you this week?"

Domini smiled against his chest, elated he couldn't get enough of her. "I sure hope so." After one last kiss to his amazingly hard pectoral, she rolled up. It was heartening to see him lounging naked, not trying at all to cover up his prosthesis as he watched her dress. But his gaze turned suspicious. "What?"

"Nothing. I just like to look at your hot body, Cam."

"You don't hafta stop at lookin', princess. You can touch any time you want to."

She leaned over to peck him on the mouth. "Thank you for a great night."

"So you had fun?"

"Yes."

Cam glanced over his shoulder when the shower kicked on. "Would you be up for doin' it again?"

"Honestly? No."

He went still. "No? Why not if you had a good time?"

"It's...hard to explain."

"Try."

"Fine. It's like eating rattlesnake. Fun to say you did it once but not something you'd want to repeat."

Cam didn't say another word. He appeared to be lost in serious thought.

"Anyway. Good night."

Domini had plenty to think about on the drive back to her apartment in Sundance.

Although Cam wasn't scheduled to work for a few hours, he popped up at the crack of dawn. Habit he supposed. But the truth was he didn't sleep much after he'd crawled in bed alone.

The hallway floor creaked and Cam braced himself to see his friend. Who'd fucked his girlfriend. He swallowed a snarl.

The fact Brock looked a little haggard cheered Cam considerably.

Petty, McKay.

"Mornin'. There's coffee," Cam offered.

"Thank God." Brock snatched a mug off the dish rack and poured.

"You ready to head out?"

"Just about." Brock rested his backside against the counter and studied Cam curiously. "How are you after last night?"

Pissy. "Good. Why?"

"Wondered if you still had the urge to beat me bloody."

Shit.

"Spray-painting your name on her couldn't have stated it more obviously you consider her yours. Or maybe...it could've been your continual demands she focus only on *you*."

Cam said nothing.

"I ain't gonna get into the dynamics of having three people involved in a sexual situation, but if you didn't want me to touch her why in the hell did we even mess around last night?"

"Domini wanted it." He shoved a hand through his hair. "Or I thought she wanted it. I'm not so sure I did the right thing by pushing her to try it. I know I can't go through that again. No offense."

"None taken." Brock sipped his coffee but his eyes never wavered from Cam's. "Does Domini know you're in love with her?"

"No."

"You are planning on telling her?"

Cam shrugged.

"Jesus, McKay, don't be a fucktard about this."

That got Cam's back up. "What's that supposed to mean?"

"It means I never would've believed you'd allow a woman to get that close. I ain't only talking physically. You didn't bat an eye about letting her see every part of you. You didn't bat an eye about letting *me* see how she reacted to that missing part of you. "

"So?"

"So, the last time I saw you, I worried you'd never get over whatever stupid embarrassment you have about being an injured vet."

"It's not stupid, Brock. You have no fucking idea what it's like to be—"

"Yeah, yeah, we've beat that conversation to death. So fucking sue me; I worried about you okay? I worried you'd never have a decent relationship and then Domini walked in. I'll admit when she first showed up I gave her a hard time."

Cam fought the immediate surge of anger. "Why?"

"Because she's not like the women you used to date. She's...reserved."

"Which you took as to mean what? She's stupid? She's a doormat?" Even thinking those words in the same breath as her name had Cam seeing red.

"Chill out. I thought maybe she was one of those freaky amputee fanatics."

Cam scowled.

"Hey, we both know those women are out there."

"They're few and far between in Wyoming."

"Anyway, I changed my mind about Domini after I spent

time talking to her—"

"And let's not forget how much more appealing she is after she's been sucking your cock," Cam retorted.

Brock wagged his finger at Cam. "Don't go there. The three-way was a mutual decision last night and has no bearing on this conversation. All's I'm saying is Domini gets you, in ways most people don't. I didn't have to be part of a threesome to pick up on that. And you'd be a fucking idiot if you didn't snatch her up right now."

Cam's shoulders slumped. "Which is all great, but we've been dating for like a week. I'm supposed to beat on my chest, drag her off by her hair and demand she marry me?"

"You'd do all those things if you thought she'd say yes."

"In a fucking heartbeat."

Brock sighed.

"What?"

"Cam, man, I love you like a brother. Do me a favor. Be selfish. Just this one time. Don't think about anybody but yourself and what you want. You don't have to put a ring on her finger right now, but make sure you do *something* besides giving her a fucking hickey so she knows you consider her yours." Brock ditched his coffee cup and retreated to the bedroom to get his duffel bag.

Cam followed him and petted Gracie as they watched Brock load up. "Drive safe, buddy."

"I will. Thanks for letting me crash here." Brock grinned. "Thanks for letting me fuck your girlfriend."

"You're *not* welcome to her ever again."

"Good. Tell her how you feel. Go all caveman on her ass. At least one of us has a chance at being happy. Do something crazy and impulsive for once in your life."

Cam was on his way to work when Keely's F-250 extended cab diesel truck blocked him in. "What's up, sis?"

"Can't a girl stop by her favorite brother's house and tell him she misses him?"

He snorted. "What do you want?"

"Nothing. I'm headed to Cheyenne. I wondered if you

needed anything from the VA while I'm there."

"No." He squinted at her behind his shades. "What're you doin' at the VA again?" For the last couple years Keely spent at least one week out of every month at the VA in Cheyenne, but she never divulged the details to anyone, which was completely unlike her.

"Moonlighting. They're short staffed and I'm short on cash so it's a perfect partnership. I work PT two days this week, then I'll be back." A weary sigh escaped. "I sure am tired of living out of a suitcase with Mom and Dad while I'm working out the details of going to work for Doc Monroe."

"Sucks to be you." Now he knew what was behind her impromptu visit.

"Cam, I'm just gonna say this flat out. Please let me live with you until I get my own place. I'd pay rent. I'd cook and clean and—"

"Keely, darlin'. Stop. I love you. But it won't work. I need my own space."

"Space to do what? To keep your family out? How long are you going to make Mom and Dad and our other brothers suffer and hope you'll pull your head out of your ass and join the goddamn family again? How much longer are you going to wallow in misery? Jesus. Why don't you build a fuckin' moat to protect yourself from us? Do you really need this much space to hide in?"

No, I need it to fuck in was on the tip of his tongue but he bit it back. "That smartass answer ain't helpin' your cause, little sis."

"Sorry. But—"

"But nothin'. I'm not exactly a hermit. I am seeing Domini. And Brock crashed here last night—"

"Brock was here? Really? How is he?"

"Good. Why?" With Keely's suddenly chipper disposition, followed immediately by her hesitation, Cam guessed the truth. "For Christsake! You slept with him!"

She drummed her fingers on the steering wheel—the adult equivalent of jamming her fingers in her ears and singing *la la la*.

"When?"

"Cam—"

"I don't believe this. Jesus, Keely! He's like, ten years older than you. He's my best friend and you...what the fuck were you thinking?"

Keely lowered her sunglasses and glared at him. "I'm thinking I'm not twelve, Cam. Yeah, Brock and I made mattress angels when he visited you in Cheyenne. I could bullshit you about how we comforted each other because we were torn up over your situation, but the truth is...Brock is really freakin' hot. He's sweet and sexy and I like him a lot. I trusted him. It sort of just happened. We both knew it'd never go anywhere, and I have not a single regret."

Brock and his sister. Surreal.

"Please don't go all psycho big brother on him and threaten to kick his ass or anything, okay? I know he's your best friend. I would never do anything to sabotage that friendship because I know how important it is to both of you. Which is why neither of us said anything."

"Fine." He pointed at her. "But this is the reason you can't live with me."

"Because I slept with Brock?"

"No, because your behavior drives me insane. And my house is the one place where no insanity exists."

"You suck."

"Yep." Cam smiled. "Drive safe."

"I always do."

Her tires spit gravel for twenty feet before the rubber caught pavement.

Safe. Right. Keely was a menace. He oughta write her a damn ticket.

Domini was restocking the pie case after the lunch rush when Deputy McKay strolled in.

Normally he'd wave off the waitress and head to his favorite booth if it was unoccupied. Not today.

Today Cam strode directly to her. The gleam in his eye was unmistakable.

No hello. No smile. Cam just planted his lips on hers and kissed her with passion, hunger and total possession.

In public.

The only place they touched were lips and tongues until Cam reached for her hand, sweeping his ragged thumb across her knuckles. Domini's knees threatened to buckle. This man could undo her with a simple touch.

Finally, he eased back and smiled at her. "Hi."

She blinked at him. Their faces were close enough his breath teased her damp lips. Seeing such pleasure in his eyes, his smile, even his posture, made her throw caution to the wind. She returned his kiss with the same potent lust.

Cam's growl was too low for anyone else to hear, but to her it sounded as loud as a lion's roar.

Domini broke the kiss in tiny nipping increments. She smiled up at him. "Hi yourself. What are you doing here?"

"I needed coffee."

"Have a seat and I'll bring you a cup."

He squeezed her hand. "That was a lie. I needed to see you. I need to talk to you."

Her stomach cartwheeled like a tumbleweed. "About?"

"Last night." Cam tossed a look over his shoulder. "Is there someplace more private than the dining room?"

Domini glanced around. Only three tables had customers, but everyone was watching them. The rumor about Cam's surprising public display of affection would fuel the gossip fires all day.

"Can't this wait?"

"No."

"My office is in the back, but I'll warn you it's the size of a coat closet."

"That's fine."

She stopped at the waitress station and poured two cups of coffee, handing one to him. They wove through the cardboard boxes of produce stacked in the prep area. She unlocked her office. "I'll get another chair."

Cam pushed the door closed. And locked it. That unholy gleam was back in his eyes. "No need. I'll sit in the chair. You sit on the desk facing me."

His posture read: don't argue. Domini shoved aside the papers littering her desk and kicked the chair against the wall giving them both room.

But after Cam's ass hit the seat, he rolled the chair up to the desk. Right into her space. He didn't touch her. He studied her intently as he nonchalantly sipped his coffee.

"What? You're making me nervous."

"Are you okay after last night's threesome?"

She blushed.

"Does that blush mean you're *not* okay with what happened?"

Domini focused on him, but his eyes were flat, as if he were interrogating a suspect. "If I wasn't okay with it what could I do about it now? It's over." Her hands tightened on the coffee mug. "Unless that's why you're here? You're wanting to demand a three-peat?"

"Fuck no." He gulped his coffee and set the cup aside. He curled his hands around her knees. "After you left I wondered if the situation with Brock bothered you...if I'd gone too far because you practically ran out of my house when it was over."

"And if I say yes, you'd gone too far. What then?"

"Then I'll ask your forgiveness and assure you it won't happen again."

The conversation sent a jolt of power zinging through her. Rather than remind him she'd already confessed she wasn't a threesome girl, Domini decided to do something bold for a change and...toy with Cam a little. Make him sweat. She gazed at him with aloofness, casually finishing her coffee. "And if I say...no? If I admit I liked it? What then?"

The muscle in Cam's jaw popped he'd clenched his teeth so hard. His nostrils flared. His eyebrows were squished together. Yet for all his agitation, the pressure of his hands on her legs didn't increase at all.

When he didn't respond, Domini prompted, "What then?"

Cam inched toward her. "My answer is still no. *Fuck. No.* I had plenty of time to think about it, too, and know what I've determined, princess?"

Holy moly. Maybe she shouldn't have taunted him.

"I don't like to see another man's hands on you. I don't like to see another man's cock in you. Last night with Brock I realized I don't like to share, especially not you. And you don't need two men in your bed to satisfy you. You need one man. *Me.*" He pushed out of the chair and crowded her. "Any questions?"

Was the thrilling sense of belonging only to Cam McKay...wrong? If so, too bad, Domini absolutely gloried in it.

"I said, any questions?"

"No."

"Good. Now c'mere. I'll make you forget every man's touch but mine."

Cam's mouth was hot and controlling. He clamped his hands on her behind, yanking her forward until barely an inch of her butt cheeks rested on the desk. He broke from marauding her mouth to demand, "Undo your pants."

After loosening the drawstring, the white chefs pants were baggy enough Cam easily snuck his hand inside.

He lightly traced the seam of her panties before his fingers slipped beneath the lace band. He parted the wet folds of her sex and probed her entrance with one finger, then two. "I love how fast you heat up for me." He pressed his fingers deeper and trailed openmouthed kisses down her throat. "I love to make you come. I wish I had time to spread you across the desk and lick away all this sweet cream. Make you come against my tongue. Then I'd do it again, making you wetter and hotter. Making you come over and over until I had to carry you out of here because you couldn't walk. I'd carry you straight upstairs to your bed and fuck you until you screamed."

She let her head fall back and withheld a moan when Cam slid his middle finger to her clit and started the rapid flicking that caused her whole body to vibrate like a tuning fork.

"More?" he murmured.

"Yes."

Between his blistering kiss and the attention to her clit, Domini's speedy climax bowled her over. She whimpered through each pulse, grateful Cam's mouth muffled her cries.

When she opened her eyes, Cam was staring at her. Very possessively.

"I can look at you from here on out and know no man has touched you but me."

That statement was true in so many ways.

"I want your hands on me, Domini. Now."

She unhooked his belt buckle and lowered the zipper. The weight of his gun and cuffs on his pants dropped them to his hips. His cock jerked against her fingers as she slipped her hand beneath his briefs and circled his hard shaft.

He hissed. "Stroke me hard. Don't squeeze too tight but pull harder and faster than you think you should." He put his hand on top of hers. "Like this."

Oh wow. That was more forceful than she dared try. But with Cam's guidance she created an unbroken rhythm that brought forth his deep groans and gave her that heady sense of power again.

He buried his lips in her hair and his choppy breathing drifted over her ear. His hips started pumping faster, "Yes. Don't stop. I'm right...there. Jesus." He cupped his hand around the tip as she kept stroking until warm, thick liquid coated both their hands.

Domini squeezed one last time and he grunted.

Cam's lips sought hers. His kiss wasn't sweet, but flirty. Teasing. He smiled against her mouth. "I didn't show up here hoping that'd happen, but I won't complain it did."

"Me either." She reached for the box of tissues and cleaned both their hands while she continued the playful kisses.

He stepped back and righted his clothing. "I want to see you tonight. I'm giving you fair warning that you're mine. *All* mine."

"Got big plans for us?"

"Yep." Cam flashed a devilish grin. "But first, turn around and close your eyes."

Her heart skipped a beat when he brushed her hair from the nape of her neck. Cool metal caressed her collarbone. Automatically her hand rose to touch it.

"Cam? What is this?" She looked down at the delicate silver links that formed a chain necklace.

"A gift."

"You didn't have to—"

His strong, warm hand closed over hers. "I wanted to give you something that's a symbol. A reminder."

"Of?"

"Me," he whispered silkily. "Will you wear it for me, Domini?"

Was this necklace a tangible symbol of his...ownership? And why in the heck didn't that very idea bother her? Why was she absurdly touched?

Domini squeezed his fingers. "Yes, I'll wear it for you, Cam."

She felt him grin against her cheek. "Good. I'll pick you up after my shift ends tonight. Be ready."

Chapter Fourteen

Three hours left on his shift. What a long boring night. Thank God he could spice up his dull thoughts by replaying last night's events.

Talk about a blazing encounter. He'd taken Domini to his favorite spot, an overlook where the view of the high plains stretched for miles. The stars were bright, the air was cool and her body had been red-hot. Being in the great outdoors had stirred the beast in him. He'd answered the call of the wild and shown her a truly dominant male.

Cam had made her strip then spread her out on a blanket in the back of his truck. While feasting on her juicy pussy, he'd introduced her to one of his favorite toys—a beaded butt plug. After she came with a sexy shriek that echoed across the plateau, he fucked her so hard the truck bounced. After he roared his release, he heated them both up again with the rough kisses and insistent caresses she craved. Then Cam removed the plug, pushed her over a fallen log and reamed her ass, riding her without mercy, keeping her head down, keeping his hand around her throat, around the necklace that was proof of his possession.

She'd loved every second of her total surrender to him. He'd made sure of it.

"Deputy McKay, please respond."

Snapped out of his lewd thoughts, he responded, "This is Deputy McKay, dispatch, go ahead."

"Multiple vehicle accident on Highway 74A. Officer on scene is reporting multiple fatalities. We've called in all available units, as well as first responders from Search and Rescue from Weston County. They've confirmed they're en route."

"What happened?"

"A temperature inversion at the bottom of Shep's Canyon caused heavy fog. Due to slick road conditions, a semi misjudged the curve and jackknifed, blocking both lanes. Approaching vehicles didn't see the accident until they were right upon it. Sayzers is reporting at least four vehicles are involved at this point, two confirmed DOA, so use extreme caution when approaching scene."

"What am I looking for?"

"Mile marker forty-one."

"Has the fog lifted?"

"Affirmative."

"My ETA at mile marker forty-one is approximately six minutes."

"Roger that. And...Deputy, please be aware that if another law enforcement choice were available, we wouldn't be sending you to deal with this...situation."

Cam's knuckles went white on the steering wheel. Son of a bitch. That was dispatch's way of warning he knew the victims.

Fuck. He tried to rein in his fear as his mind checked names off the list of possibilities. His parents were home. Ditto for Colby, Cord, and their families. Carter and his brood were in Canyon River. Keely was in Cheyenne. Colt and Indy were at an A.A. meeting in Sundance and wouldn't have reason to be on the back road going into Moorcroft.

His stomach twisted into a mass of knots. Kade traveled this road every day. As did his wife, Skylar. He swallowed hard against the bile rising in his throat.

Didn't mean it was them. It could be anyone.

That thought didn't alleviate his fears.

He looked up just as mile marker forty passed by. Less than a mile now.

There was no way to mentally prepare himself, but there was no way to blank it out either. The darkness of the isolated location morphed into an eerie otherworld as red, blue and amber strobe lights flashed. He slowed.

Pieces of twisted metal, chunks of plastic taillights littered the road. His gaze landed on the semi. One white mega-cab pickup was embedded in the side of the semi-trailer. His gaze tracked the headlights spilling across the road from an

167

unnatural angle. Another car was upside down on the shoulder, the front end crushed into the front seat. The roof was caved in and glass from the broken windshield covered the roadway. Two workers were attempting to remove the driver's side door and they weren't hurrying.

His belly lurched. Chances were slim whoever was in that car had survived.

Orange cones and flashers lined the perimeter, although no one manned the area. Leaving his flashers on, he donned his reflective vest and forced himself out of the patrol car.

Cam's feet were dragging—for once not because he had an artificial leg. He'd seen car accidents in his time as a deputy. Hell, he'd witnessed some damn gruesome car bombings in his years in the army, but none of the incidents involved someone he knew.

Fred, the part-time EMT, motioned him over. "Deputy, are we taking the victims to the hospital?"

The guy didn't mean to the hospital for treatment; he meant to the hospital since it also housed the county morgue. Cam cleared his throat. "Yes."

"I'm supposed to tell you to track down Sheriff Shortbull right away."

"Where is he?"

"He's on the other side of the semi, dealing with the accidents over there."

A two-lane highway meant wreckage on both sides. His eyes flicked over the body on the stretcher, covered with a sheet.

As Cam debated the fastest, safest way to proceed to the other side, Sheriff Shortbull appeared around the front end of the semi. The normally gregarious man was dragging his feet too.

"McKay."

"Sheriff."

Pause.

Shortbull rubbed his top lip with the back of his hand. "Did Jolene tell you—"

"No. She didn't tell me anything besides to prepare myself."

"There ain't any easy way to say this."

"Then just say it flat out." *Just don't say Kade. Or Skylar.*

Or Buck. Or anyone else in my family. Please. Don't say it.

"One of the confirmed victims on the other side is Luke."

Cam's chest constricted. "Luke? As in my cousin Luke McKay? You're sure?"

"Yes. Dammit, Cam, I'm so sorry."

Jesus. What the hell was Luke doing out here? That thought vanished and Cam's head snapped up. "Was his wife Jessie with him?"

"No. He was alone."

"Ah fuck. Ah Jesus. Ah Christ. I can't believe…" Tears smarted. Cam couldn't think beyond *dead dead dead*. This tragic shit happened to other people, not to his family. Not this many goddamn times. First Dag. Now Luke? Fucking senseless accidents. Jesus. He spun away, clenching his hands into fists, shoving the anguish into the corner inside himself where darkness and misery dwelled.

"Under normal circumstances, I'd notify next of kin. But in this case…are you up to doing it?"

It never occurred to Cam to say no. It was his duty as an officer and a family member. "Yeah. It ain't gonna be easier on Jessie or my cousins or my uncle and aunt if the bad news comes from me."

"I wish to fucking God you didn't have to do it at all," Shortbull said wearily. "But I'll be making plenty of late night visits to other families."

A couple of shouts sounded, breaking the surreal silence.

"Does that mean the other victims have been ID'd?"

"Luke and the truck driver both positively ID'd. There's an Indian guy on the other side we can't get info on. He didn't carry a wallet and the car is registered to the tribe, so that's no help. The couple in the crushed car…theirs was the first vehicle to hit the semi. Due to speed and lack of visibility, they hit hard and flipped. It's a real mess."

Still reeling from the news his cousin Luke was dead, Cam barely nodded to show that he was listening.

Deputy Sayzers trotted over with a piece of paper. "We've got a registration name on the car."

"Who?"

"Rex DeMarco."

That caught Cam's attention. "Who did you say?"

"Rex DeMarco. Do you know him?"

"Not personally. His ex-wife put a restraining order on him a few years back before I started working here. He had issues with domestic disturbances."

"Now I remember. So the woman in the car...who is she?"

Grimly, Cam said, "I'd bet money it's his ex-wife, Nadia DeMarco."

"Why do you say that?"

"Domini is friends with Nadia, and Nadia recently started spending time with her ex again. As a matter of fact, Domini agreed to watch their son tonight so they could go out."

Shortbull whistled. "That poor kid. With both his parents dead, who's his next of kin?"

"No one. Nadia emigrated from Bosnia so she's it as far as family."

"And the father?"

"No local family for him either."

"I'll make the call to Social Services and give them the heads up." Shortbull sighed. "That boy is gonna go through hell."

Cam's brain was stuck on breaking the bad news. But something in Shortbull's tone jarred him. "You ain't gonna make him ID his parents?"

"No! Jesus, McKay. What kind of monster do you think I am?"

"I don't. I just..." Cam dry-scrubbed his face. "Shit. Sorry. I ain't exactly thinkin' straight."

"Understandable."

They trudged back to the other side. Emergency lights blinked. The ambulances waited silently as the Search and Rescue guys worked on getting Rex's and Nadia's bodies out of the car.

Thirty minutes ticked by. Cam paced so much his shirt was damp from sweat and his prosthesis hurt like a bitch. The tow trucks loaded the smashed vehicles onto flatbed trucks. This time of night there wasn't much traffic, but cars were lined up both directions. Cam had to get to Jessie before someone in the community recognized Luke's wrecked truck and called her to ask about it.

Dread weighted him down as Sheriff Shortbull said, "Other

people can handle this part. You'll have enough trauma and drama to deal with."

Cam barely remembered driving to Luke and Jessie's place—a doublewide trailer on the far edge of the McKay Ranch. A porch light burned. He glanced at the clock before he climbed out. Ten thirty. Christ. Had it only been two hours since he'd gotten the call? It seemed like a lifetime ago.

He lumbered up the steps, inhaling a deep breath before he knocked on the door.

Lexie, Jessie's dog barked inside the house. A voice hushed her, then a squeaking, sucking noise sounded as the inner door swung open.

Is that what he'd remember of this night? The sound the door made before he gave Jessie the news that'd change her life forever?

A pajama clad Jessie blinked at him with total confusion. "Cam? What are you doing here?"

"Jessie. There's been an accident."

Her gaze widened at his deputy's uniform, realizing he was there on official business. The blood drained from her face. "Luke?"

Cam nodded.

"Is he all right?"

"No." Cam forced his body and his voice to stay steady. "Luke didn't survive. I'm so sorry."

"What? Luke is..." She swayed but righted herself before Cam could get to her. "When?"

"About two hours ago."

"Where did this happen?"

"A semi jackknifed in Shep's Canyon. Because of the fog...there was really nothing he could've done. It happened fast."

"Was anyone else with him?"

Cam shook his head. "There were fatalities in other vehicles that also hit the semi, but Luke was alone."

"Did you tell Luke's folks? Or his brothers?"

"Not yet. I wanted to let you know first. I'm sorry."

When Jessie started to cry, Cam knew the sound of the squeaking door wouldn't stick in his mind, but the hiccupping sobs Jessie didn't try to hold in.

Without another word, Cam wrapped her in his arms. She clung to him and for the first time all night, he let himself grieve.

Time was a black void of sorrow, but eventually Jessie eased back and looked at him through red-rimmed, horror-filled eyes. "Will you come with me to tell Brandt? He'll—we'll—need to tell Casper and Joan right after, but it'd be...better coming from him than from me."

"Of course."

"Let's get this over with." She stumbled down the deck steps.

Cam said, "Jess, sweetheart, you're gonna need shoes."

She froze and stared at her bare feet. Then back at him with an expression Cam recognized as shock.

"Oh. Shoes. Right." She reversed course and slipped her feet into a pair of muddy ropers that were propped on the welcome mat. Wrapping her arms tightly around her middle, she trudged to the passenger side of the patrol car.

Neither spoke on the short, miserable drive to Brandt's place. She stared out the windshield as tears dripped down her face.

By the time Cam hit the end of Brandt's driveway, Brandt waited on the porch steps. Not a lot of social calls this time of night. Cam parked, but neither he nor Jessie attempted to get out of the car.

Jessie's voice was barely a whisper. "I don't want to tell him, Cam. This will ruin him. Brandt and Luke are so close." Her voice caught on a sob. "*Were* so close. Oh God. I can't do this."

"It's okay. Stay here. I'll take care of it." Cam forced himself to open the door. Forced himself to walk the twenty feet to where his cousin stood. Forced himself to look his cousin in the eye.

They stared at each other. Then Brandt said just one word. "Who?"

"Luke."

A pain-filled sound cut the night air.

It sliced Cam to the bone. He whispered. "Jesus, Brandt. I'm so sorry."

Brandt's gaze zoomed to the passenger side of the car.

"Where's Jessie?"

She was out of the car and sobbing in Brandt's arms before Cam could answer.

He had to look away. He had to *get* away. Yet, he couldn't leave if they needed him. So he waited in hellish silence as Brandt and Jessie tried to hold one another up.

"Cam?" Brandt said hoarsely.

"Yeah?"

"Can you do something for me?"

"Anything. Name it."

"Give me a couple hours to talk to my folks and my brothers before you tell the rest of the family?"

"Sure."

"Thank you."

"Anything you need, either of you, just ask, okay? We're all gonna be here for you. Every one of us in the McKay family. Count on it."

"I appreciate it." Brandt draped his arm around Jessie and they disappeared into the house.

He'd been given a momentary reprieve on the family side of being the bearer of bad news. But he still had to get through the conversation with Domini.

With a heavy heart, Cam climbed in his car. But a mile from Brandt's place he had to pull over on the shoulder. He rested his forehead on the steering wheel and wept.

Domini recognized the leaden tread coming up the stairs. Cam. Not Nadia.

She frowned at the clock. Eleven-thirty. Nadia was never this late picking Anton up. She'd tried to call Nadia's cell to tell her just to leave Anton over night, but Nadia didn't pick up. Which was odd.

She released the deadbolt and opened the door for Cam. Without looking at him, she headed for the living room. The climb up the stairs took a lot out of him and he hated her looks of sympathy. "Anton is still here, so I—"

"Domini."

The way he said her name, so seriously, so full of regret and sadness had her spinning toward him.

Her awareness jumped to full alert at the grief etched on Cam's face.

"What happened?"

"There was an accident tonight. A bad accident."

"And you were called to the scene?"

"I wasn't first on scene, but everyone was called, including help from other counties."

She touched his arm, wanting to appease him, not knowing if he'd welcome it. "Oh, Cam. I'm so sorry. That had to be rough."

"Makes it rough when the victims are someone you know."

Her stomach lurched. "Someone you knew? Who?"

"My cousin Luke, for one."

"Oh my God. What can I do?"

Cam shuffled his feet. "Can we sit down? I've been on my feet half the damn night."

"Sure." Domini led him to the sofa. She wanted to snuggle up, smooth the frown lines from his brow and erase the haggard look from his eyes. But something about his posture made her keep her distance.

"I just left Luke's wife, Jessie, with his brother, Brandt." He shuddered. "It about tore me up to tell them. It was just so goddamn surreal. Like this is all happening to someone else."

"*You* had to tell them?" Jessie's sweet face flickered in Domini's mind. The poor woman. What an awful thing to deal with.

"It's part of my job." He took her hands in his. "There's no easy way to do this. So I'm just gonna say it flat out. Luke wasn't the only victim tonight."

The first niggling of fear crept in.

"It was a multiple car crash with multiple fatalities. Not so uncommon in Wyoming, sad to say." Cam briefly ran down what'd happened. As he relayed the information, he seemed to be watching her very closely. Too closely.

"Who else was in the accident, Cam?"

"Nadia and Rex."

Stunned didn't begin to describe her thoughts. "What? No. You're mistaken."

Cam shook his head. "I'm sorry. It's been confirmed."

"No. It can't be. She'll be here any minute."

"Rex owns a red Taurus, right?"

"Lots of people drive red Taurus's."

"The car was licensed to him."

"So? That doesn't mean—"

"Nadia was out with him tonight, wasn't she? And she hasn't come to pick up Anton. And she's not answering her cell phone. You know that's not like her."

Domini stared at him, the horror expanding in her chest. The room started to spin. White dots danced in front of her eyes. A din of pain pealed in her brain. Her heart seized as her throat closed. "Oh no. Please no."

"I'm sorry."

"Oh God, I'm going to be sick."

Cam placed his hand on the back of her neck and gently shoved her head between her knees. "Breathe. Nice and slow. That's it."

Her tears plopped on the carpet. She swallowed over and over to keep the bile down. Gagging on her disbelief.

And through the maelstrom of emotions, Cam's constant, soothing caresses drifted up and down her back.

Finally, she managed to sit up. "This isn't a bad dream."

The awful truth filled Cam's eyes.

"Nadia. I can't believe... How can she be dead? I just saw her a few hours ago." Domini went straight from a sick feeling to pure panic. She began to hyperventilate through her tears. "I can't—"

Cam swore. Then his hands held her head and he was in her face. "Breathe, baby. Come on. Look at me. Focus on me. Just breathe with me. Inhale slowly. Good. Now exhale. That's it. Three more times."

After three long breaths, she started to speak, but he put his thumbs over her mouth.

"Huh-uh. We'll talk when I know you ain't gonna pass out. Just look in my eyes and breathe with me. That's all you need to do right now."

Domini let him calm her. It took a while.

He murmured, "Better?"

She nodded. Inhaled once more. "What about Anton? How am I supposed to tell him his mother...is never coming back?"

"I don't know."

"What will happen to him? Nadia had sole custody. She has no family. Anton has no one...but me."

"As far as I know, in situations like this, Social Services will step in and—"

"No!" Domini jumped to her feet. She shot a look at the closed bedroom door where Anton was sleeping. Then she whispered fiercely, "He is *not* going into foster care. Ever."

"Domini, be reasonable."

"You can't possibly expect me to be reasonable when I know how bad state care is."

Calmly, Cam said, "Really? How?"

"Because my parents died when I was eleven," she snapped. "With no family, I was shoved into an orphanage."

Shock crossed his face, followed by anger. "You were orphaned? Holy hell, Domini, why didn't you tell me?"

"Because I don't want to be pitied even more than I am."

"You're not—"

"You think I don't know what people say about me? What they've said my whole life? Poor Domini, she's so quiet she must lack a backbone. Poor Domini, she's scared of dogs and her own shadow. Poor Domini, she lost her parents and grew up unwanted. Poor Domini, she can't have—" She stopped midrant, cringing for the near slip-up. "I didn't tell you because I don't want pity from you."

"Pity is the last goddamn thing I'd *ever* feel for you." Cam softened his tone. "Besides, you're coming up with worst-case scenarios. Foster care here is nothing like what you dealt with living in an orphanage in a foreign country."

"That's your reasoning? I'm supposed to turn him over to an agency that knows nothing about him? I lived with him for two years, Cam. I'm a much better candidate to take care of him than some random person who's only fostering kids for the money!"

"You'd take him on, just like that?" Cam demanded. "Give up your life as you know it to raise him?"

"In a heartbeat." She stared at him. "Wouldn't you do the same? For Brock? If he died and left a kid behind, wouldn't you want to make sure he was taken care of?"

"Of course."

"Then you do understand. You know that nothing you or

anyone else says will change my mind. Anton belongs with me."

"Sit."

Domini paced as her feet tried to keep up with the jumbled thoughts in her head.

His voice was sharper. "I said sit down. Now."

"Fine." She perched on the very edge of the cushion, legs bouncing up and down impatiently.

"Sheriff Shortbull knows the victims left behind an unattended minor."

"How in the world does he know that?"

"Because I told him."

Her mouth dropped open. "Why would you do that to me?"

"I didn't do it to you."

"It feels like it." God. This was a nightmare. She knew it wasn't Cam's fault but she couldn't stop from lashing out at him.

"Wrong. Goddammit. No matter what I feel for you, Domini, I am an officer of the court and I have an obligation to uphold the law. Making Social Services aware of Anton and his situation might not be what you'd do, but it's what I *have* to do."

Domini studied Cam like she'd never seen him before. "And I'll do what *I* have to do."

"What's that supposed to mean?"

"I'll take him away before I'll turn him over."

He snatched her hands again. "Don't tell me shit like that because I can't just ignore it! What you're talking about is illegal."

"What you're talking about is unjust."

They glared at each other, which wasn't what they needed right now. In the last twenty minutes her whole life had been turned upside down. She began to cry.

"Hey." He brought his knuckles to her cheek and wiped her tears. "Sorry about yelling at you. Just don't scare me like that. After what I've seen tonight I can't stand the thought of you—" His voice broke.

Cam had lost a family member tonight and he was trying to keep it together for her. He deserved her sympathy, not her anger. "Cam. I'm sorry. I'm scared. For him. For me..." *For us* went unsaid.

"We'll get through this. I promise." He stroked her jawline. "Let's take it a day at a time, okay? Tomorrow morning you'll tell Anton about his mom. Get through that first."

"But shouldn't I tell him tonight?"

"No reason to wake the boy to bad news when tonight is probably one of the last nights of sleep he'll have for a long time."

Domini's head spun. She just wanted to curl into Cam and let his solid presence surround her and reassure her.

"Come here." He hauled her onto his lap and buried his face in her hair. "I don't want to fight with you after the day I've had and the shitty days in front of me."

"Me either."

Silence stretched as they held each other.

She whispered, "I wish you could stay with me tonight."

"Me too. I promised Brandt I'd wait awhile before I told our family about Luke. It's been a few hours so I've got some calls to make—"

"You told me not to wake Anton up to bad news, but you're going to call your brothers and other family members and do the same thing?"

He sighed. "No. I guess you're right. It'll keep." Cam's hold locked them together, even as they were mired in their own separate, anguished thoughts.

He cocked his head back to look at her.

And Domini was lost in a million conflicting emotions when his mouth pressed to hers, helpless to keep the tears from falling when he kissed her so sweetly, like she was the most precious thing on the planet. The kiss lingered, almost as if they knew it'd be a while before they'd get the chance again.

Cam rested his forehead to hers. "I want to make all the hurt you've ever suffered go away. I want to make sure you never hurt again. I want to pull the covers over our heads and wake up to find this was all a bad fucking dream."

"I wish we could."

"The next few days are gonna be pure hell for both of us. Will you keep in touch with me? Promise you won't do anything rash or crazy like grab Anton and leave in the middle of the night?"

"I promise."

"Good. Because I will hunt your ass down and drag it back here if you try it."

Chapter Fifteen

Telling Anton about Nadia's death was every bit as horrible as Domini imagined. He repeated words "fault" and "blame" and because his sobbing was incoherent, Domini wasn't sure if Anton was blaming Rex or Nadia or himself.

The poor boy wept until he passed out from exhaustion. He refused to let go of her hand. What would she do when Social Services came calling and tried to take him away?

Grateful as Domini was for the outpouring of support from the crew at Dewey's, she had no idea what to do next. Did she handle memorial service arrangements for Nadia? Was there a will? Did she pack up Nadia's house and bring Anton's stuff here? Did she need to hire a lawyer? Would they give her custody—even temporary—if she wasn't a blood relative?

And while all the scenarios raced in her head, she grieved. Nadia had been her friend, her roommate, the closest thing Domini had ever had to a sister. Now she was gone. Every single time she thought of that, she cried.

Soft knocking on the apartment door forced Domini to wipe her tears and get off the couch. She shot a look to her bedroom and listened, but the noise hadn't disturbed Anton.

Domini opened the door to Skylar McKay. Nadia's boss. Her eyes were swollen, her face was puffy. The second their gazes connected, more tears spilled from Skylar's eyes.

"Come in," Domini said. "Anton is sleeping in my bedroom."

"How is he?" Skylar squeezed her eyes shut. "Stupid question. That poor sweet boy. We're all just heartsick. I closed the plant for a couple days."

Nadia had loved working at Sky Blue. She'd gotten close to the other employees after she'd divorced Rex. And because Sky

Blue maintained onsite daycare, everyone knew Anton.

Skylar clasped Domini's hands as she sat across from her. "What can I do?"

"I don't know. I have no idea what to do first."

"We should plan Nadia's memorial service. The girls volunteered to clear out Nadia's house and bring Anton's stuff to you, including any paperwork. I doubt Nadia had a will and that brings me to my next question." Skylar leaned forward. "What happens to him?"

"I don't know. Nadia had no other family. I have no idea how the American system works, if Anton becomes a ward of the state or what." Domini looked away, sickness churning in her belly as awful memories from that turbulent time in her life resurfaced. "Right after my parents died in the Ukraine, I was turned over to an orphanage."

"Oh Domini. I'm so sorry. I had no idea."

"It's not something I'm comfortable talking about. But you can understand why I don't want him to end up in foster care. Ever. I'll do whatever it takes to get custody of him, Skylar. I love him. I lived with him for two years. There is no one alive who knows that boy better than me. He needs me."

"And I think you need him," Skylar murmured. "That should work in your favor. But I do think you need to hire a lawyer." She unearthed a stack of post-its from her purse and scrawled a number. "Call Ginger Paulson. You met her at Keely's party. She's done corporate legal work for me. Since she's a single mom, my guess is she'd be a bulldog on this case."

Domini tucked the note into her pocket. "Thank you. I think Ginger was Nadia's divorce attorney."

"Then she'd already have legal paperwork about Rex. It might speed things up." Skylar glanced at her watch. "I have to run. I'm meeting Indy, AJ, Channing and Libby. We're going over to see Jessie. Which is just another horrible situation."

"How awful for her to lose her husband. Cam was really shaken up last night after having to tell her and Luke's brother. Then he had to come here to tell me about Nadia... Sometimes I think he has the worst job in the world."

"It boggles my mind. He never wanted to be a rancher because it's a thankless job, and yet he's a cop, which is even more thankless." Skylar squeezed Domini's hand. "Despite all the bad shit that's gone down in the last twenty-four hours, I'm—we're—really glad that Cam came to you last night, Domini. He's kept his distance from most of his family since returning from Iraq."

Domini couldn't fathom why, but she had more things to worry about than Cam's sticky family situation. "Is Jessie getting a lot of support from Luke's family?"

"No." Skylar's face turned hard. "I never understood the riff between Casper McKay and his brothers, but now I see why—that man is a plain mean bastard. Jessie is the sweetest girl in the world, who's just suffered a huge loss and she doesn't deserve any of this bullshit about Luke's stake in the McKay Ranch..." Tears pooled in Skylar's eyes. "Sorry. I have to get control of myself. The last thing Jessie needs is more angry people around her." She stood. "Keep in touch. Please."

"I will. I promise. Thanks, Sky."

Domini had barely closed the door, when she heard, "Mom?" drifting from the bedroom.

She took a deep breath and wandered in to the room and perched on the edge of the bed. "Hey. You hungry? I've got cookies."

Anton had a death grip on his fleece blanket. "Where's my mom? Is she coming to get me soon?"

Domini swallowed a sob. "No, sweetling, your mom had an accident, remember?"

He stared at her. Confused. "I thought it was a bad dream."

"No, I'm sorry."

"It's not fair."

"I know it's not. And I know just how you feel."

Angrily, he said, "Oh yeah? How do *you* know?"

"Because when I was eleven both my parents died."

His mouth made an *O* of surprise. "Where did you live after they died?"

In hell. She swept the hair from his tear-stained cheek and changed the subject. "Are you hungry?"

Anton shook his head. "Am I gonna live here with you now?"

"I sure hope so. I'll do everything I can to keep you with me."

He rolled over to face the wall.

Domini didn't push. She just stayed with him as he cried himself to sleep once again.

Four days later...

With so many people filing in and out of her apartment, Domini considered leaving the door open. But she would've triple locked it if she'd known Social Services would darken her doorstep.

The agency woman resembled every supervisor Domini had dealt with in the Ukraine: older, gray-haired, her sharp eyes were only second to her sharp tongue.

"Sorry for the lack of notice about this visit, Miss Katzinski. The case file from Sheriff Shortbull came to us late."

Had Cam played a part in delaying the information? Probably not. Since that would've been wrong, and Deputy Cam McKay always did the right thing. "I've been expecting this visit."

"Well, then, let's get straight to the point. Anton DeMarco is currently in your care, following the death of his mother, Nadia DeMarco and his father, Rex DeMarco. Do you consider this a temporary arrangement?"

"No. I intend to file for permanent legal custody of Anton."

"And what of the boy's father? Rex DeMarco has no surviving relatives that might be interested in retaining custody?"

"I'm not certain. But I do know that Anton's mother retained sole custody in the divorce, which was not contested by Rex."

"I see. And what was your relationship to Nadia DeMarco?"

"She was my best friend. We were housemates for a couple years. During that time I helped take care of Anton." *I helped her raise Anton.*

"What is your occupation?"

"I'm general manager of Dewey's Delish Dish, a family restaurant. It's right downstairs."

"How long have you lived in Sundance, Miss Katzinski?"

"Almost four years."

"Do you own property in Sundance?"

What did that have to do with anything? "No."

"Where did you live previous to moving to Wyoming?"

"Denver, Colorado."

"How long were you in residence in Colorado?"

"Three years."

"Where did you live previous to Denver?"

"Lubbock, Texas."

"How long were you in residence in Texas?"

"Six months."

"Where did you live previous to Lubbock?"

"Miami, Florida."

"How long were you in residence in Florida?"

"Six months."

"Where did you live previous to Miami?"

"Charleston, South Carolina."

"How long were you in residence in South Carolina?"

"Six months."

"Where did you live previous to Charleston?"

"Hershey, Pennsylvania."

"How long were you in residence in Pennsylvania?"

"Six months."

"Where did you live previous to Hershey?"

"Cincinnati, Ohio."

"How long were you in residence in Ohio?"

"Six months."

"Where did you live previous to Cincinnati?"

"Chicago, Illinois."

"How long were you in residence in Illinois?"

"Three years."

"Where did you live previous to Chicago?"

"Kharkiv, the Ukraine."

"Could you spell that for me, please?"

Domini did.

Scribble, scribble.

"You immigrated to the United States from the Ukraine nearly twelve years ago. You became a naturalized citizen of the United States six years ago. In twelve years you've lived...eight places. Is that correct?"

"Yes."

Scribble, scribble.

"Do you have family in the Ukraine?"

"No. I was orphaned at age eleven."

"Do you have family in Sundance or any of the other seven locales you listed as former residences?"

"No." Domini's hopes were sinking. When faced with the cold hard facts about her nomadic life, even though she had valid reasons for the continual relocation, she felt her chances of keeping Anton were getting smaller and smaller.

Maybe he belongs with a real family.

No! She was his family.

Mrs. Beesman glanced up. "I'd like to speak with Anton now."

Domini nodded. She poked her head in the small bedroom and gestured for Anton to come out.

Anton sat right next to Domini and gripped her hand. He was trying so hard to be brave but his bottom lip quivered and Domini almost lost it.

"Anton, I'm going to ask you some questions. Be as truthful as you can. If you feel you could be more truthful if we were having this conversation somewhere else, just between you and me, we can stop right now until I can arrange that."

She ground her teeth. The boy was seven years old. He still believed in Santa Claus for godsake. How was he supposed to understand the implication Domini might be somehow coercing him?

"Domini, don't leave. Don't make me go somewhere else away from you. Please."

"I won't, sweetling. I'm right here."

Mrs. Beesman's questions for Anton were neutral. But when she asked him why he thought Domini wanted custody of him, he simply said, "Because she loves me and she already knows how to take care of me."

Domini didn't bother to hide her tears.

Just like that the interview ended and Mrs. Beesman bustled out.

Neither she nor Anton spoke for a while. When he started swinging his feet—a nervous habit he'd always had—she knew something bothered him. "Hey, buddy, what's going on in that smart head of yours?"

"I think I told her a lie."

Fear skittered down her spine. "About what?"

"About when she asked why you wanted me."

"You said exactly the right thing, the true thing. I *do* love you. I *do* know how to take care of you."

His blue eyes filled with such confusion and pain her heart nearly stopped. "But do you think I shoulda told her that you want me because no one else does?"

Those broken words sent her heart plummeting to her toes. "Don't ever say that. Don't ever think that. Anyone would be thrilled to have you, but I don't want to give anyone else a chance because I want you most of all, understand?"

He nodded. He crawled into her lap, clinging as if he were afraid to let her go. She understood the feeling.

Not for the first time, Domini thought if the court ruled against her for custody of this sweet, needy little boy, she'd take Anton and run.

And she had a sneaking suspicion Mrs. Beesman from Social Services had come to the exact same conclusion.

*

Cam hadn't seen Domini for days and he was going insane.

Before they'd hooked up, Cam had seen Domini every day. Sometimes twice a day. He wasn't about to walk away when he'd come to terms with how he felt about her.

In addition to setting up Nadia's memorial service, Domini was taking care of Anton fulltime. He'd dealt with his cousin Luke's funeral and all the family shit that went along with it, which reminded him why he tended to avoid all that unpleasantness.

Might not be PC, but Cam could give a crap how Anton reacted to him being at Domini's place. Far as he was concerned, the kid better get used to seeing him.

Cam knocked twice. The fifteen-second wait for her to unlock the door was excruciating. Then Domini, his sweet, beautiful, wonderful Domini, stood in front of him, close enough to touch, close enough to kiss. He hugged her hard, kissed her hard and was totally hard.

"Come in the kitchen. You hungry? There's leftover casserole."

"No. I don't have much of an appetite lately."

Domini brought them both a beer. He was a little surprised when she parked herself on his lap.

They stayed that way, not speaking, just being together. Cam had never known anyone as comfortable with silence as Domini. He'd never known anyone like Domini period.

This awful week without her had just reinforced the truth: Cam was totally head over heels in love with her. Nothing had ever felt so real, so right.

Too bad his timing was all wrong. Domini had so many life changing events to get through, he didn't want to burden her with his declaration of love. When the time was right, he'd blurt out everything in his heart. Every sappy thing.

"Cam?"

He leaned back to look at her. "Sorry, I was kinda spacing out. What did you say?"

"I—I..."

"What's wrong?"

She fingered the necklace he'd given her. "Come to bed with me. Please. I know you can't stay, but I need to be with you, even for a little while."

Touched by her sweet hesitation, Cam clasped her hand and directed her to the bedroom, locking the door behind them.

She stripped. She helped him strip. She left his prosthesis on and pushed him on his back. After she straddled him, she ran her hands up the insides of his arms and pinned his arms above his head.

"My way," she said and kissed him.

Holy shit did Domini kiss him. Seductively. Wantonly. Relentlessly. She licked and bit his lips as her tongue tasted and teased. Her kisses destroyed him, turning him into a raging beast; her caresses tamed him into a junkie who craved her touch. His body burned from the light stroke of her fingertips over his skin. He bowed up from the silken rasp of the pads of her thumbs across his nipples. The bite of her nails into his scalp stung as she held him in place and kissed him stupid.

Domini locked her gaze to his. She grasped his cock and impaled herself in one deep stroke.

She kept the pace fast enough to excite but slow enough to tantalize. When she whispered, "Put your hands on me and help me ride," Cam gritted his teeth against the urge to flip her on her back and fuck her through the mattress.

But he let her choose the pace. He let her love him with the desperation they both felt. Domini didn't drag it out; she took them both to the brink and kicked them into sweet ecstasy.

"I needed that," she panted against his throat.

I needed you.

Domini kept touching his body, as if trying to memorize his shape. Then she sighed and nestled deeper into him. "I could fall asleep like this."

"We'll have to try it sometime." He stroked her back and waited for her get whatever was bugging her off her chest.

"Cam, can I ask you something?"

"Sure."

"I mean, I'd understand if you'd say no—"

"Just ask me."

She blew out a breath. "Will you come to the lawyer's office with me tomorrow?"

"What time?"

"Two o'clock."

He was pretty shocked she'd asked him because she never asked him for anything. "I'll be there."

"Thank you."

Cam started to drift off. It was tough forcing himself to leave the warmth of her bed, the comfort of her body and the serenity she brought him. It was tougher yet when she kissed him goodnight and it felt as if she was kissing him goodbye.

Maybe it had been a goodbye fuck, because Domini had warned him she'd run with Anton if things didn't go in her favor.

Fuck that.

No way would she leave here. No way would she leave him. He'd do whatever it took to make sure she stayed.

Whatever. It. Took.

Chapter Sixteen

"Domini, Deputy McKay. Good to have you both here, have a seat." Ginger Paulson indicated two tweed wingback chairs in front of her desk. She scooted her leather chair in and donned a pair of glasses.

"Without violating confidentiality agreements, I will tell you I filed Nadia's divorce. When it appeared Rex might contest it, which is a rarity in this day and age, I had Nadia on record discussing the domestic violence issues that'd plagued their marriage. I requested a copy of the police records. At the last minute, Rex agreed to the terms of irreconcilable differences. He also agreed to sign over sole custody of Anton DeMarco, to Nadia, with the stipulation he was no longer responsible for child support, which Nadia agreed to."

Ginger peered over the rim of her glasses. "Domini, it is your intention to file for permanent legal guardianship of Anton?"

"Yes."

"Well, that's going to be tricky."

"Why?"

"As much as I hate to admit it, the state does have sound reasons for the recommendation of Anton's immediate transfer from your temporary care into a foster home."

Domini compressed Cam's hand painfully.

"What are the reasons?" he demanded.

Ginger looked right at Domini. "You aren't a blood relative nor are you licensed for foster care. You are a single woman. You don't own property. You don't have family in the area. You have a history of transient behavior. Any one of those is a strike against you. But all of them?" She shook her head.

"But there were circumstances with the church group who sponsored me to the U.S. that I had no control over. They moved around a lot and since I was here with them on a work visa...I didn't have a choice but to follow them wherever they went."

"The biggest concern the state has right now, even if you were licensed for foster care, is you are considered a flight risk. A high flight risk."

Cam said, "Bullshit," but he noticed Domini didn't immediately deny it.

Hope drained out of Domini's face. "I'm going to lose him, aren't I? The state workers will show up and drag him to a stranger's house where they don't know he hates carrots and he loves to draw and he has to have his Cars blanket at night or he can't sleep and he's scared of the dark..." Her tears fell.

Cam felt as if he'd been gutted. Dammit, it was his fucking job to uphold the law and he hated these situations existed where the law was utter bullshit. Domini was the best person to have custody of Anton. She loved him, and she'd be a great mother to him. So what if she didn't have the official foster care certification? So what if she didn't own a house? So what if she was single?

A light bulb pinged and the "Hallelujah Chorus" rang out in his head.

Bingo. Why hadn't he thought of it before?

Because you were dealing with your own family issues.

"But if Domini was married to a local law enforcement officer, who has taken the required Social Services classes regarding foster care, who owns property, who has family ties to the area for several generations, what would her flight risk be considered then?"

"Practically zero," Ginger answered.

"Fine. Domini and I will get married. Today."

"What? Cam. No. What are you doing?" Domini was flustered and pale and about to start hyperventilating.

Cam aimed a cool look at her and faced Ginger. "Could you give us a minute alone please?"

Ginger didn't bat an eye at his request. "Certainly."

As soon as Ginger was gone, Domini blurted, "Cam, what are you doing?"

Cam said, "Do you want Anton? Yes or no?"

"Yes! But I don't want him temporarily. I want him permanently."

"I know. You can have him if you marry me."

She gaped at him. "Us? Married? But...I thought we'd break things off now that everything in my life has changed."

Don't bite her head off for thinking so lowly of you. "Domini. I'm not the kind of man who bails when things get tough. You should know that."

"But married? Us? Really?"

"Do you have a better solution?"

"Umm. No."

Was that hope or panic glazing her eyes?

"You'd do that for me, Cam?"

I'd do anything for you. "Look, I know you've sworn to never get married. Neither of us envisioned this kind of scenario. So this solution makes perfect sense for a situation that was thrust on you. If you marry me, you get to keep Anton."

"Would this be temporary?"

Fuck no. It's for good, it's for real, it's forever and ever amen. "Is the thought of marrying me, even for a little while, so awful?" he asked softly.

Domini shook her head.

"Then marry me."

She stared at him, a million questions in her eyes. "Will anyone know the real reason we're getting married?"

"No. We'll keep it strictly between us."

"Why are you doing this?"

Because I love you. Because you'll think I'm being selfless. Because by giving you the one thing you want so badly, Anton, I get the only thing I want: you.

"Cam?"

He cleared the emotion from his throat and told a bald-faced lie. "Because it's the right thing to do."

Domini didn't smile. She didn't fling herself into his arms. She didn't happily shriek the word...*yes.*

Sweat broke out under his collar. Cam figured the lie was about to bite him in the ass. If he confessed the truth, shouting his love for her to the rafters, would that sway her to say yes? Or scare her into saying no?

"So what's your answer, princess?"

"Yes, I'll marry you."

Cam could've floated out of the room.

When Ginger returned, Cam announced, "We're getting married as soon as possible."

"Congratulations!" Ginger beamed at both of them. "However, the courthouse is closed today."

"Tomorrow then," Cam insisted.

Domini's face went pasty white.

"After I receive confirmation of the marriage, I'll file a rebuttal with the Department of Social Services, requesting Anton DeMarco immediately be placed in the foster care of Cameron and Domini McKay." Ginger grinned again. "I do so love a happy ending."

Cam wondered if Ginger's happiness stemmed from figuring out a way to buck the legal system. Lawyers got off on shit like that all the time.

"Stick around Wyoming the next couple of weeks until we're through the preliminary foster care assignment process. Then you can jet off for a romantic honeymoon."

"Understood. Thanks."

Cam helped Domini to her feet. She seemed to be having a hard time functioning.

Not Cam. Cam felt like doing a jig.

Domini wobbled to Cam's truck on jelly-like legs.

Domini and I will get married. Today.

She'd almost passed out hearing Cam's matter-of-fact tone. Like it was no big deal. Like it was already a done deal.

By this time tomorrow Cam McKay would be her husband.

Unreal.

She sagged against the front bumper of his truck, twisting the necklace chain around her finger. As soon as they'd walked out the door, Cam's cell phone rang with police business and he instructed her to wait for him. So, they'd had no chance to discuss this bizarre development.

What was she supposed to say to him anyway? Ask him why he was suddenly willing to take on the responsibility of a wife and a child? A child he didn't know?

It made zero sense. Why was he volunteering to turn his life upside down? Cam loved his privacy. He loved living by himself to the point his own family was rarely welcomed into his sanctuary. Why would Cam offer to open his home and his life not only her, but to a rambunctious boy with emotional scars?

Sex. Pure and simple.

It might've been different if Cam had confessed his undying love for her. But he hadn't. He'd merely resigned himself to doing the right thing.

When Domini asked him if the marriage was temporary, he'd hedged. So maybe Cam wasn't treating this as a lifetime vow. Maybe the spectacular sex was enough incentive to keep up the appearance of a real marriage for a while. But once she started the adoption process, his "do the right thing" mission would be successful and he'd be free to move on.

If that was the case, then there was no reason to tell Cam anything about her medical issues because it wouldn't matter. She'd be his wife for as long as it took her to adopt Anton.

Now that made perfect sense. She'd consider this a business arrangement. She'd keep her finances separate. Keep her job. Keep everything simple.

Domini just had to keep herself from falling in love with him.

A Cam-sized shadow fell over her. "Sorry about that. I traded with Sayzers to get the next two days off." He touched her face and offered a dazzling smile. "The ceremony is one o'clock tomorrow afternoon."

Ask him why he's doing this. Force him to give you a real reason.

But Domini couldn't get her tongue unstuck from the roof of her mouth.

"Talk to me, princess. The look on your face is scaring the holy hell outta me."

"I-I can't..." White specks wavered in front of her eyes. She couldn't suck enough air into her lungs. Blood whooshed in her ears. Her heart threatened to beat out of her chest.

Oh God. Please, not now.

"Domini? Baby, what's wrong?"

"I can't breathe." She flapped her hand in front of her face as if that would help.

"Shit." Cam hauled her to her feet. He put his palms over

her ears and tipped her head to look directly into her eyes. "Breathe with me. Nice and slow, okay?"

Below her line of vision, she could see his chest expand as he inhaled. She followed his lead. *In. Out. In. Out.*

"Good. Three more. Come on, you're doin' great."

Finally, she felt calmer, but she was still embarrassed. She focused on the placket of his uniform shirt and tried to blink the tears back. "Sorry."

"Don't apologize." Cam kept stroking the side of her face. "Should I be worried you had a panic attack at the thought of marrying me?"

Domini's gaze flew to his. "No! It's not you! It's me. This happens when I'm stressed and I can't remember ever being more stressed in my life. I want Anton, but what do I know about raising him? Babysitting isn't the same as living with him every day for the next eleven years. What if I'm not the best choice? And then you offer to marry me, which you've got to admit—"

"Hey now. Relax." His hands tightened on her scalp. "No reason to get worked up again. Breathe."

She concentrated on breathing slowly.

"Does this happen often, princess?"

"Not as much as it used to." Her eyes searched his. "I'm not exactly a prize, Cam. I have issues and baggage and...damage that I don't know if I'll ever get over."

"I have plenty of my own issues, most of which you've already seen and dealt with, so I think that makes us pretty evenly matched." He wiped a tear from the corner of her eye. "So are you feeling calmer now?"

"No! I am getting married tomorrow! I don't have a wedding dress. My best friend is dead and I don't have anyone else to talk to. I don't have a clue if I'm supposed to pack everything tonight. Are we moving in with you right away? Do you want me to tell Anton we're getting married, or should we do it together? And who all is coming to the wedding? What about the other legal stuff? We hardly discussed that with Ginger—"

Cam placed his finger over her mouth, stopping her tirade. "You can really work up a head of steam, can't you?" He traced her lips with the pad of his thumb. "One thing at a time. You and Anton will be living with me as soon as we exchange I do's. You can tell him the happy news because I'll be wrapping up a few things at my place tonight to get ready for you to move in.

"As far as the ceremony? You and me are the only ones who matter. We'll need witnesses and I'd like Colt to stand up for me. I can talk to Keely and see if she'll help you figure out some of the girly stuff since she's been through a dozen weddings."

"But—"

"Ah-ah. I ain't done. Now, what haven't we addressed as far as legal issues?"

"I think we should have a prenuptial agreement."

Cam's eyes narrowed dangerously. "Why?"

"Because I don't want your money if this doesn't work out. I will want sole custody of Anton and I won't expect you to pay child support for him. And Skylar mentioned legal issues Jessie's dealing with, as far as Luke's stake in the McKay Ranch—"

"Forget it. None of that shit matters. We'll figure it out as we go along." Cam leaned in so they were nose to nose. "You are changing your name."

Not a question.

"You think I want to keep Katzinski?"

Cam granted her the slow, sexy smile that turned her knees weak. "Now that we've got that settled..." He kissed her. Lord did he ever kiss her.

After he released her mouth, he nuzzled her cheek, her hair, her neck. "Domini, I..."

"What?" she whispered, feeling the urgency in his tone.

"I-I've gotta go." His breath drifted across her ear. "I'll call you later and I'll see you at the courthouse tomorrow."

Cam smooched her forehead and climbed in his truck.

Evidently what he'd meant to say hadn't been so urgent after all.

Cam had chickened out telling Domini he loved her and none of the legal stuff mattered because their marriage would be real in every sense of the word.

It'd been hard seeing her caught off balance, seeing her struggle. She wasn't sure of anything.

But Cam had never been more sure of anything in his life.

His first call was to his sister. "Hey Keely, I need your help."

"Big surprise."

"Seriously. This is important. Can you keep a secret?"

A beat passed. "I'll keep your secret if you forget what you saw at Colt and Indy's wedding reception and we never ever *ever* bring it up again."

He frowned. "You haven't talked to him about it?"

"No! I hate him! *Hate him,* understand? And if I ever see that smug, self-serving, self-righteous prick again, I'll cut off his limp—"

"Okay, okay, I get it. So, if you help me, I will erase my memory of the incident in question."

"Deal. What's up?"

"Domini and I are getting married tomorrow." Cam grinned like a loon. He couldn't help it. By this time tomorrow that Ukrainian princess would be his. His wife. In his bed every night. Forever.

Keely squealed. "Get out! That is so awesome." She went quiet. "Dammit, Cam, you're not telling anyone else in the family, are you?"

"Nope. Well, I'm gonna ask Colt to stand up for me at the courthouse. Which means Indy will know."

"Why the big secret?"

"The McKay family can be overwhelming. With Luke's death, and what Domini is going through after Nadia's death, and dealing with Anton...we decided to keep it simple."

"Who's standing up for Domini?"

"Umm. I don't know. I don't think she knows."

"Oh, pick me, pick me! I couldn't stand it if I didn't get to be in your wedding, Cam. Please?"

"That's Domini's choice. If you get over to her place right away and help her, she'll probably pick you. She was kinda freaked out, to be honest. She doesn't have a dress or flowers, and the rest of that girly crap I don't know nothin' about."

"Say no more. I will take care of it pronto." She sniffled. "And can I just say I'm really really really happy for you?"

"Yeah, you can." His wild child baby sis was such a softie. "Do you still have Grandma Dinah's wedding ring?"

"Yeppers. Why?"

"I know Grandma left it to you and all, and obviously I'd pay you for it—"

"Cameron West McKay, you'll do no such thing as pay me! I

don't know why the hell she ever left it to me anyway, unless she thought it was the only wedding ring I'd ever get."

Cam laughed.

"I'd hoped one of my brothers would want it."

"As I am the last male to get married, it ain't like you've got a choice on which brother," he said dryly.

Even though Keely was mute on the other end of the phone, he heard the gears churning.

Why the sudden marriage? Why was he denying his family a chance to share in his happiness? Especially when he'd had so little of it in the last few years?

Cam heard her intake of breath and he braced himself.

But Keely's train of thought had nothing to do with his impending nuptials. "So if Domini is moving in with you right away I totally call dibs on her apartment."

Chapter Seventeen

"...by the State of Wyoming, I pronounce you husband and wife."

"Can I kiss my bride?"

"By all means, Deputy."

Cam flashed Domini a devastating, possessive grin. Then his hands were cupping her face and he kissed her with such melting sweetness, with such pride and intent, Domini knew she'd start bawling if he kept it up.

She murmured, "Save some of those kisses for tonight when we're alone."

"Got plenty more where those came from. Now that you're mine, I can kiss you pretty much any time I please, *wife*."

Colt clapped Cam on the back. "Congrats, bro." He hugged Domini. "Welcome to the family."

"Thank you."

Cam took Colt aside to talk to him.

"Domini, you look gorgeous, fabulous, radiant all those bridely type words," India said. Her curious gaze zoomed to the chain circling Domini's neck. "Where'd you get the necklace?"

"Cam gave it to me last week." Lord. It seemed like a lifetime ago. But Domini had gotten so used to wearing the necklace, she felt naked if she took it off.

"I never would've guessed Cam was so...generous." Indy traced the satin sleeve banded across Domini's biceps. "And wow. Who would've thought this color would be perfect for a wedding dress?"

"Keely thought of it." She'd shown up yesterday afternoon with three wedding dress choices. This one stood out—a simple, short silk sheath in aquamarine.

"Doesn't it match her eyes exactly? I knew there was a reason I was compelled to buy this classy dress last year...it just wasn't for me," Keely said.

"Keely, I can't thank you enough for all you did to get me ready. The dress. The hair. The makeup. The bridal bouquet." Driving her to Spearfish so she could pick out a wedding band for Cam.

Her husband.

Oh God. She'd really done it. She'd really married him.

"Don't sweat it. We're sisters now." Keely hip-checked Indy and whispered, "So now that Domini is officially a McKay, let's figure out where you're gonna tattoo her."

"What? I have to get a tattoo?"

"Ssh. India has tattooed all the women who've married into the McKay family with the McKay cattle brand. It's something we started with AJ." Keely grinned. "Since we didn't throw a bachelorette party before AJ's wedding, we had a private tattoo party afterward at Indy's new studio. Channing and Macie's brands are 'tramp stamps' on their lower backs. Mine is on my hip. Indy did hers on the inside of her left thigh last year. Skylar's is on her shoulder.

"At the McKay branding we convinced Libby and Jessie to get 'em too. Which was when I came up with the brilliant idea for the first annual Cowgirl's Night Out." A moment of silence passed as they all thought about Jessie, and how much everything had changed since that night. Keely squeezed Domini's hand. "She'll be happy for you and Cam, I promise."

"Everyone is going to be happy for you two," India added.

"Once they all get over being pissed off they weren't invited to the wedding," Keely said.

That had bothered Domini. It was like Cam was...embarrassed to be marrying her. Or maybe he wanted to save the big family celebration for when he got married for real.

Anton wormed his way between India and Keely. "Domini?"

"Hey, sweetling." She smoothed his cowlick. "You were very good during the ceremony."

"Are you really married to him now?"

"Yes, I am." Domini held out her left hand. The large, square pale blue stone glimmered in the light. She definitely planned on asking Cam where he'd found such a stunning ring—on such short notice. "And tomorrow we're both moving into Cam's house. Tonight—"

"We have a special sleepover planned for you, Anton, to officially welcome you into the McKay family."

Confused, Domini looked up at Keely. "What? But—"

India crouched down and spoke to Anton. "All the ladies at Sky Blue miss seeing you, sport, and they know how much you miss your mom. They miss her too. So Skylar set up a pizza and movie night tonight with your friends from Sky Blue daycare."

"Just babies," he scoffed.

But Domini could tell he was interested.

"No, Ky, my nephew, is spending the night with you at Kade and Skylar's house." Keely whispered, "Ky is ready to hang out with you because all of his other cousins are younger. A couple of them are even—gasp—girls!"

"Ky's okay," Anton said. "So is Eliza." His eyes pleaded with Domini. "Are you gonna be there?"

"Not tonight," India said firmly. "But we will bring you back to her and Cam first thing in the morning."

"You promise you aren't going nowhere? You promise you'll come for me tomorrow?"

"You have my word, Anton." How was she supposed to leave him?

"Just one night," Keely assured him.

"Well...okay."

"Good. We'll swing by Domini's apartment and load up your stuff, and then you, Indy and me will hit the grocery store for serious junk food. I hear you like cookies." Keely started to lead him away.

They'd made it about ten feet when Anton stopped. He barreled back to Domini and threw his arms around her, nearly knocking her over. "Promise? You promise I'll see you tomorrow?"

"I promise." She squeezed him tightly and for once he didn't try to squirm away.

"Where's my wife?" Cam's voice boomed in the small space.

Anton jumped back and looked up at Cam.

"Hey, Anton. Have fun tonight and we'll see you tomorrow, okay?"

He nodded and didn't cause a fuss when India herded him out.

"He'll be fine," Keely said.

"When did you...why...?"

"It's your wedding night. You need to be alone with your husband without worrying about a seven-year-old boy. And considering all that Anton has been through, Indy and I knew he'd be comfortable at Sky's place."

These people, this family was so thoughtful it brought a lump to Domini's throat.

"But I did have to tell Sky and Kade you guys were getting married so she could do some planning. Cam said it was okay."

"It is wonderful. Thank you so much."

"Yeah, thanks." Cam kissed Keely's head. "You are the best sister ever."

"You know it." She smirked. "Now can I tell everyone?"

"Have at it. Be nice to have good news to hear about our family for a change."

"Amen." Keely gave them both a quick hug and practically skipped out, cell phone at her ear.

"What do you say we go home, Mrs. McKay?"

Domini let her gaze linger on him. Talk about outrageously handsome. Cam had worn his dress green Army uniform rather than a traditional suit for the ceremony. With medals and patches adorning his chest and arms, and a burgundy beret on his head, he looked every inch the warrior soldier. And he was all hers.

At least for a little while.

She smiled. "Lead the way, Mr. McKay."

Cam's house didn't look different. And yet, it looked completely different. Because this was her home now?

"Hang on, lemme come around and help you out so you don't get that pretty dress dirty."

He lifted her from the truck, and managed to steal a kiss. She had a sneaking suspicion she should get used to it. Mr. Tough Guy Cam was more publicly affectionate than she'd ever dreamed.

Once they were on the deck, Cam swooped her up into his

arms again.

"Cam! What are you doing? Your leg—"

"Is fine. And I'm carryin' my bride over the threshold, which is tradition in case you didn't know, bein's you're Ukrainian."

Touched beyond measure, she buried her face in his neck.

Cam pretended not to notice her tears. "There now, that wasn't so bad, was it?" He set her down and hugged her from behind. "Welcome home. Anything you want to change around here, feel free."

This place was perfect and he knew it. "I shall endeavor to suffer through the lack of amenities until I am able to make the much needed changes."

He laughed.

Domini sniffed. "What is that delicious scent coming from the kitchen? Did you cook?"

"Princess, I'm about the worst cook on the planet." Cam grabbed her hand and towed her to the kitchen.

They both froze.

The table was covered with a crisp linen tablecloth. Two place settings, china dishes, silver, crystal wine and water glasses, were cozied side by side. An enormous bouquet of colorful wildflowers anchored one end; unlit candles in several sizes, shapes and colors anchored the other end. A bottle of champagne poked out of a silver bucket, alongside two beribboned champagne flutes, which read *bride* and *groom*. A piece of stationery was balanced between the salad plates.

"Did you do all this?"

"Wish I could say, yes, but I'm afraid not." He pointed at the note. "Bet that'll tell us who did."

Domini flipped it open and read:

"Congrats to the newlyweds! We took the liberty of preparing your wedding supper—Swiss steak and scalloped potatoes are in the crock-pots, salad and chocolate cheesecake with raspberry sauce are in the refrigerator. Enjoy them at your leisure. Welcome to the family, Domini! Channing and AJ

PS - Macie says congrats and you're on vacation for the next three days..."

She met Cam's gaze. "I'm...stunned."

"I shoulda figured those crazy females would do this after I told my brothers we were getting married today."

"You told them? I didn't think we were telling anyone."

"I couldn't help it. I wanted to beat Keely to the punch. I'm just so damn happy."

"But...the only reason we got married was because—"

Cam's mouth cut off her protest. Then his hands were in her hair, tearing the hairpins out, shaking her hair free and loose, as he preferred it. Domini was adrift, drowning in his passion.

"Since supper will keep, I'm taking you to bed. Right now."

In their bedroom, after he'd peeled her out of her wedding dress, Domini stood before him naked, feeling strangely shy.

"You all right?"

"It's silly that I'm nervous. I mean, we've done this before."

"Never as husband and wife."

"Are you nervous?"

He snatched her hand to kiss the skin above her wedding ring. "Just anxious."

She tugged him toward the bed. "Maybe we should do it fast."

"You always wanna do it fast," he drawled.

"You always wanna do it slow," she retorted. Domini stretched out on the bed with her arms above her head, one knee up, one leg down, back arched, breasts thrust up, knowing the wanton pose drove Cam crazy.

After Cam removed his prosthesis, he rolled on top of her. "Are we havin' our first married-couple fight about sex?"

"No, but I think it's important we learn to compromise right away." She traced the line of his broad shoulders and down that muscular back, to those oh-so-wonderfully tight buns.

"I'm listening." He nuzzled her throat in the spot that instantly made her wet.

"How about...you start out nice and slow, and then at the end we can go as fast as I want?"

"I believe that's a compromise I can agree to."

"See? That wasn't so hard."

"Oh, I disagree wife, I'm very hard." Cam angled her hips and eased into her one excruciating inch at a time. "However, I think we've got this compromise thing down pat."

*

Cam stroked Domini's head as it rested on his chest, content to hold her, content she was finally where she belonged.

She picked up their joined hands and studied them. For the third time. "It was such a surprise."

"What?"

"My wedding ring. It's perfect, Cam."

"I'm glad. But now you're gonna ask me where I got it, aren't you?"

"Unless you tell me a story like...you gave it to the first woman you ever loved. She broke your heart but you kept the ring...then you can skip it."

I did give it to the first woman I've ever loved.

She lifted her head. "Cam?"

"Nothin' that sinister." Cam swept his thumb over the stone. "This ring belonged to my great-grandmother, Dinah. After my great-grandfather died, she took it off and never wore it again. As the only girl, Keely inherited it, but she passed it along to me."

Something akin to alarm flared in her eyes. "You gave me a family heirloom?"

"Is that an issue? You'd prefer a newer ring?"

"No! It's gorgeous." The platinum shone around the aquamarine stone. "But are you sure I should wear it?"

"You're my wife. My brothers already bought their wives rings. Who else should have it?"

Domini didn't answer. She rubbed her finger over the plain platinum band on his ring finger. He admitted it looked good next to the empty space where his left pinky used to be. It made his hand look...complete.

"Now I know why Keely insisted on this color for your ring. She was trying to match it to this one."

He held their hands side by side. "Looks like a perfect match to me."

"It is." She kissed his pectoral. "Let's eat. I'm starved."

Cam insisted Domini wear one of his dress shirts and nothing else. He lit the candles and cracked the champagne while Domini dished up the food. They toasted. They kissed and nuzzled and were drunk on champagne and on each other. It was intimate and sexy and romantic and Cam couldn't imagine a better wedding supper. Or a better woman to be married to.

He was hard as concrete after licking raspberry sauce off her nipples. "Let's go back to bed."

"But the dishes—"

"Will be right there in the morning. I think you get a free pass from doin' dishes on your wedding night."

Domini gave him a saucy look and ran to the bedroom.

He shoved his crutches by the nightstand and centered himself on the bed. "Come here and kiss your husband, your lord and master."

Domini slunk across him, sexy as sin and straddled his groin. "You called, master?" She giggled. "I can't even say that with a straight face."

He fingered the necklace dangling from her neck. "Have I lost all control over you, wife?"

"No." But she sobered quickly.

"Something wrong?" Cam twined her soft hair around his fingers. "No secrets between us now."

A bleak look flitted through her eyes. She broke eye contact and kissed the inside of his wrist. "Everything is going to change between us when Anton is living here tomorrow. No more sex on the dining room table. No more bending me over the couch. No more plastering me against the refrigerator. We won't be able to be as spontaneous with sex. Will that bother you?"

"Yes."

That grim expression crossed her face again.

"But having you in my bed every night more than makes up for it, Domini."

"Really?"

"Really."

"You won't have a problem being sexually creative and commanding with a seven-year-old down the hall?"

Cam frowned. "You think being confined to this room will make me boring in bed?"

"Never." She lapped at his nipple. Slowly. Thoroughly. "But why don't you show me something new, Mr. McKay, to allay my new bride jitters."

"Marriage has made you cheeky, Mrs. McKay."

She smirked. And kept licking as she trailed her fingers

down his belly until they circled his erect cock. She jacked him a couple of times, then rolled his balls between her delicate fingertips.

"Move down and use your mouth."

Domini inched toward his groin.

For the briefest second he had a flash of panic with Domini being so close to his stump. But she didn't pay any attention to it. Her eyes were devouring his dick.

"Suck it."

Immediately heat and wetness surrounded the head, then the soft tissues of her mouth. She formed a firm seal around his shaft as she pulled him deep.

"That's it. Show me how much you love to drive me crazy with that wicked mouth of yours."

Domini hummed and began the unbroken rhythm he'd taught her.

Cam withheld a groan. Damn. It felt amazing. But he wanted something more. To teach her a new trick. He clamped his hands around her head, stopping the bobbing motion.

Puzzled, she glanced up with half his shaft still in her mouth.

"Get the lube in the nightstand drawer and a towel."

She let her teeth drag along the sensitive underside of his cock as she released him from her mouth. Once the tube of K-Y and a washcloth were in her hand, that puzzled look returned.

After she was back in position, he said, "Suck my balls."

Her breath teased the taut globes. Then she sucked them, one at a time, until both were resting on her tongue. She sucked experimentally. She sucked perfectly.

Cam's pelvis bumped up. "Oh hell, Domini."

The humming response buzzed up his cock.

Damn. If she kept that up he'd shoot, guaranteed. "Stop."

His balls slipped from her mouth with an audible pop. She licked the length of his shaft, ready to suck him off.

"I'll let you blow me to heaven in a second, but here's the new part you were wanting to try."

That caught her attention. "What's that?"

"You're gonna massage my prostate as you're sucking me off. You ever done that?"

Domini shook her head.

"I'll teach you how I like it, so lube up your finger first and then you'll spread some lube on the seam of my ass."

A smile curled the corners of her mouth and her eyes glittered. She cracked open the tube and coated her index finger, leaving a very big glob on the tip.

Cam felt the cool, slick gel on the strip of skin between his balls, and then the gentle circles she rubbed directly on his hole. "Jesus." He forced his ass to unclench. "Now palm my balls as you're working the finger inside a little at a time."

Her tongue rimmed the head of his cock as she slowly swirled her finger in his ass.

The burning sensation vanished the second her finger connected with the gland. "Oh fuck. Christ, that's it. That's *so* fucking it."

As Domini swept her finger back and forth over that magic spot she sucked his cock until the crown bumped the back of her throat.

Cam figured he'd last about a minute, maybe less. He came with a roar, pumping his hips and Domini made a soft purr as she swallowed every drop of come. Once the throbbing, pulsing orgasm ended, she removed her finger from his ass.

Holy fucking Christ. His mind blanked. His whole body shook.

Domini kept kissing and licking her way up his torso.

He cracked open his eyes. "Come here."

She straddled his pelvis.

"Huh-uh. Knees on either side of my head and put that pretty pussy on my face."

"You still going with the 'new' theme?"

"Yep." He used his heel to drag himself further down the bed. "Hands on the headboard."

"Cam. I don't know about this—oh!"

He sucked her clitoris and then rubbed his face on her inner thighs. "Mmm. Juicy. You are sopping wet, princess. And lucky for you, I'm parched." He opened her up with his fingers and burrowed his tongue in as far as he could reach. He speared into her over and over. Until her scent coated his face. Until her taste glazed his lips and coated his tongue and flowed down the back of his throat. He basked in her, bathed in her, and lost himself in bringing her—his wife—pleasure.

When Domini was grinding her wet sex down and her whimpering moans escalated, he sucked her clit hard and she came all over his face.

Then he did it again.

After her last climax, she collapsed on the bed. After a bit she snuggled into him on his left side, her right knee below his stump, her toes drifting up and down his calf. Domini sighed dreamily and fell asleep in his arms.

Cam kissed the top of her head and mouthed, "I love you," before he joined his wife in dreamland.

Chapter Eighteen

Gracie started barking. "Sorry, girl, you're gonna have to go out back for a bit."

She whined.

"At least he doesn't have a dog he's bringing to invade your space."

Invade your space. Was that how Cam felt? Domini didn't want to start the day out on a bad note, so she said nothing and went out to meet Anton.

After Cord McKay's pickup parked, Ky jumped out of the passenger side, followed by Anton. The relief on Anton's face when he saw Domini brought a smile. "Hey guys."

Anton hustled up the steps and hugged her. Hard.

"Did you have fun last night?" she asked around the lump in her throat.

"It was okay." The door opened behind them and Gracie was jumping and yipping around Anton.

Domini froze. "Cam?"

"Gracie! Settle down. Sit."

"Aw, she's not hurting me," Anton said, blocking Domini from the dog. He crouched down and stroked her head. "She's pretty. But Gracie is a kinda weird name."

Gracie allowed Anton to pet her.

Kyler leapt onto the deck beside them. "Ain't Gracie great? I wish she wasn't fixed so she and Rascal could have puppies."

"Puppies would be cool."

Cord ambled up and smiled. "Congrats to both of you."

"Thanks. Please tell AJ the dinner was so thoughtful and very delicious."

"Will do." He focused on Cam. "How are you?"

"Never better. You?"

Cord smiled. "I recognize that look."

Domini blushed.

"Are you loadin' up the stuff from Domini's apartment today?"

"Hadn't thought about it, but I guess I should or else Keely'll throw it out the window in her desperation to move outta Ma and Dad's place."

"True. That's why me'n Colby are offerin' to drag stuff up and down the stairs for you."

Cam's smile flattened. "Nah, that's okay, I can get it."

"You sure? It won't take—"

"I said I can handle it," Cam said tersely.

Silence.

Cord pushed his hat back and stared daggers at Cam. "Ky, why don't you show Anton where Cam keeps the four-wheelers."

"Okay." Ky and Anton rounded the deck toward the garage. Gracie whined on the deck.

Anton stopped and looked at Cam. "Can she come with us?"

"Sure. Say 'come' and pat your leg. But if she jumps up on you, bump her aside with your knee and make her sit. I don't need her knocking me over."

"Come, Gracie." Anton slapped his thighs. Gracie took off like a shot, tail wagging.

The air between Cam and Cord was heavy with tension.

"Don't be stubborn, Cam. Us wantin' to help you ain't a reflection of your disabilities. There's no sense in you fightin' them stairs when you don't have to."

Cam crossed his arms over his chest. "I appreciate the offer."

"But you're turnin' it down flat," Cord said.

"Yep.

"Goddammit. This is asinine. We all just want—"

"To humiliate the cripple?" Cam snapped. "Hell, why don't you invite Colt, Kade, Buck, Quinn and Ben too? So everyone in the whole fuckin' family knows that I can't take care of—"

"Cam. Stop." Domini planted herself in front of him. "Take your brother's help."

He scowled. "I don't need it."

"Yes, you do. And if you don't take it, I'll move all the stuff by myself."

"Like hell," Cam and Cord said simultaneously.

"See? You two can agree on something."

Cord's smile was as slow and as lethally sexy as Cam's. "I am so gonna love sayin' 'listen to your wife' little bro, since you get such a huge fuckin' chuckle outta sayin' it to me all the damn time."

Cam relaxed. Smirked. "I can't wait."

"Seriously. Let us help you."

"Fine. As long as it's only you and Colby. Not Ma and Dad, not anyone else."

"Not a problem."

"There's not much anyway, maybe one load, I don't have much," Domini said. "And Anton's stuff is still boxed up in the entryway so that'll be easy."

"Maybe we oughta just go get it done now." Cord's look challenged Cam. "Will it piss you off if I suggest you stay here with the boys?"

"Yep."

"Then I'll say it." Domini stood on her tiptoes to whisper, "Stay here and save your strength for tonight because you're gonna need it, husband."

He growled.

"We won't be long. And if Anton and Ky get hungry, just feed them mac and cheese."

Domini and Cord returned three hours later. Cord stacked the boxes on the deck and Cam insisted on taking them into the house. Once Cord's truck was unloaded, he and Ky took off.

Anton sat on the steps with Gracie.

"She seems to like you," Domini said.

He didn't answer.

"We picked up your stuff from your mom's house."

No answer.

"Want to see your room?"

"I guess."

Domini wondered why Anton was surly. She showed Anton his room. "The bathroom is across the hall."

"Where is your room?"

She pointed. "Right there. I'm not far."

"I'm hungry."

"Didn't Cam feed you?"

"Yeah, but he burned it. Tasted so crappy the dog wouldn't even eat it."

"Anton! That's not nice."

"But it's true."

"Come on, I'll fix you something." She whipped up a couple grilled cheese sandwiches. While Anton devoured the entire plate, she jotted down grocery items. Good Lord the man was a bachelor to the core when it came to food. That'd have to change.

Cam entered the kitchen through the sliding glass door. "I thought I smelled food."

"You want a grilled cheese?"

"Sure." He came up behind her and kissed her neck, sending a delicious shiver through her. "Better make it two."

"We'll need to hit the grocery store later."

"I figured."

Domini looked over at Anton. "Anything special I need to put on the list?"

"Oreos. Chips. Mountain Dew. Cap'n Crunch."

"No, no, no, and maybe." She'd seen a box of Peanut Butter Cap'n Crunch in the cupboard, so she knew Cam liked it. "Name something healthy."

"Why?"

"Because eating that stuff is bad for you."

"It's what I like. My mom never said I couldn't have it."

Anton already played the "my mom" card? "Your mother and I had very different ideas about food, remember? So for now, we're doing it my way."

"Your way sucks."

"Hey," Cam said sharply, "let's get one thing straight up front. You don't get to talk to her like that. Ever."

Anton hopped down from the breakfast bar.

"Where you going?" Domini called out.

The slam of his bedroom door was the answer.

"That went well."

Cam tugged her into his arms. "It's going to be an adjustment. I'll cut him a little slack because he just lost his mother. And now he's living in a strange place. But I won't stand for him disrespecting you. Or me. Let's just let him be for now and see what happens, okay?"

"Okay."

He brushed his mouth over her ear. "I want you."

Her belly fluttered.

"I know it ain't gonna happen until he's tucked in for the night, but I can't help myself. I can't get enough of you."

"I should hope you haven't gotten enough of me, since we've only been married one day."

"He goes to bed early, right?" he murmured.

Domini figured her own bedtime had just gotten a lot earlier too.

Week Two...

"Anton. Why are there still markers all over the floor? I've told you three times to pick them up."

"I'm doing it. Geez, you don't have to get all freaked out."

Domini counted to ten. "Yes, I do, because Cam could slip on any one of these and fall."

"You always take his side," he muttered.

"Side? What side? Safety and consideration have a side?"

After Anton shoved the markers in the box, he said, "Can I go out and play with Gracie now?"

Yes. Please. And stay out there for at least an hour so I don't snap at you.

"Don't go far."

"You say that every time."

"That's because I worry."

Anton snorted. And slammed the door on his way out.

The first week of marriage had been the week from hell. Anton showed extremely bratty behavior at every opportunity. Cam worked overtime to make up for the days he missed, leaving Domini to deal with Anton and Gracie. Oddly enough, Gracie was the least of her problems.

Domini had the mixer whirring on full power, so she was surprised when she turned around to see Cam leaning against the counter watching her.

Would she ever get used to the way this hunky man

devoured her with unabashed hunger? His very smug, very male grin indicated he too, was reliving last night's sexcapades.

Those sinfully sensual memories bombarded her. Facing each other in the Jacuzzi as the heat and the steam created a sultry haven. The rushing sound of the water jets and the darkness formed an erotic cocoon. The feel of his slippery chest gliding against hers as he fucked her slowly. His mouth sucking on her neck. On her breasts. The naughty words he growled in her ear. Cam's hands gripping her ass as he lifted and lowered her. How the tight binding around her wrists left her completely at his mercy.

She'd loved every second of it. And she couldn't wait to see what Cam had in store for her tonight. Anton's presence down the hall seemed to challenge Cam to become even more inventive when it came to sex. She smiled and walked straight into his arms.

"Mmm. Now that's a welcome home a man could get accustomed to."

"How was your day, Deputy?"

"All the better now that I'm here with my wife." Cam bussed the top of her head. "How was yours?"

Trying.

Don't burden him with Anton's issues, her internal voice cautioned. While another countered with, *why not? Anton is as much Cam's responsibility as he is yours.*

But as many times as Domini reminded herself in the last two weeks, it'd never fully sunk in. Mostly because Cam seemed to...tolerate Anton. He wasn't unpleasant, but he didn't go out of his way to engage the boy in conversation, either.

Be patient. These changes will take time. You've had two years to get to know Anton, Cam has had two weeks.

"Domini?"

"Sorry. I've been distracted all day."

"Distracted thinking about our water games last night?" he purred in her ear.

"Uh-huh. And I'm wondering what you've planned for tonight."

Cam chuckled. "I ain't telling."

The timer on the oven buzzed and she pushed away from him. She punched the "off" button and grabbed the potholders.

She set three loaves of bread on the wire cooling racks. When she looked up, Cam wore the strangest expression.

Domini stood in his kitchen wearing smiley face oven mitts. Smiley face oven mitts for Christsake.

The unfamiliar rush of love for her contracted his heart.

Tell her.

"Cam? What's wrong?"

Nothing. Everything is utterly perfect in my life and I don't want to fuck it up by doing or saying something to make you leave.

"Don't you like wheat bread?"

He cleared his throat. "No, I like it." He pointed to the mixer. "More bread dough in there?"

"No, silly. Bread dough is best when it's hand kneaded. I'm also making cookies."

"For Anton?"

"And for you. White chocolate chip macadamia nut are your favorite, right?"

"Yeah. How'd you know?"

Domini lightly smacked him with the oven mitt. "Need I remind you of all the meals you've eaten at Dewey's the past two years? I've memorized your favorite foods and the ones you hate."

Cam lifted an eyebrow. "Now you have me worried, princess."

"Why?"

"Because if we ever have a fight, I'll come home to a plate of liver and onions for supper, won't I?"

"Yep, so don't tick me off."

He snagged her around the waist. Cam swallowed her surprised squeak, kissing her with coaxing, dreamy kisses until she melted into him.

The sliding glass door whooshed open. Gracie yipped and her toenails clattered as she tore around the corner of the breakfast bar. Domini froze. Cam had a split second to shove Domini behind him before Gracie jumped up on Cam's left side.

"Gracie! Sit. What the hell is wrong with you?"

Gracie whined and cowered on the floor, recognizing her master's angry tone.

Domini's hand clutched his shoulder. "Cam. It's okay."

"No, it's not. She never used to do this. Took me damn near a year to get her trained not to jump up." His gaze zoomed to Anton. "Have you been letting her jump on you?"

"She just does."

"And you haven't tried to stop her like I showed you?"

Anton shrugged. "I don't mind."

Fury charged Cam's system. He managed a curt, "*I* mind. And you'll either follow my rules concerning my dog, or I'll separate the two of you, understand?"

A stricken look settled on Anton's face.

Cam knew Anton had bonded with Gracie, which was good for both boy and dog, but he wouldn't put up with Anton's blatant disregard of Gracie's training or of the rules he'd laid down.

"Cam, I think—"

He held his hand up, stopping Domini's interference, as he spoke to Anton. "I asked, do you understand?"

"Yeah, I get it." Anton walked off and his bedroom door slammed.

Jesus. That kid pushed his buttons. And it pissed him off that Domini just let Anton retreat to his room whenever he got mad, instead of forcing him to talk. But once again, Cam said nothing. Domini would take the kid's side, guaranteed.

Gracie whined. He said, "Stay," sharply, and faced his wife.

Domini rubbed his biceps. "You okay?"

Every time she touched him with concern or caring or passion, he could almost believe she loved him.

"I'm fine. Just not looking forward to trying to break Gracie's bad behavior again."

"Do you have to do it yourself?"

"I always have before."

"We're here now. How about if we help you? After supper, you can show Anton and me how we should correct Gracie if she veers from her training. That way we'll all know the right way to keep her in line."

"Why would you do that?" He frowned. "You don't like dogs."

"I'll admit Gracie's grown on me." She sent Gracie a fond look, but her face was serious when she looked back at him.

"We need to figure out a way to make this work for all of us."

Cam knew Domini wasn't just talking about the dog.

Chapter Nineteen

Week Three...

"Domini, it's Ginger. I have good news! Anton DeMarco has officially been released into the foster care of Deputy Cameron McKay and Domini McKay, by Wyoming Department of Social Services."

Domini sagged against the counter. "That is good news, Ginger, thank you. Now what?"

"Now you adjust to parenting a child full-time. Social Services will check in periodically. That's about it."

"No, I mean when can I start the paperwork for adopting him?"

Ginger's hesitation was apparent even through the phone line.

A strange feeling of foreboding flowed through Domini. "What?"

"There are a couple of things to do before you take that permanent step."

"Like what?"

"First, I recommend you hire a private detective to track down Rex's remaining family."

Domini frowned. "That's necessary?"

"Covering all our bases from the start is very necessary."

"But I don't know anything about hiring private detectives."

"If you're interested, I can handle it out of my office at my standard rate."

"Yes. Please. Whatever I need to do, I'll do it. I don't care how much it costs."

Ginger chuckled. "Darlin', don't ever say that to an

attorney."

Domini smiled. "So say the detective tracks these relatives down, what happens after that?"

"Then the private detective gives the family official notification of Rex's death, of financial windfalls of said death, of which I'm going to assume none, and financial responsibilities of said death."

"Which would be...?"

"Funeral costs. Payment of any outstanding debts. The recipient cannot have the gains without the bearing the losses, understand what I'm saying?"

"Yes. Then what?"

"Once that's done, we see if there's any interest in adoption from his relatives."

Her stomach clenched. "What are the odds that will happen?"

"Slim. However, it is a possibility. You and Cam have a minimum of six months of Anton living with you as a foster kid before you can even think of applying for adoption. And it'll take the detective at least that long to do the first stage of the legwork on a case like this. Especially if you don't want to pay through the nose for it."

"So we should get started right away?"

"Yes. Would you like me to get it set up?"

"Please. And one other thing." Domini hesitated. "Can you call me with updates? And send your bills to me at the restaurant?"

"Not to your home address?"

"No."

Ginger was quiet a minute and then she sighed. "You're keeping Cam out of this?"

"For now. He's already done so much and this isn't something he needs to think about until we are actually closer to the adoption process, is it?"

"No. You are the client and I can set it up however you want, but I strongly recommend you include Cam in every step."

"Why?"

"Because he's your husband. Because he will be Anton's adoptive father. Because keeping secrets is never a good thing,

Domini."

How well Domini knew that. "I appreciate the advice, Ginger. Keep me updated."

Week Four...

Cam dragged ass. Talk about a colossally shitty day. He wanted to tear off his uniform, ditch his prosthesis, stand under a scalding shower, drink an icy cold beer and fuck his wife for an hour.

In that exact order.

He opened the door and chaos whacked him in the face.

His house—his haven—was utterly trashed. Blankets and sheets were draped across every surface. Hell, he couldn't even see his furniture. The stereo blasted some classical crap with a billion weeping violins. Neither Domini nor Anton were in sight. His blood boiled when he noticed the small bronze statue his brother Carter had sculpted tipped on its side on the floor.

"Domini?" he shouted over the music, picking up the statue.

Her head popped up from beneath a yellow sheet. "Hey! Hang on." She disappeared beneath the blankets. The music stopped. She reappeared holding the stereo remote. "How come you're home so late?"

Cam clenched his teeth at her accusation. "I was busy."

"Anyway, Anton and I were just playing—"

"Pigs in a blanket?"

"No. That's food, not a game..." Domini frowned. "Not nice, Cam."

I'm not feeling very nice.

"What's the matter?"

"I'm tired, I've had a shit day, and I just want to get out of these clothes and have some peace and quiet."

"You're at the wrong place for that."

She'd meant it to be funny, but it struck a sour chord in him.

"Are you hungry? I saved a plate for you in the kitchen."

He scowled. "How am I supposed to get to the kitchen? I

can't even get across the damn living room." *Of my own damn house,* he silently tacked on. Be just his luck if he tried to ford his way through the maze only to land in a big heap on the floor. Perfect capper to his awesome day.

Domini kept her tone cool. "Anton? Playtime is over. We need to get this stuff picked up. Now."

Due to static from the blankets, Anton's hair stuck up every which way. "Aw, do we have to? It took forever to set up."

"I know, sweetling. We should've asked Cam first before we created such a mess in his house."

His house. That barb crossed the room, sharp as an arrow, and hit him dead center. "For Christsake, Domini, that's not fair and you know that's not what I meant."

She scalded him with an "Oh really?" look and vanished beneath the blankets.

Fucking fantastic.

He exited through the front door, grumbling as he trekked to the backside of the house and scaled the rear deck steps. He paused at the sliding glass door to rub the section of skin where the sock was chafing his stump. He couldn't wait to get the goddamn thing off. He snagged two beers from the fridge, ignoring the piles of dishes stacked everywhere and headed down the hallway, which was blessedly free of blankets. And dishes. And people.

Cam shucked his clothes, removed his leg and used his crutches to propel himself to the bathroom. He froze in the doorway.

Whoa. Looked like a Revlon factory exploded in here. Lotion, powders and creams were strewn across the countertop. Did Domini really need all that crap? And would it have killed her to put it away when she was done with it? Especially when it seemed she stashed his shaving stuff in a completely new drawer every damn time he turned around?

He ground his teeth. He was not a neat freak, not any more than any other guy who'd spent a dozen years in the army. But he hated shit piled everywhere. He'd learned the hard way not to leave wet towels, empty soda bottles and magazines scattered around after he'd tripped and fallen on his ass a few times.

A shower didn't calm him.

He slipped on a pair of frayed sweat pant shorts and cast a look of loathing at his prosthesis. No way was he putting it back on tonight. No fucking way.

Now what? He was in a pissy mood. He wanted to be alone. The living room wasn't an option, neither was the kitchen. With no other recourse, he flopped on the bed.

Cam reached for his beer on the nightstand. His knuckle clipped the edge of the fan attached to the headboard, nearly knocking it off. That'd be great, if he'd have to crawl underneath the bed on one goddamn knee to plug in Domini's pacifier.

Okay, maybe it was mean to call it that, but Domini couldn't sleep without the damn thing on. The white noise from an oscillating fan calmed her. Which wouldn't have bothered him, except she had to have the air blowing directly on her. Which meant it blew on him. All night. He'd woken up freezing on more than one occasion.

When he'd tried to joke, "Luke. I am your father," into the fan in his best Darth Vader imitation, Domini hadn't laughed. Maybe their senses of humor didn't mesh.

Maybe nothing about this situation meshed.

Cam expected adjustments. He expected changes. He thought he'd done fairly well, considering the double whammy of a taking on a wife and a young kid all at once.

Honestly, his relationship with Domini wasn't causing friction. When they were locked in their bedroom, locked body to body, everything was perfect.

But that's not realistic. Your lives can't revolve around the few hours you spend in bed.

Yeah? Her life shouldn't revolve around Anton, either.

Talk about a stalemate.

He finished the first beer. Maybe he should've crashed in Anton's room. At least he could've watched TV. That was just another thing he and Domini disagreed on. Cam didn't think the kid needed a damn TV in his room. Domini claimed Anton needed his own space, his own things, and not a bunch more drastic changes in his life right away.

So Cam had given in. Sucked up his resentment. How did people do this parenting shit without going bonkers?

Most parents started out with a baby, not a surly seven-year-old. Maybe things would be different when he and Domini started having kids of their own. Right. If she stuck around that long. She'd already been making contingency plans to adopt Anton on her own and that sucked ass.

Just by happenstance, Cam discovered Domini had hired Ginger to start Anton's preliminary adoption process paperwork. He'd been waiting in her office and noticed the bill on Domini's desk. He hadn't brought it up with her because he hadn't known what to say. And part of him wanted Domini to explain, of her own volition, not because he forced the issue. Might be a long damn wait.

Cam sighed and closed his eyes. Allowing himself to drift off. Just for a minute.

The sound of approaching helicopters echoed in the distance. Extraction was here. His two young charges, still green as far as live fire ops went, popped up out of their hiding places. He motioned for them to stay put. But the lead guy misread the hand signal and started across the open field. Keeping low, like he'd been trained, yet Cam was horrified. The kid wasn't supposed to cross an open field. Ever. Too much shit could go wrong.

Frantically, he made the "stay" signal again. Which the rear guy also misread and he followed his buddy through the exposed field.

Cam wanted to shout and drag those dumb little fuckers out of danger by their ears. But he could only watch helplessly, concealed in his own hiding place, sweating pure fear, praying they got lucky and cleared the field without incident.

The landmine shook the ground and took out the first guy. The second guy ran pell-mell through the smoke and dust, screeching for his partner and setting off another landmine.

The words, your fault, it was all your fault, screaming in his head.

Wait. The screaming sound was outside his head too.

He looked to the sky as the whistling noise of a surface to air missile hit the helicopter. The explosion distorted reality, creating a ball of orange fire that knocked Cam flat on his ass. Parts rained down on him like metal raindrops. But when he saw the broken helicopter blade flipping end over end toward him like a deadly boomerang, he broke his silence and screamed.

And kept screaming.

"Cam?"

He jackknifed, not knowing where he was. He attempted to roll away and run from danger.

"Cam!" Hands slapped his cheeks. Legs pinned him down. "Wake up."

He blinked in the near darkness until the face belonging to the voice swam into view.

Domini.

"Domini? What are you doing in..." Shit. He wasn't in Afghanistan. The force of the old nightmare hit him anew and the shakes started. Sickness roiled in his belly. "Oh fuck."

"Ssh. It's okay. I'm here. I've got you."

"I can't—"

"I know. Lay back."

"I—don't, no—"

"Ssh. I'm here." Domini cupped his face in her hands. "Look at me. Let me help you."

"Okay," he whispered. "Don't go."

"I'm right here, Cam. I'm not going anywhere. I promise. I'm right here."

She turned him on his side and covered him with the quilt after pressing her body tightly to his. Domini settled her right palm on his chest directly over his heart. She placed her left arm behind his head on the pillow and tenderly stroked his clammy forehead with her cool fingers. She murmured in his ear. He couldn't tell if her words were Ukrainian or English.

It didn't matter. Cam closed his eyes and focused on her voice. It soothed him. Her gentle touches, her sporadic sweet kisses, her presence was a healing balm to his soul.

Domini nuzzled the back of his neck and stayed with him through every second of his meltdown.

He seemed to regain some semblance of control faster this time than the first night they'd spent together. Might make him a needy bastard...but he just didn't want her to let go.

And she didn't. Domini didn't ask questions or babble to fill the empty air. Without doubt, if he did decide to spill his guts, she wouldn't judge him. She accepted him and he felt safe with her. At peace.

Goddamn. He loved her so fucking much.

She deserved better than the shitty way he'd treated her when he'd first walked in the door. He rolled to his back and she was still touching him. Still offering him solace. Still acting like she cared. Like she loved him.

Cam swept her hair behind her ear. His voice was thick with emotion. "You're beautiful. I'm the luckiest goddamn guy in the world to get to come home to you every night. Thank you for staying with me through that."

"You're welcome. You better?"

"Much, thanks to you."

"I'm glad." She smiled softly and sweetly stroked his scarred face.

"I'm sorry I was such an ass earlier."

"You *were* an ass."

He sighed. "I'll work harder on bein' less of an ass, okay?"

"I appreciate the apology and I forgive you. So, I'll put the liver and onions I had planned for dinner tomorrow night on hold."

He smiled.

Before he drifted off, he murmured, "Thank you."

"You're welcome. Rest, Deputy. I've got your back."

When Domini reached up and switched on the fan, he didn't mind a bit.

Chapter Twenty

Week Six...

Exhausted. Domini was just plain exhausted.

The fatigue wasn't from her randy husband keeping her up until the wee hours proving his sexual mastery. No, his big body hadn't been in bed next to her for the last three weeks.

Since Cam had started his month long assignment to third shift—ten pm to six am—she wasn't sleeping well. Add in the upheaval at Dewey's after firing Bobby and she'd been working eleven-hour shifts. Naturally, none of her days off coincided with Cam's days off. It drove her crazy to think she'd seen more of Cam *before* they'd married.

Cam was equally frustrated at their lack of time together. He suggested she quit working at Dewey's, even going so far as to hint he earned enough money to support them and her job wasn't necessary.

Not necessary? Keeping her job was essential, not only for financial reasons, but her own sanity. She was good at her job. Not all women had the burning desire to stay home, bake muffins, iron clothes and pop out kids.

Like the last one was even an option.

She'd pointed out they hadn't discussed the issues before their hurry-up wedding, so it shouldn't have shocked him they held different perspectives. Add Anton into the mix and it was turning out to be a very messy soup.

Anton's surly behavior had mellowed, but whenever his new reality hit him, he'd become inconsolable. Domini feared she was doing a lousy job mothering Anton, but she couldn't share her concerns about her lack of parenting skills with Cam. Cam had even less skills than she and it didn't seem to bother him.

Granted, the six-month waiting period to start formal adoption was good in that Cam and Anton needed time to establish some kind of relationship—because right now, they had no relationship. What if it didn't get better? Would she have to choose between Cam and Anton?

It'd been a rocky start all around.

She mixed the taco seasoning with the ground beef and layered it over the noodles. After sprinkling the casserole with cheese, she slid it in the oven and set the timer.

Her arms were elbow deep in dishwater and she was lost in thought when a muscular body pressed against her, the thick forearms braced on either side of the sink.

"Mmm, I like you like this. Confined. You can't really move without splashing yourself. So I can do this—" Cam rubbed his lips on the back of her head, "—and this—" he nosed aside her hair to flick his tongue across her nape, "—and especially this—" he dragged openmouthed kisses up her neck.

Goose flesh broke out.

Cam continued his sensual assault with his heated breath, clever mouth and questing tongue. She closed her eyes, absorbing every sensation, craving this side of her dominant husband.

"My wife, my Domini," he murmured, "I want to fuck you. Just like this. No time for you to think, no time for you to move. I'd drop your pants and drive into you hard."

She moaned.

"Since you like it fast, I'd go slow. So." Kiss. "Very." Another kiss. "Very." Another kiss. "Slow."

"No. Please—"

"But I'd let you choose which side of your neck I sink my teeth into. This area makes you squeak," Cam fastened his mouth to the left dip between her neck and collarbone and sucked.

Domini did squeak.

"But attention on this side elicits a throaty purr that makes my cock hard as steel." Cam scraped his teeth up the right side of her nape. "My fingers would stroke that sweet little clit. I'd fist the other hand in your hair so I can angle your neck however I please." He threaded his fingers through her hair and lightly tugged. "And there's not a damn thing you can do about it."

"Cam. Please."

"Am I turning you on? Telling you how I plan on taking what's mine?"

"Yes." She needed him. Needed to feel that rush of pleasure only he could give her.

He growled. His grip increased on her hair. His right hand slid around her hip and stroked between her legs. Then he spread his big hand on her abdomen as he ground his erection into her ass. "Right. Fucking. Now."

"Cam—"

"Huh-uh. I make the rules, you follow them."

"We can't—"

"Don't force me to get rough, Domini."

Oh how she'd love that. In private. "Stop."

"You don't want me to stop."

True. Domini spoke firmly through the lust tightening her throat. "Please. Cam, no. Don't. I'm—"

"Leave her alone!" Fast footsteps smacked behind them.

She felt Cam's entire body stiffen as he was shoved hard into her. The sounds of slapping flesh followed.

"Don't you hurt her!" *Whack whack whack.* "Don't you touch her!"

"Whoa. Hang on—"

"No!" Anton shrieked. His fists connected with the side of Domini's torso as he pummeled Cam.

"That's enough!" Cam backed up.

"No!"

Domini spun around.

Cam tried to deflect Anton's blows, but Anton was undeterred as he kept hitting him. Face cherry red, fury darkening his eyes.

"Anton—"

"Domini, stay out of this," Cam snapped.

Anton resembled the Tasmanian devil, his limbs flailing as he attempted to corner Cam. He was repeating, "No, no, no."

"Listen to me, Anton—"

"No!" he screamed and rushed Cam, putting his head down low, aiming for Cam's groin.

The wounded animal wail coming from Anton ripped a hole in Domini's heart. She slapped her hand over her mouth, forgetting about the water and suds covering her hands until liquid dripped down her chin.

Cam dodged Anton, and held the boy's hands at his sides. When Anton tried to twist out of the hold, Cam pulled Anton's wrists behind his back and kept a wide stance in case Anton started kicking.

"You done?" Cam said coolly.

Anton's chest rose and fell as quickly as a trapped bird's. He was crying in great big, gasping sobs. His hair covered his face.

Cam waited a minute and repeated, "Answer me. You done?"

Anton nodded.

"Good. Now I'm going to walk over to the chair and sit down. If I let go of your arms and you run, or try to hit or kick me again, and we're gonna have a serious problem, understand?"

He nodded again.

Domini watched as Cam sat and brought Anton around to face him, not sure if she should get in the middle of it.

"What was that attacking me crap about?" Cam asked.

No answer.

"Anton. Look me in the eye and answer the question."

Defiantly, Anton lifted his head. "You were hurting her. She said no, I heard her. And you didn't listen, you just kept doing it! Just like him." Tears tracked his face.

"Cam wasn't hurting me, Anton," Domini said softly.

Cam shot her a look that clearly said *stay out of it.*

"That's what my mom said too, but she lied! He always hurt her, always, even when she said he wasn't!"

What this poor boy had been through made her want to curl her body around his and protect him from the world. "Oh sweetling, it's not the same..."

"Domini. Will you please let me handle this?"

"Fine." But could Cam handle it? When he'd shown no interest in Anton whatsoever? Good or bad?

"First off, sport, I wasn't hurting Domini. I'd never hurt her. Ever. We were just kinda goofing around like...you did with Ky a couple weeks back."

Anton's teary eyes were filled with skepticism.

"Second, not all men are like your dad. Most men aren't like your dad. I'm not like your dad. Just because I'm big doesn't mean I'm...well...*mean*. But I will not put up with any hitting in this house."

Cam's firm, yet gentle tone stunned Domini.

"So there will be consequences for your actions of taking after me. We clear on that?"

"Uh-huh."

"The two of us are gonna take a walk. Wait on the back deck for me."

Anton slunk out the sliding glass door without looking at Domini.

Her gaze connected with Cam's and she knew he read every question in her eyes.

"Before you say a word, understand this, I won't hurt him. I won't berate him. But it's time he learns how things are gonna go around here. It needs to come from me, not you, so I'd appreciate it if you'd give us some time."

Cam left her staring after him. She thought she'd wanted him involved with Anton on a deeper level. Now she wasn't so sure.

"Let's head over to the corral."

"I'm in trouble, huh," Anton said quietly.

"Yep."

Even Gracie was subdued as they traipsed along. When they reached the fence, Anton blurted, "Didja bring me out here so Domini won't see you whippin' me?"

Cam scowled at the kid. "I'm not gonna whip you."

"You're not?"

"No. When I said I won't tolerate hitting in my house, I meant for everyone. Including me."

"Oh."

"Look. I ain't gonna pretend to know what you were thinking when you saw me and Domini in the kitchen. It was a private moment between a husband and wife you misunderstood and I'll leave it that."

Silence.

"Now you wanna tell me what's really goin' on with you?"

More silence.

Shit. Cam had no idea how to do this. How did he get the kid to talk? About what? Or did he start right in on the lecture? Just as he was about to give up and detail specific punishment, Anton spoke so softly Cam struggled to hear it.

"He used to come into the kitchen when she was cooking and pull her hair. Then he'd take her by the hair into the bathroom or the bedroom. I heard her cry. Even when I put the pillow over my head I still heard her."

Cam withheld a wince. He'd had his hand in Domini's hair, no wonder Anton freaked out, it probably flashed him right back to those bad memories.

"He hurt her, my mom."

Interesting that Anton never said *Dad* or *Rex*, only *he* or *him*. "I know."

"If you knew then why didn't you stop him?" he demanded. "You're the police! You're supposed to help people."

Goddamn if that comment didn't knock the fight right out of him. "We tried. And I don't understand either, because I'm sure she didn't like him hurting her."

"She didn't." Anton kicked a clump of dirt through the bottom of the fence and Gracie whined. "So why was she happy he was coming around again?"

Because that's how the cycle of abuse works. "I don't know. When he was with her, was he...pulling her hair and stuff?"

Anton shook his head.

"How long had he been coming around?"

"Since Valentine's Day when he brought her flowers," Anton sneered.

So Nadia had lasted a whole two months after Domini moved out before she hooked up with her ex.

"Mom made me go to my room when he came over."

"Every time?"

"Uh-huh."

Cam frowned. Why wouldn't Rex want anything to do with his son?

Because Rex didn't need to win Anton over; Rex needed to win Nadia over. And if Rex was ignoring the kid, then in Nadia's frame of mind, that probably meant Anton was safe. Or if parenting issues with the kid had been a problem before, Rex ignoring Anton would've been some sick kind of proof that he'd changed.

Fucked up. But most domestic abuse cases were.

"I hate him."

His focus snapped back. "Excuse me?"

"I hate him more now because he's the reason she's dead."

"Anton—"

"Don't you get it? If she hadn't been with him on a stupid date, she'd be alive, I know it."

Cam understood the logic, he understood the rage. He just didn't know how to help the kid see the world didn't work that way. And he sure didn't tell him that Nadia had been driving.

"It's his fault!"

He thought Anton was gearing up to let rage fly again, but the boy started crying so hard his narrow shoulders shook. He babbled and snuffled like Cam'd never seen from the surly kid.

A kid Domini claimed had rarely been surly.

Cam didn't need a detective's shield to realize something was up. Something that didn't have a damn thing to do with him and Domini. Something had gone down with his folks. Something big that little Anton had been keeping to himself. Cam put his hand on Anton's back, unsure what to do, and offered the kid a reassuring pat.

Which was the signal Anton needed to launch himself at Cam.

He buried his face in Cam's stomach, wrapped his thin arms around his waist and sobbed.

Jesus. Cam's emotions shifted from fear to resolve back to fear. What if he and Domini didn't have the skills to help Anton deal with his grief and guilt and abuse issues? Especially when they both had plenty of their own issues to work through?

The sobs abated. Cam pushed the thick blonde hair from Anton's damp forehead. "So, sport, you wanna tell me what really happened?"

Anton vehemently shook his head. "You'll think I'm bad."

"No, I won't."

The kid's internal debate lasted barely fifteen seconds. "When my mom left me at Domini's, I was mad at her about him. I wouldn't kiss her goodbye when I got out of the car. I wouldn't hug her either. And now I'll never get the chance to hug her or kiss her again! Or tell her I'm sorry and I didn't mean it!"

Cam's heart ripped in two. The burden Anton carried was heavy for anyone, but for a confused seven-year-old kid it probably felt like the end of the world. In some ways, it had been the end of his world as he'd known it. No wonder he'd been acting out—he'd been reaching out. "Have you talked to anyone else about what happened? Maybe your teacher?"

"No."

"Why not Domini?"

"Because I don't want her to think I'm bad."

"But it doesn't matter if *I* think you're bad?"

"You already think I'm bad. You were mad about Gracie. You don't talk to me unless I say something to hurt Domini's feelings and then you get mad at me. You think I'm a pig and you get mad at me when your house is a mess."

Dammit. Cam's cheeks burned with pure shame. Why did he think the kid wouldn't notice or care about his distant behavior? Had Domini noticed?

Yes.

Cam would be wise to remember the only reason Domini had agreed to marry him...was standing right in front of him sobbing his heart out. If Cam couldn't come to terms with Anton, he'd lose Domini.

You deserve to lose her. You took advantage of her. She never wanted the marriage or you. She just wanted Anton.

"Sorry I hit you and stuff," Anton said quietly, interrupting Cam's derisive thoughts. "I thought it was just like before. With him."

"I know. Apology accepted, okay?"

"Okay."

"Look, sport, maybe I have been ignoring you. It ain't because I think you're bad, it's just...well, I haven't spent a lot of time with kids."

"What about Ky?"

"Sure, my brothers and cousins have kids, but bein' around them for a couple of hours once a month isn't like living with them. When I was growing up, my dad was either yelling at me or ignoring me. So maybe I thought ignoring you was better than yelling, but now I can see that isn't any better."

"What did your dad yell at you about?"

"Mostly about not getting my chores done."

"Do you really got a fake leg?"

For once Cam didn't mind the abrupt subject change. "Yep."

"Huh."

Cam half-expected him to ask to see it.

"There's a kid at my school that gots a fake arm." Anton squinted at Cam's leg. "But he doesn't hide it. Why do you hide yours?"

Because I'm embarrassed. "Because it makes people uncomfortable. And because I'm a cop, everyone is already on edge around me, so it's easier not to draw attention to it."

"Jeffrey doesn't care. He just whips it off in class. He scares the girls because it grosses them out."

Yeah, it'd probably gross them out long past second grade.

"One time, he hit Doug in the butt with it. He got sent to the principal's office for that."

"I imagine so."

"He said his dad doesn't whip him anymore 'cause he feels sorry for him. When you were bad as a kid, did your dad whip you?"

"Nope. I didn't lose my leg until a couple years ago. Besides, there were a lot of other shitty things he could make us do to get his point across that didn't involve smacking us."

"Like what?"

"Like the same kind of consequences I'm gonna give you for whaling on me today."

Anton looked afraid again.

"You're on dog doo-doo duty, which means you're gonna pick up all of Gracie's dog crap in the backyard and haul it to the hole behind that big tree over there." Cam pointed to a half-dead elm. "I ain't talking about it bein' a one time thing, neither."

"Really? Like chores I hafta do all the time?"

Why did the kid sound so...happy about doing chores? "Yeah, why?"

"Kids at school talk about having to do chores when they get home."

"Plenty of chores around here."

Anton smiled sweetly, maybe for the first time since Cam had known him. "I can do chores. Sometimes I help Domini sweep up at Dewey's."

"You'll be on broom detail then. As for your other consequence, I'm gonna hafta take the TV outta your room."

"Oh, man." Anton's shoulders slumped. "Really?"

"Really. When you come home from school you should be doin' your homework, or chores, or outside playin' with Gracie."

Gracie barked and they both looked up to see Domini walking toward them.

"Don't tell her about what I said about my mom."

"I won't. It'll be our secret. But I think you probably should tell her."

Anton nodded.

"Hey guys. You've been out here awhile. Is everything all right?"

"Yeah, except I'm getting my TV taken away," Anton said glumly. "And I hafta do chores every day."

"That sounds fair," she said cautiously. Domini gazed at Anton with such softness and sweetness Cam was a little jealous. She loved the kid. She was good to him. Good for him.

"Maybe you should get a head start on chores by clearing a path in your room for when we haul the TV out," she suggested.

"All right." Anton tapped his leg. "Gracie. Come." Boy and dog tore off.

Domini nestled her face in Cam's neck. "I'm sorry."

"For?"

"For you having to deal with that. Not only him hitting you, but his anger."

"Which is entirely justified." He clasped his hands together on her lower back, bringing her closer.

"It's not the first time he's been that upset, but I've always been able to calm him down."

Guilt socked him in the gut. Domini shouldn't have to deal with Anton's issues alone. "Who calms you down?"

"You. When you're not heating me up."

Cam kissed the top of her head, working his way to her succulent mouth.

The unhurried kiss soothed rather than inflamed.

Domini shivered and he forced his lips from hers. "It's getting chilly. We should go in. Supper's done anyway."

"Mmm. Think we can pick up where we left off after he goes to bed?"

"If I can stay awake. I'm so tired lately."

"I've got plenty of ideas on how to keep you up," he murmured.

"Isn't that supposed to be my line?"

"Smarty. Just for that, I think I'll drag out the nipple clamps tonight."

"Promise?"

Cam swatted her on the ass. "Feed me, woman. I'll need to keep up my strength."

Chapter Twenty-one

Two weeks later...

"Please no. Come on." Domini turned the ignition key again.

Nothing.

"I don't have time for this. I really don't."

The next try had the same result of an empty click. The damn car was dead.

Domini wanted to beat her hands on the steering wheel in pure frustration. She knew nothing about cars. Nothing. At least the stupid thing had broken down in the school parking lot and not in the middle of the road.

"What are we gonna do?" Anton asked.

"Walk to the diner, I guess. And hope the repair shop can look at it tomorrow."

"Why can't Cam look at it now? He probably knows a lot about cars."

Domini froze. She'd handled every little thing in her life for so long it never crossed her mind to ask someone for help.

Cam's not someone. He's your husband.

She reached for her cell phone and dialed. She was patched straight through to him.

"Hello, wife. You never call me at work. What's the occasion?"

"Nothing that will make you happy. My stupid car died."

"Where are you?"

"In the school parking lot."

"Hang tight. I'll be there in five."

"But—" and she heard a dial tone. She looked over at

Anton.

He smirked. "Told ya."

As soon as Cam arrived, he checked the engine and did mysterious manly stuff beneath the hood. Then he sauntered over to where Domini and Anton waited.

"What's wrong with it?"

"The starter is shot. The repair shop will have to order the part so it looks like we're carpooling for the next couple days."

"That won't work. I need my own car. I have to be—"

"Well, princess, we don't have a choice about sharing a ride, unless you stashed another vehicle someplace I don't know about?"

Domini shook her head.

"Then that settles it."

"I'm working from five until close tonight. Do you really want to wake Anton up at eleven and drive back into town to get me?"

"No, but I'd do it." Cam's eyes held a challenge. "What's wrong with you driving my truck tonight?"

"You'd trust me with it?"

"I trust you with everything, Domini." Cam touched her cheek. "Every. Damn. Thing."

When Cam uttered such sweet words she wanted to burst out in song.

Anton sighed. "Can I sit in the truck if you guys are gonna kiss and junk now so I don't hafta watch?"

"Do you have all your stuff out of Domini's car?" Cam asked.

"Yeah."

"Then climb on in, sport, and close your eyes 'cause there's gonna be some serious smooching going on."

She smiled when Anton sighed again.

Cam situated them chest to chest. "I wish we had time for kissing and junk, but I know you have to work. I'm off duty now, so why don't you drive us home and bring the truck back into town."

"You're sure?"

"Yep. Nowhere I need to go tonight."

"What will you guys be doing?"

"I dunno. We'll think of something."

"That's what worries me." Domini kissed his chin and snatched his keys.

✳

"More?" Cam asked Anton.

"Nope." Anton pushed aside his empty bowl.

Cam rolled the wax pouch and shoved it inside the Cap'n Crunch box. "This was a new box and now it's half empty. Domini is gonna know we had cereal for supper."

"We could tell her it's gone because...it spilled?"

"Lying is never a good choice. We'll have to come clean if she asks, okay?"

"Okay. But only if she asks, right?"

Cam smiled. "You're learning. You rinse the bowls and I'll take the garbage out." Cam practically dragged the bag he was so dead on his feet. After dumping the trash, he trudged up the back deck. Maybe Anton wouldn't mind if they just called it a night right now.

He snorted. Yeah, nothing seven-year-olds liked better than hitting the hay at six thirty. As Cam tried to think of something entertaining he and Anton could do, he misjudged the next step and fell on his ass with a loud crash, painfully twisting his bum leg in the process.

"Fuck!" He hissed against the sudden pain. "Fuck fuck fuck! Motherfucking piece of shit!"

The sliding glass door opened. Footsteps vibrated the wooden deck as Anton raced toward him. "Holy crap. Are you okay?"

No. Fuck no. Cam couldn't put pressure on his stump even if it hadn't detached from the prosthesis. "Can you run into my bedroom and get my crutches?"

"Um. Sure. Where are they?"

"By the nightstand."

He ran back inside.

Less than a minute later Cam heard the clatter of metal and opened his eyes. Anton held out the crutches. "Here."

"Thanks." Cam struggled upright. With the aid of the crutches he made it into the house without falling on his ass.

Anton stayed behind him. Watchful. Sometimes the kid was

so much like Domini he was surprised Anton hadn't sprung from her womb.

His stump hadn't detached, but it'd been wrenched hard enough Cam knew in order to wear the prosthetic at work tomorrow, he couldn't wear it for the rest of the night.

So much for hiding in his room. He couldn't leave Anton unattended.

"Cam?"

He glanced over his shoulder and realized he was blocking the doorway. "Sorry." He hopped sideways. "Can you get by now?"

"Yeah. Do you need any more help?"

"Nope. I've got it," he replied briskly.

Anton's smile slipped. "Oh. So what're you gonna do now?"

"Go to my room, get changed and take this off. Why? Did you need something?"

Anton shrugged. "I need help with my homework."

"They're giving you homework in second grade?"

"Spelling. You just have to read the words and I write 'em down."

"I can probably handle that. Get your stuff out and set up at the breakfast bar. I'll be right back."

Cam ditched his uniform and slipped on an old army PT shirt and a pair of sweatpants altered into shorts. They hung low enough that the fabric covered his stump completely. He stared at himself in the bathroom mirror. Why was he afraid of the stares and questions of a seven-year-old boy?

Talk about ridiculous.

Still, he was uncomfortable shuffling into the kitchen.

Anton's head lifted. He automatically focused on the empty space below Cam's left thigh. Then when he realized he'd been staring, his cheeks reddened and he quickly turned back to his notebook.

Cam took the barstool to the left of Anton. He propped his crutches on the support beam that framed the breakfast bar area and leaned across the countertop. "So? Whatcha got?"

Paper rattled and Anton slid a sheet in front of him. "Read me those words on the left."

"Starting with *imagine*?"

"Yep." Anton waited, pencil poised above the wide-ruled

lines, car-shaped eraser at the ready.

"The first word is: delight."

He frowned. "That's not the first word. The first word is *imagine*."

"I like mixing things up. Keeping you on your toes. Making sure you can spell them out of order."

"Domini doesn't do it that way."

"I'm not Domini."

It didn't take long and they were through the list.

"The last word is: antidisestablishmentarianism."

Anton's blue eyes bugged out. "What? That's not on the list."

Cam grinned. "I'm kidding. When I was in school that was the longest word in the dictionary. I'm sure there's something worse than that these days. I just wanted to see if you were paying attention."

"I bet I could spell it."

"I bet you could too. The last word is *resist*."

Anton smiled when Cam checked his paper and he'd gotten all the words right.

"You are a great speller."

He blushed and ducked his head.

Cam knew nothing about Anton's school activities besides when the bus let him off. That was pretty sad actually.

So change it.

"I'll bet you're good at math, too?"

"Yep."

"I never was worth a crap in math."

"Any more homework?"

"Nah." Anton's legs swung beneath the barstool.

Silence filled the air except for the hum of the dishwasher.

Man. He sucked at this.

You're never going to get better if you don't try. Start simple.

Cam sighed. "You wanna watch TV with me or something?"

"Sure."

When Anton plopped down on Cam's left side, close enough their hips touched, Cam didn't mind the invasion of his space as much as he'd thought.

Chapter Twenty-two

Week Eight...

The queasy feeling wouldn't let up.

Domini ate crackers, drank soda water, but every time she stood up too fast, she got dizzy.

"Domini, sweetie, you okay?" Neva asked.

"Just a little lightheaded. I'm sure it'll pass. I haven't been getting much sleep."

Neva smiled in her sweet, grandmotherly way. "Child, with all that you've been through in the last two months...not to mention being a newlywed...I don't imagine letting you rest is on the top of the deputy's agenda."

How true that was. Cam was insatiable. He was fabulous. And Domini was so crazy in love with her husband it wasn't funny.

She patted Domini's hand. "If you need anything, you let me know, okay?"

"Thanks, Neva."

Domini noticed a spatula underneath the prep station and bent to pick it up. When she stood, spots danced in front of her eyes, her hearing muffled, and then everything went black.

A lifetime later she heard, "Domini? Can you hear me?"

She was cold. Her head hurt. And why couldn't she open her eyes? "Yes."

"Stop pissing around with this, Dave, and call the ambulance."

That brought Domini out of her stupor. "No. I'm fine, you can't—"

"Easy." Gentle hands pushed her shoulders down. "We'll

get you taken care of."

"What happened?"

"You passed out, that's what happened," Beatrice snapped. "Dammit, you went down like a sack of potatoes."

"I don't remember."

"Which is why we need to call the ambulance, because something ain't right with you."

Domini opened her eyes. "You can't do that. Cam is on duty and all ambulance calls go through dispatch first. He'd hear it and freak out."

"Honey, he is your husband. He should freak out. He should be there when you talk to the doctor."

"No. He's got—" *no idea I've been keeping something really big from him,* "—too much going on today to hold my hand when I'm perfectly fine."

Bea wouldn't let up. "I don't know what your deal is, Domini, but you're not perfectly fine. I'll agree not to call an ambulance, if you let Neva drive you to the hospital. Right now."

Dave and Neva murmured their agreement with Bea's assessment.

"No hospital."

"The doctor then. I'll call Doc Monroe. I know she'll get you in right away."

Damn. Doc Monroe was the last person Domini wanted to see, but it appeared she'd have no choice. "Okay. Call her." She looked at the concerned faces hovering above her. "But no one calls Cam, got it? I will talk to him after I've seen Doctor Monroe. There's no reason to make him worry."

"Neva. Get your car and bring it around back."

Neva disappeared. Bea left to make the call, leaving Domini with Dave. She attempted a smile. "Help me up?"

Dave extended a hand and Domini slowly rose to her feet.

"See? I'm fine."

He just shook his head. "No. You're stubborn."

At the doctor's office, Domini convinced Neva to return to Dewey's to help with the lunch rush. But Neva walked her into the clinic, making sure Domini didn't skip out on her appointment.

She filled out the medical forms, intentionally leaving some sections blank. Although medical records were supposed to be confidential, in a town the size of Sundance, Domini wasn't taking chances.

A young nurse called out, "Domini McKay?"

Domini followed the nurse back through the maze of exam rooms and ran straight into...Keely. She couldn't go anywhere in this town without running into a member of Cam's family.

Keely's blue eyes narrowed. "You look like a ghost. What's wrong with you?"

"What are you doing here?"

"Doc Monroe and I are working on a project together and I'm wrapping a few things up. Where's Cam?"

"At work. What project?"

"Nice try, *sis*, with the bait and switch, but you didn't answer my question. What's wrong with you?"

"Maybe she didn't answer because that's none of your business," the nurse retorted. "This way, Mrs. McKay." She led her into an exam room in the farthest corner and shut the door in Keely's face. The nurse gave her a tight smile. "I'll get rid of her, don't worry."

"Thank you."

The nurse weighed her, took her blood pressure and her temperature. Then she drew a vial of blood. She gestured to the gown on the exam table. "You'll need to get undressed completely. Put the gown on with the opening in the front. The doctor will be in shortly."

Domini perched on the exam table. Before too long her eyes began to droop and she laid back. The last thing she remembered was the crinkly sound of the paper beneath her bare butt as she tried to get comfortable.

Two sharp raps on the door startled her awake.

Doctor Monroe strode in and smiled. "I'd ask how you are, but the fact you're here is pretty much my answer." She sat on the rolling stool and flipped through the papers on the clipboard. "Why don't you tell me what's going on?"

"It's silly I'm here at all. I passed out in the kitchen at Dewey's, my coworkers panicked and offered me the choice of the emergency room or you, so here I am."

"Mmm-hmm." The doctor didn't look up. "Your medical history seems to have quite a few gaps."

"I'm not sure about some of it."

"Because...?"

"I was orphaned at age eleven and they didn't have my full medical history. Then my medical records were lost in the immigration paperwork."

"Mmm-hmm. Understandable." Doctor Monroe shut the folder. "But complete and total b.s. So why don't you tell me the truth if you expect me to help you?"

Startled, Domini stared at her.

"First thing, strictly off the record, I assure you I've never had designs on Cam McKay, which you might've mistakenly believed. Cam is a patient. I don't date my patients. Period.

"Secondly, I take my patient's confidentiality very seriously. No one works for me I don't trust. Access to medical records is strictly monitored. No one on my staff will blab any part of your medical history to anyone. I guarantee it. So whatever you tell me, will be held in the utmost confidence."

"You won't tell my husband?"

"Not without your consent." Doctor Monroe stood and pulled out the table extension. "Lie back. Let's see if we can't figure out what's going on with you."

Good thing she already had her blood pressure taken, because right now it was through the roof. Domini closed her eyes and flinched when the doc's cold hands started poking her abdomen. She knew the exact moment the doctor figured it out.

"Do you have a uterus?" She poked the area above Domini's hipbones.

"No."

"You still have ovaries." She traced the scar above her pubic bone. "Surgical rather than vaginal removal?"

"Yes."

"Please sit up."

Domini gathered the edges of her gown together. She heard the doctor return to her chair. Heard the squeak as the chair rolled toward the desk. Heard her flipping through the scant paperwork looking for answers.

Doctor Monroe's pale red eyebrows were drawn together. Her teeth were digging into her lower lip. She seemed...agitated. "I don't have to ask if you're having problems with your menstrual cycle." She looked up. Her eyes were compassionate, yet held resolve. "Will you please explain to me why a perfectly healthy thirty-year-old woman has had a hysterectomy?"

"It wasn't by choice."

"Excuse me?"

She might as well tell the whole sordid story. "I'm not sure about all the technical medical terms, but I started having issues with my menstrual cycle when I was fifteen. I had no one to talk to. My caregivers at the orphanage didn't care, so I suffered through it. Halfway through my sixteenth year, I could feel these...lumps in my abdomen. The pain was excruciating. Whenever I brought it up, I was told it was part of being a woman. Until one day I passed out from the pain. Someone called an ambulance and I ended up in the hospital. I was in and out of a drug-induced haze when the doctors did tests. I remembered thinking maybe my appendix had burst."

"What did they find?"

"Uterine fibroids. The orphanage director was called in." Domini fought back the anger. "I was a minor. When the doctors told him the best option was removal of my uterus, he didn't question it. He just signed the paperwork. I didn't know any of this until after it happened when I woke up two days later."

"There are so many other options besides the most extreme one! Especially at your age! Why didn't they—"

"What could I do? The orphanage made the choice for me."

"And you had something taken from you without your consent. My older patients who've gone through a hysterectomy have emotional issues with the physical loss of part of their womanhood. But to deal with that loss at age sixteen when you were just a girl? Just becoming a woman—" Her voice broke, and she looked away.

Domini watched in shocked silence as Doctor Monroe's tears dripped on her white slacks. Not the reaction she'd expected.

What did you expect? She'd call Cam and tell him she could give him the babies you can't?

Finally Doctor Monroe composed herself. "I'm sorry. It makes me so angry that there are monsters in the medical field all over the world who can just play God and take away choices..." She inhaled. Exhaled. "I get a little worked up sometimes."

"It's okay."

"Did they have any idea what might've caused the fibroids? It's fairly uncommon at that age."

"There were a lot of medical abnormalities after Chernobyl. Some immediate, some issues that didn't show up until years later. Of course, no one will admit that disaster had long term affects on any of the Ukraine people."

"Of course not. Who monitors you?"

"A gynecological specialist in Denver. I see her once a year."

"Good. But now that I'm aware of your condition, if you have any issues you're not sure of, I'd be happy to treat you. I'm not a specialist, but I am determined to make rural healthcare top notch."

"Thank you." Domini fidgeted with the folds of the gown. "Cam doesn't know."

Doctor Monroe frowned. "Why not?"

"Because when we'd just started dating my friend Nadia died and left her son Anton an orphan and I couldn't let him go into foster care. I'd have a hard time getting custody of Anton as a single woman so Cam suggested I marry him."

"He did?"

"It was spur of the moment. As a cop Cam has had foster care training. His logic was if I married him, I wouldn't be a flight risk and Anton wouldn't have to go into foster care. So I said yes. I'm so selfish." Domini started crying. "Cam is the best man in the world and he deserves so much better than me, especially with his brothers and cousins all having kids. If he stays married to me that'll never happen, he'll never have kids of his own and I don't know how to tell him."

"Ssh. Hey. Here." The doctor handed her a tissue. "Take a deep breath. I can't tell you what to do, because you already know what you should do. I don't believe the only reason Cam McKay married you is so you could get custody of Anton. No one is that selfless."

"You'd be surprised."

"There's no other reason?"

Domini blew her nose. "Well, the sex between us is pretty spectacular."

"I don't doubt that. Look, obviously you've dealt with the issues concerning Cam's handicap. I can't imagine he wouldn't be as understanding when you tell him about yours."

"But—"

"Do you think any less of him because his leg is gone?"

"No!"

Two raps sounded on the door and the nurse poked her head in. "Umm. There's a very agitated, very large, uniformed man out here demanding to see his wife. He's armed and he's scaring me."

Domini's gaze zipped to the doctor's. "How did Cam find out I was here?"

"Don't look at me. I didn't call him. Send him back." Doctor Monroe patted Domini's knee. "For now, let's concentrate on—"

The door opened and Cam barreled in. "Domini, are you all right?"

"I'm fine, Cam."

"You scared me half to death." He cupped her face in his hands. His eyes searched hers frantically. "Why didn't you call me?"

"You're busy and—"

"I'm never too busy for you. Never ever *ever* too busy for my wife." Cam glanced at the doctor. "What's wrong with her? Is it serious? Is she gonna be okay?"

"She's anemic for one thing. Which explains the lightheadedness and fainting spells."

"You fainted?" Cam said incredulously.

"Just once."

"How many times do you have to faint before you see it as a problem?" Cam turned to the doctor. "What else?"

"Nausea. It sounds like she hasn't been eating right or sleeping much."

"Anything else?"

"Hypertension. Stress can create all sorts of different reactions in the body."

"So what do I do to make her better? I'll do whatever it takes."

Her tears pooled again. She didn't deserve this man.

"For the anemia I'll prescribe iron tablets. For the hypertension, bed rest for a couple of days." The doctor clasped the chart to her chest.

"Thank you, Doctor Monroe."

"Yeah, thanks, doc, for seeing her right away. I owe you

one."

She smiled. "Remember that when you see the bill. Take care. Both of you."

When the door clicked shut, Cam's mouth was on hers, bestowing the sweetest, gentlest kiss that brought tears to the surface again. "Thank God you're okay. I don't know what I'd do if something happened to you, princess. I'd absolutely lose my fucking mind."

"Listen—"

"No, you listen. I'm taking you home and you will not do a single goddamned thing but lay in bed for at least two days."

"Cam—"

"I ain't kiddin'. When Dave called me—"

Domini placed her hand on his chest. "Wait. *Dave* called you?"

"How do you think I found out?"

So Keely hadn't tattled. "It doesn't matter."

"Oh, but it does matter. I should've found out from *you*."

"Sorry. I just...wasn't thinking straight."

"Lucky thing you won't have to think for the next two days, because, princess, I'm gonna be stuck to your side like a burr. So get dressed so I can take you home."

Cam made no move to leave the exam room. "Why don't you wait out front? It'll just take me a minute."

"Huh-uh. What if you fainted? And hit your head? I am not taking the chance that anything will happen to you."

"Fine." She dressed quickly. Cam paid the doctor's bill and escorted her—heck he practically carried her—to his truck. The sun burned her eyes. She slipped on her sunglasses.

About halfway home, Cam said, "When I heard you'd passed out and were nauseous, I thought...maybe you were pregnant."

Domini froze.

"I know we haven't been married long, but if it'd turned out you were pregnant, I...well, I wouldn't have minded. Not at all. I just wanted you to know."

She faced out the window. She had to tell him the truth.

And if Cam decides to walk away?

She loved him. Now she knew the true meaning of selfishness because she didn't know if she could let him go.

✳

Cam tucked Domini in bed, called the station and requested a couple of sick days. He jotted down a grocery list. He paced until it was time to pick up Anton.

At the school, he rested his butt against the passenger side of his pickup and kept his eyes peeled for the boy. Cam whistled and Anton looked his direction. The kid smiled as he hustled toward him. "Hey, Cam."

"Heya, sport."

"I didn't know you were picking me up today."

"Your lucky day, huh?"

"Uh-huh. We doin' something fun?"

"Not really, unless you love grocery shopping."

Anton groaned and hefted himself into the cab.

"How was school today?"

"Okay."

"Have any homework?"

"Nope. Where's Domini?"

Cam turned the corner and waved at Mrs. Jackson walking her toy poodles. "She's at home. She ain't feeling too good."

Anton was quiet. Too quiet. "Is she gonna have a baby?"

"No." He sent Anton a sideways glance. "What makes you say that?"

"People have babies after they get married. I thought maybe now she's got a baby in her tummy."

I wish. Maybe then Cam could believe she'd stick around. She hadn't called him today when she'd gotten ill, but she had called him when she had car trouble? That bugged the crap out of him. Add in the fact she wouldn't share a bank account with him, she insisted on buying all the groceries and Cam wondered if they had a marriage or a business arrangement.

It is a business arrangement. She only married you for Anton. Once she gets him she'll be gone.

Cam didn't believe that. He half believed Domini loved him. But the last thing she needed right now was the added stress of him demanding to know how she felt about him.

"Cam?"

"Hmm?"

"What's wrong with her?"

"She's tired and it's making her sick."

"What do we hafta do to make her get better?"

Cam smiled at Anton's use of "we" and his offer to take care of the woman who took such good care of both of them. "Make sure she rests and eats right. We'll be eating a lot of steak. And burgers."

"Who's cooking?"

"Me. Why?"

He blurted, "Because you're a really bad cook."

Cam said nothing.

A hint of fear shone in Anton's eyes. "Are you mad?"

"Because you told the truth? Hell no. But you're right, sport, I'm a shitty cook." He shot him a look. "Sorry, I'm not supposed to swear in front of you."

The kid actually rolled his eyes.

"So, I'm a bad cook, yet I need to feed my wife...what do you think we oughta do?"

"Eat at Dewey's every day?"

"Nope. Try again."

"We could ask Dave to help us. He knows everything about cooking."

"That's a great idea."

Anton's face lit up. "Really?"

"Yep. We've gotta stop at Dewey's and get Domini's purse anyway, so we'll see if Dave can give us some pointers."

Armed with detailed instructions, Cam and Anton picked up several steaks before they headed home. Domini was sitting on the front deck when he pulled up.

Gracie barked and waited by the truck for Anton. Damn dog was completely smitten with the boy. And Anton had done a one-eighty when it came to Gracie's behavior. The dog minded Anton better than him sometimes.

Cam unloaded the grocery bags. Anton hauled them in the house, leaving Cam alone with Domini. He climbed the steps slowly. "You wanna explain what you're doin' out of bed, Mrs. McKay?"

"I was lonely for my boys. Gracie was antsy so I thought I'd sit out in the fresh air."

My boys. He leaned down and kissed her. "Getcha ass back

in bed, woman. Now."

"I love it when you go all caveman on me, Deputy. Makes me all tingly."

Does that mean you love me?

Not going there. Not now. "I could toss you over my shoulder and drag you inside."

"Will you wear a sexy jungle print loin cloth too?"

"You have a filthy mind, woman. That's why I—"

Love you.

Shit.

Domini's eyes narrowed. "That's why you what?"

"That's why I plan on doing nasty, raunchy, dirty things to you for hours when you're better. Now get in bed."

After Anton finished chores, which the crazy kid seemed to enjoy, they unwrapped the meat and fired up the barbecue. They read through Dave's instructions—twice—but it didn't help.

By the time they finished "cooking" the steaks were burned beyond recognition. Both he and Anton stared at the charred chunks of meat. Finally Anton said, "We suck."

"Yep. We seriously suck."

"I don't think Gracie will even eat it."

Gracie whined.

"Can I make a suggestion?" Domini said from the doorframe.

Cam wheeled around. "You're supposed to be—"

"In bed. I know. I'm anemic, not an invalid. You don't have to wait on me. And I'm thinking it might be best if you don't try to cook for me either."

Cam and Anton exchanged a glum look.

"Here's the deal, how about if I cook and you guys do everything else." She shook her head at the burned disks. "Was that...steak?"

"Uh-huh."

"Choice cut steak."

She winced. "We definitely cannot afford for you guys to massacre any more meat. Do we have a deal?"

"Deal."

✳

"...sparsely..." Anton looked up at Domini. "What does that mean?"

"Umm...very little?"

She glanced over at Cam and he nodded.

"You don't know?"

She bumped Anton with her shoulder. "English isn't my native language, remember? It takes a minute for me to translate."

"So when you're thinking in your head, are you thinking in Ukrainian? Or in English?"

"When I first moved to the U.S. I only thought in Ukrainian. But the longer I've been here away from people who speak my language, it's English that pops into my head first. But there are always words that throw me off. Like sparsely." She tousled Anton's hair. "Did your mom speak to you in Bosnian?"

"Nope. He didn't like it."

"It's about time for bed, sport."

"I know." Anton jumped off the couch, securing his book under his arm, and lingered in front of Domini. "Are you gonna tuck me in?"

"Yes. Then I'm tucking myself in."

Anton opened the front door and Gracie bounced in. Her tail wagged so hard her body swayed as she followed Anton down the hallway to his bedroom.

"Sometimes I forget that English isn't your native tongue," Cam murmured. "Will you teach our kids to speak Ukrainian?"

Domini let her head fall back on the cushion and closed her eyes. "Do you think Anton will ever talk about Rex? Or will he just avoid the issue if we let him?"

Kind of like she'd sidestepped his question. Cam decided not to push it. "Give him time. I know we all wanna be one big happy family from the get go, but it'll take us all time to adjust."

"Are you adjusting, Cam? Now that you've got a kid and a wife? Do you want us to be a big happy family? When all this chaos you never wanted is destroying the serenity of your haven?"

No, now I've got everything I ever wanted.

Domini wasn't the only one who'd mastered the art of

deflection. "I'll double check I shut the grill off while you tuck Anton in."

Domini was already in bed when he returned to their bedroom. Cam stripped, unfastened his prosthesis and slid beneath the covers.

Immediately Domini wrapped herself around him. She kissed his biceps. And his collarbones. Her lips skimmed his throat. "Cam?"

"Mmm?"

"Touch me."

"Domini. Baby, you're supposed to take it easy."

"So love me nice and easy. And slow. You love to torture me. Take your time with me, Cam." She sank her teeth into his earlobe. "Please. I need you."

Cam was helpless to resist. He didn't want to resist. He kissed her. Teased her. Showed her with his hands and his mouth and his body how much he loved her.

When he slid inside her, surrounded by her warmth and softness and strength, he realized she made him a whole man and it didn't have a damn thing to do with his missing leg. It had everything to do with filling his heart.

Chapter Twenty-three

"We don't have to go. In fact, I think we oughta stay home. You *have* been sick."

Domini tied the laces on her tennis shoes. "Not sick, Cam. Anemic. I'm feeling much better after being babied by you guys for the last two days. I want to enjoy the gorgeous day. I'm tired of being cooped up inside."

"There are gonna be a million people there," Cam warned. "And my family will grill both of us on our marriage, if we're gonna start havin' kids—"

Her stomach knotted, but she tossed out a breezy, "Maybe they won't, since we already have a kid."

Anton and Gracie burst into the kitchen. "Is it time to go yet?"

Domini gave Cam a we-don't-want-to-disappoint-Anton look.

Cam sighed. "Fine. But if you look the slightest bit faint, we're comin' home and I'm tyin' you to the bed for a solid week."

She stood on tiptoe and kissed his cheek. Her lips slid to his ear and she whispered, "Is that a promise, Deputy?"

"Yep."

"Good because I miss that side of you. You've been too careful with me lately. You know I won't break."

He eased back to look at her face. "Domini, I—"

"Are you two gonna suck face or are we going?"

"Suck face. Definitely." Cam teased his mouth over hers and her heart jumped.

"Yuck. We're outta here." The sliding glass door slammed.

Domini stepped back. "We'll be lucky if any of the doors in

this house survive until his teen years."

Cam went still.

"What?"

"Ah. Nothin'. I just can't imagine Anton a teenager."

That was weird. Didn't he expect to be around then?

Maybe you won't be once you tell him the truth.

"Do we have everything?"

"I guess." Cam caught her staring at his pants. "What?"

"I've never seen you wear those." His baggy dark khaki pants appeared to be made out of shiny, lightweight parachute material, with cargo pockets everywhere and elastic bands at the knees and ankles. "Are they new?"

He snorted. "Hell no, they're old. I couldn't face wearing jeans today, sweats are too casual and every other pair of pants is in the hamper, so this is what was left."

"I'm sorry I didn't have a chance to do laundry this week. I'm slacking on all sorts of wifely duties."

Cam tipped her chin up. "I didn't marry you so you could wash my clothes, Domini."

No, you married me because you're selfless, perfect and a good man.

He pecked her on the mouth. "Let's go before I find another reason to stay."

"Another?"

"Tyin' you to the bed and keepin' you there all day is mighty tempting."

Outside, Anton was already in the truck bed with Gracie.

"Come on, hop in the front," Domini said.

"Aw, do I have to? Everybody rides in the back of pickups with their dogs."

"Everybody except for you."

Anton turned his puppy dog eyes to Cam.

Cam shrugged. "I don't see the big deal. It's only ten miles."

"In the back of a bouncy pickup on a gravel road!"

"So he'll be dusty. He won't be the only one."

"Ky rides in the back of Cord's truck all the time," Anton added.

"We all did. We all turned out fine."

She knew she was outnumbered. And when she really

thought about it, they'd been siding together a lot in the last week. "All right. But you stay down. No hanging off the side, I mean it."

"I promise."

Domini couldn't help but turn round every couple of minutes to check on Anton.

"Stop worrying. He's happier than a pig in shit," Cam drawled. He plucked up her hand from the middle seat and kissed her knuckles. "Is the honeymoon over? We've only been married two months and you're not sitting close to me in the truck anymore."

She scooted closer. "Better?"

"Much. I'm always better with you by my side."

A sigh of contentment drifted out. She rested her head on Cam's shoulder. He draped his arm across the back of the seat and lightly stroked the outside of her arm. Sometimes the silences between them were more revealing than words.

Vehicles crowded the yard at the Carson McKay ranch. Kids and dogs ran everywhere. With all the questions they'd be facing about future kids, she wished she'd talked to Cam before they'd left home.

Anton beat on the window. "Can I get out now?"

"Go ahead."

Suddenly shy, Domini kept a death grip on Cam's hand as they wended through the chairs and tables.

Carolyn McKay hopped up the instant she saw them.

Because Domini's schedule and Cam's schedules hadn't meshed, they'd missed out on all the McKay family dinners in the last two months, so this was Domini's first official family function as Cam's wife.

"Cam! Sweetie, it's good to see you."

"Hey, Ma."

She hugged him for a long time. Then she hugged Domini. "It's good to see you too, Domini. I heard you've been under the weather."

"She's anemic, which makes her tired. She's taking heavy duty iron."

"Oh, you poor thing!" Carolyn said. "What can I do?"

"Don't be upset if we leave early. I have to take her home and get her back in bed."

"Spoken like a true McKay man," Keely said.

Domini blushed.

"I hope you'll stick around for a little while," Carolyn said. "I hardly get to see you. I've thought about doin' something wild to get myself arrested by you, just so we'd have time to chat."

"Great plan, Ma."

"You are welcome to stop by our house anytime," Domini offered.

Carolyn gave her a puzzled look, almost as if she didn't believe Domini's invitation. Not that Domini blamed her. Cam wasn't known for his hospitality and Carolyn probably assumed Domini was the same way, especially since she and Cam had little to do with his parents since they'd gotten married.

A herd of boys, ranging in age from eight to three, barreled up. Domini was happy to see Anton in the thick of things.

"Grama, can we please have some cookies? We're starvin'," Ky pleaded.

"Of course, I can't have poor starving kids runnin' around. What would the neighbors think? I left the cookie jar on the back porch."

A chorus of "Thanks!" broke out. Boots thumped, dust kicked up and dogs barked as the group tore off.

"Cookies? Before lunch?" Cam mock-chided. "You're getting soft. You never would've let us have cookies that early."

"Grandbabies are different. I can sugar them up and send them home with their parents." Carolyn strolled off when Kimi McKay shouted for her.

"Come on, let's make the rounds so we can leave right after lunch," Cam murmured.

The first people they approached were India and Skylar. India swayed with a blanketed bundle tucked against her body. A toddler with auburn ringlets was cocked on Skylar's hip. Colt stood behind India talking to Kade, who also had a toddler clinging to him. Cam released her hand and moved between his brother and cousin.

India smiled. "We didn't know if you guys would make it. Anton is off running with the boys?"

"And girl," Skylar said dryly. "I don't know why Eliza is so determined to keep up with her boy cousins."

"Because she *is* a girl, that's why. I remember it well." Keely snuck in the group and held her hands out. "Shannie, come with Aunt Keely and we'll go see what the pack is up to."

Shannie practically jumped into Keely's arms.

Domini wasn't surprised when India and Skylar's discussion returned to business. "It pisses me off she had to go looking for work at all."

"Carolyn didn't invite Casper and Joan, did she?"

"No. I know she invited Jessie. I don't know about Tell and Dalton. But if Jessie shows up Brandt will probably be with her. I'm so glad they're helping each other through this."

Domini didn't have a clue what they were talking about. Should she ask? If she didn't would they think she didn't give a damn about Cam's family?

Skylar must've sensed her curiosity. "Sorry. I don't know if Cam told you about what happened with Jessie after Luke's funeral?"

She shook her head.

"Casper kicked Jessie out of the trailer she'd shared with Luke and he told her she had no financial claim on any part of the McKay Ranch and she was on her own."

"No."

"Afraid so. Jessie had nowhere to live, no job, no place for her horses or her llamas. Poor girl. Her dad is still chasing the rodeo circuit. Her mom has remarried and is living on the Shoshone reservation with her new husband."

"If she needs a job I could always use extra help at Dewey's—"

Skylar squeezed her arm. "You are such a sweetie, Domini, to offer. I needed to hire someone to replace Nadia, so Jessie is working for me at Sky Blue. Brandt tracked down a rental place outside of Moorcroft with a small pasture so she's kept her animals."

"That is so awful. I didn't know." Domini wondered why Cam hadn't told her. Wouldn't that be something you'd tell your spouse?

Like you have any right to judge him on keeping secrets.

"Cam keeps to himself and generally stays out of family—I mean ranch—business. Anyway, Casper's behavior caused another big rift with the McKay families. Even Casper's sons are pissed off at him. So in addition to losing their brother…"

Hudson fussed and Colt was right there. "I'll take him."

India handed the baby over, but followed Colt to the house anyway.

Skylar sighed. "My sister is absolutely smitten with her son. She's as bad as Chassie was."

"Did someone say my name?" Chassie inquired sweetly behind Skylar.

Domini and Skylar turned.

Chassie shifted her roly-poly baby boy from one hip to the next. One chubby hand gripped Chassie's long braid. "Westin, honey, let go of mama's hair."

He cooed, blinked enormous hazel eyes and blew a big spit bubble.

"Blowing me kisses won't charm me, buddy boy." She kissed the top of his blond head and attempted to pry his fingers off her braid.

"Need some help?" Domini asked.

"It'd be great if you'd distract him."

Domini made goofy faces. Poked his round belly until he giggled while Chassie freed her hair.

"Thanks." She smooched Westin's plump cheek. "You should show Domini how good you are at giving kisses."

"I'll take a kiss," she said, leaning in. She caught a whiff of powdery baby smell as Westin's cool mouth connected with her cheek, leaving a drooly wet mark. She laughed and looked up to see Cam staring at her.

The soft, wistful look in his eyes caused her to break eye contact. Caused her stomach to lurch with dread. Caused an immense amount of guilt.

Skylar said, "I haven't been into Dewey's in ages. It's a nightmare to take three kids to a restaurant."

"Not much has changed."

Westin wiggled in Chassie's arms. When she shifted her hold, he arched his back and protested loudly.

"I am not putting you down, so stop fussing." Chassie flicked her hair aside as Westin tried to snatch it again. "He's already trying to walk. It's driving me nuts."

"You want them to walk and you don't realize how easy you had it when they weren't walking." Skylar smiled. "We weren't anxious for Peyton and Shannie to start walking at all, after dealing with Eliza, the pink tornado."

Westin pushed on Chassie's chest and attempted to either throw himself to the ground, or shinny down her body. When neither option worked, he wailed with full lung power.

"Look at what you've done now with that caterwauling. Daddies are gonna come running."

Sure enough, Trevor and Edgard were both there instantly.

"What's wrong?" Trevor said as Westin dove into his arms.

Edgard rubbed Westin's back. "He sounds tired."

"He's mad because I won't let him roll in the dirt."

"Shoot, Chass, boys get dirty. He just wants to be runnin' with his cousins."

Chassie rolled her eyes at Edgard.

The dinner bell clanked.

"I should track down Anton and make sure he eats something besides cookies," Domini said.

Cam's hands landed on her shoulders. "Let him be. I'm sure he's havin' a great time. Plus, I need to make sure *you* eat."

When Domini and Cam were in the food line, she felt guilty seeing Macie, Keely and AJ running around behind the serving tables helping Carolyn.

"I recognize that guilty look, princess," Cam murmured. "Next time, when you're feeling better, I'm sure Ma would appreciate your help."

Sometimes it amazed her how well Cam read her.

The kids got in line. Red faced, sweaty, dirty. Carolyn kicked them out of line and sent them to the pump to wash up. Grama ruled the clan with a velvet fist.

She turned to follow Anton's blond head in the crowd of dark-headed boys and found herself looking into Carson McKay's face. Into blue eyes identical to Cam's. Uncanny, how all Carson's offspring had his eyes. He gave her a dimpled, charming smile. "We're glad to have you here, Domini."

"Thanks."

Carson cocked his head at Cam, who towered over his dad by a good five inches. "Son, I understand you and Domini just got married, and you're figurin' out how to be parents and balance your jobs. But your mother and I sure would like to get to know your new family."

Lorelei James

Every McKay family member had gone out of their way to make her feel welcome. So Cam's…standoffish attitude toward his family bothered her and she wanted to let Carson know she appreciated his genuine interest in welcoming her and Anton into the McKay family. "I'd like that, Mr. McKay."

"Shoot, darlin', call me Carson."

"We will definitely find a time to get together soon, Carson."

"Good enough."

Cam whispered, "Nicely done, wife."

Anton didn't sit with them. Colby and Cord stood back from the kid's table, keeping an eye on the kids, while they talked and held yet more dark-haired babies.

This was one fertile family.

Libby plopped down beside her. "How is Anton faring with the multitude of McKay males?"

"Good I guess."

"I forgot. Not all males." She pointed. "Look at Eliza."

Her face was sweaty and smudged with dirt. Weeds poked out of her pigtails. Grass stained her flowered shirt. And she was grinning from ear to ear.

"And they thought Keely was hell on wheels. I say look out for her."

Domini scanned the picnic tables, but she didn't see Channing. "Where's Channing?"

"Lying down upstairs." Libby chuckled. "Can you believe she's pregnant again? Some of us can't even have one baby and she's knocked up every time I turn around."

She didn't press Libby on her *some of us can't even have one baby* comment, but she was curious as to why Libby just blithely tossed it out there.

She can tell a stranger about her fertility issues but you can't even tell your husband about yours?

"This is their fourth in six years. Miles is only six months old." Libby gave her a droll stare. "FYI: Channing is blaming the cherry bombs for her current state. Said she got home, got naked with Colby and neither remembered a condom."

Domini couldn't help but laugh. "If it's a girl, I hope they consider naming her Cherry."

A beat-up Suburban pulled up. Carter McKay exited the driver's side. A tall, muscular guy Domini vaguely remembered

262

from Colt and India's wedding reception sauntered around the front end of the vehicle.

Talk about gorgeous. Talk about impeccably dressed. He wore tasseled loafers, black dress pants, and a gray cashmere sweater layered over a black mock turtleneck. His dark hair was a little long, but created a sophisticated, bad boy, devil-may-care aura that added to his dazzling looks.

Carter's oldest two boys ran up and hugged their dad and then Mr. Overdressed, who grinned and didn't seem to care if the dirt on their clothes transferred to his.

Domini glanced at Cam, but Cam's eyes were narrowed at someone behind her.

"For Christsake, what the hell is he doin' here?"

"Keely!" AJ said.

Domini turned around. Keely had worn that same furious look the night of the bar fight. Not a good sign.

"I'm not kidding. Who invited him?"

"We did." Macie took her youngest son, Spencer, from Keely's arms as a precaution. "He's staying with us for a couple days. What were we supposed to do? Leave him at home?"

"I'm sure he'd love to spend the day staring at his perfect face in the mirror. Or combing his perfect hair. Or figuring out how he can be even more of a perfect dickhead. Oh right, that's not possible for *Jack-off*, because he's already the biggest dickhead on the planet."

"Keely West McKay, that's enough." Carolyn came up behind Keely, set her hands on her shoulders and whispered furiously in her ear.

"No. Not possible. You are dead wrong, Ma, and I'm ticked off you even suggested it." She wheeled around and hustled into the house.

Carolyn and AJ exchanged a look. AJ sighed and chased after Keely.

Oddly enough, Cam said, "Excuse me," and left the table too.

Confused, Domini faced Libby. "What was that about?"

"Keely used to date Jack's younger brother. No love lost between them, which is awkward since Jack is Carter's best friend. Keely and Jack are constantly sniping and one of these days they're gonna kill each another."

"Oh." Quinn and Libby jumped into a heated discussion with Buck and Kade. When ten minutes passed and Cam hadn't returned, she dumped her plate. Anton was nowhere to be found. Babies cried. Kids shrieked. Dogs barked. People were everywhere. It was chaotic and loud.

What would it be like to really be part of this boisterous family? To understand the rivalries and alliances? To build relationships that would last beyond the length of a job? To have roots in not only a place, but with people?

She'd put down roots in Sundance, more so than in any other place she'd resided, but the temptation to leave existed. She had nothing to keep her here.

What about Cam? He wants to give you all this.

He should give it to a woman who can give the same thing back to him—babies, family, that long-term community connection.

Isn't it up to Cam to decide that? Aren't you doing what you hate; taking away someone's choice?

It hit her. Her reproductive problem wasn't the total issue. She'd used it as an excuse. She'd been more than willing to share her body with Cam, but her heart? No.

Why had she demanded so much brutal honesty from him but she'd not done the same, except for when it came to sex?

She wandered to the section of the yard between the house and the barn. On edge. Wanting so much to come clean, to have the kind of marriage with Cam she didn't think existed. To have a real chance with him. Not for Anton's sake, but for hers.

"Domini?"

Speak of the devil. Warmth suffused her body. Not surprising he'd tracked her down when she needed him—the man was inordinately attuned to her. "I was just thinking of you and here you are."

He turned her toward him. "What's wrong?"

"Everything."

Cam's grip increased on her shoulders. "Are you sick? Do we need to go home?"

"No. We need to talk."

"Right now?"

"Yes. I didn't want to do this here, with your family around but I have to do it before I lose my nerve."

Cursing, Cam dragged her around the corner of the house, out of sight. He braced her spine against the trunk of an old oak tree and framed her face in his hands, not saying a word, just watching her with those dark blue eyes.

Domini attempted to push him back because he was crowding her, but he didn't allow it. "Talk."

"I haven't been...honest about something. Something big. Something that will probably change everything between us."

"What?"

Breathe. Own up to it. Just say it straight out like he would. "You know that scar on my abdomen?"

He nodded guardedly.

"It's not from getting my appendix taken out. It's from getting my uterus taken out." Domini detailed the short version of her medical history. She finished by saying; "I know I should've told you I can't have children before you married me. I'm sorry. It was selfish. You deserve better, Cam. You deserve more. You deserve a woman who's as selfless as you are and I understand if you—"

"Stop. Talking. Now."

She froze.

Cam's hands dropped. He spun on his heel away from her and retreated to pace like a caged animal.

Her heart pounded with pure fear. Was he resetting the distance between them with each step?

Finally, Cam got right in her face. "Listen to me very carefully, Domini McKay. I don't mean to be flip or make light of your medical condition, but guess what? It doesn't matter to me. Should you have told me sooner? Yes. Would it have made a damn bit of difference when I asked you to marry me? Hell no. I'm taking the fact you're telling me this now as a good sign that you haven't dragged me behind the goddamn house to tell me you're leaving me."

She blinked at him, unable to formulate the words *leaving me* out loud. Cam thought she wanted to leave him?

"Havin' a mini-Cam running around isn't important to me. *You* are important to me." He flattened his palm on her lower belly. "This isn't why I love you." His hand slid up to cover her heart. "This is."

Domini choked out, "You love me?"

"Yes, I love you. Why do you think I married you?"

"Because of the foster care issue with Anton. Because it was the right thing to do, you told me that yourself in Ginger's office."

"That was a total lie."

Her head reeled back as if she'd been slapped. "What?"

"I told you what you wanted to hear. You were so...mired in grief about Nadia and worried about Anton's future you weren't thinking straight. I seized my chance to get what I wanted."

"Which was?"

"You."

A shiver worked loose at his forceful tone. "Me? But—"

"You think me offering to marry you was selfless?" His grip increased on her shoulders and he shook her a little. "Wrong. I'm a total selfish bastard, Domini. I used the legal system I'm supposed to be upholding to benefit *me*. Despite the shitty circumstances of Nadia's death, it made me happy you had no choice but to marry me without delay if you wanted Anton. Even now I wouldn't change a goddamn thing. How fucked up is that?"

She forced a hoarse, "Why?" through her dry throat.

Cam's eyes searched hers. "Because I hoped if you were around me every day as my wife you'd fall in love with me, given the chance. Don't you understand? I'm not the one who always does the right thing, princess. You are. You're the one who's selfless, taking on a grieving boy and a handicapped man all in one fell swoop."

"Cam—"

"Let me finish. I fell in love with you so goddamned hard and fast my ass is still sore. The thing is, I fought it from the first time I set eyes on you, which is partially why I tried to just stay friends with you."

"Partially?"

"The other part was I didn't think you could handle my sexual needs. Boy was I ever wrong." He smiled cagily. "Then you told me what you needed in bed and gave me everything I'd dreamed of—and more—in return. The night you called my bluff, refusing to let me hide my body from you, I knew you were meant to be mine.

"You fill a part of me that's been empty since before I lost my damn leg. For the first time in my life I feel like a whole man. Not because you accept my handicap, but because you accept *me*. All of me." Cam's hand shook as his knuckle drifted down the side of her face. "You own my soul, Domini. You are my heart."

Domini studied his handsome, serious face for a long time, mustering her courage, because her next confession would be the hardest one.

"Say something," he insisted.

"I'm sorry. All this time we've been together, I demanded something from you that I wasn't prepared to give in return. I've given you my body without hesitation, but not my..." Emotion engulfed her.

"Sweet Jesus, Domini, baby, why are you crying?"

"Because I'm an idiot. I tried to protect my heart from you, but it's safe with you, isn't it?"

"Yes, baby, it's safe with me. I'll always keep it safe."

"I love you. I think I've always loved you."

Then his mouth was on hers. Kissing her with sweetness and tenderness so rare for him. Her tears fell with each gentle glide of his lips, with each heartbeat, with each shared breath. When she broke the kiss to whisper, "You make me feel whole too," he clutched her like he'd never let her go.

After he'd squeezed the breath out of her, he laughed. Hard.

"What?"

"Did you really think I'd trade you in for a model that wasn't missing parts?" He swept her hair behind her ear. "I'm missing parts. That hasn't mattered to you, has it?"

"No."

"Then why would you think it'd matter to me? I married you for real, for keeps, forever. I want to spend the rest of my life loving you, not making babies with you."

"You're too good to be true."

"Nah. Just crazy about my wife." Cam kissed her again. "Besides, if we ever get a handle on how to parent the kid we've already got, and if we decide we want more, we can adopt. After what we've seen the world over...we both know—you probably better than anyone—that there are kids all over the world who need a home."

"You want to adopt Anton?"

"Yes. I know you're surprised."

"That's putting it mildly."

"It's taken me time to adjust. Maybe you should've kept me in the loop as far as what legal steps you were taking alone, with the help of Ginger Paulson, on lining up Anton's adoption."

Her face flamed. "You knew?"

"Only because I saw her bill on your desk at Dewey's. Were you going to tell me?"

"Maybe. Probably. I guess I wanted to see if you'd change your mind."

"Princess, I'm damn stubborn. Once I set my mind to something, I don't change it. Since you've been sick and I've been hanging out with Anton I had an epiphany of sorts. I realized I really like the kid. I also understood that for the last two months I tried to get along with Anton for your sake. That's unfair, not only to you, but to me, and most of all to Anton.

"It's scary shit being entrusted with the care of a child, but you've bucked up to the challenge so can I. Anton deserves better than my half-assed attempt at being a father figure. He needs a real father and I intend to be one to him if he'll let me."

Domini closed her eyes. She was half afraid if she reopened them she'd find this was all some kind of cruel dream. One of those where everything she'd ever wanted was within her grasp and as soon as she reached for it, it'd vanish into mist and she'd wake up.

"Domini? Say something."

"Am I dreaming?"

"No baby, this is as real as it gets."

Chapter Twenty-four

Everything Domini said, everything that'd come out, gave Cam an unbelievable sense of relief their marriage was real—and finally on the right track. When Domini insisted on helping his mother clean up, he'd been grateful for a few moments alone. Not that it'd last long. Sure enough he heard, "Cam?"

He glanced up at Jack Donohue's approach. Cam tried not to scowl at the man his sister hated, who was also his brother's best friend. "Hey, Jack. What's up?"

"Not much. I'm looking for..." Jack jammed his hands in his pockets and scowled at his shoes.

Cam knew who Jack was seeking out, but no way would he point the man in Keely's direction. But he would let the poor sucker off the hook. "You looking for Carter?"

"No, I know where Carter and Thane are. They're partnering up for the games. Are you joining in?"

His mother loved games. Which meant she subjected her children to games, even as adults. "I haven't decided. Why?"

"I saw Anton sitting by himself on the porch swing."

His eyes narrowed. Did Jack's tone sound a little judgmental?

"Jesus. Do all you McKays practice that fiery death stare from the cradle?" Jack demanded.

"Yep."

"Awesome. I'd hate to think that foul-mouthed cowgirl cornered the market on dirty looks in this family." He sighed. "Anyway, I just thought you should know about Anton." Jack sauntered off.

Cam headed for the front of the house, discreetly rubbing

at the top of his socket. He was sweating like crazy and the damn thing itched today.

When he saw Anton with Gracie's head in his lap, the dejected look on the kid's face released a flood of emotions, none of which he knew how to handle.

Figure it out.

"Why so glum chum?" Cam asked from the bottom of the stairs. "Why aren't you playing games with the rest of your—" *cousins*, but Cam amended it to, "—buddies?"

Anton didn't look up. "I don't know how to throw a rope. How to hook something with a rope. How to tie something up with a rope. I don't know how to do any of that ranch and cowboy stuff."

"That's all they're doin'?"

"No. There *was* a foot race. I got third. Colt got first and Ky got second."

Cam bit back a groan. Colt's competitive streak would never go away. "Third is damn good."

Anton finally looked at him. "You really think so?"

"Sure. What other games does Grama have planned?"

"Some pin chaps on the cowboy for the little kids and a three-legged race."

Cam's stomach did a loop-de-loop. Anything but that. He managed, "Do you want to enter that one?"

"Yeah, but Domini's sick and she can't do it."

Don't say it. Don't even think it. You will fall on your ass and embarrass yourself in front of your entire family.

But Cam's mouth opened anyway despite the warning of self-preservation. "We could partner up for it."

"It's okay. I know you don't wanna do it and you're trying to be nice to me."

The kid's dead-on assessment of his attitude stung. "Why would I offer if I didn't mean it?"

Anton shrugged. "All grownups say things they don't mean."

The truth left shame coiling in his gut. Cam had sworn to Anton he was nothing like his father. But he acted just like Rex—he ignored the boy the same as Rex had done.

Hellfire and damnation. Cam wished he could erase the last two months. But since he couldn't, the best he could do was to start fresh.

"Look, I could feed you full of crap, offering excuses on why I've kept my distance since you moved in with us. I could make promises about how everything will be ponies and puppies and sparkling rainbows from here on out, but you're a smart kid. You've been burned by those lies before.

"So I'll just tell you I'm sorry. I will do better, not *try* to do better, but I'll actually be part of your life. Every day, not just at family picnics or when I've got no other choice because Domini is working. It'll take time to prove to you I'm in this for the long haul, but luckily for us, neither of us is going anywhere any time soon."

Anton ruffled his fingers through Gracie's fur.

"I understand if you don't wanna partner up with me, bein's I have a peg leg and all, but I used to whup butt all the time in races when we were kids."

That caught Anton's attention. "You're serious about being in the three-legged race with me?"

"Yep. We're the ringers, no one expects us to compete so I think we've got a shot at winning."

Anton smiled. Shyly. "Maybe we do."

"Come on. Let's go."

The area in front of the pickups had been cleared. A section of orange rope was used as the starting line. The course curved and ended by the old outhouse. His family members had already paired off and were tying orange ropes around their "third" leg. Cord with Ky, Colby with Gib, Carter with Thane, Kade with Eliza, Buck with Hayden. Colt and Jack were helping Colby's second son Braxton, and Carter's second son Parker, get set up.

"Got room for us?" Cam asked.

Everyone stopped. All eyes zoomed to him and Anton. Anton half-ducked behind him. Damn. He knew just how the kid felt.

"Of course we do!" Carolyn said. She walked over with Miles cocked on her hip. "There's the rope. Help yourselves."

While they readied for the race, the crowd grew. His sisters-in-law, assorted cousins, aunts and uncles stood on the sidelines. But there was only one face he searched for: Domini's.

When she smiled, her eyes shone, her face lit up as her gaze flicked back and forth between him and Anton. She gave them both a thumbs-up.

Once his and Anton's legs were tied together, they took a couple practice steps. Shit. That hurt. He clamped his teeth together and rode out the pain. He'd done it before. For months. And months. He could do it for five more minutes. He forced a smile. "Ready?"

"Yep. Are you?"

Hell no. "Yep." He wrapped his arm around Anton's shoulders; Anton brought his arm around Cam's waist.

Keely made a big production of starting the race with a long green scarf. "On your marks. Get set. Go!"

Cheers erupted and the race was on.

Cord and Ky took the early lead. Cam kept his head down and focused exclusively on his footing and the terrain beneath his feet. *Heel first, step* kept repeating in his head. *Heel first, step. Heel first, step.*

Cam and Anton built up a good rhythm. They weren't winning, and Cam was in pain, but Anton seemed to be getting a huge kick out of it and that's what mattered.

Then two things happened simultaneously. Parker and Braxton veered off course, directly into their path. While Cam attempted to avoid mowing over the little boys, he wasn't watching his footing and the toe of his prosthetic foot caught in a gopher hole.

Panic and inevitability seized his lungs. If he landed on his nephews, he'd crush their bodies. Ditto if he hit Anton with his full weight. So he took the logical course of action and jerked to his left so he crashed on his hip and prosthetic leg.

The familiar agonizing pain assaulted him. Too much sweat caused the rubber sleeve covering his stump to loosen and slide down. The vacuum suction popped and gave way. Then his prosthetic was flopping around inside his pant leg. He was completely helpless.

Fuck.

It seemed dozens of hands touched him at once. Dozens of voices spoke to him. Cam gritted his teeth and kept his eyes closed. He didn't want to see the looks of pity and concern from his family. He wanted everyone to leave him the fuck alone.

"Cam?"

Her soft voice cut through the chatter, but he still flinched at the idea of his wife seeing him lying in a big goddamn pile in the middle of the fucking yard.

"I'm here. Look at me. Just me."

He squinted at her even though her face was only inches away.

"How bad is it?" she asked.

Hurts like a motherfucking son of a bitch. "Bad enough. It detached."

"Okay." She moved back and quickly unzipped the section of his pants that turned them from pants into shorts.

"Let me see." Keely bulled her way in beside Domini and dropped to her knees.

"That's not—"

"Did you bring your crutches?" Keely demanded.

No. He'd forgotten them.

"Of course you didn't. First we need to get it completely off."

"I know. That's what I'm doing," Domini said.

"Has it been coming loose a lot lately? You need to trot your stubborn self to the VA and have it refitted. Bodies change. I think—"

"I think I've got this, Keely, thanks," Domini said tightly.

"But do you know—"

"Yes, I know what my *husband* needs, so I suggest you back off so I can give it to him. Now."

Silence.

Keely's hands went up defensively.

Cam was stunned when Domini took it a step further. She addressed his family. "Thanks for your concern. We'd appreciate it if you all gave Cam space right now."

Everyone backed off. Including Keely.

Despite the stitch in his thigh, he shifted toward Anton, sitting cross-legged beside him. Tear tracks streaked his dirty face. Alarmed, Cam said, "Anton? Did you get hurt?"

Anton shook his head.

"Then why are you crying, sport?"

He whispered, "Because I'm sorry."

"For what?"

"For making you do the race. You knew this would happen, huh?"

Cam wanted to toss off something clever, but he hurt too fucking bad to try. He hated the throbbing pain in the aftermath of a fall. Guaranteed his stump would be bruised and it'd be damn painful to walk for the next week.

"Did you get hurt?" Anton asked in a small voice.

"Nah." He reached over and brushed dirt off Anton's knee. "I'm fine. Don't worry about it, okay?"

"Okay."

"I wish I could send you for my crutches like last time. That was a big help."

"Maybe next time I could remember to put them in the truck for you when we go somewhere," Anton offered.

"That would be great. I can't seem to remember shit like that." He looked up at Domini expecting her to spear him with a dark look because he'd cursed again.

"Wait a minute. What did you mean by last time?" Domini repeated. "What happened?"

"Cam fell down on the back deck. I got his crutches and helped him up. Then he showed me his fake leg."

Her mouth dropped open. "You fell? Why didn't you tell me?"

Cam exchanged a look with Anton. "Because it was no big deal and us guys gotta have some secrets. Plus, I was in a lot of pain and cussin' up a storm. And I know you don't want me swearing around him."

"True. So maybe you'd better give us a minute alone, young secret keeper and crutches fetcher," Domini said to Anton.

"Aw, I don't think he's gonna swear that much," Anton said.

"Maybe I'm going to swear at him," Domini replied coolly.

Cam muttered, "Shit."

Anton raced off.

Smart kid.

Domini didn't bat an eye as she removed his stump from the socket. "Keely has a point, Cam. You've been having issues with the fit since before we got married." She peeled the socks off. "You're using five socks? Instead of two?"

"The damn sleeve is really slippery lately. I need the extras to mop up the sweat but it doesn't help and it still hurts like a bitch."

Shoulda Been A Cowboy

"You in pain now?"

"Yeah."

"How bad?"

"It's been worse."

Domini rattled off a Russian phrase.

Hell, she only swore in Russian when she was really pissed. He attempted to remove his stump from her hands. "Let me do this. I...you know my · family ain't ever seen me—"

"Vulnerable?" she supplied. "The injured war hero Cameron McKay has a chip on his shoulder the size of his missing leg, when it comes to letting his family see his stump."

Cam's mouth dropped open in shock.

But his wife wasn't finished. "I can see how you'd hate all the love, support and help they've offered you. That has to suck."

"Domini—"

She got right in his face. "I understand that you don't want to show your stump to the world at large. But these people—" she gestured to the group watching them very closely from afar, "—aren't the world at large. They care about you. They always have, they always will. What don't you get about that?"

"You sent Keely away," he pointed out.

"I'm not talking about Keely. Besides, if I wouldn't have told her to back off, you would have."

True.

"Your inability to let your family see, just once, what the damn war did to you physically, makes you emotionally handicapped, and that is way worse than losing your damn leg."

A hot wave of shame washed over him.

What could he say? Domini was exactly right. Yet, no one had dared say it to him before now. Ballsy, this soft-spoken woman he married.

He turned his head, but instead of facing away, he looked toward the family members who hadn't gone far after the directive from his suddenly bossy wife.

In truth, his family never had gone far. They'd rallied around him from the second he'd been back on American soil. Never complained when he'd banned them from the hospital.

Understood when he claimed the need for privacy. Had they resigned themselves to the fact he'd never be the man he was?

You aren't the man you were and maybe that's not such a bad thing.

Talk about a day for epiphanies.

Domini touched his face. "You mad at me?"

He kissed the inside of her wrist. "Yeah, I hate that you're right. So what do I do? Lay here and let them file over and gawk at me like..." *I've always feared they would?*

The pack of dogs chasing a squirrel brought Ky running past. He skidded to a stop. Behind Ky were the rest of his nephews. His whole body stiffened as he braced himself for their stares. And questions. And disgust.

Ky peered at his stump without apology. "So did it hurt when they chopped it off?"

"I don't remember, but it hurt afterward."

Gib asked, "Didja cry?"

"Yep."

"I prolly woulda cried too," he said solemnly.

Out of the mouth of babes.

Thane edged closer to the prosthetic. "Is that a robot leg?"

"Sort of."

His hazel eyes went wide. "Like in *Transformers*?"

"If it was like in *Transformers*, Uncle Cam could turn his leg into an arm," Ky chided.

Before Cam answered, Gib said, "Wouldn't it be cool if he could turn it into a machine gun?"

"That'd totally be cool!"

"Yeah! Or how about some of them knives?" Thane said, adding a slashing motion.

The boys wandered off, debating the merits on the coolest robotic body parts.

Cam frowned. *That* was the extent of it? That was what he'd worried about? Sort of anticlimactic.

Soft fingertips gently traced the red marks on his stump. Domini said nothing; she just touched him and he felt it clear down to his soul. He mouthed, "I love you," and she gave him that special serene smile.

Four shadows fell across him. He looked up as Carter, Colby, Cord, and Colt crouched down.

A tense minute passed when no one spoke.

"Sorry about the boys. They were...curious," Carter said.

"No harm. I can't say as I blame them. We'da all done the same thing at their ages."

"I've said it before, and I'll say it again, it sucks ass that this happened to you, bro," Colt said.

Murmured agreements.

Colby poked the fake leg. "How in the hell you walk on this every day is beyond me."

"Obviously I didn't do such a bang up job of walkin' on it today."

Another bout of silence.

Cord cleared his throat. "I admire the hell outta you for even tryin'."

"We all do," Carter added. "But as long as you're a captive audience, we ain't letting you up until we've had our say."

Fucking awesome.

"Since you came back you've forced us to see things in a new light in this family. So it's ironic you can't see what's right in front of you," Carter said.

"Did you think we'd look at you differently just because you're missing a goddamn leg?" Colby's eyes bored into him. "Did you honestly fucking believe that we'd somehow see you as...weak?"

"Yeah, I did. Look at me. I'm sitting in the fucking skunkweed. I can't get up by myself. That makes me weak."

"No, that makes you stupid," Cord fired back.

"Picking on the cripple, that's nice, bro."

Domini didn't pipe in to defend him. She stayed silent and watchful.

Colby's arms were crossed over his chest. "I think what Cord—and all of us are sayin'—is we're goddamned glad you ain't dead. If anyone is weak in this family, it's us, because we haven't kicked your sorry ass before this. We just let you be. Well, that bullshit is over, little bro, I guarantee it. You're part of this family whether you're ranchin' with us or not. Whether you like it or not. So get used to it. We're gonna be in your face and in your life like we should've been all along."

Cam stared at Colt. Then Cord. Then Colby. Then Carter. His embarrassment at how he'd treated his brothers vanished when he understood how goddamn lucky he was to have them. How he had a chance to make this—another thing that'd gone wrong in his life—right.

"Don't you have something to say?" Colt prodded.

"You wanna know what sucks worse than ranching?"

"Nothing?" Carter offered.

Chuckles broke out.

"No. It was worse having to face Brandt and tell him about Luke. Losing his brother...I never want to go through that. Ever. Jesus." Cam stopped, afraid he'd start bawling. Domini's steady grip on his hand encouraged him to go on. "I never realized how hard it must've been on you guys, especially in the beginning, when you didn't know if I was alive or dead. Then I get back here and I'm not the same guy."

"Believe it or not, none of us are the same guy since you left when you were eighteen," Cord said. "You'd know that if you weren't bein' such a reclusive asshole."

Cam winced. "I deserve that and more. Christ. I'm sorry."

"We've all had our bad moments, that's for damn sure." Colt flashed him a challenging grin. "So now that all the touchy-feely crap is over...question is: do you need help up?"

Say no. Scream no.

Cam swallowed his pride and his fear. "Yeah. Since I forgot my crutches, that'd be great."

"See? That wasn't so hard."

His brothers carried him to the porch like it was no big deal. He didn't point out they should've carried him to his damn truck so he could go home.

All of a sudden his brothers took off like their boots were on fire. When a sharp gasp sounded, he knew why: his mother stood behind him.

"So, is it worse than you thought?" he asked brusquely, fighting the temptation to cover his limb.

"No. The worst part was not knowing what it looked like."

Cam tipped his head back. Tears rolled from the corners of his mother's eyes. Shit. "Ma. Don't—"

"Don't you tell me how to react when I see my boy's blown-off leg for the first time, don't even try, Cameron West McKay."

He bit his tongue, letting her to harangue him because he deserved it.

"After they told us you were gonna live through your injuries, I'll admit after the immediate feeling of relief, I was pissed off at you."

"Caro..." his dad warned.

She waved him off. "I thought if you would've stayed here on the ranch, being a cowboy like your brothers, that this wouldn't have happened to you.

"But then I think of poor Dag. And now Luke...and what their families—what our family is going through and how it's ripping them apart on so many levels. Stupid accidents happen everywhere. All the time. No one is immune. No one is ever really safe." A small sob escaped. "I realized I can't protect you any more now than when you were my sweet baby boy who was determined to run before you could even walk."

"Ma."

"But it doesn't change the fact I hate that you're embarrassed about your stump. I hate you don't understand how I see that stump—not as not a flaw, but a miracle." She reached for Cam's hand. "You don't want to hear this, but I'll say it anyway. When you went missing..." Her voice cracked. "That was the worst week of my life. Or so I thought."

Cam frowned.

"But in some ways, it's been harder having you living in Sundance. When you were in the army, you had an excuse for not being here. I could tell myself you *would* be with us if you could. Now that you live ten miles away and we still don't see you, I know it's your choice to stay away. The lie no longer works and that's what hurts the most."

"I never meant to hurt any of you."

"But you did."

"I'm sorry."

"I know you are. And I forgive you even when I still want to paddle your butt." She kissed his forehead. "But it needed to be said."

He owed her more than a perfunctory *I'm sorry*. He owed his entire family more than that.

"Being kicked around by my family when I've been down today has been a good thing, believe it or not." He smiled at Domini. "I don't want to go back to being the man I was because some changes are for the better."

"That's good to hear and I'm happy for you, son. Let us share in your happiness, okay? Let us get to know the different man you've become."

Cam nodded.

"I meant it when I said you're welcome at our house any time, Carolyn," Domini said. "You too, Carson."

Carolyn squeezed their joined hands. "That means a lot. Cameron's been back in Wyoming for a while but it took you to really bring him home to us. Thank you."

His dad just patted his shoulder and then Domini's. Twice. Then he slipped his arm around his mother's waist and murmured to her as they walked off by themselves.

As soon as his folks were gone, the screen door slammed.

Keely wrapped her arms around Domini from behind, setting her chin on Domini's shoulder. "Relax, I'm not gonna choke you for ordering me away from my own brother. I deserved it. I just wanted to ask if you're glad you took my naked advice?"

Domini blushed when Cam lifted an eyebrow at her. "Very glad. The best advice I ever had."

"Good, because I'll be honest, Domini, I wasn't sure if you were...assertive enough to handle my tough-as-nails brother."

Sometimes his sister had the tact of an ape. "Keely, what the hell is wrong with you?"

"No, it's okay, Cam, let her finish," Domini said, running her hand down his forearm.

"See? That's why you two fit so perfectly." Keely leaned into Domini. "You're quiet and sweet, but that's deceiving because you have an inner core of pure steel. I always thought Cam would need a woman who is as hardheaded and tenacious as he is. But Cam needs someone like you, a woman who gives him a soft place to land as well as quiet strength. You understand him in ways none of us ever have." Keely's eyes filled with tears and Cam felt himself tearing up. "I will always be grateful to you for that. And I am so happy you found each other."

Domini murmured in Ukrainian.

"What? Are you swearing at me after I spilled my guts?" Keely demanded.

She laughed. "No, I just remembered a Ukrainian proverb:

she who weeps with joy for others will find joy in return."

"Sometimes I wonder if I'll ever get married. Being around these McKay males, I have very high standards for a man and no man has ever come close."

Anton and Gracie bounded over.

"I wouldn't mind having kids though. Just girls." She smirked. "You guys gonna join the McKay baby parade soon?"

Cam said, "Nah. We've already got a jump on our family." He ruffled Anton's hair. "One kid is plenty, right?"

Gracie barked in agreement.

"Since the boys had such a great time today I thought I'd offer to take Anton for an overnight. Ky's coming. So are Gib and Thane. It'll be fun."

Cam looked at Anton. "You interested?"

"I dunno. Do you want me to go?"

"I thought maybe we could chill out at home. Pop some popcorn, check out that *Transformers* movie so I can see why Ky and Thane and Gib were all fired up about me having robot parts."

Anton grinned. "That'd be cool."

"There's your answer, sis. We're goin' home. But if Domini and Anton are okay with it, maybe sometime soon we could have the family over for a barbecue."

"Just as long as you're not cookin'," Anton said.

"Amen to that," Keely said and low fived him.

Domini helped him to his feet. They inched their way to his truck, Anton on one side, Domini on the other. The pain made him dizzy. Domini held him up, she held him up in so many ways. His wife. His sweet, strong, perfect miracle.

No man—cowboy or otherwise—had ever had it so good.

Epilogue

One year later...

"Watch me."

"Hang on," Cam yelled over his shoulder. He flipped the burgers and shut the lid on the grill, praying they wouldn't catch fire the second he turned his back. Although he'd drastically improved his cooking skills, they all preferred Domini's food to his. But the woman deserved a night off now and then, so he'd bucked up and learned the basics.

"Dad! Seriously, look at this!" Anton shouted.

Cam felt that catch in his heart and in his gut. His eyes got a little damp whenever Anton called him Dad. He'd get used to it eventually—the word was still new even if Cam's paternal feelings for the boy weren't.

The change from *Cam* to *Dad* happened gradually, not in some sappy Hallmark moment. At the school's fall open house, Anton had introduced them to his new teacher as his mom and dad. Poor overwhelmed Domini had hidden her face against Cam's chest and cried. Cam managed to man up—barely—he'd been pretty bowled over himself.

There were times in the last year they'd all struggled to become a real family, not just on paper, but in their hearts and everyday lives. When Anton had taken that last step on his own, Cam knew the struggle had been worth it. They truly were a family now—by choice, not by circumstance.

"Dad!"

He leaned over the deck rail. "Okay, son, I'm watchin'."

Anton's black cowboy hat was almost as big as he was. He adjusted the rope, started twirling it above his head, and let fly. It landed in a perfect loop on the practice horns on the sawhorse. Then he quickly cinched the rope tight and let out a whoop. Gracie barked happily at his bootheels.

"Lookin' good. You're gonna give Ky a run for his money at the junior rodeo tomorrow."

Anton beamed...and returned to practicing. The kid was obsessed.

"You know he's going to be a total cowboy," Domini said, behind him.

"Hard not to be one, growin' up in Wyoming."

"It's not Wyoming that's his influence, silly man, it's you."

"Me?" Cam cocked his head at her. "Princess, I'll remind you I'm not a cowboy."

"I disagree. You might not be wearing chaps, riding a horse, roping steers and showing off all those external cues." Domini moved into his arms and placed her hand over his chest, over his heart. "But inside? Where it really counts? You're all cowboy, Cameron McKay."

"Dom—"

She briefly laid a finger over his lips. "You've always done the right thing, whether you were a ranch kid, or a soldier, or a cop, or a member of the notorious McKay clan, or now as a husband and a father. That's who you are, that's who I fell in love with." She stood on her tiptoes and kissed him lightly on the lips. "A true cowboy."

This woman had quite a bit of cowboy in her too. He curled his hands around her face and rested his forehead to hers. "I love you so damn much."

The moment was sweet... And short-lived when Anton sicced Gracie on them.

Domini laughed and shooed the dog away. "Before I forget, you're supposed to call Remy back."

"He say why? Is there a problem?"

"Everything is on schedule, worrywart, he just wanted to go over a few things about taking care of Gracie before we leave on Monday."

Cam glanced at the markers surrounding the new concrete slab, as well as the skeletal walls and ceiling trusses. His cousins were adding on a new section to the house that'd double the size of their current living space.

Which made sense, since he and Domini were about to

double the size of their family. His stomach fluttered when he considered the next step in their lives together. Adoption. Anton would officially become a McKay the same time as his new siblings. It'd all happened so fast. Normally adoption took forever, so they were surprised when everything fell into place in record time. They'd taken it as a good sign.

"So, are we all set for the trip?"

"Yes. We're meeting them Thursday. If all the paperwork is at the orphanage and the embassy, which Ginger assures me it is, then we should have them out of Romania and be back in Wyoming within two weeks."

Cam smoothed her hair behind her ear. "You nervous?"

"Yes. You?"

"Terrified."

"It's not too late to back out."

"Domini, I don't want to back out. I already think of them as ours. I have since the first time we saw their pictures."

"Me too."

"Plus, Anton is looking forward to bein' a big brother. And it kills Ky that his cousin is getting a brother and a sister all in one shot." Fourteen-month-old twins. Yeah, he and Domini would be hitting up everyone in his family for parenting advice.

"How do you think Anton will do on diaper duty?"

"Horrible. Just like me. But just like everything else we've done in this family, we'll learn together."

About the Author

To learn more about Lorelei James, please visit www.loreleijames.com. Send an email to lorelei@loreleijames.com or join her Yahoo! group to join in the fun with other readers as well as Lorelei: http://groups.yahoo.com/group/Lorelei JamesGang

The world is waiting for her…and he's waited long enough.

Wander*lust*
© 2009 KyAnn Waters

Meg Snow is having hot and wild sex with Cory Traven…in her dreams.

Four years ago he had his chance for a relationship with her. Instead, he joined the military, leaving her to endure Milcott, South Dakota on her own. Now it's her turn for adventure and a chance to banish those erotic Cory fantasies once and for all—on a singles cruise to Jamaica.

Cory has come home for what he'd denied himself four years before. Meg. But she's made it clear she wants anyone except him. There's only one way to show her that what she wants and what she needs are different things. How? Storm the beaches of Jamaica. Infiltrate his way into her bed. Breach the walls of her heart.

And show her that paradise is not in the Caribbean, but in his arms.

Warning: This title contains scorching sex on the beach, in the shower, in bed, and against a wall. A hot hero with a wicked tongue who goes after what he wants and a heroine who gives it to him…again, and again and again.

Available now in ebook and print from Samhain Publishing.

GREAT
CHEAP
FUN

Discover eBooks!

THE FASTEST WAY TO GET THE HOTTEST NAMES

Get your favorite authors on your favorite reader, long before they're out in print! Ebooks from Samhain go wherever you go, and work with whatever you carry—Palm, PDF, Mobi, and more.